Scoff At The Mundane

Scoff At The Mundane

Bill Kalman

Copyright © 2009 by Bill Kalman.

Library of Congress Control Number: 2009908914
ISBN: Hardcover   978-1-4415-6973-8
              Softcover   978-1-4415-6972-1

All rights reserved. No part of this book may be reproduced or transmitted in any form or by any means, electronic or mechanical, including photocopying, recording, or by any information storage and retrieval system, without permission in writing from the copyright owner.

This is a work of fiction. Names, characters, places and incidents either are the product of the author's imagination or are used fictitiously, and any resemblance to any actual persons, living or dead, events, or locales is entirely coincidental.

This book was printed in the United States of America.

To order additional copies of this book, contact:
Xlibris Corporation
1-888-795-4274
www.Xlibris.com
Orders@Xlibris.com
66378

For my Ashby McHale,
Whoever you are.

"I shall assume that your silence gives consent."

-Plato

1

AFTER A LONG, puzzled stare, he finally greets me with, "Um, is there any particular reason you're not wearing any shoes?"

There is in fact a reason why I'm not wearing my shoes, but I'm still debating whether or not I should unveil the truth to my therapist. The thing is I've just started counseling sessions with Dr. Polk, and although I think he's a decent enough guy, I'm still not exactly sure how I feel about him as the examiner of my innermost thoughts. After I reminisce about the series of events that led up to me sitting in his office with my shoes outside, I eventually calm down and begin to recount the story to him. "Good morning, Dr. Polk," I tell him with mild aggravation. "Well, what happened is that I was taking a walk earlier this morning and running some errands." Yes, contrary to popular belief, some people really *do* walk in L.A. "I was actually at the post office not too long ago and just decided to come straight here instead of going back home first. And, well, long story short, I stepped in some dog poop and didn't have time to clean it off. So I scraped off most of it with a stick, and when I got here, I took my shoes off and left them outside, since I didn't want to make a mess of your lobby."

Trying to be what I assume is analytical, he responds with, "Hmm, I see. That's quite a dilemma. Have you always had this strong dislike for pets in general, or is it just dogs that bother you?"

What the fuck does that mean? How did he equate me stepping in dog shit to harboring a hatred of all animals? This is a textbook example of why I'm not fully comfortable telling him about my life. I'd say on a scale ranging from amoebic dysentery to a piñata full of strippers, this guy is about as pleasant as soda that's gone flat: you really want to get rid of it, but there is something inherent in the flavor keeping you hooked.

My history with animals is complicated to say the least. You probably won't find me adopting any strays, but by no means do I hate them either. If I wanted to rant with my therapist about things I really hated, I'd talk to him about teenagers, tacky clothes (sartorial ineptitude as I like to call it), or how the post office always gives you those Sacagawea gold dollars for change, leaving you with seventeen coins just clanging around in your pocket.

Although I have my reservations about him, after talking with my friends, I've decided that I'm going to give Dr. Polk at least ten sessions before I make my ultimate assessment on whether or not he's a good fit for my id. We're now on session number five, and things don't look very good for him at the moment. I mean, during our first session, I explained to him that I had a friend who sought therapy to help treat his condition, and it worked rather well. When I mentioned to Dr. Polk that my friend suffered from agoraphobia, he responded by telling me that a fear of heights is a very common thing. If you're keeping score, *acro*phobia is a fear of heights. I guess it is a little irrational to expect a man who charges as much as he does to know the difference. In all fairness, the two words do sound similar, so I dismissed it rather quickly. Unfortunately, my psychologist is just so oblivious I'm beginning to wonder if the 713 degrees and plaques on his wall are genuine or if they're just reproductions. Did this guy really do his undergrad at New York University, gaining his Master's at Brown, followed by a PhD from Harvard?

I will certainly concede that this morning doesn't exactly put dogs in my best graces right now, as I don't think anyone likes having their brand-new Pumas ruined. But that's really the owner's fault more than the animal's. Actually, I used to love dogs growing up. Unfortunately, when I was five, I was at the playground, and one of my buddies got bit by a dog after coming down a slide. It was nothing too serious, but when you're that young, the screams make it seem infinitely more painful than anything you could imagine. The way this kid was whaling made it seem like he was not so much knockin' on heaven's door, as much as he was trying to ram through it with a tank. So I grew up always being a little nervous around animals, especially dogs. I don't run in fear, and I would never wish them any harm. But I do get a little apprehensive when they try to lick me. Despite the fact that the conditions I've just listed might make excellent discussion topics for my therapist, this is not why I'm here. But since I'm still trying to get a feel for this guy, I decide to test the waters a little bit. I like to throw him curveballs, just to see if he is in fact paying attention.

"Well actually, I don't think I started really disliking them until I was about eight or nine." He begins writing on his pad. "I think it all happened suddenly during a week I was ill and stayed home from school. Obviously, I couldn't go outside and play, but I could definitely watch as much television that a little kid could handle. And the *Price is Right* was always one of my favorites. I think what excited me more about being sick was not so much the missing school but the fact that I could watch people play *Plinko* and spin that huge wheel." He gives me a slightly quizzical look, wondering how this ties into animals. "And at the end of every show, Bob Barker would always say 'Help control the pet population. Have your pets spayed and neutered.' It didn't bother me at first, but after a while, I just really wanted him to trip up and say something to the effect of 'Help control the pet population . . . run over a stray cat.' Or maybe he could end it with 'Feed your puppies lead pellets.' I don't know; anything along those lines would have been great."

I look over at him, and he is writing frantically. Lying to him certainly makes me feel a bit despicable, but it's so funny watching him eat my fabrications as if they were a bowl of Lucky Charms. For some reason, I get caught up in it and decide to go with it. "And I don't think it's because I really hate animals, but for some reason, I've always wanted to eat panda meat."

"I'm sorry, did you say panda meat?"

Trying not to break out in uncontrollable laughter, I bite my tongue and continue, "Well yeah, I mean think about it. There must be some reason they're on the verge of extinction now. Seriously, they must make for some really delectable stew or panda burgers if they're going away so quickly, right? And I know I'd look pretty good in a panda skin fur coat, especially if I ever make a rap video you know?"

I think he has finally caught on that I'm exaggerating and my sarcasm is begging to grow old, but he's far too passive to call me out on it. More than likely, that breaks some kind of therapist code of conduct. After I remain silent for a while, he tries to get me talking again by asking me about my job.

"So how are things at work? Film anything exciting lately?"

For the record, I'm a fucking photographer, not a cameraman. This is our fifth session, and he still does not know what I do for a living. Although this was much closer, both professions do in fact involve a camera. Last time I was a chef and the session before that a pilot. I think after two more meetings, he will actually get it right.

"Actually, I'm a photographer. I do still shots, not movies or television," I say.

"Really?" he counters. "Did you ever tell me that?" OK, seriously, what is he writing on that stupid notepad, because it's obviously not my occupation. Perhaps, he's making a list of the people on earth more competent that he is, which is the only logical justification to explain his constant scribbling.

Here's how I know I told him about my line of work: In our first session (and pretty much every session since), I explained how I'm a photographer for *Velvet Rope*, a fashion magazine. I was not at all surprised that he'd never heard of it, but I also told him that I have my own web site of stuff I shoot in my free time. My favorite subjects are bridges and skyscrapers. I have always been a fan of architecture and engineering. I am also a sculptor, but more for fun and as a hobby. I receive great fulfillment through the process of a project and eventually seeing it completed. The way a bridge is constructed, all the parts that are integral to its success, I find the process very similar to my fabrications.

"That's great, what's the site?" he asks.

"Oh, it's www.antonbradleyphoto.net" I say.

Yes, my name is Anton Bradley, and despite being named after a Russian literary genius, I am very much American. My parents were both actors for many years. They met while performing in *The Cherry Orchard* together back in college. They're the most nostalgic people I've ever known, so they named me after the play's author Anton Chekhov, although they've never been to Russia. However, I'm sure they could at least locate it on a map. I'm not so sure about Dr. Polk on the other hand.

"Well good for you," he says. "The Internet is a great tool for promoting your work."

No shit, welcome to the nineties.

Then, he follows with "My brother-in-law has done some stuff with the Internet as well. He's made a killing."

"Oh yeah, what's he do?"

"Have you ever heard of eBay?"

"Of course, does he auction off stuff on that site?" I reply. "I know a guy who would buy kitschy Americana stuff in bulk and resell it. He raked in big money with it."

And after baiting me into giving an answer that everyone he asks this question inevitably replies with, he gives me "No, he actually started it. He started eBay." I wonder how many times he has had this brief conversation with someone; it must be scripted in his head by now.

Now, I'll concede that starting eBay is in fact impressive . . . if you're his brother-in-law. But for some reason, Sigmund Fraud over here finds a way to work irrelevant topics such as eBay into every conversation we've ever had. While I admit that the ability to not only purchase a used mop is truly remarkable, it is trumped only by the fact that I can also "buy it now." No wonder this guy never stops talking about someone else's accomplishments, they're truly the bedrock of a better world. Where would I be if I weren't able to find a movie poster for *Over the Top* autographed by Sylvester Stallone?

So why am I here? Why am I spending so much time, and even more money, talking to someone who appears to have no marketable skills? Why don't I try to find another therapist? There are many of them out there; maybe I just haven't met my "fit." I think my situation is comparable to someone wanting out of a relationship. They might not be miserable, but something just isn't clicking. But by moving on and looking for someone else, they give up that comfort zone, of always having someone, even if it's not the right one, to talk to.

No, I think the reason I don't look for a new shrink is because I know I have an issue I need to deal with, and by going to a "licensed professional," I give the impression that I'm taking strides to work at my problem. However, I am also fully aware of my personal issues. I know exactly what is causing me stress. I guess this is just my way of pretending I'm confronting the situation, without having to do anything about it. And by sticking with the same guy, I can at least tell myself that I'm not waffling.

So why am I here? The answer to that is incredibly simple, yet more complicated than anything I've ever dealt with. I'm here for the same reason millions of people have sought therapy since the beginning of time. The reason once thriving civilizations were reduced to rubble. This is why I'm here:

Women. Or I guess, the plural isn't even necessary. It's really just *one* woman.

I do think that within two or three more sessions, I'll actually be able to tell Dr. Polk what is really bothering me, and then I'll be able to really assess whether or not he can actually help me, because as much as I like to complain about him, he is a really nice guy, and that's got to count for something in this world. It's not very fair for me to complain about him and his ability to help me when I'm not really giving him the full story. Right now, he thinks I'm in here because I have PTSD (posttraumatic stress disorder) from the time I witnessed the World Trade Center go down. That part is true; I really was in NYC that horrific day. It was certainly awful, and it shook me up for a while. But I'm a photographer; I've seen some pretty gnarly stuff doing what I do. I don't want to say I'm desensitized, but it's certainly possible. Yeah, I hated seeing that happen and almost feel guilty for making money off of it, but it's my job.

No, Dr. Polk has no idea why I'm really here.

He has no idea about Ashby McHale.

2

"Can I get some water before we continue? I'm sorry, but the sun is just killing me."

I say no problem, we can take ten before moving on. I need to change lenses anyway. I've had my fair share of crap jobs in this life, and as much as I hated them at the time, they were all worth it because I love where I am right now. I can't really imagine a better way to spend a Tuesday than photographing a beautiful woman on a beach near the Equator. I mean, it is viciously hot, even in the shade, and I did have to get out of bed at 4:30 a.m., but somehow I manage to get by. This sure beats my first job taking out trash and cleaning toilets at a family fun park twenty minutes from my high school. It wasn't all bad; I mean I did get a free thing of popcorn every shift, so I really have no right to complain.

All joking aside, today is a beautiful day, and I'm photographing one of the most famous swimsuit models in the entire world on Brazil's Eastern Coast. Alicia McGrath is a very popular name in fashion, and contrary to what I've been told, she's actually very easy to work with. Yes, I love this part of my job, but I've also grown accustomed to it because it is in fact how I earn a living. Being surrounded by gorgeous women several days a week does not take long to adjust to, and it really never gets old.

Despite the fact that after countless shoots for numerous magazines and web sites all these models begin to look the same, that has had minimal impact on my desire to sleep with them. And I have in fact slept with a rather large number of them. Now, I hate when people complain about having "too much meaningless sex," and I honestly never thought I'd be one of them. But I'm finding out firsthand that there is more to life than sleeping with gorgeous women. However, I have enjoyed every bit of this ride . . . until now. It did take sometime for me to get where I am, and my success didn't happen overnight, but it certainly happened rather abruptly.

Back in my first year out of college, when I was working at the Office Depot to pay bills while trying to get my freelance photography career off the ground, something incredible happened. I was a regular at the Starbuck's two shops over, which is where I met Jenny Desmond. She was a knockout in every sense of the word and had just graduated cum laude from Clemson with a degree in economics. But all she talked about was her interest in modeling. I know it sounds strange, but it's what she wanted. We regularly joked that one day I would be a big photographer and she'd be a famous star, and when that happened, I would be the one behind the camera for her debut in *Playboy*.

To me, it was just a little flirtation between friends, and although she never asked me to take pictures of her in the nude, she did come to me with an idea.

"*HEO* magazine is accepting pics of girls in Halloween costumes for their upcoming October issue," she adamantly tells me while shoving the July issue in my face.

"Interesting. What does that mean?"

"Anton, this is *it*! This is a chance for both of us! It's really quite simple, you big goof. You take a picture of me in some costume, I have a couple ideas, and we'll submit it to *His Eyes Only*." Her eyes are lit up like it's her fifth birthday and she's about to open the first of one hundred presents. She is literally jumping up and down.

"Um OK, yeah that sounds great," I say with a combination of skepticism, confusion, and intrigue. "I don't think that should be a problem. When are you available to shoot?" I ask her. Her overt enthusiasm already lets me know her answer will be "anytime, anywhere."

"How about Wednesday night around eight? I would say tomorrow but I close, and we can't do it tonight because I don't have a costume chosen yet, but two days should be perfect right? Can I come over to your apartment then? That's where all your stuff is right?"

I'm not sure if this is an excuse to get naked in my apartment or if she's trying to make a move or what, but because I have a penis I say of course, that would be fine. I go home and just check that all of my equipment is in working order, that I have plenty of film, all the normal things I look at before a shoot.

The next night, around 9:30 p.m., I get a call at home, and it's Jenny. "Can you meet me at Starbuck's at eleven forty-five tonight?" she asks very quietly, probably trying to keep this conversation secret since she is still at work.

"Huh, what?" I say very confused. "I guess, but why? Do you need someone to walk you home?" This was not uncommon. I lived rather close, and sometimes on nights she closed, she would ask me to walk her home since she did not leave until after 11. I found it strange on this particular night though because she normally asked me the day before or at least at the beginning of her shift.

"Oh no," Jenny tells me, "Just bring your camera and whatever else you need for the shoot we talked about . . . I've got an idea. See you at 11:45, bye!" and she hangs up before I can say anything or ask any questions.

I'm not really sure what she has in mind, but I don't work Wednesday mornings, so I figure I might as well go, and if nothing else I can escort her home. I gather up my things so I'll be ready to leave at 11:30 p.m., and just read until it is time to meet her.

When I get there, another employee in a green apron is just leaving and locking the door. I've seen her several times, but we've never engaged in more than general conversation involving my *chai latte*. I walk by her giving the obligatory head nod and good night greeting. She does the same, but she's just had a long shift, so I really don't think she recognizes me or cares who I am. As I approach the door, it's very dark inside with a light on near the espresso machine. No one is inside, and I assume that Jenny just went home anyway. I look inside a little more carefully, when suddenly I get a tap on the back of my shoulder, "Hey there," Jenny says, as I jump toward the building and almost crash through the glass walls of the coffee juggernaut.

"Damnit! I thought you were inside. Don't do that to me!" I say in a scolding tone.

"Yeah, I 'left' the store about ten minutes before the manager. She thinks I've gone home." I can tell something is obviously up. I'm a little nervous at this point.

"So why did you have to hide from her?" I ask, not really wanting to know the answer.

"Come on in and I'll show ya," she says as she puts her key in the lock and opens up the door, looking left and right to make sure her manager is no longer around, even though I saw her ride pick her up a couple of minutes ago. "You've got your camera right?"

"Right here" I say as I pat my bag and step inside the store.

"Great, follow me, and don't touch anything. We just cleaned, and the people who open tomorrow expect it to be spotless," she orders me as if I were a toddler.

"OK, so could you please tell me why you wanted me to meet you here since you don't need a walk home?" I plead.

She says, "Oh fine, you take all the fun out of things," and opens up her body-length coat, displaying her green apron, black hot pants . . . and nothing else. The coat drops to the floor, and she is standing in front of me wearing nothing other than that spectacular green cloth, accented by a minor scrap of black fabric. "Happy Halloween, do you like my costume?"

"Um . . . yes." I would give up oxygen for a month to be that fucking apron.

"This is my costume for the *HEO* photo submission Anton. I'm a slutty barista."

I love my life.

"Oh, what a relief! I thought you were gonna try to get me to help you rob the place," I awkwardly chuckle while she looks at me admonishingly. "Um, well just give me about two minutes to get set up and we'll start shooting."

Over the next couple of minutes, I snap about one hundred exposures. As I pack up, she puts on her coat, much to my dismay, and I walk her home.

After I develop the photos the next day, I invite Jenny over to see them and select the one she wants us to send in to the magazine. After about two hours of viewing and deliberating, we reach an agreement as to which photo will hopefully be seen by horny American men. I send it out the next day, and then do what all freelance artists do . . . wait with great optimism, not really expecting much though.

Over the next couple of weeks, I go into Starbucks to get my *chai* and sometimes a scone, and every time Jenny sees me enter the store she shoots me a look hoping that I've heard something from the magazine, and every day I tell her that unfortunately I have not. This pattern continues up until the last week of September, when I'm reading at home and the phone rings.

I pick up and say hello. "May I speak to Anton Bradley please?" the voice on the other end inquires.

"Speaking, who is this? Sorry, may I ask who's speaking?" I correct myself trying not to seem too rude.

"Hi Anton, my name is Jessica Conrad, calling from *His Eyes Only* magazine. You submitted a photograph to us several weeks ago correct?"

What I say is "Yes, that is correct," even though I'm thinking "abso-fuckin-lutely," while trying to force back a massive grin. I know exactly what she's calling to tell me. I'm pretty sure that this is how it feels to hump a rainbow.

"Great, well, we really like the photo of the barista, and we would like to purchase it and put it in our Halloween issue. I assume this is fine with you? Our standard rate for this is $400. Is that OK with you?"

This is now the greatest moment in my young photographic career, overtaking the time I took pictures of the Homecoming pep rally my senior year of high school. The class president, Natalie Thomas, walked up from her seat to give a speech, but was tripped accidentally by a rowdy bunch of juniors that were just trying to show everyone in the gym that they were more spirited than everyone else. That was not the good part. I actually do not take pleasure in the misfortunes of others, and thankfully no one was hurt. However, when she fell, she landed a little funny, and my first instinct was to start snapping away; it's just inherent in my nature. For whatever reason Natalie decided the Homecoming assembly would be a great day *not* to wear underwear beneath her sundress, and I ended up with about four photos of her snatch in my camera. I thought about selling them to kids in school, but never let anyone see them fearing the backlash that would have ensued if they ever got to that poor girl or the principal. It was hilarious because I didn't actually notice it in real time. Not until I developed the film did I see her hoo-ha staring back at me.

That was good, but this is way better.

Trying not to sound overly eager and pretending this is totally common for me, I coolly reply "Oh yeah, that's fine, do you need me to sign anything?"

"Yes, I'll fax the forms over just as soon as you tell me where you'd like them sent." I didn't have a personal fax machine at the time, so instead I had it faxed to work but told her not to send it until tomorrow, because I didn't want to get disciplined for using company property for personal business.

I held off telling the good news to Jenny until I received, signed, and returned the contract, just to make sure I wouldn't get her hopes up if something went wrong. Fortunately, it only took a couple of days to get all of that taken care of, and shortly afterward I got the check in the mail. I immediately went to my bank to deposit it, and on my return trip stopped by the coffee shop, trying to look bummed so as to not give anything away to Jenny.

"Hey Anton, *grande chai* today?" she asks casually. She has given up on the dream of appearing in a national publication sporting only a green apron at this point.

"No, you know what, make it a *venti*. I feel like celebrating."

"Oh really? What are you celebrating?" she asks, not having a clue.

"Well, I just sold a photo of mine for $400," I tell her.

"Anton, that's great! Which one was it? Don't tell me, let me guess: The Golden Gate Bridge at sunset? That lightning storm from a few weeks ago? Um, one of those concerts you're always going to? Your trip to Walden Pond?"

"Not quite, this one was a picture of a coffee shop," I tell her, trying to sound aloof.

"A coffee shop, that's kind of boring, what was it of? The outside of the building? The pastry display?"

I'm looking down at my shoes trying to appear calm and modest when I explain "Well, it's actually a picture of an espresso machine in all its glory, really artsy shot with great focus on it but a distorted surrounding . . . and I think somewhere in the foreground is a beautiful blonde wearing nothing but an apron." My head is still pointed down, but my eyes look up to her to see her reaction, assuming she's figured it out by now.

"Shut the fuck up!" she yells loud enough for everyone outside to hear. Everyone turns to stare at her like people always do when a profanity is uttered with that much gusto. Luckily, her manager was not around, and no one seemed to mind, so she continued in a much more subdued tone, "Anton don't mess with me. Are you serious?"

"Of course, I'm serious," and I pull the contract out of my bag as well as my deposit receipt for $400. "I think half of this money is yours though. I guess they didn't contact you since only my name was attached to the photo with a copyright, but don't worry, I gave them your name and you will definitely be credited in the magazine," her smile is ear to ear at this point.

"When does it come out?" she eagerly inquires.

"Well, it hits the stands in three days I believe," her smile drops because to her this must feel like an eternity. "Luckily, *HEO* sent me an advanced copy," and mid-sentence she goes from looking defeated to appearing to have just won the lottery. I pull the magazine out of my bag, "Page 55, hope you like it," I sarcastically say, knowing very well it will be framed and on her wall by sunset.

Jenny frantically tears through the pages and eventually lands on 55, and she is the happiest woman in the world. "I can't believe it! I mean, there are lots of other pictures around it, but it's a start!" Pause. "We have to celebrate. How about dinner tonight at the nicest restaurant in town?" The picture is only about the size of a baseball card, and there are four other women on the same page, but she is right, it is something, and both of our names are in a national magazine.

"Well, that's great! But the nearest Cracker Barrel is about two hours away. Can't we just go to Applebee's?" I suggest and quickly shield myself to avoid a potential beat-down.

"Ha-Ha," she says dragging out each syllable in an exaggerated dry tone. "I was thinking something like *Carte Blanche*," she says, in a much better mood than during my recommendation.

"Well, that's a great idea Jenny. But aren't they booked at least a week out? I can make reservations right now for next week if you'd like," I say as a consolation, assuming that in her current state she has forgotten how impossible it is to get into the fanciest restaurant in town.

"Normally yes, but the manager is a regular here. We chat a few times a week. He gave me his card a couple weeks ago and told me if I ever needed anything, to not hesitate to call. I guess making his espresso a double and only charging him for a single turned out to be a good idea after all."

"Well, great then, make the reservation and let me know where I should meet you and when," I tell her, slightly bummed because this guy is obviously on the fast track into her panties.

"OK, Anton, you got it. I get off at five. I'll call you soon, but I've got to get back to work. Ooooh! tonight is going to be so much fun," and the look on her face makes me forget all about how smooth this manager is, and how I wish I could seduce women by allowing them to order flirtinis and calamari without a reservation.

"Bye Jenny, and congratulations, this is great for both of us."

A few hours later, I get a call from Jenny, and she tells me we have dinner at 9:00 p.m., and she will grab a cab at her place and swing by to pick me up on the way at 8:30 p.m. From my place, it is maybe a seven-minute ride, but I can understand her not wanting to be late.

I put on my nicest suit knowing that Jenny will be nothing less than a knockout, so I want to look at least a little bit like I belong. The cab rolls up right on time as Jenny said; I open the door, and my jaw drops. As expected, she is looking flawless; I will be the envy of every man in the city.

When we get to the restaurant and approach the host to let them know we are here for our 9:00 reservation, Jenny is immediately greeted by François, the most sharply dressed Frenchman I've ever seen. He and Jenny exchange that fake double-kiss on each cheek thing they do in Europe, and immediately I am comforted by the fact that François is more likely to try and get me drunk than Jenny. He is quite nice, and I thank him endlessly for doing this huge favor for us.

Jenny and I have decided to spend the $400 we received from the photo on just this night. I was hesitant at first, but it is truly a big deal. I figure it would be fine to splurge just this time. Personally, I am a beer person, but Jenny loves her wine and orders a bottle of one of the most expensive Pinot-Noirs on the wine list . . . four times. I don't even remember if dinner was good or not, but that wine was quite spectacular. It's probably not necessary to detail the rest of the evening, but I will, just out of decorum, because I feel that I epitomize the word.

Long story short, we flirted, joked, and laughed for the next two and a half hours, and when all was said and done, we had just enough of the $400 remaining to take a cab downtown. We walked around a little bit while I held onto her waist. She kept her arm around my shoulder, mainly just to prevent herself from falling down, but also because that's what pretty girls in nice dresses do . . . they drive men crazy, and she could be the queen of Daytona the way she is working me.

With all the photo money spent, I use my credit card to get a room at some hotel downtown, and you can imagine the rest. Fortunately, the next morning was really not awkward at all. We got breakfast and discussed what had happened. After a really long talk, we discovered there had been a mutual attraction for months.

"I don't know why you never asked me out. I gave you plenty of signs," Jenny tells me as if I'm supposed to know everything.

"What can I say? I'm a guy . . . and I'm kind of clueless."

After all of that craziness, we started dating pretty seriously, for about the next month anyway. Then, things took a turn. Despite the fact that the "slutty barista" photo was not much bigger than 2"x 3", Jenny was a hit. Readers wanted more; they kept writing *His Eyes Only* inquiring "who is this girl?" and demanding more of her. Soon enough, Jenny's phone was ringing off the hook. They wanted her for a full-page photo with a paragraph about how she was the "next hot thing." The timing couldn't have been better for her because Starbucks fired her as soon as corporate found out about the photo. Actually, it wasn't the photo that upset them. Stuff like that is actually great for business. But they were definitely not thrilled by the fact that she went into the store after hours for personal use.

I think it's a sacrifice she was willing to make. This was great for her, but crappy for us. We were both sad to see it end so quickly, but I knew this was what was best for her. Jenny did demand however that I be her photographer for the full-page shot.

The rest is history; she is big-time now, but she hasn't changed, at least not when it comes to talking to me. Over the last few years, I've shot a few spreads for various magazines with her, and we still get along great. It's not like things turned out badly for me either. I'm somewhat famous, at least in the fashion world. I mean, I don't expect someone in front of me at the grocery store to be flipping through *Velvet Rope* and know who I am, but I do OK for myself. Right when Jenny's career was starting to take off, she gave me several compliments in her interviews, always acknowledging how much I helped her career. Now that she is one of the hottest people in Hollywood and she still mentions my name occasionally, well let's just say that has paid dividends—Alicia McGrath being a prime example.

"Thanks Anton, I needed that, I'm ready now. You're really great to work with by the way, so helpful and carefree," Alicia tells me with a not-so-subtle subtext.

Every woman I work with knows that I have slept with Jenny Desmond. By my calculations, in their minds, this puts me just below Oprah and slightly ahead of Scott Baio. Jenny is still a great friend; we talk on occasion, but simply having dated her has allowed me to do nothing short of sleep with any model I want.

This is why after we're done shooting for the day Alicia McGrath is going to ask me if I'm doing anything tonight. This is why when I say "no," she is going to invite me to a party. This is why after five Maker's and gingers, I am going to have my way with her. This is why I am unstoppable. This is why I love my life.

And this is why I am in therapy.

3

"I'M SORRY, DID you just ask me if I minded you referring to me as 'The Dark Horse'?" Dr. Polk asks me with a puzzled look on his face. It's an expression I've grown quite familiar with coming from him.

I flew back in from Brazil less than six hours ago. I'm running on very little sleep, and my questions and comments are a little suspect. However, I deliberately asked him this to test whether or not he is actually paying attention to me: I feel like I'm analyzing *him*, that our roles are reversed.

"Yeah, well I think that would be cool. I mean, it's definitely founded in logic. I didn't pull it out of nowhere," I defend my stance. "Your name is Dr. Polk, and that instantly makes me think of James K. Polk, one of our nation's earlier presidents. His nickname was 'The Dark Horse,'" I explain to him.

He begins writing vigorously, probably his shopping list.

"So Polk is your favorite president?" he asks, and continues. "I'm just curious because a person's preferred leader often says a lot about their personality."

This is interesting. It *almost* sounds like he's trying to draw some sort of conclusion about me. Is this progress? I sure hope so. I'm now on session seven and don't feel much different than the first time we spoke.

"Actually," I say, "It's Roosevelt, FDR that is. Nothing against Teddy, but I have a sentimental connection to Franklin Delano Roosevelt. And he's the only president to ever serve three terms. I think that helps to distance him from the rest." This is actually a very compelling story, which means Dr. Polk is likely to change subjects.

"Good choice, mine is Thomas Jefferson," he tells me with no enthusiasm whatsoever. "I'm from Virginia, so he is placed on a pedestal, and we're taught to love him. I even have a portrait of him hanging by the window over there," he points to a painting about 20" wide x 30" tall.

"Pretty cool," I say to humor him. "Was that passed down through your family?"

"No, I bought it on eBay. I get great deals on eBay. Did I ever tell you my brother-in-law started that web site? It's really great," he relays to me for the fifteenth time. My eyes roll back so far into my skull I momentarily see my brain and all of its bizarre contours.

Why does this guy never shut up about eBay? And why does he always remind me that his brother-in-law started it? It's almost as if he assumes my memory has the longevity of a virgin teenage boy in a gangbang.

I have to change the subject, or I'm gonna pull a Sweeney Todd on this jackass, so I say "I had another episode while I was in Brazil."

His eyebrows raise, giving the illusion that he is interested in what I am about to say. "Really? What happened this time?"

I'm completely caught off-guard, and I have only myself to blame. I told him a while back that I have PTSD. But really, it's just an excuse to see him and talk about the things that are really bothering me. Normally, when I tell him about my "episodes," I conjure them up the night before so they have some appearance of coherency. But this was just a reaction, and I'm not sure what to say.

"Well, I had a dream I was playing pinball on the rings of Saturn. But even though it's outer space, there were vending machines all over the place. For some reason, I distinctly remember there being Skittles and Doritos on the rings of Saturn." I have no idea where this is coming from; he begins writing on his notepad. "Just when I feel that I am doomed to be lost in space forever, I spot an airplane in the distance. I begin to wave frantically," I have been watching too much television, which is odd since mine is broken. "Somehow, the plane spots me and begins coming toward me, and as it approaches me, it begins its descent." You can tell I fly a lot because that is the terminology they use to announce that we are near our destination . . . well, that or "approach." "The plane is now only a few feet above the height of my head, and it's coming right at me. It's not slowing down or changing paths, and I'm frozen there," I continue but add a pause for dramatic effect. "I don't know what to do. The plane is going to hit me and I'm scared to death, and just as it is about to hit me, I wake up."

After about fifteen seconds of silence, Dr. Polk inquires, "Is there anything else?"

"No, that's all I remember," I say, hoping that he doesn't detect any impurities in my account. "But falling back to sleep is nearly impossible after that," I tell him.

Another long pause, he continues to write.

"And no one else was on Saturn with you?" he wants to know.

This is my chance; I can finally segue into the reason I'm *really* here. "Well actually, there was a woman there, beautiful, but not anyone specific in my life. I don't remember anything physical happening in the dream, but I was definitely under the impression that we had been intimate earlier on." I am somehow able to make this sound halfway reasonable. I mean, I would believe it if it were being recounted to me.

"Hmmm." He writes some more. He seriously must keep the Bic pen company in business with his product consumption alone. "That's interesting. I'm not sure what to make of that."

His aloofness has now hit a new plateau. I am furious. I glance at a clock on the wall, not even recognizing what time it actually is. "Oh, I'm sorry, I have to go. I completely forgot that I have to be somewhere in ten minutes," he can almost certainly see through my fabrication, but I do not care at all. "I'll see you in two weeks," I tell him and stomp out the door.

"Good-bye Antoine," he screws up my name, and I am seriously considering locating this guy's house and peeing in every container in his pantry. I will receive great satisfaction knowing that one morning he will be eating pancakes in which the acid of my urine provides that extra special flavor. Seriously, my name is not that difficult to remember.

As I leave, I stop at a small shop to grab a coffee and a bagel. I am in a terrible mood, but also egregiously unaware that I am doing *exactly* what Dr. Polk wants me to do.

4

"Excuse me, Mr. Brown?" the new girl two desks over and one up from me says as she raises her hand.

"Um yes, you have a question?" he pauses and looks at the attendance sheet on his desk. "Miss McHale, is it?" the chemistry teacher responds, looking very proper in his bow tie, lab coat, and safety goggles, preparing for a demonstration.

"Yeah, is it true that you can get mono from inhaling carbon monoxide?" she sarcastically says, trying very diligently not to burst out in laughter. The rest of the class is not so disciplined, and chuckles are heard around the room.

"No, that's not true at all. However, many other bad things can happen as a result, so be careful around it. CO can be a very dangerous gas," he states in a very professional tone, assuming she really is that clueless.

Although I am very shy, I take this cue and run with it, prolonging the foolish conversation with, "But carbon *di*oxide is the stuff in sodas right? Isn't that what makes it carbonated?"

"Yes, that is correct." The new girl is staring at me, wondering where I'm going with this pointless inquiry.

"Well then, since carbon monoxide is bad, but carbon dioxide is fine, does that mean that if I'm ever in a situation where CO is pouring into a room, if I can somehow find a way to double my intake of it, I'll just get a caffeine buzz?" I wonder, trying to appear as genuinely clueless as my question indicates.

Now a little ticked-off and sensing we are just trying to delay the lesson, he simply declares, "No, that won't happen. Now, as I was *about* to say " . . . and he continues pouring random chemicals into various tubes and flasks. I am in another world. Mr. Brown and his Bunsen burners are the farthest things from my mind. Right now, my eyes are fixed on this girl, who is smiling ear to ear because of my joke. Luckily, she doesn't notice me because she is actually trying to learn something, so I stare for about ten seconds and go back to my notebook. My heart is racing unlike anything I've ever felt before.

Chemistry was my least favorite class in all of high school. I fought tooth and nail with my advisors about taking it, but I was merely delaying the inevitable. They convinced me that in order to get into a "good college," I would need that on my transcript, despite the fact I knew when I went to college, science would have nothing to do with my major. I had no idea that being coerced into chemistry, my sophomore year would be one of the greatest things to ever happen to me.

The bell finally rang, and Mr. Brown dismissed the class. I took one final glance at the new girl, picked up my backpack, and headed off to my next class. The rest of the day dragged on forever. I couldn't concentrate on anything else. For the remainder of the day, my brain was focused on this new girl, contemplating why she was in this school, pondering if she was new to town. Naturally, the ever-critical potential of a boyfriend weighed heavily on my mind too.

As the bell rang and I left my fifth period geometry class, I heard someone yelling at me from behind. "Hey, Franklin, wait up!"

OK, so I know that everyone calls me Anton. And it is my name . . . sort of. It is actually my middle name, and Franklin is technically my first name. I'm confused as to who would be calling me by that name though. None of my friends call me that; I've asked all the teachers to call me Anton. Out of intrigue, I turn around, and it's *her*, walking straight toward me. My heart stops momentarily, I panic, she must have me mistaken for someone else.

"Hey, you," she says with a smirk on her face.

Trying to maintain my composure and not freak out that this girl actually wants to talk to me, I give her my coolest "Hey, what's up?" I have just set a new personal record for number of words I've actually spoken to a girl to which I was not related.

"Franklin right? You were pretty funny in chemistry today. I don't think Mr. Brown knew we were goofin' with him. I felt kinda bad being a smartass on the first day, but being in a new school is odd for me, so I had to break the ice somehow."

"Oh yeah, that was pretty rad!" Did I just say that? "I mean, I was just following your lead. You were really the funny one," I tell her, waiting for the moment I break down and freak out that this is by far the longest I have ever spent in the presence of a girl.

"Ashby," she says confidently, extending her right hand for me to shake.

"Oh, um, Anton," I mumble, shaking her hand, impressed by her fierce grip.

"Oh, I thought your name was Franklin?" she tells me with a quizzical look on her face, eyebrows slanted indicating confusion. "Isn't that what Mr. Brown called you when he took attendance?"

"Ha, about that, Franklin is my legal first name, which is why that's what's on all the teachers' lists. Anton is my middle name, and that's what everyone calls me. No one calls me Franklin, but I mean, if you really want to call me Franklin, you can. I mean, that wouldn't really be a problem . . . I prefer if you call me Anton because I get annoyed when other people call me Franklin," I am speaking a mile a minute. My mouth refuses to shut off. There is no doubt this girl thinks I am such a nerd. I am a deer in headlights.

"Well, thanks for your permission, but I was gonna call you Franklin whether you liked it or not," I've never heard words spoken with such conviction. "Congratulations, Franklin, you're my first friend here at this school . . . in this city actually. Well, I gotta get to my next class, but I'll see you around right?"

Is this happening to me? "Um, yeah, you know it." She starts to walk away, and I'm able to force out a final, "Nice to meet you Ashby."

Jeeringly, she states, "You too Franklin! Don't go huffin' any CO_2 without me all right?"

I am left alone in disbelief. "Did that just happen?" I nervously squeal under my breath. As I head off to my next class, I know I'll be late due to my conversation with Ashby. But there was nothing in this moment in time that was going to drag me down, not a scornful glance from a teacher, not detention, nothing.

I am on top of the world. I am invincible.

5

Everyone is familiar with the phrase "A picture is worth a thousand words." Well, that's great I guess, but when you photograph things for a living, words don't really pay the rent or put food on the table. My web site has some of my personal work for sale, available in a wide range of sizes, prices, subjects, and finishes. I've been staring at the same pictures for what feels like hours. I'm finding it very hard to focus on my work when all I can think about is my crazy therapist. It has been less than a full day since I last saw The Dark Horse. Due to his lack of competence, I have begun refusing to call him by his name. I actually prefer to save proper nouns for people who I respect at least a little bit. I already want to go back and lay into him with a verbal lashing unlike anything he has seen or heard before. Sadly, I leave for a shoot tomorrow, and he is fully booked all day today.

After I finish some odds and ends on my web site, I decide to go to my favorite place in town. This is where I can shut out all the hassles and aggravations that I encounter in daily life. It is a metal and woodworking shop about two miles from my condo. I have been making stuff there on and off for a couple of years. I'm really good friends with Ross, the owner of the shop, and he lets me use his tools for personal projects from time to time. He doesn't even charge me for materials or shop maintenance, which is really generous of him. All he wants in return is an occasional print to hang up in his house or give to a friend. There was also the one time I had to shoot a full session of him in sexy modeling poses as a birthday present for his wife . . . I would have gladly just bought my own brand-new tools, but as I said, he's a close friend. There are two absolutely hilarious facts about Ross that I tell everyone I know when his name comes up: first, he has the largest laser-disc collection in the world. Even though it was a technology that was popular for a year at most, Ross has over two hundred of them. Many of them are still unopened. The second little tidbit, which is my personal favorite, is Ross's view on politics. He has probably told me the story twenty times, but it never gets old. When Ross was in his early twenties, he was working in Chicago. The machine shop that employed him at the time was located on Van Buren and LaSalle, or somewhere in that neighborhood. Well, for reasons that seem arbitrary but according to Ross are quite relevant, he really took a liking to former President Martin van Buren. Whenever anyone asks him what was so great about Martin van Buren, Ross always responds the exact same way. He looks them square in the eyes and asks, "Have you ever seen a more intimidating pair of muttonchops? Would you fuck with a country led by a man with facial hair that can't be controlled?" What makes this story even better is that every year, Ross hand writes, not just types, letters to his two U.S. senators and congressional representative. The message is always the same, but it's worded differently every year. He simply tells these three elected officials that they should seriously consider growing muttonchops because they are "a trademark of noble leadership." And yes, he still writes this letter to female members in Capitol Hill. I don't think he's won any of them over just yet, but I think our current congressman is warming up to the idea.

It has been a couple of months since the last time I was in Ross's shop, but I have some great sketches of a new piece I want to work on. It will definitely require about fifty hours or more of work on my behalf, and with my schedule, I'll be lucky if I can finish it in three months. That does not bother me though, because I am just overjoyed to go into that shop, and crank up the stereo with Social Distortion playing at full blast. There are few things I find more pleasant than welding scorching hot steel with Mike Ness's scratchy vocals blaring all around me. The guys who taught me the basics of metalworking loved Social D. So it was a good thing I enjoyed them too, because I heard *Mommy's Little Monster* more times than I can count when I first started working with steel. I think they might even give out free copies of that record when they issue California drivers' licenses; knowing Social D is kind of a prerequisite for living here.

    I get into the shop and shoot the shit with Ross. We spend time catching up since we haven't seen one another in a couple months. Everything is where it was last time I was there, which is actually astonishing, since Ross loves to move things around every few weeks. I think it's an OCD thing, but I never question it. He does let me use the stuff for free after all. I grab the metal I need to start my newest project and begin to clean the grease off. Not even forty-five minutes into my project I get a text message from my editor, I read it, and my heart sinks.

> Change of plans. John is sick. You're off VDL.
> New project details coming via e-mail. See you at DFW
> Tomorrow morning.–JW

    I am furious for multiple reasons right now. Before John got sick, I was scheduled to go to Paris in three days for the Victoria's Secret Fashion Show. VDL is my boss's clever way of abbreviating "Vicky's Down Low," which is her preferred way of referencing the Goliath of unmentionables. Obviously, I am pretty annoyed at missing the fashion show, but I have been once before, so that is not the killing blow in this scenario. No, what is eating at me most is that tomorrow I'll be in . . . Dallas . . . as in Dallas, Texas . . . as in every stereotypical thing one can imagine, I have witnessed firsthand in the Lone Star State. Clearly, I'm not bitter.

    I would be downplaying my career by saying I travel a lot. In fact, I am probably on an airplane an average of one hundred days out of the year, so I spend far too much of my life in airports. Now, everyone has things about traveling that annoy them, their little pet peeves that make them tick. Maybe it's the guy in the middle seat hogging the armrest, or the kid across the aisle blasting his iPod. Although I'm not very fond of any of those things, my most profound annoyance pertains to the overhead cabin.

    My aunt on my mother's side is a flight attendant, so I have heard countless stories about passengers on airplanes. It is no secret, you're allowed one carry-on and one personal item (whatever that means) to bring with you on-board the plane. Should you decide to travel with large luggage, you must check it and retrieve it at the baggage claim like everyone else. Sadly, it is inevitable that on *every* flight, there will be at least one, yet I've seen as many as five, passengers that try to stuff their entire wardrobe into that compact space just above the heads of travelers.

Yes, I feel awful for the 105 pound flight attendant, who can't be much taller than five feet two inches, who is coerced into lifting this monstrosity of a "carry-on" above her head as if she were a Norwegian competitor for the world's strongest man. I would even go so far as to say I feel compassion for them, and I want to help. But I'm already buckled in, and the seatbelt sign is illuminated. My hands are tied.

Today's flight to the cultural Mecca of Dallas is no different. Seated a few rows ahead of me in first class is a man wearing a five-gallon hat, blue jeans, and sporting a button-down shirt displaying the most intense jungle of chest hair I've ever seen. Magnum P.I. would be genuinely intimidated. His facial hair is keeping the pace too. Las Vegas is probably giving odds at 2:1 that this guy gives a better mustache ride than Friedrich Nietzsche. So Mr. Six Shooter is attempting to stuff what appears to be his latest kill in the wild into the overhead bin, and true to form it is not fitting. To his credit, he is attempting this himself and not making our flight attendant Tinkerbell do it. As much as this frustrates me, it is at the same time very humorous. Every time I see someone attempt this near-impossible feat, I get the image of someone trying to stuff a watermelon into a briefcase. I think this is like reverse pregnancy, and sadly it is the closest any man will ever come to empathizing with that aspect of a woman's life.

After that scenario is finally settled, a man and a woman holding hands approach me virtually on cue. The middle seat next to me is vacant, and before he opens his mouth, I already know what he's going to ask. These two both got stuck with middle seats and are hoping that I'll be nice enough to give up my aisle chair and sit a few rows back. I've never understood why couples make such a fuss over sitting together on airplanes. I mean, they've got the rest of their lives to sit together. What's three hours in the grand scheme of things?

As advertised, my editor was waiting for me at Dallas-Fort Worth airport. As was explained to me in the e-mail she sent me, we are here for a piece on the Dallas Cowboy Cheerleaders. This is certainly great news. The inescapable caveat however is that I must attend the football game where they will be entertaining. We are going straight to the stadium for some pictures as Friday morning nears noon. The game is not until Sunday, but these shots will be in a studio setting, similar to a calendar. Then, we will go to the game on Sunday for live-action shots, a little more candid, although these girls know how to pose in everything they do. As I will find out a few times this weekend, they really do pose for *everything they do*.

I'm barely awake for the Friday shoot, and it drags on forever. However, I am well rested come Saturday morning, and things are much more interesting. The girls are all very cooperative and flirty, which is always a great combination. Several of the girls introduce themselves and invite me to a party that evening where many of the players will be as well. Even after they announce that second part, I still gratefully tell them I will be there. When I travel to a city for a work assignment, I frequently have copious amounts of free time to kill. The scenario usually plays out as this: work really hard nonstop for a few hours, take several hours off. Work several hours again without any break, and then I am given a few more hours for myself. This often works out great because I commonly use this time to explore the city and snap shots for my web site and portfolio.

But I'm in Dallas.

Dallas, Texas.

So I consider exercising my second amendment right and begin looking for a firearm store. Surprisingly, people in Texas don't even wince when you buy a soda at a convenience store and immediately after paying say "Have a nice day. Do you know where I can find a shiny new Ann Berretta?" This question is just as common as asking for directions to the freeway. Guns are big in Texas.

I decide against purchasing a gun, but do ask to hold several of them. You know, when in Rome . . . Since I am big into stereotyping, I know I won't be satisfied until I find a place to eat dinner that serves the biggest steak I have ever witnessed. I do in fact find such an establishment. It costs $77, and had I paid for it, I would have considered myself cheated. Luckily, dinner is on *Velvet Rope*. Oddly enough, the two greatest words in the English language are of Latin origin: per diem. By my estimate, since I began working for the magazine, I have purchased food with my own money somewhere in the neighborhood of three times. It also comes in handy going on dates in cities where I'm only working for a couple of days.

After dinner, I head back to my hotel room to change for the party and grab my gear as well. One of the many things I've learned about this industry is that even when I'm not working, I am still "on the clock." I have to be ready for anything, especially when alcohol, pretty women, and athletes are involved.

The soiree is a typical "who's-who" of the sporting world, particularly in the state of Texas. What exactly they are celebrating, I have no idea, but I do know this: I met Nolan Ryan at the dessert table while eating the most scrumptious cheesecake that has ever entered my mouth. He is by far the greatest pitcher of all-time, my childhood idol, and for a moment I contemplate going gay. I figure that the evening has peaked already, that there is no possible way for it to get any better. And I am in fact correct with my assumption. However, what ensued following my encounter with a legend should not be taken lightly. In many ways, this evening will play out like it almost always does . . . with notable exceptions.

Tonight was a Wild Turkey kind of night, which usually means I'm in a good mood. I caroused with several celebrities, the Cowboys' players, even spoke with Jerry Jones for a bit; he's very charismatic, I have to hand it to him. Most importantly, though I conversed with several of the Dallas Cowboy Cheerleaders more in-depth, as always, there was one in whom I was particularly interested. Or should I say, I met Tara.

Upon first meeting her, my impression was that she was going to be an airhead and a bitch, and I was blatantly wrong on both of my presumptions. We flirt and dance for quite a while, exchanging the requisite generic details of our lives before we can go back to her apartment in good conscience. The cab ride is very short. We probably could have walked, but being a little drunk, getting a ride was the right call.

In the few short hours I've known Tara, I am truly intrigued by her. For the most immeasurable instant in time, part of me wishes I lived in Dallas so that I could actually take her on a date like a real person. She really only has one flaw in my opinion: her Scottish terrier, Brady. Although Tara is from Pittsburgh and works for the Cowboys, like most women, she has a huge crush on Tom Brady. The dog is the drawback, not her crush on Tom Brady.

She pours me a glass of wine as I sit on her couch and pretend with every fiber of my existence that I do not want to throw her dog out the window. For the next forty-five minutes, we talk, and to my shock, I do not get bored or even try to make the first move to "speed this along." She is actually interesting and rather insightful. Most impressive is that she has a Master's in English from UT-Austin.

"Follow me, I want to show you something," she tells me, and naturally I assume that this is her coming onto me. I was wrong. She does in fact take me to her bedroom, but for another reason. The walls of her room are covered with approximately fifteen beautiful paintings. "What do you think of the paintings?" she asks shyly.

"Oh nice, who did them?" I say, as my physical desires have trumped anything logical happening in my brain.

"I did, I love to paint. I was actually an art major at Carnegie Mellon back home in Pittsburgh. I don't get to do it nearly as much as I'd like, but hopefully I'll be getting back into it more. I mean, dancing for the Cowboys is great and all, but I know I won't be young forever. And painting is what I love the most. I've been doing it since I was eight," she informs me.

My eyes open wide, nearly popping out of my head. At first, I was just trying to move the conversation along, but I am quite impressed at the works of art I see in front of me. That is saying a lot too, because I am an artist as well, working in both 2D—and 3D forms. There are few artists as pretentious about their work as I am, but I love her paintings. "Tara, these are incredible," I tell her with absolute conviction.

"Hey thanks, Anton." I can tell by her inflection that she does not believe me. This is almost certainly due to the fact that every other man she has shown these paintings to has told her how impressive they are, merely to sleep with her.

As I look at them more intricately, I notice that many of them appear to be fictional characters from popular literary works. I see *Huck Finn*, *The Three Musketeers*, and what appears to be the balcony scene from *Romeo and Juliet*. The most noteworthy to me is of a young boy perched atop a large rock, blowing into a seashell, and he is surrounded by a swarm of young boys. "Hey, that's Ralph from *Lord of the Flies*, right?"

Her eyes light up with unparalleled astonishment. "Wow! um . . . yeah. I'm impressed; no one ever gets the reference." Again, this is likely attributed to the fact that most of the men who pursue her don't know there is a difference between the masterpieces by William Golding and J. R. R. Tolkien.

"How about that one?" she says, pointing to a portrait of a boy in a red hat.

"Please, how 'bout a challenge? Houndstooth jacket, red hunting hat. There's no way it's anyone other than *The Catcher in the Rye*, Mr. Holden Caulfield."

Without saying a word, she removes her jacket, and I can tell she is impressed.

All of a sudden, I start to think that maybe sleeping with Tara might not be as great as it first seemed moments ago. Then, I notice all the books she has on a shelf next to her television. As I browse through her collection, I see some very laudable titles: *War and Peace*, *Les Miserables*, and just about everything ever written by Dickens, Emerson, and Thoreau. She even has three different editions of *Moby Dick*. Then, my eyes catch a glimpse of *The Complete Works of Anton Chekhov*.

"You know? I was named after him," I tell her as I pick up the book, pointing to the title on the binding.

"Really?"

"Yeah, my parents met in college while performing in a production of *The Cherry Orchard*," her eyes are now devouring me. It has been a very long time since any woman looked at me with such intense passion. I think that in her mind, men like me do not exist. I'm getting the impression that for some reason, I am the manifestation of her innermost desires.

"*The Seagull* is my favorite play from Chekhov, so romantic while so tragic," she says coquettishly, and as I open my mouth to tell her that I am a fan of *Uncle Vanya* personally, she grabs me behind my head and kisses me. At this point, I don't have the strength of conviction or the moral character to do what I should do, and leave. I don't necessarily feel like I'm using her because we are both well aware that this will not continue past Sunday, but something about it feels weird. As gorgeous as she is, that is not the thing drawing me to her.

She kisses me, points to a painting of a green light on a dock. I call out *The Great Gatsby*. Her shirt is off. I reach for her bra, but she stops me. "What's that one?" she asks while pointing to a frame containing what appears to be a swirled windmill.

I never thought paying attention in Mrs. Welch's freshmen English class would come in handy, but somehow I actually find myself utilizing info I picked up that year. With a smirk on my face, I tell her it's *Don Quixote*, and her bra hits the floor. And for what it's worth, her version is *way* better than Picasso's. I massage her back, and she reciprocates. I have an amazing grip. My massages drive women wild, and Tara is no exception. Eventually, I grab a condom out of my wallet, and as I'm about to put it on, Tara says something very strange to me.

"Baby, I want you to cum on my stomach," she orders me in a deeply seductive voice.

My heart stops. Not that I've never done such a thing. Under normal conditions, I would take her up on her offer and do my best Jackson Pollock impression all over her upper body, but all of a sudden this thought disgusts me. Again, her statement is likely a product of all the other men she has slept with completely disregarding any emotions Tara has.

"No," I say, "I'm gonna enjoy every second of this with you. It's not just all about me." Who the *fuck* am I? Where is this shit coming from? Someone must have slipped a Nicholas Sparks audio book into my stereo while I was asleep one night because these are definitely not my thoughts coming out of my mouth.

Tara looks at me intensely and says, "Whatever gets you going, Anton."

And for some reason, I am stricken with the unshakable compulsion to respond with what I perceive to be a rather clever flirtation, "Please . . . call me Ishmael." Right then, her eyes lit up as if Herman Melville himself was in her bedroom wearing only a thong and a cape. If you ever want to make a bookworm howl at the moon, say this to her in bed. I had no idea how effective it would be. She took this as a cue to essentially mention every major work of literature throughout our night of passion. I heard allusions to Roskalnikov, Yossarian, and I think I even caught a *Harry Potter* reference, but I'm not certain . . . I'm still not sure how I feel about that.

The next morning is a little uncomfortable, but really I'm more bummed than anything because this girl is actually very nice and fun to be around. She has to leave early to get to the stadium, but tells me I can leave whenever I need to, just make sure I lock the door on the way out. I walk her out to her car and kiss her good-bye, hoping that the game will not be torturous on my soul while I'm photographing her and her coworkers during the game.

As she drives off, I can't help but feeling slightly guilty, even though we both fully understood the situation. I mean, we really used each other for the night, knowing deep down that this was just a way of satisfying a deeper need: a short-term solution to a much more profound problem. And although I hated it when Jenny used to speak of everything in economics terms, I am certain they apply here. She would always refer to situations in terms of its "comparative advantage," its "cost-benefit ratio," or its "opportunity cost." It drove me crazy as an artist because I hate quantifying everything. I do not appreciate it when the mental and emotional aspects of things are disregarded.

However, I know it is appropriate here. Although I know sleeping with many women just because they are gorgeous makes me feel like a bit of a jerk, it also feels really good physically. Now, sadly I am thirty-two and have never had a real girlfriend. Obviously, I've dated women for a few weeks, but I don't think I have ever even kissed a girl for the first time where alcohol was not involved. Do I want a serious relationship? Absolutely. But that is much easier said than done. And it's sad to say, but maybe I feel that what I would have to give up to get what I want is just no quite worth it, since there are no guarantees that is.

SCOFF AT THE MUNDANE

I eventually get myself to the stadium and onto the field and begin snapping away. Tara shoots me a quick wink and a smile that shows no signs of resentment, nor is she staring at me the entire game as if she just found the love of her life. We understand the gravity of the situation, and I am relieved. Unfortunately, the rest of the game is not nearly as pleasant. Football fans are obnoxious, but football fans in the state of Texas are a different breed entirely.

"What are you doing? *Sack him*!!!!"

"Quit dropping the ball, you idiot!!!!"

"Tackle him! Come on, *get him*!!!!"

"Don't run straight into the defense, stupid!!!!"

The next four hours of my life are filled with statements similar to these. I have never heard as many rhetorical questions in my life as I hear at sporting events. Every fan seems to have a better idea of how to play football than the people actually doing it, and they go to great lengths to let them know it. Although it's not as if any of the players or coaches can hear their taunts with all of them coming at once. I would really like it if some day one of the players or coaches, after making a poor play, would ask the ref for his microphone right in the middle of the game. I can just see a star linebacker walking to the middle of the field and saying, "Um, yes, you see I definitely *could* have sacked him, but I let him go, just to spite you . . . yes you, fourth row, foam finger, and nachos, let me do my job."

Honestly, if anyone ever told my buddy Ross or any of the guys who work in his shop how to do their jobs, there is no way they would stand for it. Those guys would ream you so damn fast you wouldn't know what to do. As I once heard Ross's friend and coworker Joey mouth off to someone talking out of turn: "Hey, I don't show up where you work, and slap the dick out of your mouth . . . let me do my job."

Those who can, do . . . those who can't, criticize those who can. The only thing more humorous than people who yell at athletes in a noisy stadium is people who shout at inanimate objects. I've never quite understood that one, although I have to admit that sometimes I talk to my camera when it's not cooperating.

It got even better though. I'm certainly used to redundant statements regarding the performance of athletes, that I can handle. But since I am spending most of my time near the cheerleaders, I have to listen to all the moronic statements coming from the guys around me.

"I'd fuck her."

"Nah, her thighs are too thick. The brunette on the end though, I would definitely bang her."

"What? She's a stick, probably weighs ninety pounds. I need a girl with some meat on her bones."

It went on and on. I heard those same thoughts repeated with minor variations throughout the course of the game. Now, I won't be hypocritical or almighty and even pretend for a second I've never said things like that . . . I have, and I'm an asshole for it. But I would not describe any of the men saying these things as "a catch." I honestly think that if they had a picture of a stair-master and a proton accelerator placed in front of them, they would not be capable of differentiating the two.

It hits a little closer to home on this day though given what happened the night before with Tara. I mean, I'm not going to marry the girl, but I definitely have an attraction to her that extends beyond physical appearances.

Eventually, the game ends, and I am able to get out of that stadium. Tara texted me shortly after she got off the field and asked if I was doing anything. I ended up waiting for her outside for about thirty minutes, and we went to dinner. I was amazed when Tara took me to one of the best sushi restaurants I have ever been to. I never thought in a million years that I would be eating sushi in a state famous for its livestock, let alone actually enjoy it. The *edamame* was incredibly salty too, which really hit the spot.

After dinner, we went back to Tara's place. We opt to forego the conversation and get naked moments after closing the door. Unfortunately, neither she nor I had any condoms. Nicely put, the evening's festivities were confined to a strictly Clintonian nature, but still incredible. I didn't mind, and this time I gladly honored her request from the night before. We talked and cuddled (seriously, what does Texas put in their barbeque sauce?) for a little while after, and then she took me to the airport.

The entire time on my flight back, I think about the weekend, and how many emotions were rushing through my head. I honestly think I have made great progress in understanding why I do the things I do. I was brutally honest with myself this past weekend, even bordering on an epiphany. The more I put the weekend in context and compare what I have realized to what I tell Dr. Polk, I conclude I do not need him. I can figure out all of my problems with women on my own. Certainly, I could just cancel my next appointment, but that would be too easy. No way am I letting the Dark Horse off the hook like a punk. Dr. Polk is owed a fierce verbal onslaught, and I'm going to give it to him, even if I have to pay for a session in order to tell him what's on my mind about him and eBay and everything else. Oh yes, this next session is going to be great. I envision him writing down all of my insults as I'm delivering them to him, and a huge grin takes over my face.

As I am about to fall asleep, I hear the captain say, "Ladies and gentlemen, I have just illuminated the seatbelt sign. We're about to encounter some turbulence up ahead."

Yes.

Yes we are.

6

"ALL RIGHT, OPEN 'em!" Ashby yells at me with excitement.

I open my eyes, and in front of me, staring right back at me is a tiny light green turtle. It is my eighteenth birthday, and Ashby and I are at our favorite diner. We have probably been to Roxy's Diner almost two hundred times over the past three years; this is definitely "our" place. Although I absolutely love hanging out and sharing milkshakes with Ashby, I would be lying if I said I was happy being "just friends" with her. This is definitely not a date, just like it was not a date the few hundred times we hung out since we first met.

That is not to say that I only talk to her because I want to get with her. I really do enjoy Ashby's company; she is probably my best friend, and certainly my best female friend. Very early on in our friendship, Ashby told me about her boyfriend that still lives in Minnesota. I did a good job hiding my disappointment, but like all guys in high school, I still fostered a shred of hope that someday that might change. At this point, she is still with him, and I am a little bummed out by that. I've actually met the guy, and he's nice and respectful, but the fact of the matter is he isn't me.

As much as it sucks spending so much time with Ashby and not having kissed her even one time, that is far from the worst part. I don't think anyone will ever enjoy rejection, but I like to think that I can at the very least handle it with some maturity. The worst part is that everyone in high school knows how close we are, and naturally everyone but Ashby can see how blatantly obvious my attraction to her is. So of course every time anybody sees us together, the moment we go our separate ways to class, I immediately get bombarded with "Good luck dude, you know you're never gonna hit that." Or maybe it's simply "Anton, she's sooo out of your league, just give up."

Ashby McHale is one of the most popular girls in school; there is not one person who does not smile when she is around. She is a genuinely nice person and is insanely intelligent. Her popularity wasn't widespread immediately, but after only a few months at our school, everybody knew who she was. Now, by no means am I an unpopular person, but I am far from the Prom Court. People know who I am. I get a lot of head nods in the hallways, but that's about it. So when one of the most popular, beautiful, witty women I have ever witnessed kept asking me to "do something" after school, I did what any other adolescent boy would do: I succumbed instantly, and the word "no" dropped straight out of my vocabulary.

I have never even kissed a girl at this point in my life, much less had a girlfriend. Spending time with a wonderful girl was uncharted territory for me; I had no idea how to act or what to do. So when all the kids in school made fun of me and put me down, at first, I thought they were right. I figured Ashby just needed someone to be friends with in a new school, and after a couple of weeks, she would forget who I was. That was the furthest thing from the truth, and over time my crush only intensified. However, my confidence also grew tremendously over the years. It got to the point that when people would mock me, at first, I defensively said things like "fuck you," or "shut up dummy." But after I heard enough of those remarks, I got really good at brushing them off and reciprocating with a clever quip.

I'm not really sure what feels worse: wanting something and not feeling like you deserve it, or feeling like there is absolutely no reason in the world why you shouldn't have what you want, but still not achieving it. At first, I could rationalize her not wanting to date me because my confidence was subpar. Over time though, I saw how much fun she had around me, and I still have no idea why she doesn't want to be with me "in that way." I mean, I have no experience dating girls, but I know if I tell her what's on my mind, she will undoubtedly say, "That's sweet, but I don't want to lose you as a friend."

Male-female relationships are a frightening and wretchedly confusing thing. The best comparison I can make is relating them to a "prisoners' dilemma." Essentially, each person is in a situation where someone will have to compromise at least a little bit of happiness, if not both people. The options appear to be:

1) Guy likes girl, and wants to date her
2) Girl wants to be just friends
3) Guy and girl are not friends or in a relationship, they simply don't speak.

In each of the scenarios above, if 1 or 2 are fulfilled, one of the people is not getting what they want. Sacrifice must be made by one of the parties involved in situations 1 and 2. In situation 3, both people give up some happiness, and neither gets what they want. There is no option 4 that says "Guy likes girl, girl likes guy, and they date exclusively." If option 4 were available, then 1–3 would not even need to be considered. It's really very tricky, and I'm sure it has complicated the lives of many people since the beginning of time.

"Happy birthday! Do you like it?" she shouts with a childlike enthusiasm.

She knows I don't like it. Ashby knows how much animals weird me out, and she loves to make fun of me for it. She constantly tells me that it is her goal to get me to adore animals one day. For some reason, Ashby loves animals. She wants to be one of those people who swim with dolphins at Sea World or something like that. As close as we are, this is one area where we definitely do not see eye to eye. However, I really can't say anything negative to or about her.

"A turtle? Whoa," I say, feigning excitement. I was really hoping for the deluxe version of Scrabble, but I guess this will do.

"I knew you'd like it Franklin," she says in a very obvious mockery of my phobia of animals. "But technically, he's a tortoise. Turtles are aquatic, whereas tortoises are terrestrial. Come touch him," she commands me as she picks up the slimy shell out of the box she brought him in. She is holding this thing like it's a wad of hundred-dollar bills. I shakily stretch out my hands to take the pet from her, fearful of how slimy and gross this will feel on my bare skin. But it's Ashby . . . she could ask me to swim in an active volcano, and all I'd say is "let me get my snorkel."

As expected, this thing feels so gross. He can tell I'm apprehensive, and he ducks back into his shell. This actually puts me at ease because now I feel I'm merely holding an inanimate object instead of a living thing. I move the shell around slowly, twisting it in my hands looking at it from various angles. It's actually kind of cool, and I start thinking of ways that I can get this thing to stay inside forever.

"What are you gonna name it? Come on, give it a funny name, and Franklin is already taken."

"Ha-ha" I say sarcastically as I continue to roll the shell around in my palms. I notice on his belly or underside, whatever that part of the tortoise is called, that there is a little scar in the shape of a keyhole. Maybe it's a birthmark; zoology is not my field of interest. "That's a good question. I'll have to think about it for a minute."

"OK, but you have to decide before we leave though," her power over me is unreal.

I think about it some more, and I really like that little mark on its stomach. I want that to have something to do with his name, because I'm a big fan of defining characteristics. "I really like this little mark here," I tell her as I point to his belly. "It makes him unique. I mean, this is uncommon right? Or do all turtles have this on their shells?" I ask her, somewhat jokingly, but rather sincerely.

"Yeah, that's way cool Franklin! You definitely have to incorporate that into his name. What could it be? We need something cool like Lock and Roll," she tells me jokingly. "Oh, I've got it! How about Matlock?"

I stare at her with a blank face, "Seriously Ashby? You're better than that, come on. Give me a minute though, I'll think of something good."

As we're debating the matter, throwing out random names that rhyme with lock, our milkshakes arrive. Roxys' Oreo shakes are hands-down the most delicious things I have ever consumed. All the flavors are tasty, but the Oreo shake borders on euphoric. As I unwrap my straw and place it into my shake, I am lost in thought about coming up with a good name for this turtle.

"Thank you, Ronald," Ashby says to the waiter as he sets down our basket of fries. "You're the best waiter ever."

Detecting her dry sense of humor, but also mildly appreciative, Ronald brazenly tells her, "Oh you know, I do what I can, just fulfilling my end of the social contract."

And right then, it clicks. "I've got it!" I exclaim. "I know what I'm going to name the turtle." Ashby shoots me a look, intent on preventing me from using the two words interchangeably. "Sorry, I mean, tortoise. I know what I'm going to name . . . the tortoise."

"Oh great, let's hear it," Ashby says with strong intrigue.

"Leviathan."

"Huh? What does that mean? Where did that come from? That has nothing to do with a lock or a keyhole or anything like that Franklin," she tells me admonishingly, but also with an element of curiosity to see how I will respond.

"Oh, it makes perfect sense. You see, he has a keyhole-shaped thing on his stomach, and that made me think of the famous philosopher John Locke. Well that, and our waiter mentioned social contract theory. It's like fate or something." We had just been discussing Locke and similar trains of thought in government class the week before. "Well another famous philosopher often mentioned in the same sentence with Locke is Thomas Hobbes. And Hobbes wrote a very famous work titled *Leviathan*."

"That's good, I guess, but why not name it after a work of John Locke's?" she asks me.

"Well, I could, but most of his book titles are very long, and I don't think *Two Treatises of Government* is a very good name for a pet," she smirks at me, and I forget for a moment how to speak. "But also," I gather my thoughts, "Leviathan also means 'a large aquatic creature.' So it kind of makes sense, since some turtles live in water and land. I'm not sure if all of them do, but I know that some of them do. And yes, I realize this one does not live in water, but I think you can give me the benefit of the doubt here."

"Wow! That's kind of cool, actually. I like it. Leviathan it is," she sits up very straight and confers upon me her approval of the name I have chosen. "I know I told you he is a tortoise, but I'm not an expert on animals yet either. I will say thought that I am 99 percent certain he's not an aquatic turtle, so don't go flushing him or take him swimming with you, OK?" The look on her face tells me she is kidding, but also a little concerned I might try one of those options. Had anyone else given me this stupid thing, it would be lost before lunchtime tomorrow. However, since Ashby gave it to me, I'm going to try my hardest to keep it alive for at least two weeks.

"OK, that's fair," I tell her, and we start slurping down our shakes, racing to see who can get the first brain-freeze.

I conveniently forgot to mention to her that Leviathan in the Bible is also associated with the devil. The name I chose was very intentional.

As karma would have it, that word also means "a thing that is very large or powerful." I thought I was just giving my new pet a clever name. I had no idea that this turtle would prove to be more influential in my life than I initially anticipated. Maybe two weeks isn't enough time. I think this little green guy deserves at least a month . . . six weeks tops.

7

SLEEPING ALL DAY has got to be one of the greatest activities of all time. I rarely get to participate, but when I get the chance, I go all out. After my flight from Dallas got in, I went straight home and slept most of the day away, one of my rare days off, but well deserved. This is particularly helpful because it is always beneficial to be in a refreshed state when going to therapy. Well, actually it's probably better to be in a really screwed-up frame of mind, but since I plan on slaying the Dark Horse today, I want to have a level head. Truthfully, I have calmed down a little bit and decided not to just yell and scream and threaten him, but I'm going to tell him that it just is not working out. My voice may get a little stern, but it won't be an all-out tirade. It is difficult to tell if my therapist and I don't get along, or if *therapy* and I don't mesh well.

"Anton? Dr. Polk will see you now," a peppy receptionist taking a break from her most recent edition of *Vanity Fair* tells me. If I were not so well rested, I would rip that crappy publication from her hands and hit her with it; it's garbage. I've met their photographers, and they're terrible . . . No, I'm not bitter that they didn't hire me, not at all. I give her a cutting stare and snarl, but I don't think she notices. This walk down the hall will be my last. Well, when I leave, it will be the last, but this is the calm before the storm; I'm soaking in everything around me. The posters advocating safe sex; telling one how to help a friend with an eating disorder; they will soon be a distant memory. The only thing I want to remember about this experience is the fact that I actually took a stand for myself and decided to walk out of an unhealthy situation, which is ironic since that is usually what brings people to places like this.

"Hello Anton, welcome back. Please, sit down. How was your latest trip?" my psychologist asks me with an apparent interest in my life.

I sit down and immediately want to start talking about Tara, but I simply come out with "Oh it was fine, nothing too unusual. I had to go to Dallas."

"Oh Dallas huh? I've been to Dallas many times. My sister lives there. Nice for a visit, I doubt I would ever like to live there though."

Oh shit. I know I shouldn't ask this, but for some reason, my lips do nothing to refuse my tongue from enunciating it. "Oh really? Small world. Is that the sister who is married to the guy who started eBay?" Fuck. Did I really just ask him that?

"Ha-ha, oh no, they live in Silicon Valley now. Apparently, computers are big out there. Have you ever heard of Google?" he asks me with absolute ignorance. Does this guy think I live in a cave? I know I told him about my dream on Saturn, but I never meant for him to assume I actually grew up on the outer edge of our solar system.

"Um, yeah, I think I've heard of Google," I tell him in my most condescending voice as I grind my teeth trying to remind myself that he is the idiot, and I shouldn't take his ludicrous questions personally.

"Oh, I just love that site. You can find just about anything you need there."

Including your degrees?

"Oh, you'll appreciate this. I actually Googled your name to try and find your web site." What? Did he just say that? Is my therapist actually taking an interest in my life by investing some of his time outside of our sessions in my work?

"Yeah? Really?" I say and perk up like a dog whose owner has just walked through the door with a Frisbee made from newspaper and kibble. "What did you think?"

"Excuse me?" he says.

"You know of my site? Did you like my web site and my photos on there?" I say anticipating a compliment or something that resembles an encouraging statement.

"What? Oh! I didn't actually make it to *your* site. You see, Google gives you so many random things mixed in with whatever it is you are searching for. And, well Anton, a link to digital cameras came up at the top of the page, and I have been thinking of purchasing a new camera. So I decided to check out that site and before I knew it I had been comparing prices for almost an hour. At that point, it was getting rather late, and as I'm sure you can understand I needed my rest and went to bed."

Was I really hearing this? I would not have been insulted if he had *never* gone to my site, or had he told me he had gone there and *hated* my work. OK, I would have been a little annoyed. But why the fuck did he go out of his way to tell me he was about to check out my site and got sidetracked? My fury is reaching a record high. There are few occasions in my life I can recall being this angry with someone. Although I had told myself I was going to make this a peaceful parting between the two of us, this was the last straw. I do not even know how to put into words how frustrated I am. If I grabbed a thesaurus and listed every word for "angry," and then I looked up each of those words in said book and wrote them down, and then repeated the process fifty times, that would not be enough to properly illustrate my rage.

What came out of my mouth next was the most cathartic moment of my life. I am steaming with unmitigated angst. I cannot even properly describe my emotions. To label my feelings as "raging anger" would be like referring to World War II as a "disaster." I know that I personally have a tendency to speak in hyperbole. I have found that exaggeration makes things more interesting. However, I am completely justified with the given circumstances.

"Excuse me? You went shopping for cameras?"

"Yes, that's right. I got a great deal on a new ten mega pixel too."

A very long pause.

I take a deep breath.

In a very somber tone I inquire, "Dr. Polk? Can I ask you something?"

He has no idea what he is about to unleash. "Of course Anton, that's why you're here isn't it?"

Another long pause.

One more deep breath.

"Are you out of your *fucking mind*?" Judging by his facial expression, one would assume I had just sacrificed a live animal on his office floor, or perhaps crapped right on his desk while dancing to *Manic Monday*. "I mean, this is what, the tenth time I've seen you? I don't even know, I lost track around two or three when it became very obvious to me that you are quite possibly the most oblivious, ignorant, and clueless person I have ever met." He is shocked. "And yes, I know that I'm being redundant, but I want to drive home the point about how . . . how . . . how completely frustrated you make me. I mean, I come here to talk to you about my problems, and inevitably we will end up talking about eBay or some bullshit web site that of course I have heard of, but bares no relevance to the conversation whatsoever." I look above his terrified face, which has now acclimated itself to my rage and notice some of his degrees hanging on the wall.

Pointing to a framed piece of paper with a bunch of fancy writing, I say, "These are impressive. I mean, how many degrees do you have? I would loooove to get my own PhD from Yale, or maybe Harvard, possibly even MIT. Do you think your brother-in-law could set me up with a good deal on one from eBay? While he's at it, I could also use another digital camera. It's not like I have some of the nicest equipment available on this planet, but you know it's always nice to have a spare." He has begun writing again, and now appears very demure as if this is just business as usual.

"I really have no idea how you were able to convince a panel of people that your thesises, or theses, or however you pluralize the word 'thesis' . . . how you were able to convince some academic big shots that you were worthy of not just a Master's but a fucking doctorate blows my mind." I get sidetracked, as if this entire rant is not just one big tangent. "You know, I've never understood why there are so many 'doctors' out there. Do you know how to cauterize a wound? Could you deliver a baby? Could you even spot herpes if it were staring you in the face? This is the company you are in: Hunter S. Thompson is a fucking doctor, and that dude was out of his mind, but at least he was somewhat entertaining. His life was nothing but one huge acid trip, and he's a doctor. Can just anyone be a doctor? Can I be a doctor? I'm pretty good at photography; can I have a PhD from Polaroid University or Kodak Tech? Seriously, have you ever read *Fear and Loathing*? That book is totally messed up, and a doctor wrote it. Think about that. That work of literature was the product of someone on your level, albeit a different area, but still respected in his field. Well I'm tired of idiots being admired for no apparent reason."

I pause to drink some water from a bottle I brought with me; Dr. Polk is still scribbling notes on his pad. I calm down a little bit, but not entirely, and continue with "Dr. Polk, I'm sorry for blowing up, but in all honesty, I came here to talk about my problems, mainly concerning my relationships with women . . . well, lack thereof, but my situation with women. And any time I seem to approach the subject, you completely divert me and I freak out. I honestly think that just about anyone could see that I am a mess, I need help, which is obviously why I'm here, but I still don't necessarily feel comfortable with you rambling about whatever nonsense you desire."

I take another long breath, calming down even more now, still not very pleased about the situation. "For example, I've told you about how sleeping with women has not been a problem for me, at least not in the last few years." He nods to acknowledge that he actually recalls the stories, and I go on, "But I've never even had what I would consider a girlfriend. If I can say that at my age, there has to be something seriously fucked up with me, and I need you to tell me what to do about it. And if you can't, then I need someone who can. There probably aren't too many people who would complain about having meaningless sex with women who have appeared in fashion magazines wearing little more than pieces of tape in certain areas, and I don't want to sound like I haven't enjoyed it, but I need a change."

All of this has come out so quickly. I am breathing rather heavily and even though I have much more to say, I need to stop for a minute to take a break.

"Anton, may I interject for a moment?" Dr. Polk asks me without any concern in his voice that I might snap again. He has most definitely witnessed episodes like this before, and many of them much greater in scope I'm sure.

Breathing heavily, I wearily give him the go ahead, "Yeah sure, whatever you want."

He stares at me for a while, looks me up and down, licks his lips, and taps his pen. He must be doing this on purpose, trying to drag out whatever he wants in order to test my patience to see if this recent incident was a one-time thing or if I have more in the tank.

"Congratulations, it's about fucking time . . . It took a little longer than I had anticipated, but you *finally* spit out what you've been wanting to say for a long, long time."

Huh? No disciplinary words? He isn't going to have me dragged out in a straightjacket? Is he actually encouraging me? And did he just drop an f-bomb?

"You see Anton, I am fully aware that our sessions up until this point have been, well, fruitless at best. Although many therapists disagree with my method, my approach to our conversations is part of my process, and you have just now hit a major milestone on your . . . well your path to solving whatever it is you want to figure out."

I can't focus now; I start feeling a little dizzy. Is this guy messing with me? His method? Part of his process? Am I some sort of science experiment, a control group, or something like that?

"I'm sorry, what do you mean by 'your method,' Dr. Polk?"

"Well, is it safe to say that you came here wanting to talk about things that troubled you, but your reservations were preventing you from discussing exactly what was on your mind?"

"Uh, well, yeah," I say with confusion, wondering where he is going with this.

"Right, well, when people go into therapy, they usually fall into one of the two main categories. There are people who seek counseling and from the first words with their therapist, they just talk a mile a minute. They have no inhibitions talking about anything and everything that is bringing about tension. However, there are also those who have great apprehension. Which, correct me if I'm wrong, I believe you fall into the second category?"

"Well, yeah, but it's not easy to talk about all this stuff to a total stranger," I tell him in a highly defensive tone, almost feeling accused of something.

"That is completely understandable, and as a therapist, I realize that many people are not comfortable bearing their innermost thoughts with me right away. But it would also be ineffective and irresponsible of me to force it out of them. In order to help people, they need to move at their own pace, telling me what they want, when they want to. I hope I've never given you the impression that any topics were off-limits, Anton."

"Well, no, but I mean it seems like you were always talking about something stupid or irrelevant, such as eBay," my tone on the last words resonate with bitterness.

"Oh that," he says with a chuckle, clearly amused and giving me the impression that I am on a hidden camera show. "Anton, I know you're not here because you have a posttraumatic stress disorder." I give him a shocked look, and he catches himself, "I'm sorry, let me rephrase: I highly doubt that is the reason you are here, but I could not have just come out and said that when you were talking about it, because there is certainly the slight chance I could be wrong."

Although he's right, I'm kind of enraged at what is tantamount to calling me a liar. "What makes you think I don't have PTSD?"

"Well Anton, you have told me numerous times how frequently you travel and fly for work. I find it very unlikely that a person with PTSD related to two airplanes crashing into skyscrapers would be able to fly as often as you do. Many people with such a disorder feel an enormous amount of anxiety surrounding the topic at the root of their problem. For you that was airplanes, for many war veterans I counsel, it might be something such as a car engine triggering a memory of a land mine exploding. Please understand that I am not suggesting that you did not witness the events of September 11 in person. I do believe, however, that they were not as destructive to your mental health as you originally claimed." He looks at me, as I have now dipped my head in embarrassment. "Please feel free to correct me if I'm wrong. I am only human after all."

Although I am seriously ashamed of having flat out lied to my therapist, the one person to whom I should be able to say anything, I like where this is going.

"No . . . no, you're right . . . Wow! you're far more observant than I had given you credit for."

"Well, I am a doctor . . . I can't 'cauterize a wound,' but I do know a thing or two about how people think." Oh great, now he's mocking me. Not only does he call me out on my bullshit, he is now making fun of me. Apparently, I'm being counseled by Bill Cosby. At least my psychologist has a slightly better fashion sense, but now I'm really wanting a pudding pop.

I just sit there in silence for a moment with my hand over my mouth, trying to comprehend what exactly has just transpired. Dr. Polk decides to break this silence that has now gone on longer than I can handle.

He continues to explain his method. "You see, I could tell that you were having trouble opening up, which as I said is normal. However, in order for you to benefit from therapy, you have to be able to speak freely and without any qualms. Please forgive me if I upset you, but part of my method is to try and gently nudge people toward opening up, without blatantly forcing them to talk. It's a fine line I try to walk. Sometimes, I walk it just fine, but I make mistakes and misread people too."

I am now rather impressed with this jackass. He was playing me the whole time. Although I want to hate him, I admire his gusto, and now I genuinely feel comfortable talking to him. I start to feel as though Dr. Polk is going to work out just fine for me.

He stands up and initiates one of those introductions that are symbolic of a fresh start, a new beginning. Reaching out to shake my hand, he says, "Hello, Anton. I'm Dr. Polk, what can I help you with?"

8

THE KNOCK ON the door starts off rather calmly, but then gradually ascends to a maddening pounding that I can no longer ignore. What makes it even more obnoxious is that the door is not locked, which is why I refuse to get up and open it. I also know that it's my roommate on the other side, and although we get along just fine, he needs to learn not to do things like this while I'm trying to work. After about thirty seconds of pure pummeling on the door, the knob finally turns and in walks my roommate. Not out of character, especially for a Friday night, he is very drunk.

"Anton, what are you doing dude?" he slurs while stumbling and dropping himself down on the couch next to me.

"Um, I think it's pretty obvious Brent," I say as I hold my book up in his face.

"Dude, Anton! Why are you reading," he takes a few seconds to focus his vision and actually read the cover of my book, "*Civil Disobedience*, on a fucking Friday night? Come on man, it's the first week back and it's time to party. Classes just started a few days ago. You can't have homework already," he says in an aggravated tone. "And who in the world is Henry David Thoreau?"

Although Brent is a pretty nice guy, and very good at math, he is not what I would describe as well read. Yes, he is right in that I really do not have much work to do seeing as syllabi were just handed out on Tuesday and Wednesday, but I came to college to learn. If I wanted to learn about plants, I would have majored in botany or horticulture, instead of Brent's method that involves puking in every variety of shrubbery on and around campus.

"Um, he's this really great author, totally up-and-coming. This book of his just came out about two months ago. I think it's really going to jumpstart his career." Lying to my roommate is really fun when he's wasted because he will believe just about anything I say, and I enjoy seeing how far I can take a foolish tale before he finally calls me on it. "It's for my political science class though, I'll have to write a paper on it in a few weeks."

"A few weeks!" He is in awe that I am thinking that far ahead. Right now, in Brent's (and just about every other coed in the area) opinion, the only thing I should be worried about writing is my address on a slip of paper so that when someone finds me passed out in an alley, the police will know where to return me. "Anton, put the book away, and come to this party with me. I know a few chicks that are throwing this killer welcome back fiasco. And the best part is we can walk there in like five minutes. They live on Durant just off of Telegraph. Please, just come with me. I'll buy your Fat Slice on the way back." Offering me pizza late at night is my weakness, and Brent knows this. He is well aware that bribing me with pizza is a surefire way to sway me to do things I am on the fence about. However, this is a little different, because I know Brent will not be coming home tonight. He will either sleep in a strange woman's bed, or pass out on a lawn. There is no way he is making it to Fat Slice tonight.

"Man, I can go get my own in a little bit. I don't feel like partying tonight," I'm hoping he will understand that I'm trying to gently tell him to leave me alone.

His rather cheery although drunken demeanor has now gone stale. He quickly sobers up and lectures me sternly. "Anton, listen to me. You know you're my boy, but seriously man, you have got to lighten the fuck up. You went to like two parties all of last semester. This is your first year in college . . . college man, the best years of your life, and you're wasting them reading on a *Friday night*! Your whole 'I don't need alcohol to have fun' routine was cute for a few weeks last semester, but honestly bro, you are not having fun. I can tell you're miserable." I am getting really irritated right now, and if we did not attend the university with the highest hippie per capita ratio in the nation, I would probably hit him. I really do not want to deal with attending anger management classes or talking to my

RA because my drunken roommate wouldn't let me read my book on subverting the government.

"Brent, I am having fun. Reading *is* fun, leave me alone." Everyone in my dorm knows this is a fucking lie. I might have believed it myself for a few months last semester, but I can't kid myself anymore. Brent really is right about my tension. I need to relax. The big problem with appeasing him is then I have to deal with my drunken roommate constantly reminding me that he got me to drink, and he's the "reason I'm having fun."

"Bullshit Anton! Seriously, I'm not asking you to drink a case of beer or drive a car drunk. But I know you want to drink Anton. I wouldn't keep trying to get you to do it if I didn't honestly believe that deep down. You are at least a little curious . . . come with me to this party, have *one* beer, and if you hate it, or are having a bad time, you can walk right back to the room and read your book. Please Anton, it will be fun."

I am fighting a huge internal battle at this point. Despite the fact that he is very drunk, Brent is making a lot of sense and saying several things that I have thought personally just never verbalized to anyone. I can't believe I'm actually considering this.

"OK, Brent, I'll go with you, but when I hate it there, I'm gonna leave. And I'm *not* drinking," I say to assert my individuality, a notion I have desperately been clinging onto since I first set foot on the campus of UC Berkeley.

"Sure Anton, whatever you say," he says in a sarcastic tone, implying that he has heard that a million times, and every time it has resulted in a failure to follow through with the given proclamation. "Dude, I'm gonna get you laid, maybe not tonight, but this semester, you're gonna get some ass, and it will be awesome." I try to pretend to be insulted at his reduction of women to nothing more than an objective, but I am also a little excited by the thought. A small smile starts to break out across my face, and I attempt to suppress it before Brent can see it, but it's too late. "Ha-ha, yeah, that's what I'm talking about. Let's do this."

I've never been a party animal, but I was definitely not always this uptight. But going to a really ritzy high school where every kid drove a BMW made me really just want to get far away when I went to college. For whatever reason, I have always has this tendency to go against the grain. When everyone in high school was driving fancy cars and talking about prom, I decided to get a job at Orange Julius and basically skip out on almost every major social function. Again, I was not a misfit or an outcast, but I just felt like focusing my efforts on other things. I simply did not see why people got so worked up over that dance.

I was really proud when I took all that money I made blending delicious fruit-flavored beverages and bought my own used Chevy pick-up. I mean, the thing was by no means glamorous, but something about pulling up to school in a truck that I bought with my own money made me appreciate that vehicle so much. I would take that truck any day over any Mercedes Benz. Well, in all honesty, I was a little jealous of the kids who drove those cars, but like I said, I always had to go against the grain. I'm sure this mentality reeks of insecurity, but it's who I was, and still a big part of who I am.

It was also really cool being one of probably five kids in high school who purchased their own vehicle. Mine was definitely the least glamorous, but the scrapes and dents on that truck were like a badge of pride. The best part of it though was the fact that Danielle Silver and I shared something in common. One day in the middle of senior year, she pulled up to school in a brand-new Jaguar that everyone was drooling over. Up until that day, throughout all of high school, she would walk to school, about a mile or so. That might not sound so bad, but some kids made a commute half that distance in sedans worth more than many houses. A mile walk to a teenager in high school is virtually a light-year. Some people laughed at her for that, never to her face, but I'm sure she caught on. Much to her credit, she always remained at least pleasant though. You see, Danielle was a knockout. Every guy in school was in love with her, but she didn't really hang out with anyone at our school, let alone date them. The fact that she was a bombshell probably did nothing to reduce the remarks about her financial situation. I think she thought they were all too stuck up and spoiled, and about many of them I would probably agree. I rarely exchanged words with her, other than the occasional "hey" and "what's up" that came about in some of our classes. My entire view of her changed on my eighteenth birthday though. Well, I never really had an opinion about her other than that it bothered me when she cheated off my math tests, but when you're in high school and a gorgeous girl is showing you attention, no matter what kind, you don't question it.

A lot of rumors began to spread about how Danielle was able to purchase such a car. Obviously, lots of drug references and pornography jokes ensued, but most of them went by the wayside. Well, on my eighteenth birthday, I found out how she did in fact pay for that car. As a rite of passage, almost all guys go to a strip club for their eighteenth birthday, just like they go get drunk on their twenty-first. Mine was no exception. I was actually older than the majority of my guy friends. However, I was able to round up a couple guys to hit *Stiletto*, a strip club just outside of our hometown of Mission Viejo, for my entry into adulthood. Being in high school, none of us had much money, but my friends were nice enough to pool their money together and buy me a lap dance. I think it cost them $20 total. I went to the restroom, and when I came back, they had a girl waiting to take me back to a private booth. I was a little surprised they had done it, but it was my birthday after all, so I wasn't completely shocked. What really threw me was who was waiting for me. I wonder how many young men Danielle had to show her breasts to in order to purchase that car. My first thought was "what a slut," but the more I thought about it, I thought it was kind of cool. Now, obviously being a young male "adult," I'm likely to think favorably of naked women. But the thing I thought was really cool was that she was making money and buying things for herself. Most of those kids in that school drove cars that their parents bought doing things that might be considered more socially acceptable, but were by no means morally superior. That is just putting it nicely.

When our eyes met, it was so uncomfortable, but Danielle, or Renee as she was called at the club, knew she was at work, and she quickly got back into character. She grabbed my hand and led me back to the private booth.

"Hey Danielle," I said with the most annoying crack of my voice. Had any bouncer heard that he surely would have suspected me of being prepubescent, and likely would have kicked me out. "Um, you look . . . uh, you look nice?" I tell her trying to make this less awkward. "You don't have to do this, I mean, you probably don't want to, I know this is kind of weird."

"Hey Anton, shut up OK," she snaps at me. "Your friends tell me it's your birthday." I nod, "Well happy birthday. Is this your first time in a strip club?"

"Uh, yeah it's my first time. This is a really nice place though,"

"It's a shit hole. You can say it, and I'm not offended. But it pays the bills, and it's not like my knowledge of verb conjugation is going to make me rich" she says jokingly as she unsnaps the back of her bra. "And although it ain't the greatest gig in the world, it's *almost* worth it seeing the look on those shitheads' faces when I pull up in that shiny Jag, you know?"

"Yeah, well I can sort of relate. I bought my truck with my own money too, and I can tell those kids go home and jerk off thinking about my ride," I joke, drawing a laugh out of Danielle, who is now topless and gyrating her hips on my lap. I have no idea how to analyze or describe this situation. Part of me is very aroused. I want to feel embarrassed and ashamed, but part of me also takes some pride in the fact that I'm helping her get back at those kids who talk so much trash behind her back. It's kind of like my going to the strip club is an indirect way of rebelling against boring conformist culture.

It's as if every dollar I stuff in her g-string is striking a blow for the working class. I'm sort of like Cesar Chavez, and that makes me feel good.

I'm a true patriot, my country should be proud. Perhaps, this was what Thoreau had in mind when he wrote *Civil Disobedience*. I can't say for sure though, I only got through about three pages when Brent interrupted me. Going from my high school where cash is king, to Berkeley, California, is about as radical a transition one can make. Don't get me wrong. Cost of living here is outrageous, and the difference between the haves and the have-nots is quite apparent. However, the most obvious contrast is that people in Berkeley at least seem to care about the homeless population. From what I've witnessed, people here are quite generous and progressive about the situation.

Another huge disparity between the two towns separated by merely a few hundred miles is that back home, looks and image dominated. That is not to say that everyone in Berkeley is so above material things. It is still home to an infamous university, and college kids like to buy stuff they do not need. But in Berkeley, people are much more open-minded and accepting than any place I've ever been. It is undoubtedly more welcoming to all kinds of people than the town I grew up in, that's for sure.

As a political science and journalism major, I get a major hard-on just thinking about all of the stuff that has taken place in this community. I live just a few hundred feet from People's Park, home to some of the most impressive protests in this state's history. After just one semester here, my entire worldview was turned around. This is the ideal school for someone such as myself who likes to swim upstream. The truth is that is why it is both ironic and sad that in a place known for promoting diversity and equality, I actually became *less* respectful of women. Not more than three hundred yards from where WoLF, the Women's Liberation Front, fought for women's rights in the mid-1980s, I would start down a road I told myself I'd never go down.

"Dude, Anton, you are not gonna regret this. We're almost there; it's just up ahead three more houses on the right. Do you see the one with all the people on the porch with the Columbian flag?" Actually, it was the Tibetan flag, not uncommon in Berkeley. I do not blame that on Brent's drunken state though; I highly doubt he would get that correct under any circumstance.

"All right, well, let's get this over with," I tell him with a mix of resentment and intrigue. "So who do you know here?"

"What?"

"The girls who live here, you said you know them. Which ones are they?"

"Oh yeah. I was just saying that to get you to come with me. I didn't think you would come otherwise."

"What? That's crap Brent, I'm outta here," I tell him with my teeth clenched as I turn around and begin to walk back to my dorm.

"Anton, I'm kidding," he says as he grabs my arm and pulls me back. "The girls who live there are in my philosophy class. Their names are Samantha and Josie. Come on I'll introduce you. But I call dibs on Josie," he tells me matter-of-factly as if it's a done deal that he and Josie will be hooking up in virtually no time.

"OK, fine. Can we just go inside?" I plead.

"Yep, follow me, and remember this moment . . . the first night of your new life." I follow Brent up about four steps through a swarm of people and into the house that is blasting some kind of reggae-jazz mix, I'm not exactly sure what it is, but I would probably really enjoy it if it were played at a reasonable volume. "Excuse me, comin' through. Come on Anton, keep up," Brent says as he commands his way through the crowd to the backyard, where a group of people is swarmed around a keg. "Ladies, long time no see," Brent says in a really weird voice I've never heard anyone use before. I'm guessing and hoping these girls are Samantha and Josie.

"Brent! Hey, glad you could make it," the shorter girl exclaims as she gives him a hug, and the other girl follows suit.

"Anton, this is Samantha and Josie . . . prospectively," he says as he looks at the girl on the right, then the one on the left.

"You mean, respectively? And it's nice to meet you both," I say as I extend my arm to shake their hands.

"Ah, Anton, you're too fucking smart. Can we please do something about that? Hey Sam, please see to it that Anton gets some of that delicious refreshment right there, OK?"

"You got it Brent," she tells him as she picks up an empty cup and places the spout in it, as the beer begins to flow. "So Anton is your roommate right?"

"Yep, he's the shit, I love this kid." He has already gone into full wingman mode, wasting no time trying to get Samantha interested in me. Although I should be insulted that he thinks I can't get a girl on my own, she is very cute. And let's be honest; the stick is so far up my ass that I don't think there are many girls who would be enticed by me right now.

"Oh great, well thanks for coming . . . here's your beer," she says as she passes me the red plastic cup that matches the 350 or so just like it smashed on the ground. I had definitely planned on not drinking, but women make me do stupid things. My actions are no longer rational when breasts enter the picture. It's not fair, but it's also how I operate. I have this great idea that in my head sounds so easy to execute; I'll just hold the beer all night so at least it looks like I'm drinking. Every few minutes when no one is looking, I'll pour some out. We're outside, so it really should go unnoticed. Right after I take the cup from her and map out my perfect plan, Samantha raises her cup and says "Cheers Anton, drink up!"

"Cheers," I say as my plan goes immediately down the drain, and the crappy beer fights its way down my throat. I almost gag at the taste of it. Although I have tasted beer before, I never liked it, which is part of the reason I never drank. *"How do people do this four times a week?"* I ask myself. Damnit Samantha . . . why do your breasts have to be so, breast-like? So round and fleshy, the essence of breasts. It's not fair. I figure the only way to level the playing field and make things fair is to keep drinking. That is my indisputable logic. Well at the time it made sense, I have no idea why. "Mmm, I love this stuff," I lie to Samantha to try and cover up the fact that I am not even an amateur drinker.

"Yeah, it's OK, but I like shots. Hey!" she gets this look like she has had a revelation. "Let's go do a shot! I have a handle of Jack inside. Stay here, I'll go get it."

As much as this idea worries me, a girl with breasts just told me to stay put, and it's in my nature to follow her orders. I take a few more sips of my beer, trying to take Brent's advice and loosen up. The cup is only half empty when my vision starts to do weird things. I don't have blurred vision. I am definitely not drunk. But every few minutes my eyes will go out of focus for a split second as if I were crossing them trying to make a funny face. This is definitely a result of the Keystone Light taking its toll on my no-longer-immaculate liver and brain, and it does startle me a little bit. I do not have any time to dwell on this though, as Samantha is quickly back with a big glass bottle of brown liquid and four shot glasses.

"Hey Josie, Brent, get over here!" she screams in a commanding voice. The pair, which has wandered off about fifteen feet, catches a glimpse of the whiskey, and their eyes light up. They come rushing to the bottle like kids to an ice cream cone.

"Oh yeah, time for shots," Josie shouts. "Don't let me puke like last time, OK?" she says looking at Brent, as if he has any control over her body's ability to process booze . . . well, maybe he does, I wouldn't be surprised. Samantha sets the four glasses out on a hand railing and fills them to the top with whiskey. She passes them out, and mine spills a little on my sleeve since I am moderately nervous, having never done a shot before.

"What are we toasting to?" Samantha asks.

Brent chimes in with "To getting Anton fucked up! I told you buddy, stick with me and you'll be just fine."

"Yeah whatever ass-face. Let's just do this OK?" I proclaim in a very assertive tone, trying to make the other three believe that I am excited to do this. I can't back out now. There are four breasts looking right at me. And if I do this now, I will never have to listen to Brent harass me again. Well, theoretically, he won't bother me anymore, but even I know better.

"Yeah, drink up," Josie shouts as she raises her glass, and the rest of us do the same. We then drink the whiskey, and it becomes clear that they have all done this several times before. It takes me two tries to get all the booze down, and after I do, I start coughing hysterically. I feel like I'm going to puke, not from too much alcohol, but because it is burning my throat with the fury of a thousand suns.

"Way to go, Anton!" Brent shouts as he pats me on the back, half congratulating me, half trying to prevent me from dying. "Take it easy there, killer, the night is still young. Here, chase it with your beer," he instructs me as he hands me a red cup that I don't think is mine, but I really don't care because I need cold liquid in my mouth to cool the burning. Eventually, I recover from that episode, and probably drink about one more cup of the nasty beer before I decide I've had enough and switch to water. Despite calling it quits with the alcohol, I am actually enjoying myself so I stick around for a while. Although I probably only had the equivalent of three drinks, I am quite giddy at this point. I have never felt like this. I am not falling down, but my weight shifts from side to side without warning, and I continually have to step to the side to stand up straight.

"You OK there Anton?" Samantha asks me in a joking tone.

"Yeah, I'm good, totally fine, I'm way good, that was some good stuff," I tell her, rambling like a true novice. The way I feel right now is most definitely unfamiliar to me, and I absolutely *love* it. I start to ask myself why I waited so long to discover this wonderful potion.

"He's fine Sam. He just doesn't drink a lot," Brent butts in, also indicating to me that this girl might be interested in me. If I were sober, I would have run home screaming long ago. Despite being a freshman in college, I have never even kissed a girl. What if I miss her mouth and lick her face? She'll know that I've never done that before, and then she'll laugh at me and tell everyone at school. I can't risk that kind of embarrassment.

A few bottles of water and some stale chips sitting on top of the fridge helped straighten me out. I am a little buzzed but still feeling pretty good.

For the next hour or so, the four of us make generic conversation about school and our Christmas breaks. My three companions continue to drink at an impressive pace, especially Brent. I imagine he has a remarkably high tolerance though, so I'm not too surprised. Josie is being very flirty with Brent, and although I'm no expert I think Samantha is doing the same with me. I excuse myself briefly to use the bathroom. But I just need to pee; my stomach feels fine. When I return, Brent and Josie are in sight but about twenty feet from where our group was conversing.

"Hey Anton, you're a really good guy, you know that?" Samantha slurs as she throws her arm with a cup of beer around my shoulder, spilling some on my shirt. "I mean, you're like really, really nice." My lack of party experience makes it a little difficult to know for sure, but I am fairly certain that her repetition of the words 'really' and 'good' mean she is inebriated.

"Well, thanks, Samantha, you're pretty cool yourself," I say, trying to return the compliment. My aim is to sound flirty and not desperate, so I try to keep my words at a minimum. Brevity has never been a strength of mine.

"Hey!" she shouts in my ear as if she's just had a revelation, "Call me Sam. All my friends call me Sam, and you're my friend right Anton?"

"Oh, of course, we're totally friends . . . Saman . . . I mean Sam."

"Sweet," she says, and then without hesitation, she drops her cup of beer to the ground and shoves her tongue into my mouth. Not that I objected by any means, but it totally caught me by surprise. And it was awesome. "Hey, now that we're friends, do you wanna walk me home?"

"Huh? I mean, I would, but don't you live here? Brent told me that you and Josie live here."

"Oh no, Josie lives here with her roommates Jamie and Sarah. Jamie is out of town, and I think Sarah is at a party that her boyfriend's frat is throwing," she tells me with great precision, just to make sure that there is no doubt in my mind that she in fact does not live there. "I don't live too far from here though."

"Oh, well, where do you live then? I mean, it is late, and I wouldn't want you to walk home alone." I am confident right now that Sam is asking me to come over and make out, and if I weren't a little drunk, I would probably try to be a gentleman and wimp out. I think about it for a minute, and decide that I will walk her home strictly as a safety precaution, but I will not follow her inside. I like her, and I don't want to take advantage of her.

"I live at," she pauses, probably trying to remember where she actually lives, "at Shattuck, and Ashby."

She had to live on that street didn't she? You could imagine how much of a kick in the nuts it was that when I first arrived in Berkeley for freshman orientation to discover that one of the main streets in the town is named Ashby. I highly doubt when her parents named her that they considered this street thousands of miles from where they lived, but it wasn't entirely unfeasible. The night was going so well. Why did I have to hear *her* name just as I was finally making progress getting over the fact that she and I were never going to happen?

"Did you say Ashby?" She nods. "Yeah, I'll take you home," I tell her, and at that moment, I underwent a transformation that would have made Bruce Banner run for cover. Hearing the word Ashby caused me to throw all inhibitions and insecurities out the window. Although Sam was drunk, she didn't deserve to be treated poorly just because I was frustrated about the girl I couldn't get out of my mind. She runs over to tell Josie that she is leaving, they hug, and she walks back my way. Brent overheard the situation and looked at me with a huge smile and pointed at me with a cocky look in his eyes that said "I told you so." She grabs my hand and leads me toward the front door, and we begin our walk to her place.

"You don't have to be up for anything tomorrow morning do you?" she asks me.

"Nope. I don't have anything to do all weekend. Well, some reading to do, but it's not that big of a deal."

I think Thoreau would be proud of how this evening is about to turn out for me. Well, Samantha and I will definitely stress the "disobedience," I don't expect much about tonight to be civil though.

9

Dr. POLK'S OFFICE feels so spacious and ergonomic. Ever since my little tirade, going to treatment is an entirely different ball game. I feel so much more comfortable talking to him, and like he said, it's about time.

"So, because you are thirty-two and you are not married, you see that as a problem?" he inquires, trying to make sure he understands what I'm saying.

"No, that's not really what I mean. Well, sure, I guess I'd like to be married . . . I mean, it was only a few months ago that I ever gave any serious thought to marriage. It's probably accurate to say that until recently, I saw myself as an eternal bachelor. And for the most part, I liked it that way."

"And now you do not like the thought of that, correct?"

"Yeah, I think . . . I don't know, I just . . . I don't know."

"That's fine. No one said you have to know everything right now. You are also certainly allowed to change your mind," he says offering his reassurance.

"You know, it's just that I've always taken pride in going for the best; in getting all the things, especially women, that everyone else aspires to but cannot get."

"OK, and why do you think that is?"

After a long pause to reflect on this question, I respond "You know, it's weird because I'm not really sure." That's bullshit, because I absolutely know the reason for this, and it started back in high school. Throughout all of my sessions with Dr. Polk, it has become very common for him to ask me a question that I pause to think about. And almost always, I give him a vague response, when in reality I definitively know the answer. This is a huge problem, but I have made great progress in fixing it. Obviously, I still have a little way to go though.

My indifference might have been acceptable in the past, but now that my therapist knows I am aware that I'm hiding things, he always tries to pry it out of me. He does not however, force it out of me, just like with his eBay tactic. "Well, when the answer comes to you, you just let me know," he tells me in a tone that is two parts comfort, one part insult, with a dash of "don't be a loser" thrown in for good measure.

"What I do know is that I had no success with women in high school, and college started off much the same way. But after a few good . . . and a few questionable decisions, that changed rather quickly. When I finally started having sex and being physical with women, it completely changed me as a person. I didn't have any great enlightenment or anything, you know? But, my personality changed. My priorities shifted, and I went from just wanting to make friends, to being content with nothing less than making out with a girl."

"And this no longer satisfies you?"

"Well, yes and no. I mean, no matter how you look at it, sex is usually a pretty awesome thing. But maybe because I'm getting older and all my friends are getting married, I just start to think I need more." Where the fuck was this coming from? I never used to think like this. "I think it's also that recently I've started to view college and the lifestyle typically affiliated with it, to be, well . . . you know, sort of just a fad I guess."

"That's not uncommon. It is true that many young adults try to 'hold on' so to speak to their collegiate lives by continuing to participate in the activities they used to engage in while in school. Conversely, many of them decide that those things had their time and place. It appears that you're transitioning from the former to the latter; perfectly normal. It's also not abnormal for people to never grow out of those old habits. Everyone is different."

Despite the fact that I am developing a stronger rapport with Dr. Polk, it is exactly this kind of response that drives me up a fucking wall. But I honestly believe all therapists are like this to an extent. He is so indifferent, so passive. Whether he has an opinion about my sexual habits or not, I would never know. Dr. Polk consistently presents me with these broad statements that are so PC and unbiased I want to throw something. Why can't he just look me in the eyes and say, "Anton, it's about time you've decided to grow up. Getting drunk and sleeping with strange women is fine when you're young. But have at least a little bit of dignity and responsibility. You're not a fucking child, so stop acting like one. You are not getting anything out of casual sex." But he will never say that to me, no matter what ridiculous scenarios I tell him about in my life.

I just get really frustrated that everyone is so afraid of offending someone that they feel they have no other choice to use open-ended statements void of any finite viewpoint. My qualms with this are not to the point where I'm going to lash out like last time, but I definitely feel the need to say something.

"Dr. Polk? Can I ask you something?"

"Of course you may," he says, stressing the last word to emphasize my improper use of the words that are regularly treated as interchangeable.

"Well . . . why don't you just tell me I'm being foolish?"

"Excuse me?"

"I mean, clearly I'm telling you that I am not thrilled about the fact that I have casual sex with women simply because they are attractive. Yet all you seem to respond with are things like 'that's natural,' and 'just give it a little time.' Why don't you just tell me to grow up and act like an adult? I don't want to live like this anymore," I tell him sternly, but politely.

"Are you sure?" he asks me, implying that I'm full of it.

"What?" I ask in shock. Did he not just listen to what I said?

"I said, are you sure? You see, patients tell me all the time about things they do or do not want to do, and at the end of the day, it really comes down to one thing: you. It's up to you, Anton. If you really, truly do not want to continue having casual sex, well, don't. If you want to get married, it's up to you to start showing people that. You have to let your actions demonstrate your goals and motives. Think of it like this: If you were at a party getting drunk, flirting with every woman there, carousing freely, don't you think most people there will read that as you trying to get laid? Conversely, by asking women out on dates, women your age, with similar goals and interests, you are sending a message that you want a relationship. Not necessarily marriage right then, but that you value human interaction and a connection with another person."

Fucking. Wow! It's about time this guy gave me some good advice. This last little bit of knowledge he just dropped on me is by far the most valuable thing he has said to me. It seems so fucking obvious, but I never even seriously thought about it like that. It is up to me. It is entirely up to me.

I pause for almost a full minute, taking in and reflecting on what he has told me. And I become even more relaxed after he finally put me in my place. All of a sudden, one of the biggest things I've wanted to get off my chest is ready to come out. I can't keep it inside any longer.

"You know, as you were asking earlier, about why I say I want the best. I think it's really simple actually. I mean, I never even kissed a girl until college. That wasn't so bad, a little embarrassing, but I think it bothered other people more than it did me. No, what was really disheartening was this girl I was really good friends with in high school."

He interrupts, writing on his pad, "This is a girl whom you dated? Rejected you?"

"Oh no," I say because it's apparent I have mislead him. "No, I mean, I definitely had feelings for her. But just like most crushes in high school, I was too nervous to do anything about it. Really, the main problem is not that I never ended up with her. Of course that sucked, but just hanging out with her was fun. No, what really, *really* got to me was how all the other kids reacted to our friendship."

"I'm sorry, by 'our' you are referring to?" He leads me.

"Oh, I'm sorry, my best female friend in high school. Her name is Ashby." He nods, and now that I've sorted out any potential confusion, I continue, "You see, Ashby was really popular, everyone in school just thought she was really cool. She was very admired but also very nice to everyone. And somehow, even though I'd never even really spoken to many girls until I met her, she decided that we were going to be close friends. I didn't think much of it at the time, but she was right, our friendship was . . . is . . . one of the most important things in my life."

He's staring at me, kind of wondering where I'm going with this. "And the problem is what?"

"Well, it's not that I was *un*popular in high school, but as I'm sure you are aware, kids at that age are very judgmental. And most of them thought she was too cool to be hanging out with me. At first, it annoyed me, but I just figured everyone else was jealous. But over time, it really started to get to me. I mean, I could only listen to people talk trash to me so many times before I started to believe it."

"Do you happen to recall the kinds of things they would say to you?"

"Oh yeah, it was all pretty much along the lines of 'You know she doesn't want to fuck you right? Why are you wasting your time?' and 'Anton, she is way out of your league. You could never get with that in a million years.' And I think that really ate away at me. Over time, I think I developed the impression that in order to . . . validate myself, I had to sleep with women who were considered out of my league. I hate to say it, but I was living to impress other people. I started valuing the things they wanted me to value, and desire the girls they said I should be attracted to."

As I finish, he continues to write. Once he has finished, he looks up at me, pauses, and says to me, "Well Anton, the fact that you have acknowledged this is a huge step. Now the question is what are you going to do about it?"

Naturally, he always ends with one of those questions like he's fucking Socrates or something. Why can't he just tell me what to do? I'm not his student; I'm not looking for enlightenment. I just want to be normal.

Well, whatever normal is, I'm not sure. But I do know that whatever I am, it's not what I want to be. And like he said, this is a *huge* step.

10

JUST LIKE ALMOST every male above the age of thirteen, masturbation is a staple of my existence. Although I have always indulged in it, my free time over the last few weeks has become increasingly taken up with this habit. The sock I stash under my bed has been used so many times that it is becoming stiff as a board. It is so solid that I could hop in a kayak and row myself up a stream. I have used it so many times that it is actually beginning to chafe me. Now the obvious solutions are to either throw it away or wash it. The only reason I am hesitant to do either of those things is that after enough "uses," my sock begins to smell like baked goods. I cannot decide if it's banana bread, brownies, or a blueberry muffin, but it certainly has a much more pleasant aroma than semen glazed all over the 1000 thread-count Egyptian sheets belonging to a runway model. The smell is so good I am actually considering buying a twelve-pack of tube socks, marinating them for a few months, and then hiding them in various places around my abode. I think it might give the place a certain something extra. Truth be told, no matter how good the smell is, I do have to change socks every now and then. I even name them after girls kind of like hurricanes. First was A (and no, I didn't go with the obvious "A" name), Allison, B was Brenda, C was Charlene, and after several months, I'm on H, which I've decided to name Holly.

But all the jerking off in the world cannot change the fact that I am undergoing the longest dry spell of my life since my sophomore year of college, and it is driving me absolutely insane. I've always jerked it on a somewhat regular basis, but because I've had regular sex for the last several years, I've never been dependent on it. Now, I have Dr. Polk to thank for my deranged frame of mind. I have tried very diligently to show other people that I am ready for commitment. It has been nothing short of miserable though. This is not something simple like giving up soda because you consume too much sugar. Giving up sex with women is undoubtedly the most difficult thing I have ever done.

And I'm less than a month into it. I have no idea how long I will last. The chances of me falling off the shaggin' wagon are ridiculously high. The one thing that has made this scenario even remotely feasible is that my last few assignments have been shots with males: plenty of men in suits and ties, suspenders and fedoras. As tough as celibacy has been, these assignments have made it less of a challenge. That is all about to change though, as I am on my way to a photo shoot with Svetlana Stalin.

I am pretty comfortable in my assessment of women with first and last name alliterations: they are either porn stars or very full of themselves. Jasmine Jacobs, Brianna Banks, Tania Tyler, just to name a few. These are some of the hottest, most confident, and bitchiest women I have ever met. Svetlana Stalin is no exception. My current celibate streak is in jeopardy this weekend not only because she is gorgeous, but because she and I have indeed slept together in the past . . . twice. And to make matters worse, she is arguably the best sex I have ever had. Despite the fact that she has adamantly told me many times that she is in no way related to the Russian ruler who shares her surname, her dictatorial pillow talk and bedroom antics indicate otherwise.

The temptress in question and I met about three years ago, when she was only nineteen. Although I found her to be incredibly stunning, I told myself there was no way I was going to make a move on her; she was way too young for me. To my credit, I was right . . . initially, that is. Our rapport was strictly professional on that first shoot; however, that was not the case five months later when I was assigned to photograph her for a spread on formal wear. At some point in those five months between our sessions, she had done some kind of project for MTV with my good friend Jenny Desmond. Well, like I said, merely being affiliated with her almost ensured that I could have any woman in the fashion world that I wanted.

So when we worked together that second time, Svetlana was quite persistent to hook up with me. Although I resisted at first, I did not put up much of a fight because my libido was making all of my decisions at that time. Sadly, that has not changed a great deal. Certainly, I felt a little odd having sex with a girl a decade younger than I was, but I quickly justified it due to the fact that it was life changing. Incredible does not even begin to properly describe how wonderful the sex was. It stuck in my mind for weeks. So naturally when we were assigned to work on another project a little over a year after that, I did not even have to think twice about what was going to happen. My mind was already made up. And it certainly lived up to its expectations. It was even better than the first time.

So yeah, it's going to be monumentally difficult to resist her advances. Honestly, she has no reason to think we won't be having sex with each other tonight. She knows I want her, and she is a Russian beauty who simply needs sex more than her vodka omelet for breakfast. I have no idea how I am going to dodge this one.

After I finished setting up my equipment and performing the standard checks to make sure everything works, I head over to the pastry table to try and take my mind off of Russian women with flawless breasts. There is no way that wolfing down two apple muffins, a croissant, and two cups of coffee could ever take my mind off my current state, but they certainly help. Just as I am about to make my way over to my equipment, a young man approaches me from behind.

"How is everything sir?"

I'm assuming that this young man works for the catering service, given his nicely pressed black pants and polo shirt with a golden name tag that reads "Joey." I respond, "Oh, hey there. Um, it's delicious, thank you very much for setting this up." I really hope he works for catering; otherwise, he will probably be insulted by my presumption.

"That makes me so happy to hear that," he says to me with a wide grin, definitely mocking me because I'm sure he'd rather be playing X-Box than pampering those of us in this superficial industry. "Hey, I got a question for you."

"Yeah, what's that?" I ask him, figuring it will be something simple such as an inquiry for the time, or maybe if I can get him an autograph from one of the models.

Just to solidify my initial reaction that this kid was a ballbuster, he comes back at me with "Do you know what the best part about being the color of skin that my race is?"

Now, I do not usually make my first descriptions of people based on their race, but in this case, it is actually pertinent. Joey is an African-American teenage boy, or black, as some people like to say; my guess would be about fifteen or so. I have to pause for a second to digest what he just said because it definitely came out of nowhere. "Um, uh . . . No, what's that?" I ask hesitantly, not really sure if I want to know the answer or not.

He looks me right in the eye and very earnestly says to me, "Well, before you're born, and you're in the womb, there's a bright light on inside . . . and there are a bunch of buttons lit up, and you get to push the one for which sport you want to be good at."

I chuckle a little because the visual he has just painted inside my head is pretty funny. I humor him by asking, "Oh yeah, well which one did you push?"

After a brief pause, he responds "All of 'em." He says this straight-faced while staring me down, as if he was challenging me to a decathlon. I laugh quite a bit at his response and just walk back to my camera fearing what other strange things he might say to me if I stick around.

I am back at my camera loading a roll of film for no more than two minutes, when I hear a woman's voice behind me.

"Well, well, well. Mr. Anton Bradley, so good to see you again."

Oh shit, it's her. I know it is Svetlana because she called me by my first and last names, and when she said it, her unmistakable Russian accent distorted it to sound like "Mistur Entunn Breddlee." I am in trouble, and I have not even seen her yet. She has not even been in the room for ten seconds (to my knowledge), and I already have to subtly adjust the growing organ in my pants to avoid an inevitably awkward greeting.

I turn around as she is walking toward me to greet her. Fortunately, she is in a full-length robe, and her hair is up in a bun. She is just about ready to get her hair and makeup done, but has just come by to say hi. Even though she is fully covered, this woman is a knockout. Her accent does not help my situation much either. We exchange the general greetings and make conversation for a few minutes, but then one of her stylists gets her attention and beckons her away from me. She gives me a hug and a European kiss on both cheeks, and walks away, moving her perfectly sculpted ass left to right like a metronome with every step she takes. As she reaches the hallway she is about to head down, she turns back to catch me checking her out. She smiles and winks because she knew I would be looking. Sadly, I knew she knew I would be staring, and I kept looking anyway. My only thought is that if she looks that good in a robe, she looks one thousand times better with nothing at all.

The next hour drags by very slowly, and even though we are now starting late, I really don't think my boss would approve of me admonishing a big name in fashion. When Svetlana eventually is ready to begin, she makes her way down the hall and turns the corner into my view. I am so grateful that today is not a swimsuit or lingerie kind of day. Don't misunderstand, the tight black dress in which she is gingerly strutting toward me perched atop four-inch stilettos leaves nothing to the imagination, though it's certainly more beneficial to me than if she were wearing merely a bunny fur Russian Trooper hat and matching boots (which she actually owns by the way).

This is by far the longest shoot of my life. I do not mean in real time, because it only lasted about two hours. But in my mind, it lasted forever. The whole time, I was dreading what would inevitably ensue after I packed up my gear and Svetlana got back into her personal attire.

After I am packed and ready to leave, I bolt for the door hoping I can make it outside to flag down a taxi as soon as possible. Ideally, I can pack up and leave without being seen by the female Baryshnikov, but just as I pick up my last bag and turn around, I am spotted.

In a seductive Russian accent I hear, "Anton Bradley, I hope you're not leaving without saying good-bye."

Trying to pretend like I was not actually avoiding her, I turn around and feign my delight that she has tracked me down. "Ah, there you are!" I say, hoping she will believe that I in fact was looking for her and not the contrary. I leave it at that though because I know the more I say the more likely it is that she will be straddling me tonight. This is not me being cocky, this is just a matter of fact, because she hates being told no, and I'm not very good at rejecting attractive women.

"What is our plans tonight?" She says with great assumption. Notice she did not ask what *I* was doing tonight, she deliberately used the word *our*, because in her mind everything that leads up to the moment we rip off one another's clothing is merely a formality. Most men would be thrilled with a woman who hates the entire ritual of dinner, drinks, and some form of entertainment. Svetlana would much rather skip all of that and get down to business. And although I have not always used the best discretion in how I deal with women, I have never been comfortable sleeping with someone without at least having something that resembles a conversation. Most of the time that basically just means we talk about a random amalgam of things ranging from movies, to work, to the most recent band we saw live. Admittedly, it is rarely invigorating, and it really amounts to nothing more than protocol, but it still makes me feel more comfortable with the situation.

"Oh, um, well my flight is really early tomorrow morning, so I'm probably going to have to make it an early night. If you just want to go out without me I'll understand." This is a lie and a very bad one at that. My flight tomorrow is at 2:35 p.m., which is not asking a lot of even the most inebriated of us all.

"Oh, nonsense." Then she called me some word I couldn't understand at all. I am not fully certain, but I believe what she just called me was her "sweet." I hear her say it to everyone though, so I do not necessarily put a lot of weight in it. This is comparable to most American models referring to everyone as "babe" or "hon." Obviously, she knows my name, but I can tell she uses it around many people whose moniker she really has no desire to learn. "We go to bar near my hotel, very nice place, you like it I know this," she commands me in good but not perfect English.

Her assertiveness has quickly broken down my defense, and I respond by asking "Oh OK, well where is that? I'm staying on Lexington near the Chrysler Building."

She rolls her eyes at me, scoffing my hotel because odds are that she is staying at the Waldorf-Astoria. Even though we are staying somewhere between eight and ten blocks apart, in her mind, I might as well have booked a dumpster in Harlem.

"Hmm, cute. I am stay at Waldorf. Meet me in lobby 11:00 p.m. Not late," she tells me with such conviction, and walks off. I do not even have the chance to respond, ask a question, or decline. This is off to a really bad start.

I eventually hail a cab and drop my stuff off in my apparently tawdry hotel room in the ghetto of NYC near Grand Central Station, and take a quick little nap. When I wake up, I decide to get some lunch, maybe it's dinner. I'm not really sure because it's not terribly late, but I have not eaten much since those muffins this morning. All that I know is I need food. I drag myself out of bed and begin to wander around the city looking for some pizza. Surprisingly, despite the fact that New York is a fashion hub of the world, I have not spent a great deal of time in this city. I know how to find the major spots like Central Park, the Empire State Building, and Times Square, but not much else. Fortunately, I do not have to walk far before I spot two pizza joints on opposite sides of the street, each appearing to have a similar amount of "refinement." Since I'm not strapped for time, I opt to go for the one across the street basing my choice simply on the names. All I can think is that it's pizza in New York City, so it must be good. There is just something about the name *Moretti's* that is more appealing to me than *Frank's*. I'm sure they're both pretty good, but when it all comes down to it, I'd rather tell people I ate at *Moretti's* than *Frank's*. It's safe to say I'm not exactly what you would refer to as a discerning consumer, or one overflowing with tenacity.

As expected, the pizza was good . . . not great, nothing mind-blowing, but certainly above average. I think the best way to analogize New York style pizza served in the city itself is by comparing it to losing your virginity. Everything you have ever been told your entire life leads you to think it will be the most pleasurable thing to ever happen to you. When it finally does, you leave with a smile on your face, but you can't help but feeling a little bit let down considering all the hype surrounding the situation. That is not very fair to New York style pizza, but maybe New Yorkers shouldn't give everyone pizza blue balls.

I still have a couple of hours before I have to meet Svetlana at her hotel, and although I would love to do something touristy or walk through the city, I opt for simply watching television in my room. Nothing very entertaining is on, and I doze off briefly again. I anticipated as much, but luckily my alarm woke me up with enough time to get dressed and find a cab. With the circumstances as they are, I passed on taking a shower. I didn't forego one due to time constraints, but I want to make myself as undesirable to Svetlana as possible. This strategy might backfire though because I'm pretty sure Russians are rather rugged and unkempt, so I might actually end up arousing her more.

The thought of showing up just a few minutes late to agitate her crosses my mind, but I really do not want to deal with a one-sided verbal cold war over five minutes of tardiness. I get to the lobby of her luxurious hotel with a few minutes to spare, and not surprisingly, she is nine minutes late herself. I expected this, but it is definitely better than the other way around. One set of elevator doors open, and out steps Svetlana. As she walks toward me, every head turns and jaw drops as she passes each man on her way. It is simply unfair how spectacular she looks. A black backless dress reveals her pristine muscle tone. It is so short that any uncalculated movement might send the dress high enough to give all of New York a free peak. If that were to happen, the Statue of Liberty, New Year's Eve ball drop, and Yankee Stadium combined wouldn't have as many interested spectators as this lobby. I wish I had Dr. Polk's personal number, so I could ask for advice, but I am on my own. Suddenly, I find myself questioning whether or not celibacy is such a good idea.

She quickly walks up to me, stops about a foot away, and looks me up and down. A solid twenty seconds pass before she mutters, "You get hit by train on way to see me?"

This must mean I don't look good, so I guess my plan has at least worked for a little while.

"It is good look for you, I always thought you were too much . . . how you say? Pretty boy," she tells me. Apparently, the plan did not work out as well as I had anticipated.

I try to just go with it and respond, "Oh well, I just thought I'd try something new since I haven't seen you in so long." Shit, I just cannot seem to get away from flirting. It really is second nature to me. This is a habit I need to work much harder on breaking.

"Yes, yes. Anton Bradley, follow me," she commands as she heads for the door and waves for a cab. One quickly arrives and stops in front of us, the bellhop moves to open the car door for her, but I stop him and do it myself because I know I will get an earful if I don't. "Gilt at Palace Hotel. You know this place, yes?" she says to the driver. I catch his facial reaction in the rearview mirror, and immediately I grow suspicious.

It is not even an exaggeration to say that the cab ride lasted less than one minute. Literally, three blocks later, the cab pulled up to another swank hotel, I rolled my eyes while looking away from Svetlana, gave the driver a ten, and got out of the cab. It has nothing to do with the money, but this was more than a cliché move on her part. Everyone thinks supermodels are stuck up, and usually I defend them when people start tossing around insults. But it's things like this that really annoy me. It was not very cold out, and I would have enjoyed a brief walk.

The inside of this hotel is incredible, but to Svetlana, I assume it is just another Howard Johnson that charges way too much. She walks with great purpose toward the lounge area, always a few steps ahead of me, but close enough so that people know we're together. I spot the oval-shaped bar in the distance, and begin to think this will be a somewhat enjoyable evening. Svetlana spots a table in the bar area, but far enough away that we will not be surrounded by many people. She quickly sits down, crosses her legs, and as I begin to sit, she interrupts me by ordering me with her charming accent, "I have Stoli martini. Naked. No olive. Up. I take two of this." Short and to the point, I like that. What has me a little concerned is that she wants two of them right away. I nod at her acknowledging that I did in fact hear her, and wander over to the bar.

A man in a very nice vest and tie approaches me, lays a cocktail napkin on the bar, and says, "Good evening sir. What can I get for you?"

"Let's see. I need two naked Stoli martinis, up, without olives." He nods to me and begins to turn around, assuming that is all I want. I stop him with, "And I'll have a Maker's and ginger please." He pauses for a second, shrugs his shoulders, and goes back to making the drinks. What does he care if I'm drinking one or three drinks? It's all money and a fatter tip for him. And due to the simplicity of these drinks, they are sitting in front of me in no time.

"Would you like to open a tab or pay for this now, sir?" he politely asks me.

"Oh, um, tab please," I say as I open my wallet and hand him one of my credit cards. He gently takes it out of my hand and places it behind him next to a bottle of cognac. "Thank you," is all I say as I figure out a way to carry three glasses back to our table. Sadly, they do not yet make cardboard beverage holsters for martinis.

When I return to Svetlana, she does not even assist me with the drinks. She waits until I have clumsily placed all three glasses on the table, and grabs her first martini. By now, I'm annoyed enough that resisting her would be a relatively easy task . . . if she were wearing just a little more clothing that is. She looks incredible. I have never seen her looking bad, but she is more tempting now than ever before. Honestly, it might be my dry spell talking, but I really do think this is the most attractive I have ever seen Svetlana.

The conversation for the next ten minutes is less than thrilling, just basic chitchat about modeling and what projects we have worked on since we last saw one another. I had barely even sipped my whiskey by the time she downed both of her martinis, and pointed to the bar telling me to get two more. Not even a word out of her mouth, she simply pointed at the bar. I read somewhere that vodka in Russian means "little water." That is probably the most accurate description for how Svetlana is treating these cocktails. After an hour or so of talking about nothing meaningful, she has downed ten martinis, and I don't even think she is remotely drunk. I on the other hand have only consumed three drinks, and already I'm feeling a bit of a buzz. This does not help at all now that Svetlana has begun flirting with me, touching my face gently. Occasionally, she will put her hand on my knee and rub it, laughing at all of the uninteresting things I say. I am done for. I know it.

"Anton Bradley, please another, yes," she tells me once she polishes off her eleventh martini. Around number nine she decided she better "take it easy" and only order them one at a time. I get up because let's face it; I'm whipped. I also need another drink, despite my judgment already being less than stellar. But what I really need is to get away from the seductress for at least a minute, to make a feeble attempt to clear my mind.

By this point, the bartender just has the Stoli bottle on the bar top and when he sees me stand up, he grabs a martini glass and begins to pour. In the ten seconds or so it takes me to stagger to the bar, he has already made both our drinks. "Thanks, Greg, thank you," I tell him with a smile and a wink. He nods back with a big grin as I pick up the glasses and take a sip of my whiskey and ginger ale. As I swallow the drink, something tastes funny, so I stop and tell Greg. "Hey Greg," I say rather loudly, but not a full yell. "I mean, excuse me, Greg," he quickly walks over to me and quickly raises his eyebrows, curious as to what the problem is. "I think the ginger ale is flat or something. This drink tastes a little off." He grabs a shot glass and the beverage gun, dispensing some of the amber soda into the cup. Greg picks it up to his mouth and tastes it.

He makes a strange face as he downs the liquid, "Oh yeah, you're right. The carbonation is all screwed-up. I'll have someone check the CO_2 right away sir."

All of a sudden, something in me feels very uneasy. "I'm sorry, what was that?" I ask, making sure I heard him correctly.

"Oh, the carbonation is off. That probably just means the carbon dioxide tank is empty or something like that. But don't worry sir, I've already signaled for someone to take care of it."

And just like that, my life flashes back to the first day of my sophomore year of high school. I have replayed that moment over and over again in my mind on a daily basis ever since it happened. The moment when Ashby McHale asked our chemistry teacher if someone could get mono from carbon monoxide inhalation. That was the day I met her, I'll never forget it.

"No, Greg, don't worry about it, this one is fine," I say as I raise my whiskey, turn around and head back toward Svetlana.

She takes a sip, still appearing unfazed by the gallon or so of vodka she has recently consumed. When she finishes, she sets the glass down, and leans into me, saying very softly but not quite whispering, "I have room upstairs, fourth floor. Come with me."

OK, now is this really necessary? We couldn't just get another cab and ride back the three blocks to the most lavish hotel in New York City? She really is horny I suppose.

Honestly, if it were not for the fact that the carbonation ran out just a few moments before I ordered the last round, I would have gone upstairs with Svetlana Stalin. I would have let her pleasure me until everyone of my commie-sperm manifested all over her perfectly toned abdominal muscles. Immediately, the image of sperm cells flying around waving a hammer in one hand and a sickle in the other enters my head. Naturally, half of them are chanting "From each according to his abilities," and the other half is crying out "To each according to his needs." Well, I like to think that my sperms are more progressive than that, so I'm sure they would say "his/her" as applicable . . . on the other hand, maybe my sperm is sexist and it's better for my body to expel it before it corrupts the rest of me.

    Nevertheless, that is not what happened, and tonight, for the first time in a long time, I am going to turn down sex from a gorgeous woman. I have a brief but profound instant of introspection, and I just think to myself how proud I am that this is really going to happen (or not happen, depending on how you look at it).

    As Svetlana stands up and pulls down her dress, even though it does not accomplish much, she throws back the last few ounces of her martini, and sets the glass down on the marble tabletop with a sound that resonates loud enough for most people to notice over the music in the room. She begins to walk out of the lounge and in the direction of the elevators, and after about eight steps, she must sense that I'm not moving, and she turns back to look at me. "Anton Bradley, come, it is time for bed play."

    I take a deep breath because I know that I am on the verge of giving myself blue balls. I set my drink down and slowly pace toward her, stuttering slightly "Um, I'm sorry Svetlana, but I can't tonight. I don't think it's a good idea." Wow! Her eyes got very wide, very quickly. I might as well have just said "it's not you, it's me."

    "Excuse me?" she inquires with a tone that appears to be offering me a chance to redeem myself.

    "Um, you are . . . this is . . . I'm sorry, but I just . . . no, I can't do this."

    "Oh, silly boy. You come with me now," she declares as she grabs my hand. Part of her thinks I'm merely joking or playing a game, and the other part of her has no idea how to handle this pending rejection.

    Now, I'm rather proud to say I'm highly conversational in three languages other than English. Unfortunately, Russian is not one of them. I do however know that "*Нет*" (sounds like "net") is the Russian phrase for no. As much as I would like to assert my stance here by telling her no in her native tongue, I actually think it would prove to be fruitless, because I don't think she has ever been told "no" in her entire life.

    I become noticeably more assertive with my tone, "Svetlana, it's just a bad idea, I've got to go." I take two steps toward the door, but quickly turn back toward her and pull out my wallet. "Here, take this if you want to go back to your other hotel. I know you have a room here, but if you like the other place better, I don't want you being stuck here." I put a twenty-dollar bill in her hand, and she looks at it like it's some sort of festering animal corpse. I might as well be speaking Portuguese (which sadly I do not) because none of this is really registering with either of us. "Good night Svetlana," I say as I kiss her a single time on her left cheek. Then I sashay away from her, very proud of what I have just accomplished, and even more delighted that I avoided saying something cliché like "I'll see you soon" or "we'll be in touch."

I get outside and decide to take a cab to my hotel, because I'm in no mood to walk. As a taxi comes to a stop in front of me, I realize I did not pay my tab or pick up my credit card. I open the door to the cab and tell the driver "Hey I'm gonna be a couple of minutes. If you don't want to wait, I'll understand. But I have to run inside for something."

I walk very briskly back to the bar where I see Greg waiting for me with a leather case that has my tab in it. In the two or three minutes I was gone waiting for a cab, Svetlana had already found another "companion" for the evening. He's a silver fox, to be euphemistic. I'm pretty sure this guy was actually Abraham Lincoln's boyhood friend. He no doubt has lots of money, and he is making no effort to conceal that fact by flashing his gold Rolex and Versace suit at her. She is now drinking martini number forty-five I think, I lost track at ten. If she notices me, she is doing a good job of pretending otherwise. Oh well, I can't be mad, I brought this on myself.

I arrive at the bar, "Hey Greg, I'm so sorry man." I open the case to look at the receipt, and my jaw drops. I knew it would be expensive, but wow!

"Hey no worries brother, it happens a lot actually," Greg tells me in a tone much more casual than he has been using all night. "You want me to run it on this card or another one?" Greg asks.

Everyone of her martinis ran $15, and the total ended up just a little over $200. I have definitely spent more on one tab in a single evening; the big difference was that I was usually buying drinks for ten or more people. I open up my wallet, pull out three crisp portraits of everyone's favorite kite-flying, bifocal wearing Founding Father. "Um, neither, I'll just pay cash," I tell Greg as I throw the money down and he looks at me with awe. Probably not the biggest tip he's ever received, but it's substantial that's for sure.

"Thank you very much sir. You have yourself a great evening," he tells me as he hands me back my credit card. "Is there *anything* else I can help you with tonight?"

"No, I think I'm good Greg. Buy yourself something nice," I tell him with a wink. I have no idea why I'm acting like this. I have no one to impress, but I am certainly acting that way. Really, this must be based on my elation over my recent triumph.

I walk casually out of the bar while putting my card back into my wallet, and a small grin comes across my face. And as I exit the hotel, I'm pleased to see my cabbie still waiting for me. I really appreciate it, but if he thinks he's also getting a $90 tip, he should probably think again. I jump inside, loosen my tie, and tell him where to go. We arrive in a matter of seconds, and I give him my last twenty-dollar bill, telling him to keep the change. This was by far one of the most expensive nights of my life, at least considering what I got out of it. But when I look at it in retrospect, it was very much worth it.

Once inside my hotel room, I quickly take off my suit, throwing the tie and shirt on the bed, but having enough awareness to hang up the pants and coat. After I am undressed, I grab a full-sized towel from the bathroom, whip it out, and beat it like it's a captive KGB spy being detained for treason. Masturbation has never felt this bittersweet. When I finish, I throw on some shorts and take the towel down the hall to a larger trashcan. I know I'll probably be charged for it, but I would just feel too guilty having someone dry themselves off with that towel. I know they'll launder it, and I'm probably not the first, but for some reason I just feel weird doing that.

After that fiasco of a weekend, the trip back home is a piece of cake. I have never slept better on an airplane in my entire life. Oddly enough, when we land and I wake up, I am suddenly filled with regret. I start second-guessing myself and continually question whether or not I should have nailed Svetlana Stalin. I know it's clearly too late to do anything about it now. And deep down, I also know I did the right thing, but now my decision is haunting me to say the least.

Not that I was gone for very long, but coming home from a trip is always so soothing. I drop my bags on the floor by the front door and head straight for my bed. Regardless of sleeping well on the plane, I'm still quite fatigued. Unfortunately, when I take my wallet out of my pocket and throw it on my dresser, I knock over the small bin of Kix cereal I keep up there within a few feet of my aquarium. The little round beads of grain fall and roll all over the floor, but I am too tired to care or clean it up. All I can focus on is sleep . . . and not sleeping with the gorgeous Russian model.

My exhaustion is overwhelming, but the questions racing through my brain are even more intense. I toss and turn for almost two full hours, look at my clock, and see that it's just after 6:00 p.m. Not too late to still accomplish something today. I think about going to a movie, or maybe just taking a walk. A list of things a mile long scrolls through my mind, but when it's all said and done, I decide what I want to do most.

I get out of bed and walk back to my bags so I can grab my cell phone from one of the side pockets I usually leave it in while traveling. I flip it open and scroll through my address book, going straight for the "N" section. I find the name I'm looking for, and dial.

"Hey, Anton, what's up?" a female voice responds with minimal enthusiasm upon answering.

"Hey Nikki, I was wondering . . . you doin' anything tonight?"

11

My head is throbbing, and I'm not even close to being hungover. The sunlight seeping in through a crack in my window shades makes it impossible to stay asleep, so I roll over and look at the alarm clock. It's 10:07 a.m.

"Shit, I'm late," I say in a casual tone, but still mildly concerned that my next appointment with Dr. Polk starts in twenty-three minutes.

"Why is it when a girl says 'I'm late' to a guy, he flips out and asks 'are you sure it's mine?' But when a guy says he's late and in a rush, girls just see it as a way to have more time to themselves?" Nikki is a sassy chick to say the least. She is definitely the feistiest woman I have ever affiliated myself with. Nikki has the kind of charisma and confidence that I find way more attractive than any pair of surgically modified breasts I've ever seen. I really mean that too, there is nothing she cannot do if she really wants to accomplish it, and that is very sexy.

"Yeah, yeah, yeah, whatever Nikki. I'm not late yet, but my therapy session starts in twenty-three minutes, and I'm not even dressed. Sorry if I'm a little terse with you right now, but I've had a rough last few days, and now I have to go see my shrink. And well, I have mixed emotions about him to put it nicely," I tell her, hoping she will get the point and leave my room. There is really no way to sugarcoat it; Nikki is, for lack of a better term, a fuck buddy. Last night's booty call was by no means my finest moment, but after the last few days and what happened with Svetlana, I cracked. No excuses, I was making progress, and I dropped the ball. And for the record, Nikki and I had a solid hour-long conversation before we even kissed last evening. I just have to make that clear, not that it really makes me any more proud of what transpired. In a few minutes I'm going to cry to Dr. Polk about it, and hopefully he will chastise me like a little kid instead of taking his typical PC middle-of-the-road attitude.

"Well, I guess I'll get dressed and be on my way," Nikki tells me in a sarcastic voice. I can tell she's not mad at me, she knows last night was just about sex, nothing more. But Nikki loves to make fun of me when I get wound a little tight. After she slips on her panties that were hanging over my desk chair, she picks up one of my socks from the floor. "Hey Anton, don't forget your sock, I wouldn't want you to have athlete's foot or something gross like that," she says in a very mocking tone. She has found my cumrag, the sock that smells like pastry. "Whoa! This thing smells like the Betty Crocker factory Anton. Seriously, there must be at least two or three galaxies worth of little sperm trapped in this sock," she says as she starts batting it against the door, making sure that the knocking sound it produces is clearly audible.

"Hey, it's been a rough few weeks OK? I haven't . . . hadn't . . . had sex in like a month or something before last night," I tell her in a very defensive manner.

"Oh shit, how did you ever survive? Wow! Had I known it had been that long, I wouldn't have even stopped to get a sandwich on the way over last night. I would have hopped in a cab right away and made sure he ran every red light on the way. I'm just glad I made it here and you were still alive." Even though she is constantly mocking me, I find it rather endearing. "Hey look at me. I think I've got a better forehand than Björn Borg," she brags as she picks up a piece of trash off my desk and hits it at me like a tennis ball.

The interesting thing about Nikki is that for her, it really *is* just about sex. She's only twenty-four I think, and although she appreciates romance and monogamy, the girl likes to get down every now and then. We use one another on a regular basis, it's understood. She has actually worked for *Velvet Rope* longer than I have. She started off as an intern in human resources, and shortly afterward was an assistant to a pretty big shot executive. But her passion has always been writing (she even named her two cats Webster and Roget). Through a series of carefully determined moves, she now writes articles for the magazine, along with some other freelance work. Apparently, what set her above the other contenders was that she claims to have already had major works published. And I mean *major* works. She actually told everyone on the hiring committee that she wrote the epic novel *The Time Machine* under the pseudonym HG Wells. Nikki also mentioned that although it was obviously already published, she was visiting the future in order to do research. It's an understatement to say that one of the funniest things about her is how she keeps her creative edge sharp. Before she began writing professionally, she would often write short stories and maintain a blog about random opinions of hers. Well, she decided to take that creative writing talent and turn the world of Wikipedia upside down. Whenever Nikki is feeling the need to write something clever, she goes to a random entry in the online encyclopedia and changes the information to something completely absurd. My absolute favorite example is the one she did about Coca-Cola. Most people know that cocaine was an actual ingredient in the popular soft drink at its inception. Well, Nikki decided that during some recession shortly after the birth of the soda that cocaine was just too expensive. Rather than eliminate the drug altogether and sacrifice its addictive nature, the beverage giant opted to switch to crack, a much cheaper version of the popular narcotic. However, the company decided not to change the name to Crack-a-Cola because (1) they already had too much money invested in label printing and advertising, and (2) the name comes off as a little bit racially insensitive.

Much like I do, Nikki travels regularly, which is probably why she is single. Believe me, plenty of guys would love to date her, but her lifestyle makes maintaining a relationship difficult. Now that I think about it, I'm not sure if her casual attitude toward sex is a result of her constant traveling, or if her desire for sex is a major catalyst behind why she pursued a career that sends her all over the country on a regular basis.

"Hey not bad, I think you've got a nice career ahead of you. I can definitely see a Wimbledon championship in your future," I joke back with her, and continue to get dressed, throwing on the first pair of pants and T-shirt I can find.

Nikki puts the sock down and finishes dressing before I do, slips on her clog-style shoes, and walks over to give me a kiss good-bye, and crunches some Kix on her way over. "You know, I'm not exactly the most qualified to critique other people's living situations, since my place is a complete dump. But I'm just saying, you might want to consider not leaving cereal on your floor," she tells me, as she picks a single ball of cereal off the carpet and puts it in her mouth and chews. "Oh, and it's stale. You know Anton, girls like *fresh* cereal on the floor. No more of this stale bullshit anymore, OK?" She humorously pesters me as she gives me a hug and a kiss on the cheek. "Later babe, call me after your next trip, let's hang out, go to a movie or something."

She begins to walk out of my room, but turns around upon hearing me start my sentence. "Sounds great Nikki, I'd like that." She winks at me, and continues for the door. "Oh hey, and Nikki," I say with a quiver in my voice. She focuses on me one last time, "About last night, that thing I said. I'm really sorry, I didn't mean it. It was a total accident. You know I think you're amazing right?" I plead with her, feeling very ashamed that last night I yelled out "Fuck yes Ashby," just before I came. When she called me out for yelling a name that was obviously not "Nikki," I tried to cover my tracks by insisting that I yelled out "Ashley." Unfortunately, this is not the first time this has happened. Luckily, I've been able to convince other women that "Ashley" was just a nagging bitch I couldn't tolerate from a past job whom I would picture in my head during sex to delay orgasm. Nikki knows far too much about me to believe that though, which is both a help and a hindrance.

She responds kindly, "Ha-ha, yeah right Anton. Don't worry, I'm not offended, but don't bullshit yourself. You know you care about her, so don't pretend otherwise, OK? I know you think you're a jackass for sleeping around, and I'm not going to say it's the most charming quality, but I still know you fairly well. You're a good guy, you deserve what you want. You guys would be cute together," she tells me sincerely as she points at a picture on my nightstand of Ashby and me. It was taken a few years ago at Disneyland, the last time we hung out together.

"Hey Nikki, you're awesome. Seriously, I mean that. Thanks a lot. Please don't ever let me off the hook. If I'm acting like a moron, let me know, OK?"

"Oh don't worry, I will. But I also have to hold down a job Anton, I don't have *that* much free time you know," she says jokingly. "All right kid, I'm outta here. Have fun with your therapist. Oh, and you forgot to put your turtle back, he's in the kitchen. You really need to look after those things more closely. Lose this one and that'll make four this year, right?" she says and actually walks out the front door this time. I open the fridge, grab a can of Coke, get outside pretty quickly, and find a cab passing by right at that moment. I hop in, give him the address of Dr. Polk's office, and I make it to my appointment just barely in time.

"Anton, welcome back," Dr. Polk greets me with a firm handshake as I'm finishing my last few sips of Coke and breathing a little heavy. My edgy nature is the product of my near tardiness. I know I wouldn't have been skipped over for being just a few minutes late, but for some reason I always get afraid a doctor or dentist will say "Sorry, you're too late, please reschedule," if I'm delayed more than a few seconds. I mean, they charge you as if their time was more precious than diamonds, so I don't think my fear is totally irrational.

I shake his hand, and follow him into his office. After I seat myself, I take a solid minute to just gather myself, and calm my nerves. The caffeine probably didn't help much, but it's certainly not the core of the problem. Once I have mellowed out a little bit, I begin, "Hey Dr. Polk, good to see you."

"So, what can I help you with today?" He very frequently begins our sessions with this question or a slight variation.

"Well, last time I was here, after listening to what you said, I decided that it would be best for me to be celibate for a while. It was extremely difficult, but I went almost a full month without sex."

"OK. So when you say 'went,' I assume that means you have recently had sex?"

"Well, yeah. This past weekend, I turned down a sure thing with a girl I've slept with before. That felt great at first. I just got such a great sense of accomplishment and courage from that. I really started to feel that I was taking control of my situation. But the next day, I was a wreck. I've never been addicted to drugs, but I imagine it was like going through withdrawals or something. I was freaking out, and last night I called up a girlfriend of mine, her name is Nikki. And by that I mean a friend who is female, not a girlfriend. Well, long story short, we had sex. I feel awful. And to top it all off, I yelled out Ashby's name right before orgasm."

"I see," is all he says. Nearly a half-million dollars was likely spent acquiring all the degrees on his wall, and this is all he ever comes up with.

My agitation has already begun to build inside of me. Every time I see him, I anticipate his lackadaisical attitude. That does not stop me from being annoyed by it every single time though. Attempting to pry more out of him, I say "Well, I mean, I guess I was just really proud of myself for giving up sex for a really long time. Well, for me, it was a long time. I hadn't gone without sex for that long in many years." I slip into a more juvenile persona, "I mean Dr. Polk, if you would have seen this Russian chick, you would have been pretty shocked that I was able to turn her down."

"Oh yeah? Was she a ten? I nailed a ten once, back in college. Perfect tits, a nice tight ass. I think she ran about eleven miles a day or something obscene like that. Man, that takes me back; I haven't had a piece of ass like that in decades. If I were you, I would have hit that big time."

My heart stops immediately, and then all of a sudden, it starts pounding furiously. There are chills running all over my body. Is he *really* saying this? I cannot believe what I'm hearing. I'm feeling shocked, angry, and disgusted, all at the same time. I need to understand why he just told me that. "Um, excuse me, Dr. Polk?" I ask in a timid tone.

"Yes, Anton?"

"Well, I'm not sure what . . . I mean, I know you're a doctor, but do you . . . do you really think that what you just said was . . . well, appropriate? Shouldn't you be telling me to 'just keep trying' or 'learn from my mistakes?' Is it really good for you to be encouraging me and my imprudent behavior?"

"Well Anton, from what I've observed, it doesn't really matter what I tell you. You seem to do whatever you want to anyway. You said it yourself that last time I told you to slow down. And sure, maybe you made progress, but you came back to me with the same results: failure. Therapy isn't a first-grade science fair; I don't give accolades for trying. Well, that actually works with some of my patients, but I don't think it helps you. It honestly seems that you take what I say and just do the opposite, so maybe if I encourage your promiscuity, you'll get what you want."

I. Am. Floored. My eyelids are so wide open that to Dr. Polk, my eyeballs must be the size of golf balls. This guy is a total mind-fuck . . . *this* is what I need. It's about damn time. "Um, wow!" is the only thing that is capable of exiting my mouth after about thirty seconds of intense silence.

"Anton, I want to talk about this . . . situation, involving you and Ashby. Refresh my memory please. She is 'the one' or something equivalent to that? She is the woman consuming many of your thoughts? I just want to make sure I have things straight in my head, and I apologize, but I left my notes at home. Please forgive me."

"Oh, um, it's OK, it happens I guess." I just now noticed he wasn't writing anything down. Was this because he really doesn't care what I have to say? Or maybe he is listening even more intently and wants to focus entirely on how I say things, my facial expressions, and things of that nature. Or maybe the guy just forgot his notepad. I continue, "But yeah, Ashby, she's a longtime friend of mine. The woman I have had a crush on, or been in love with . . . the one I've had some kind of major attraction to in one way or another since sophomore year of high school. I'll be honest; this is not the first time I have called out her name during sex. But usually I'm able to find a way around it with a few carefully fabricated back-stories."

"Really? Well, would you mind sharing? I'm sure that could come in handy sometime." My jaw drops. I'm not sure if I know the person staring back at me. "Anton, I'm kidding. OK, you know what? I really feel I need to do this." I make an elaborate series of peculiar facial expressions showing my curiosity. "This is highly frowned upon, but I think it's necessary."

Interesting. I like where this is going. "Oh, well whatever you think is best," I tell him.

"Starting now, for the next few minutes, I'm not Dr. Polk. I'm Edward. Let's talk as friends, not as patient and doctor, OK?"

"Um, yeah, that sounds good I guess. How exactly does that work?"

"Well, I'm sure you've noticed this, but I don't always give you my opinion based on emotion. My answers to your questions are founded in years of study and countless case studies. But I refuse to always ignore the impact of human emotion. I think too many therapists treat patients as objects instead of people. Sorry if that sounds trite, but it's what I believe works in some instances."

"Wow! Well, I actually have noticed that, and I'm thrilled to see what you have to say," I reassure him as my interest continues to grow.

"Anton, if you want to sleep with every woman you meet, then do it. That's your right. Well, I mean, it's your life and if you want to engage in casual sex, that is your right, provided you don't do anything illegal or highly immoral. But I think you've made it clear that you are no longer satisfied by that." I nod in agreement. "So, as a friend, here is my advice to you: do something about it. No one is going to do it for you. If you want this Ashby girl, bitching to me about it accomplishes nothing. I don't know her; I've never met her. Why are you telling me all these things? You should really be telling her all . . . well, *some* . . . of this stuff. Can I share a personal story with you?"

This should be good, "Of course, please do Doct . . . Edward."

"When I was in college, I had a big crush on a woman named Janice. I talked to all my friends about how great she was. I talked to everyone of her friends about who she might like. Everyone knew I had the hots for her . . . except her. And after several months, another guy asked her out, and she said yes. Well a few months after they began dating, I ran into them at a movie theatre. When Janice saw me, she approached me and gave me a big hug. She introduced me to her boyfriend; we shook hands, and Janice told him to wait for her while she used the restroom. He and I shared an awkward pause, and I broke it with some variation of 'You better treat her right man, or you'll have to answer to me.' And this guy cockily responds, 'Oh, I see. You're into Janice aren't you?' I scowled at him slightly, and he continued by saying something like, 'That's cute man. I would have sympathy for you, but you missed your shot. You wanted something and didn't have the balls to go for it. Therefore, you don't deserve her. Tough luck kid.' And then Janice walks out of the bathroom, and they walk off to their respective theatre. Now, don't get me wrong. I eventually met my wife, whom I love dearly. But the point is no one is going to make things happen. You have to do it for yourself."

"Shit Ed, that's crazy. That guy was a dick. But I know how that must have felt."

"Yeah, it was definitely not the best I've ever felt, but like I said, I met my wife a couple years later, and I learned a very valuable lesson." He gets out of his chair and walks over to a bookshelf near his desk. After he removes a rather thin volume from the mass of literature, he says, "Anton, I want you to read this. I read it shortly after the incident I just described to you. I think it will help you in preparing for telling Ashby whatever it is you need to tell her."

"Oh, wow! That's great. What is it?"

"*The Prince*, by Machiavelli." He opens the book, flips a few pages around, and begins to read, "War is not avoided. It is merely deferred to your disadvantage." He looks up from the book, staring at me very intently, "That is my favorite quote from this book. Now, when he wrote it several hundred years ago, he was concerning himself with war and politics. But let's face it, the idiom 'love is war' didn't just appear out of nowhere. The longer you wait to say what's on your mind, the more opportunities you leave for every other man to take her away from you."

I take the book from his hand and begin to flip through it. I am sold on this epic work. I have heard many things about it, but never in regards to love and dating. I have always been of the assumption that its subject is quite the opposite. This is going to be a fantastic read. Shaking Dr. Polk's hand, I say, "Wow! Thanks a lot Ed, this is awesome. I can't wait to get home and start reading it."

"You're very welcome Anton. I hope it helps you as much as it did me."

"I'm sure it will," I tell him, having a sudden flashback to my trip to Dallas. "You know it's kind of funny, but remember that Dallas Cowboy Cheerleader I spent a weekend with not too long ago?" He nods up and down to acknowledge that he does in fact recollect my rambling about Tara. "Well, she was big into books and reading. I think she has a Master's in English or writing or something of that nature. Anyway, *The Prince* was one of the books on her shelf." There is a small pause, and I go on "I just think that's kind of funny. Pretty cool too. I wonder if she interpreted it the same way you did? Oh well, I've got to run, but thank you so much once again."

"Of course Anton, just glad to help." As I walk out the door, he stops me and says, "Oh and Anton?"

"Yeah?" I ask.

"Just remember, life ain't a first-grade science fair. 'Participant' ribbons are kind of worthless in the game of love."

12

JUST A MERE four days after my last visit with Dr. Polk, who is now apparently my new best friend, I am more relaxed than I have been in several months. Oddly enough, the source of my newfound tranquil state is the book that Dr. Polk handed to me, *The Prince*. This Machiavellian masterpiece is incredible. It blows my mind that in all my years of college I was never required to read this book. I'm equally disappointed with myself for not taking the initiative to buy a copy and critique it. Granted, *The Prince* is not a very long work. Depending on which translation one is reading, it averages around 110 pages. But I have still read it two full times since I last saw my buddy Ed. As I sit here in the middle of my favorite dive breakfast joint, *The Compote Heap*, enjoying the best apple pancakes I have ever eaten, I am thirty pages deep into my third go around.

Believe me, I was very skeptical the first time I ate here; the name is not exactly what one would think of as appetizing. But the folks who run this place, they like it that way. They know their food is amazing; they will always have a consistent clientele. They have no desire whatsoever for it to turn into some trendy spot filled with yuppies and suits. How I'm still allowed in here is beyond me.

"Hey Anton, anything else you need, man? Refill on the coffee" my waiter asks me.

"No thanks CT, I'll just take the check." I have no idea how he got the nickname "Cameltoe," but I'm sure the story is nothing less than incredible. If you asked him his real name, he would probably tell you that it's something like Curtis or Connor. Truthfully, it's Edwin. For some reason, Cameltoe flies better in this environment.

"Cool man, sounds good. Here ya go," he tells me as he pulls the crumpled paper receipt out of his pocket. "Whenever you're ready, I'll take it." Just then he notices my book. "*The Prince*, huh? Good book. The dude is kind of an asshole, but he makes some good points."

"Yeah, I'm hooked on it. I'd never read it until just a few days ago, and I can't put it down. It's kind of funny actually, but my therapist told me to read it."

"Huh, that's gnarly. How is that going by the way?"

I normally wouldn't go into my therapy situations with people who handle my food, but I've eaten here more times than I can count; CT knows almost as much about my screwed-up sex life as Dr. Polk does. Neither one of us could count the number of unbearable "morning after" breakfast dates I've sat through at this place. I usually end up saying more to him than the girl I'm eating with. But thanks to Dr. Polk, I think those days are going to be minimal, if not extinguished.

"Oh not bad, he's kind of more messed up than I am, but I think he is giving me some valuable advice too. I've seen him more times than I can count, and if you could graph my opinion of him over time, it would look a lot like a sine wave."

"Ha, that's cool man. Well I'll be right back," Cameltoe says as he takes my credit card and receipt to the register. He is only gone for about forty seconds before he returns. "OK, here you go. You know the drill, sign the top copy, bottom one is yours. So any big trips or shoots coming up?" he asks.

"Well, I'm actually going to Vegas tomorrow for a shoot. I have no idea why they're sending me. I'm taking shots of the costumes for a show opening on The Strip. But it's some show that's been open in New York for years. Normally, they just use archival footage. Who am I to complain about a free trip to Vegas though, right? It should be . . . interesting."

"Las Vegas huh? That sucks, sorry you have to deal with that." Now normally, whenever I tell anyone I'm going to Las Vegas on business, they are extremely jealous, or at the very least show some sign of enthusiasm. However, CT is one of those hippies who thinks he's above material things.

Now I love the guy, but truth be told, he's probably more of a capitalist than I am. He looks down at the materialism and greed of places like Las Vegas, but his Cannondale carbon road bike cost around $2,500. I only know this because he told me. He is the kind of guy who hates Starbuck's, even though they offer benefits to their part-time employees, but shops at Whole Foods. Don't get me wrong, I love Whole Foods, but a lot of the stuff they sell is available elsewhere for less. I can also say with relative certainty that he spent more time picking out his attire and styling his mohawk this morning than it took the farmer to plant, grow, and harvest the grains used in the pancakes in my stomach. And I have no idea why he thinks people in Las Vegas are so "governed by their vices" as he puts it. The odds are substantially high that after Cameltoe gets off work in a few hours, he's going to use the tip I just gave him and apply it toward the purchase of a couple grams of nature's finest herbal remedy. But I guess it's not a vice if it's homegrown right?

"Nah man, it'll be good for me. I told you that I'm trying to calm down and put more effort into developing a relationship. I think going to Las Vegas will be a nice test for me. You know, to see what progress, if any, I've made in looking at women for more than their bodies." I realize, this sounds like some rehearsed speech, and I even have trouble saying it from time to time, but I really do mean it.

"Yeah, OK Anton. Sure thing man. Well, have a fun trip either way. I'll see you soon," he says to me, with absolutely no confidence that I can make it to Sin City and back without engaging in questionable behavior. Ironically, Las Vegas is one of the few cities I have traveled to where I have actually never had sex. I've been there four times on business: once in college and twice for a couple of my friends' bachelor parties. Not that opportunities didn't present themselves, but the general theme that emerged was someone I was hanging out with that evening would get far too drunk, and had to be cared for until the next morning. One time it was me, once it was my friend Dan, and once it was the girl I was trying to hook up with. There are few things more arousing than making out with a girl, sucking on her chest, having her unzip your pants in preparation for a blowjob, only for her to duck down and puke on your shoes. My favorite was the time I was partying with a group of friends and the women they were attempting to lure until 7:00 a.m. In my drunken state, I announced repeatedly that it was called 'the nightlife' for a reason, and that once the sun is up it's either time to sleep or eat pancakes, so I left. There was also a time where I was making progress with a very attractive woman I had photographed earlier that day, but that night I just felt genuinely ill. Maybe it was food poisoning.

If I had to guess, I'd say I ate more than my necessary share of lobster at the buffet in my hotel.

Although that night did not quite turn out as well as I had hoped, I made a great contact in Las Vegas that has proven very beneficial. Several years back, the Hard Rock Hotel and Casino shot a series of ads that drew a lot of criticism. That is saying a lot for a town with the reputation that Las Vegas is known for. The most famous shot is of an attractive woman who is topless and wearing skimpy black underwear. The only thing covering her nipples is a pair of dice, one in each hand. Honestly, it was one of the best shoots I have ever done. Not only was the woman a knockout, she was a riot. She would keep holding the dice between her thumb and index finger, and then blow on it causing it to spin so fast it almost vanished. Then she would do things like tell her stylist to get her purse, because she wanted to play craps with the dice, then proceeded to challenge everyone in the room to a few rounds. I cannot even remember half the derogatory things she called me when I said I did not want to participate.

After talking with her for a while at the end of the session, we decided to meet up for drinks later that evening. She told me she would be bringing a friend, and although the thought of a threesome appealed to me greatly, I didn't think I was ready for that kind of pressure. Fortunately, Danny was working at the hotel that day. I'm not exactly sure what his title was, but he was very good at whatever he did. If someone asked for more water, he had a five-gallon jug there in no time. If someone spilled something, it was mopped up within seconds. His dedication and professionalism definitely made an impression on me, so I invited him out with us later that night.

Watching him operate around those two women was one of the most hilarious things I have ever witnessed. I am certain I looked just like that in my early days of talking to girls, but sitting there watching him trip over his words was just priceless. To his credit, he never said anything insulting or offensive about himself or the girls, he really just stuttered a lot. It was kind of cute actually. In fact, I know it was cute, because he called me the next day thanking him for the "best night of his life." I had to call it an early night because of my stomach, but by that point Danny and the girls had put away a few cocktails and were getting very cordial with each other.

Needless to say, Danny made sure I get in touch with him whenever I go to Las Vegas. His enthusiasm amazed me, so I gladly obliged. Like I said, Danny was a very devoted worker, so I was not surprised that every time I returned he had been promoted. Over the years, I have been comped dinners, shows, drinks, boxing matches, hotel rooms, and many other things.

Needless to say, I will definitely be giving him a call when I grace Sin City with my presence this time around.

My flight the next morning is not very early, but I still feel a bit fatigued, so I pack my suitcase and get to bed early. I made sure to call Danny and leave a message letting him know I was on my way though. Surprisingly, the temptations waiting for me in Nevada do not seem that daunting. I am feeling very confident that this trip will be strictly business and will set me on the right path.

When I wake up the next morning, I notice I have a missed call. Danny called me while I was asleep, and although I left the ringer on, it didn't wake me up. As I listened to the message, my heart sank a little.

"Hey Anton, it's Danny. Glad to hear you're coming back to town, can't wait to see ya man. I've got some great news dude; I'm a VIP host at *The Market*. So call me when you get into town, let me know where you're staying, and I'll send a limo to your hotel. Cool man, have a safe trip, see you soon."

Shit. Of course Danny would have to be a VIP host at one of the most prominent strip clubs in Las Vegas. As much as I want to say no and simply avoid any potentially volatile situations, Danny has hooked me up so many times in the past. He is actually a good friend, and I think I'd feel like I was insulting him if I passed on his offer. I guess I'll have to go for a little while and just blame jet lag for leaving early.

Now with all the traveling I do, I see a lot of cities. As a whole, Las Vegas probably doesn't even make my top twenty. But there is absolutely no doubt in my mind that there is no more impressive city to view when arriving by airplane than Las Vegas. If you were to show a random person in Europe or Asia a picture of a major U.S. skyline, they will most likely say New York City. Whether it's Chicago, Seattle, or even Los Angeles, New York is a standard response. However, there is absolutely no one who mistakes the skyline of Las Vegas for any other city in the world. Quite simply, it is unmistakable. One of the coolest things I have ever seen in my life actually happened on a rare dingy night in Las Vegas. I had seen the bright lights of Las Vegas Boulevard (aka The Strip) many times before that night, but never like this. There was an extremely thick fog hovering no more than fifty feet above the hotels on The Strip. In any other city, it would be just another gray and dreary night. But the lights from all of the properties in the area lit up the fog and painted the sky an abundance of colors. Right above the MGM Grand, the clouds were emerald green. Hovering atop the Mandalay Bay, a magnificent gold.

I knew I had to get a picture of this, but not just a normal picture that everyone else was taking that night. My gut was telling me that as impressive as this was, the view from above the clouds would be infinitely more breathtaking. I hopped in the first cab that stopped, and told the driver to take me to one of those helicopter tour places. Luckily, there are a couple of them at the south end near the airport, so I was there in practically no time. When I ran in shouting that I needed a helicopter tour right away, the guys inside kind of looked at me like I was nuts. First of all, it was late, they wanted to go home. Secondly, not that conditions were horrible, but the sky was rather crappy; not exactly ideal flying weather. In retrospect, that was the best $400 I ever spent. The pictures I took up there that evening turned out even more magnificent than I anticipated. And the prints I sold on my web site from that evening made up for the money I spent on the helicopter ride itself in a matter of days; definitely a great investment.

Unfortunately, the sky in Las Vegas is perfectly clear today, so I highly doubt I will be seeing similar results later this evening. That's probably for the best, because the last thing I need is a reason to stay out late in the world capital of decadence.

"I'll take those sir; please follow me," a bellhop says as he grabs my bags and immediately bolts for the elevators. This is my first time staying at New York New York, even though I have been there several times. When it comes to ranking things on the scale of Vegas tackiness, this one is near the top. But in all honesty, I think this is my favorite casino in the town. It has lots of live entertainment, a fun theme, and it epitomizes Las Vegas. There are places like the Bellagio, which although incredibly elegant, seem to forget which city they are actually located in. The cheesiness is part of what I love about this town, and New York New York has a nice balance of the kitschy and the luxurious. I often draw a lot of criticism with this opinion, but I really do think Las Vegas is the most honest place in the world.

The most common objection I hear from opponents of The Meadows (this is what Las Vegas translates into) is that it's "fake." I'm not sure why people get so irritated by this. I'm pretty sure that just about everyone who walks into Caesar's Palace, is fully aware that they are not actually in Rome, or anywhere in Italy for that matter. The Treasure Island is clearly nowhere near a large body of water. The L'Arc de Triumph at The Paris is blatantly not the same as the one in France. I don't stroll into Disneyland telling little kids 'Hey, by the way, Aladdin is a fictional character. And just so you know, when you're in the Haunted Mansion, the pictures don't actually get longer, you're in an elevator.'"

Seriously, everyone who comes here knows that the people who work here only want your money. They make no bones about it. Everyone knows the house holds an undeniable advantage in any game you can play. Casinos would not be in business if they didn't have this asset in their back pocket. Go to any strip club, it quickly becomes apparent to anyone paying attention that the girls there have no interest in who you are or what you do. They merely want your money and will tell you anything you want to hear in order to get it. That might seem shady, but it's also understood. Well, most people understand it. Unfortunately, there are a negligible few who actually believe what the women tell them. But as a whole, people know what they're getting from Las Vegas.

Sadly, the more time I spend in Las Vegas, the more I question the ways I have handled situations with women. Well, on second thought, maybe that's a good thing. But what I start asking myself is if how I have treated women in the past is really any different than prostitution. Certainly, in a legal sense, the two are worlds apart. But ethically, are the two separable? I can't even count how many dates I've been on where I took the woman to the nicest restaurant, took her shopping, name dropped to no end, only to ensure I would be banging her at the end of the night. Obviously, I can't speak for the woman in these situations, but I think it's fair to assume that in most of the cases it was pretty well understood that these evenings were going to be "one and done."

But these revelations have not escaped me. I cannot change what I did in the past, but I can do something about it from here on out. I find it so odd that I gain more insight into my life when I'm in Las Vegas than anywhere else I travel. It's fascinating that I undergo such intense introspection in Sin City of all places.

I am by no means a good gambler. In fact, I am awful. I apply horrible strategy in every game I play, usually opting to try and win a single big bet once than steadily win small amounts. However, to my credit, I never play with more than $100. I realize I am terrible, so the gambling is really just a way to entertain myself for a little while. After a nice two-hour nap in my room, I decide to grab a quick bite and then walk around The Strip and see some of the other casinos. Although it is several blocks away, which is an endless distance to a pedestrian in Las Vegas, I really want to see Planet Hollywood. The funny thing is, traffic on Las Vegas Boulevard is so crazy right now, I think I got there faster by walking than if I had taken a cab.

I had heard the inside of Planet Hollywood was really nice from some of my friends who recently visited Las Vegas. They were right; it's definitely flashy, but also very classy. It's a nice balance of the typical Las Vegas image as well as the more refined image the town is gradually shifting toward. Because I am so bad at blackjack, I am very relieved when I find a rare empty table in the middle of the group. The woman dealing is very attractive, definitely not a coincidence. She is wearing a corset and hot pants. My first inclination is that she is a cocktail waitress who is lost, but then I remember where I am. I come to my senses and realize she is dressed like that to lure drunken men to the table and make stupid bets while paying more attention to her chest than their cards. Say what you will, it's pretty genius. Another new strategy that Las Vegas casinos have recently started employing is go-go dancers behind the table games. Yes, there are scantily clad women dancing around poles right behind the Pai Gow and Caribbean Stud.

After redirecting my focus to the card games themselves, I take a seat at the end of the table and try to start a generic conversation with "Hi, is this table open?"

"Of course it is," the beautiful woman says back in a very cheerful tone.

I pull five $20 bills out of my wallet and say, "Can I get one hundred in chips please?" The table minimum is ten dollars, so she gives me eight ten-dollar chips, and four five-dollar chips, on the off-chance I get bold and want to bet fifteen or twenty-five on a hand.

After she puts the chips in front of me, I pull them closer, and put a single ten-dollar chip in my circle. She begins pulling cards out of the shoe, and as she flips over my first card, the eight of clubs, I ask, "So, what's your name?"

"Moxie," is all she says as she continues to deal.

"Wow! Cool name. I'm Anton. You know Moxie, you're cute and all, but you're gonna need to slow down." She gives me a weird look. She's certainly heard a lot of random things from guys in her life, but she isn't sure where I'm going with this. "I mean, I *just* met you, and you've already let me get to first base." First base is a blackjack term referring to the seat immediately to the dealer's left.

She rolls her eyes at what is certainly among the cheesiest lines she's ever heard, but is still flattered nonetheless. She tries to hold back a smile, but a cute little smirk emerges, crooked across her face. "Yeah, yeah, yeah. Not bad, I've actually never heard that one before."

And just then I realize what I'm doing; I'm flirting. This is exactly what I wanted to avoid, and I'm already falling into old habits with the first woman I encounter. Thankfully, I recognize this right away and adjust the conversation accordingly. "So Moxie, what do you want to do with your life?" She raises her eyebrows. "I mean, I'm sure dealing cards is cool and all, but what do you really want to do?" All right, maybe I didn't really adjust the conversation as much as I paved a new path, but hey, I'm new at this.

She was caught off guard by the apparent sincerity of my questioning. Although I led with a lame line, I'm actually making a genuine effort to have a normal conversation with her. Over the course of the next hour, I pretty much stick to basic strategy, betting the minimum, but every now and then betting $30 per hand. When it comes time for me to leave, I'm only down $20, but I had a couple gin and tonics, so I consider myself even. All in all, it was one of my more enjoyable gambling experiences. Sure losing a few bucks isn't any fun, but chatting with my new friend Moxie was actually really pleasant. I found out that she is currently in school working on her last few credits for a Bachelor's in psychology. After graduation, she would like to pursue a Master's Degree, but not immediately. She wants to travel first, preferably Europe. I found out a lot of nice things, but nothing about having drinks or "getting together sometime" ever came up. I'm actually kind of proud of myself. I mean, it's not a major deal, but I can also appreciate the occasional moral victory.

As I get up from the table, I come to the realization that I have delayed the inevitable long enough. I stop to grab a sandwich in the food court, but that only stalls me for about twenty more minutes. The time has come to go to *The Market*, where Danny works. I step outside to the bright lights of The Strip, and wait for a taxi. A hideously neon green Mini Cooper pulls up in front of me, and although I'm in doubt, I am pretty sure it's a cab. I walk over to the car and stick my head in to ask if he is in fact a taxi, but I can see the meter on the dashboard, so I don't even bother and just get in. Good thing I'm not carrying any personal items, because there probably wouldn't be enough room in this cab for any of my stuff.

"Hey there, what's happening?" He shrugs his shoulders, hits the button on the meter to start my fare, and pulls away from the curb. "Um, *The Market* please." Upon hearing this, he turns to me and gives me a look that is half smile, half curiosity. I'm pretty sure it's a strip club; I hope that's where I'm going. After seeing this guy's expression though, I'm not exactly certain.

Even though we probably only traveled two miles, it seemed to take forever due to all the traffic on The Strip. When we arrive, I see the words "The Market" lit up in four or five alternating colors, resting atop a building façade that has seen better days. Initially I'm concerned, but some of the fanciest nightclubs and strip joints I have ever set foot in were absolute trash on the outside. It's kind of funny that despite making their money entirely off aesthetics, the inside of a strip club conforms to the old adage "It's what's on the inside that counts." Oh the irony . . . the lap-dancing, ass-shaking, boob-bouncing irony. It's almost poetic.

After I get out of the cab, I head to the back of a short line. When I get to the front, I hand the lone bouncer my ID. He stares at it forever, mostly because it's an out of state driver's license, but I can also tell by his expression that he doesn't believe my birth date. Now clearly I'm well above age, so I'm not concerned, but even if I were way too young, this guy would let me in anyway. Strip clubs never met a horny wallet they didn't like.

"No way," the large man tells me with absolutely no variation in his voice.

"Excuse me? No way what? That's my picture."

"Not that. I can tell it's not a fake. But you don't look that old. You don't look like you were born a day before 1985."

"Oh well, thanks? I eat a lot of antioxidants. Groovy Smoothie is kind of an addiction for me," I tell him hoping he will just let me scoot on by and get this evening over with. I don't think he appreciated my "charm," but fortunately the main door to the club opens, and Danny steps out, looks around, and our eyes meet. Had I not been expecting to see him there, I probably would not have recognized him. He is dressed to the nine. His suit has to be worth at least three grand, and I would know. I think that's a real Tag watch he's wearing. But what grabs my attention most is that his hair is styled with more product than the entire male population of Long Island uses in a given weekend.

He walks up to the bouncer, puts his hand on his shoulder, and says, "Hey it's cool Tony, he's with me." The bouncer looks at him and nods without saying a word, and hands my driver's license back to me.

"Thank you," I tell the bouncer as I walk by him and into the door that Danny is holding open for me. When I step inside, I realize that my expectations were spot-on. The inside of the club looks like a palace. The lighting fixtures are all very fancy, the furniture is very clean and modern, and there are also flat-screen TVs everywhere. I'm not sure why someone would go to a strip club and watch television, but I guess people like what they like.

After we are inside, Danny sticks his hand out and says, "Hey man, great to see you. Glad you could make it."

"Yeah man, it's been too long. Great to see you too. I'm glad I could make it out tonight." The first part is true; the last part is likely requisite.

"Well, because you're my boy, you're taken care of tonight. Whatever you need, I'll make it happen. The bartender and cocktail waitresses already know who you are, so you'll drink for free all night, and you can sit at any of the roped-off tables that you would like. Unfortunately, I can't do anything about getting you free dances, but if you see a girl you like, I can probably convince her to lower her rate."

Her rate? I almost ask if she's a lawyer too, but decide against it.

"Oh, wow man! I gotta say I'm impressed. Every time I come back it seems like you've climbed higher up the ranks. You're doing OK for yourself." Although I am genuinely amazed at how professional he looks, I know that I would appreciate this situation far more if I were just a couple years younger.

"Yeah you know, I do what I can. Well, I have to attend to some other clients, but I'll check in with you later OK? Have fun playa," he tells me as he slaps my back and winks at me. "Oh, and for the record, prostitution is illegal in Clark County." I give him an odd glance. "But so is speeding, and people do that shit everyday and get it away with it . . . if you catch my drift?" He shoots me yet another wink and then walks away. When he is about twenty steps away from me, he stops a girl carrying a bowl of cotton candy that I assume is a cocktail waitress. The cotton candy is hilarious; it makes me feel like I'm at a carnival . . . a carnival of titties. He exchanges a few words with her, points at me, and then departs. The very slender woman wearing not much more than a bikini approaches me and says, "Mr. Bradley? Please follow me." She immediately turns around and marches with a very determined pace toward a table near the stage. "Here you are. What are we drinking this evening?"

Even though I'm accustomed to getting star treatment whenever Danny is involved, this is still a little odd to me. I take a seat and say, "I'll have a mojito." She nods and walks away. Under normal conditions, I would never order a mojito. For one, they take way too long to make, and it slows the pace of the bartender's way down. I don't let that stop me, because this is a fancy place that is certainly used to making elaborate drinks. But more importantly, I'm really doing it because I figure that I will likely get peppermint stuck between my teeth. I'm not trying to bring any of these girls home with me, but I have no doubt that I will be tempted. My goal with the foliage in my teeth is see if any of the dancers in the club can keep a straight face while trying to seduce me. More than likely, they can pretend to like just about anyone, but I'll take any advantage I can get.

The woman on stage when I arrived has just finished, and she picks up what minimal clothing of hers is lying on the floor. As she exits, another woman takes the stage, and the music fades out while transitioning from slow hip-hop to hard rock. Although it's been a while since I listened to their stuff, it sounds like Mötley Crüe.

"Gentlemen, give it up for Stacy," a voice over the loudspeaker announces. "Now guys, don't be stingy, those ladies work hard so tip 'em good. Got it? Now, please welcome to the stage, Pandora!" At this point, the rock goes from a moderate volume to near deafening level.

"Here you go sir," the waitress says as she puts a tall glass in front of me.

"Thank you," I say. I'm not sure if I should tip her now, wait until the end of the night, or omit tipping altogether since she didn't take any clothes off for me. I am not very familiar with strip-club protocol. She walks off before I even have a chance to pull out my wallet, so I have until the next round to reflect upon my decision.

I take a sip of my mojito and can immediately feel the parsley-like plants floating around and getting entrapped in my teeth. My plan is working. Then my eyes direct their attention to the woman spinning around the pole on stage. Both of her arms are covered in tattoos, as is the majority of her back. The more I look at her, the more assured I become that she is on the older end of the scale, probably mid-thirties, which for a stripper is kind of pushing it. But her body is very toned. Her stomach is oiled slightly, and the lights on stage are nicely accentuating her six-pack abs. I can see how a woman like this could make a lot of money in this line of work.

Unlike the woman before her, Pandora is dancing very aggressively, shaking her head so that her long jet-black hair is whipping around ferociously. It's actually quite odd because out of all the strip clubs I've been to in my life, all of the dancers moved very slowly and sensually. Needless to say, I'm enjoying her toned body move around for me, but I can honestly say that I am amazed by her athletic ability. When the song is over, the DJ reminds us to tip the girls, and since I have received royal treatment so far this evening, I think that is a perfectly practical thing to do. I pull a five-dollar bill out of my wallet and place it on the stage. Even with my fascination of feminine curves, I have never felt comfortable placing money directly into a woman's body. Most of the men are laying scanty singles in her mouth or in between her breasts. It really bothers me when classy people forget to adjust for inflation. I'm sure I was tipping with singles on my eighteenth birthday, but no one here looks younger than me, so I really don't think their stinginess is justified.

"Thanks hon," Pandora says while giving me the flawlessly rehearsed smile and wink combination that causes men to act like children. When she is done collecting all of her cash, she picks up her clothing and walks off. But right before she exits, she turns back and looks at me. Now I know that the lighting is dark in the club, and that I'm probably falling victim to the dangerous mentality that a stripper is attracted to me. Yet I can't help but feel like she looked at me in an unusual way.

Maybe seven or eight girls dance while I enjoy the rest of my mojito as well as a Grey Goose martini. Once I finish my second beverage, I make a brief trip to the restroom. As soon as I exit, a very curvy blonde wearing leopard print hot pants and a matching bra greets me.

"Hey cutie. How you doing tonight baby?"

Caught off guard I uncomfortably reply, "Oh, hey there." Then I remember where I am and quickly get into character. "I'm doing great doll," I say, as I look her up and down. "Very nice," I say and begin to walk away.

"Hey baby, don't you want a dance?" she asks in a very high-pitched voice that I'm fairly certain is not natural.

I turn around and give her my attention. "Sorry darlin', you look a little too pricy for me," I say hoping to get back to my table with my bank account still intact.

She grabs my hand and pulls me close. Leaning in she whispers into my ear, "Baby, this one is on me." After she finishes her sentence, she sticks her tongue in my ear, grabs me by the hand and leads me behind a large curtain. Most people have a spot on their body they don't like having touched, mine are the ears (I once went on a few dates with a woman who flipped out if you tried to touch her nose at all). I have honestly never understood how having a tongue in their ear arouses people. Never in my life have I met a person who enjoyed wet-willies, I'm not sure why a tongue makes it better. And the worst part is that when I return home I will have to go see an otologist for fear I have an STD hovering over my tympanic membrane.

As we pass the first curtain, I immediately see a series of velour drapes, which I assume are booths for private dances. She leads me about halfway down the row of booths, stops to open a curtain, and motions for me to enter. Once inside, this blonde bombshell staring up at me puts her hand on my chest, and gives a steady push, gently bumping me back onto the seat. She sits on my lap facing away from me, but our eyes still make contact in the mirror in front of us. "Relax baby, tonight I'm gonna make your wildest fantasy come true."

I am tempted to call her bluff, because I highly doubt that she and two of her most beautiful girlfriends are going to dress up as Snap, Crackle, and Pop and have their way with me on top of the world's largest Rice Krispy Treat. Instead, I just smile and nod.

"What's your name, baby?" she asks as she begins to slowly rock her hips back and forth.

Having finally regained my composure, I tell her with tremendous resolve, "My name is Anton, sugar. What's yours?"

"Anton, that's a hot name baby. I'm Lace." The over-under on how many times she will say the word 'baby' to me has been set at thirty-five. Any takers?

"Well Lacey, it's a pleasure to meet you."

"It's just Lace, and the pleasure is all mine baby," she tells me in the most seductive voice I have heard in years. Fortunately, I'm getting this dance early in the evening while my judgment is not yet clouded. Had she grabbed me after about three more drinks, I might actually believe that she is excited to see me.

Although this woman, who in all likelihood cannot legally purchase alcohol, is mind-blowingly hot, I still feel incredibly awkward. I'm not proud to say it, but I've probably received roughly five lap dances in my life . . . at strip clubs I mean, dances that I paid a woman to perform for me. And not once, never in all my years have I ever liked it. Honestly, I think "tolerate" is a better description. Please understand that I didn't hate the dances, but I genuinely do not see how it excites men as much as they claim it does. When you think about it, all that is taking place is a man paying to watch a woman work. I'm pretty sure if I hung out at a Krispy-Kreme donut shop and offered the employees twenty bucks to observe them glaze pastries, they'd kick me out.

When the dance eventually concludes, Lace puts on her clothes, which only takes her about fifteen seconds, winks at me, grabs my hand, and leads me back into the club. When we are back out in the main area in view of the stage, she gives me a kiss on the cheek and tells me, "Have a good night baby." She walks away, and never makes eye contact with me for the rest of the evening.

As I head back to my seat, the cocktail waitress has already placed another mojito as well as another martini on my table. She is very on top of the situation, which again is ironic since she is one of the few employees there who is only figuratively and not literally on top of things. When she passes by, I get her attention and hand her a twenty. I am fairly certain I will drink about one and a half of these cocktails and be on my way. It is better to settle up now rather than try to track her down later.

About halfway through the mojito I opted to consume first, Danny walks up to me and asks, "Hey there bro, havin' fun so far?"

"Yeah, I'm doing great Danny. Thanks a lot for hooking me up. You always take great care of me when I come into town. Oh, and thanks for the dance from . . . Lace, yeah that's it. She definitely knows how to move."

Danny looks at me with bewilderment. "Oh you mean Sarah? She is smokin', but I haven't talked to her tonight. I honestly don't know anything about any dances." After a short pause, a light bulb turns on in his head, "Oh man, I'd be careful Anton. You don't want to get involved with strippers man. I've dated three of the girls here, and well, let's just say it never turned out well."

"Huh? That's so weird Danny. You seriously didn't buy me a dance?"

"Nah man, I have no clue. But if I were you, I wouldn't be complaining about a glistening pair of Ds in your face no questions asked. All right man, I gotta talk to some other people, but I just wanted to check in. Make sure you see me before you go." Danny walks off to attend to his paying customers, which gives me more opportunity to focus on my drinks and getting back to my hotel room sooner rather than later.

Three or four dancers perform over the next fifteen minutes, but unfortunately I haven't seen the black-haired tattoo girl since that time she was on stage. I don't know what it is, but something about the way she looked at me just feels off. As the dancer is picking up her stuff, I place a five-spot next to her foot before she stands up so she won't have to bend down more times than necessary. I sit back down, look at the time on my phone, and decide that I'm out after this last dance.

"Hey guys, are you ready for this? Just what I know you have all been waiting for . . . give it up for Chloe and Ginger!" This guy also sounds strangely familiar. I'm pretty sure the current DJ used to do the introductions for Hollywood Squares.

Only a matter of seconds into the routine by the two brunettes on stage, I am startled from behind when out of nowhere I am blindfolded by a scarf. My immediate reaction is panic, but I quickly calm my nerves due to the fact that my eyes are covered by a delicate fabric, which is loosely tied around my head. After I feel a slight tug to secure the knot in the back of my head, a sexy voice whispers in my ear, "Hey Anton, I've missed you sugar." Initially, my guess would be that Lace wants to give me another dance. However, her voice sounds a little bit deeper, and she neglected to use the word "baby."

In situations like this, I go with the old standby, "Hey there, I've been looking for you."

"Follow me," she says with an impressive tone of control in her voice. This time Lace, or whoever this is, grabs me by my belt buckle and then places her arm around my waist and leads me somewhere. I'm not sure where we are going because of the blindfold, but I am fairly certain we are headed in the opposite direction of the first private room I was in. Eventually, she stops me and from what I can see through the few holes in the scarf, this room appears more brightly lit than the last one. She shoves me down rather forcefully and says, "Well, well, well. Anton Bradley, is it really fucking you?"

Why did she just call me by my full name? If I'm on a reality television show and this is my mother, I am going to be livid.

"You can take the scarf off now darlin'."

At her request, or command, I untie the cloth and see that I am sitting on a very large round cushion. It is probably ten feet in diameter. Despite looking very soft, it is deceptively uncomfortable. There are mirrors surrounding the entire room, including the ceiling. It is very erotic, but at the same time is making me nauseous. After eventually fixing my gaze on the real woman and not her ten thousand reflections, my eyes are locked with the black-haired bombshell covered in tattoos.

"Um, hi." I look around some more, but just get dizzy, so I look at this woman's shoes. Jimmy Choo's, not bad. "Um, not that I mind being taken to secluded rooms by attractive women, but could you please explain to me what's going on?"

"Anton, do you seriously not remember me?" she asks in a tone that implies she is insulted, but I can tell she is not genuinely offended.

I lift my head up from the ground and begin to look Pandora up and down. My eyes quickly concentrate on her face, hoping that maybe I can remember who she is. Have I met her somewhere? Is she someone I have slept with? Is she mad at me? And then all of a sudden it hits me. I thought she looked familiar. "Danielle? Are you Danielle . . . S . . . Silver, that's it? Danielle Silver. Please tell me it's you otherwise I have no fucking clue who you are."

"Ha, no Anton it's me. Actually, I was just giving you a hard time. Truthfully, I'm a bit surprised you remembered me at all. I have to say that when I first saw you sitting at your table, I wasn't sure who you were either. I knew you looked familiar, so I had my girl give you some personal attention to get your name and a little background info. I hope she treated you right. She's my protégée."

And just like that, the entire Lace/Sarah conundrum is solved. "Wow! I can't believe it's actually you. I don't think I've seen you since " . . ."

She finishes my sentence for me with, "Graduation. Yeah, I haven't seen many people from high school since then. Truth be told, I like it that way. But I'm glad you showed up. You were one of the few people I actually liked in that popularity contest of a school."

Am I honestly getting a lecture on image from a stripper? "Aw thanks Danielle. I really liked you too." Suddenly, I am more nervous than I ever was during my entire high school career. "I mean, as a friend . . . not that I liked you in *that* way or anything." She blushes because she can see right through me. And out of all the "compliments" she must hear in the course of a year, this one is rare because it is from the heart. I never thought I'd see Danielle again, but being right here right now feels amazing. I guess I liked her more than I thought I did back in high school. I try to draw attention away from my adolescent insecurities and ask her, "So tell me, what have you been up to since high school? I mean, have you been a dancer this whole time?"

She sits down next to me on the round sofa, and before answering my question, she notices I look a little woozy. "Are you OK, Anton? You don't look too good."

"Yeah, I'm OK, but I'd be better if I wasn't looking at an unending string of reflections."

"Oh, is that all?" She gets up and walks over to a small cabinet and grabs a remote. She points it up at a box hanging from the ceiling, hits a button, and instantly all of the mirrors become windows. "Don't worry, we can see them, but they can't see us. Some guys like complete isolation with a woman, and some kind of dig the reverse voyeurism with the windows. Does that help though?"

"Yeah, it actually feels a lot better, thanks."

She uses the remote to dim the lights a little more, and resumes her seat next to me, tossing the remote on the pillows behind us. "Well, back to your question, that would be a yes and a no." I look at her inquisitively. "Well, obviously you know that I danced in high school, as do most of the kids we went to school with. When I got to college, I had a work study that didn't pay nearly enough, so I got back into it while in Boston."

"Wow! You went to college in Boston?" Many impressions are bouncing around in my head right now. I'm impressed that she apparently went to college in Boston. Well, the fact that she went to college at all is shocking, given the fact that she used to cheat off of my tests. "Cool, where did you go?" I ask her.

"MIT. Well, technically it's in Cambridge, but I worked at a couple of clubs in Boston."

I look at her with intense cynicism. "Yeah right Danielle. No offense, but I doubt you went to MIT. Where did you really go to school?"

"Yeah, I know it sounds crazy, a stripper with a brain. But seriously Anton, I have a degree in aerospace engineering from the Massachusetts Institute of Technology."

"Well I'm sorry to ask a question that I'm sure you get all the time then, if your story is in fact true. But why did you go to a school with that kind of reputation, and go back to stripping?"

"Like I said, I haven't been dancing my entire life since high school. I worked for NASA right out of MIT. But it was way too stressful, and this pays much better."

As much as I want to believe her, I'm having enormous difficulty doing so. "But Danielle, how is that possible? I mean, you used to cheat off me all the time. I'm definitely not a moron, but I'm a long ways away from winning a Nobel Prize in physics you know?"

She giggles a little and then responds, "Oh you thought I was cheating off of your tests? Ha-ha, that's funny Anton. No, I can see why you would think that, but did you ever see my grades? I had straight As all the way through high school. I just looked at random kids' tests for a couple of reasons. Well first off, I got a kick out of reading what kind of ridiculous answers kids would try to pass off for genuine knowledge. And I don't know if you noticed this, but most of the kids in school didn't like me."

"Yeah, I know. I hope you didn't get that impression from me. I know we never hung out, but I thought you were pretty cool."

"Oh no, you were great. But not to sound cocky, I know I was a pretty girl in high school, and a lot of the popular girls resented the fact that the boys in our class liked me. It didn't help that everyone thought I was a charity case. Can you imagine how much people would have hated me if they knew I was almost valedictorian?"

I am in awe. "Wait a minute, back up. Almost valedictorian? Seriously?"

"Yeah, I was in a three-way tie going into final exams senior year. I tanked a lot of my tests on purpose to remove any possibility of having to give a speech to a bunch of mama's boys and daddy's girls."

"Really? You're fucking with me I can tell." She shakes her head no. "That sucks Danielle. I mean, I know I was a little jealous of the kids who got the best grades in school, but no one should ever have to fear success. I'm sorry."

"It's OK. It's not your fault. I still got into the school I wanted to go to, so it all worked out."

"If you don't mind my asking, what did you mean when you said we thought you were a charity case?"

"Oh about that. Well I don't need to tell you that just about everyone in our school was loaded. Almost everyone drove flashy cars and wore designer clothes. I'm not sure if you remember, but I had none of those things."

"Well, you did have that sick Jag as I do recall."

She smiles, reminiscing. "Well yeah, but I bought it myself. I actually have two Jags and a Ferrari now. But up until that point, I walked to school and wore generic clothing. Everyone thought I was from the ghetto. But truthfully, my parents were worth more than just about every other kids' parents put together."

"Yeah right. Then why didn't you have all the stuff you're talking about?"

"OK, in all honesty, I was pretty pissed at my parents for a while about not buying me all the stuff everyone else had. But the reason they did it was because they didn't want to spoil me. My parents are both immigrants from Romania who had to overcome a lot of bullshit to get where they are. They changed their last name to Silver when they got to America, sort of as a way to start fresh. But looking back on it all, I'm very happy with the way they raised me."

"Well how do they feel about what you do?"

"I knew that question was coming. Honestly, they were really mad at first. But at the same time, they realize that the world is a fucked up place. They had to do some things they aren't necessarily proud of to get where they are. I know they were definitely not thrilled about it, but they also know that sometimes in order to get where you want to go, you have to do some things that you really don't want to do."

I rub my eyes and scratch my head. "I'm sorry, this is just crazy. That's awesome, but wow! I just never expected to hear a story like this. And definitely not in a place like this."

"Well Anton, do you really think you could actually hear a story like this anywhere *besides* a strip club?"

"Good point," I tell her.

There is a long period of silence where we both just look at one another and smile. The sexual tension is off the charts. Breaking the quiet, Danielle says, "Anton, you're a really good guy. Did anything ever happen with you and that girl you always hung out with in high school? Didn't I sometimes run into the two of you at Roxy's. You guys were always drinking milkshakes. What was her name?"

I'm taken aback that she remembers anything about this part of my life from high school. "Oh, you probably mean Ashby."

"Yeah, that's it. Whatever happened to her? Do you still talk to her, or is she history?" she asks as she moves closer to me on the sofa.

"Oh we've definitely kept in touch. But honestly, we're just friends. I'm really lucky to have someone like her."

She looks right at me, rolls her eyes, and says, "Yeah right Anton. I know we're sitting in the middle of the hotbed of deceit, but you can be honest with me."

"What, nothing ever happened. We're just friends," I tell her. This is pretty much my stock response whenever anyone mentions the name Ashby.

Danielle becomes very proper and in a stern tone tells me, "Listen here OK? I saw the way you looked at her. And take it from a girl, any woman would kill to have a guy look at her the way you did. I know it was a while ago, but if you have any feelings for her, you should take a chance."

She moves closer to me again, and places her hand on my thigh near my crotch. Trying to politely change the subject, I tell her, "Well yeah, but I work all over the country, and my career is really important to me. Did you know that I've met every U.S. Congressman from the state of California? It's true I took some photos for their campaigns a few years ago." OK, I met one member of the senate and two representatives, but I really need to change the topic.

Danielle leans in closer, causing me to make a strange face, hopefully showing my discomfort. She looks at my mouth and says, "Hey, what have you been eating tonight? It looks like you're growing a spinach patch in your mouth."

"Oh, that. I'm pretty sure it's peppermint. I've been drinking mojitos."

"Ah, those will get ya every time. You know what I always say?" I raise my eyebrows in inquiry. "Mojitos, mo' problems. Come on, that was a good one right?"

I roll my eyes at her lame but amusing joke, "Yeah, I'll give it to ya, not bad, Strippy Smalls, not bad."

She says, "Well, let me help you out there." She immediately straddles my lap, grabs the back of my head, and shoves her tongue into my mouth. Although I'm a little buzzed from the cocktails, I am not oblivious to the fact that this is a horrible idea. Despite my efforts to avoid physical intimacy with women based solely on pleasure, I keep telling myself I will regret not doing this. Wasting no time, Danielle takes her top off without effort, and reaches into my pants. Her hand is so warm that my mind vaporizes.

"You wanna fuck me Anton?" I look at her and enthusiastically nod my head up and down. Thoreau once wrote "Beware of any endeavor which requires new clothes." He didn't say anything about scenarios that involve *no* clothes at all. She grabs her little purse that she keeps all of her earnings in, and pulls out a condom. I cannot believe I am about to do this. She shoves me back so that I'm staring up at the ceiling, and she climbs on top of me. As she takes my clothes off, we begin rolling around on the sofa uncontrollably, as she reaches for the condom laying on the opposite perimeter of the large circle; she falls awkwardly off of me. And immediately the windows become mirrors again. I look over and her elbow is next to that remote. She doesn't notice the change in the surface of the walls, or if she does, it is of no concern to her. Danielle climbs back on top of me, preparing to do things to my body that until this moment I had only dreamt of. But as she pulls me up, all I can see is a million reflections of our near naked bodies, and I panic. I quickly back away.

"I'm sorry, I can't do this. Believe me, I *really* want to. You have no idea how badly I want to, but I would not feel right about this."

Defensively, she goes off on me asking, "Are you out of your fucking mind? Do you know how many men would pay *a lot* of money to be here with me right now?"

The fact that she brings up the notion of money and sex in the same sentence really disturbs me. It makes me a little more comfortable in my decision. I counter her tirade with, "Danielle, look at us! You get naked for men for money!"

"Who the fuck are you to say that shit to me? Where do you get off preaching to me? I know you're a big shot photographer. One of my girls out there recognized you too, told me she worked with you on a calendar shoot. From what I hear, we're not that different. We both make money selling flesh."

"Hey, that's not fair," I yell.

"Whatever Anton. Just because the girls you photograph are wearing a thong doesn't mean you're not selling sex just like everyone else in this building. If anything, you're worse!"

"Worse? Are you crazy?"

"Yeah, that's right, worse. How much time do you spend doctoring and retouching photos? At least where I work, what you see is what you get. No more, no less."

And like a punch in the groin, I'm brought back down to earth. She is absolutely right. How have I never thought about it like that? Well, I'm fairly certain the money and sex played a significant role in my ignorance.

Calming myself down, I take several deep breaths and respond, "I'm sorry, I lost my cool. You're right though, our jobs are very similar." She nods at me as if to say "I know, I'm glad you see it my way." "But I still can't do this, not after all my therapy sessions. And not after talking about Ashby."

Quickly dropping her rough demeanor, she shouts, "I knew it! You do like her! Awesome!" She begins jumping up and down jubilantly while clapping her hands.

"OK, OK. Just keep it down."

There is a long pause so that we can both regain focus after all of the madness that has just taken place.

Danielle again breaks the silence by saying, "You know, for the record, I really don't like working here."

"So why do you do it? Is it just for the money?"

"Well, yes and no. Obviously, the money is great, but I can still make a ton working for companies that are far more revered than this dump." I give her a look this time, hopefully insinuating that she should in fact take one of those jobs. "But do you wanna know why I really do it?"

"Well obviously."

"OK, I'll tell you. As much as I hate the men who come in here, I love taking their money. For me personally, working here isn't so much about making lots of money as it is about taking cash away from the scumbags of the earth. I get a real kick out of knowing those assholes have a little less dough when they go back to their bullshit lives. And although I live a very comfortable lifestyle," she pauses to change her train of thought, "I hope you'll believe this next part."

"I will."

"Well, I give a very considerable portion of what I make to a charity that supports women who are victims of domestic violence. I don't want to say how much exactly, but my contribution is substantial."

As shocking as this is her sincerity is obvious. "Wow Danielle, you're just like Robin Hood." She smiles at the compliment. "The only difference is that you look way better naked. Well that, and the whole bow and arrow thing."

We both begin to put our clothes back on, but she is fully dressed before I even have my pants on and the belt buckled.

As I begin to button my shirt, she looks at me and says, "Congratulations Anton."

"For what? For passing up sex with a bombshell?"

She giggles once again, "No silly. Congratulations for passing my test."

"Test? What test?"

"Well, I wouldn't have stopped if you hadn't. I definitely would have jumped your hot ass. But I'm glad you put an end to what was almost a huge mistake. Now, I know that deep down you really are the nice guy I thought you were."

"Well, thanks, I guess." I'm not exactly sure how to respond to that, or if her analysis is correct.

After about fifteen seconds of wretched silence and Danielle smirking at me, she says, "So, you really wanna get this Ashby chick?" I simply nod, because she already knows the answer. "Good. I'm gonna give you some advice. I know I'm not the most credible source for what women want. But I am very knowledgeable concerning what women *don't* want. You wanna know what you need to do first?"

"Of course."

"Get as far away from this shit hole as quickly as possible. It's not helping your cause."

13

"NO WAY, WE'VE already been on the Matterhorn three times today. It's my turn to pick the ride, and I say Teacups," Ashby says to me around midday at Disneyland. We're taking a break from the Magic Kingdom to grab some food.

"OK, OK. That's fair, but it's not my fault that Splash Mountain is shut down this week for maintenance. Clearly Matterhorn is the next best option," I tell her to defend my choice.

Ashby quickly becomes animated, not angry, but very passionate. "All right Franklin, first off, the best ride at Disneyland is Space Mountain. Hands down. Secondly," she takes a look at her food, and her tone becomes much more humorous, "Why do the fries here suck so bad? And wouldn't it be cool if the hamburger patties were shaped like Mickey Mouse ears? You know, like three small patties combined into one?"

I'm glad to see that she is not bothered by my adoration for the replica of the mammoth Swiss mountain. I'm not really sure what I should say about Ashby's critique of the food though. With her intense fondness for animals, her dietary habits swing back and forth like a pendulum from one week to the next. One day, she'll be living solely on granola and tofu, but the next she'll e-mail me and tell me about her latest trip to Black Angus.

"What? The fries aren't so bad. I kind of like them."

"You would."

"Whatever. At least I'm not eating my patients, *Dr. McHale*," I tell her in a highly facetious tone.

"Ewww, gross."

"OK, sorry. But seriously, how much longer until you're officially a veterinarian?" Yes that's right, the woman of my dreams has dedicated her life to helping the things that make me very apprehensive. I can certainly appreciate the irony in that.

"Well, if all goes according to plan, it should only be about three semesters. Hopefully not this coming December, but a year and a half from now."

"And are you still liking Oregon as much as you originally did? I'll bet it's a lot different from Auburn, huh?"

"Oh yeah, Oregon and Alabama are worlds apart. Don't get me wrong. I loved my time at Auburn, but Oregon grows on me more every day I spend there. Personally, I don't think I'll stick around Corvallis after I get my degree, but I am definitely considering Portland or Eugene."

"I forget, which Oregon school do you go to?"

"Oregon State, the Beavers. The other big state school is the one in Eugene. I would rather have gone to that city, but OSU had the program I wanted and offered a nice financial package."

"Well, that makes sense. I'm glad it's all worked out for you then." She smiles in appreciation. No one can make her smile like I can. "So, speaking of Auburn, how's Mr. Bixley?"

A look of absolute awe overtakes her face. "Seriously? You didn't hear?" I shake my head no. "Chuck dumped me like three months ago." And when she says that, it's like the Macy's Thanksgiving Day Parade and Fourth of July are happening in my head at the same time. Of course I knew that, I just *really* like hearing it directly from her.

"Oh, that's awful," I say in a voice with blatant undertones of elation. "I mean, I really liked Mr. Heisman." Yes that's right. Ashby was dating Chuck Bixley, Auburn's four-year quarterback and winner of the Heisman Trophy a few years back. He's now a backup in the NFL. No big deal, really.

"I'm sure you're just devastated, Franklin." When she says this, it's like she's calling me out on having feelings for her. I've never explicitly stated how I feel about her to her face. Sure, maybe in tangential ways or the occasional "I love ya buddy" sign of affection. There is no possible way that she *doesn't* know, but I guess since I've never actually said those words, in her mind she can only speculate it. And what makes it worse is I have no idea how to interpret this. Is her subtext telling me that I should "go for it" and lay it all out there? Or is she just implying that maybe I'm a bad friend for not being empathetic to her misfortune? I have no idea how to read women. I guess that's why I'm usually drawn to the ones with low expectations as a result of being screwed over in the past.

"OK, I'm sorry, I know that sounded insensitive. I mean, I feel bad for you and all, but I didn't think he was good enough for you anyway. You know you deserve the best. And just because he was the best QB in college doesn't make him the most worthy of your affections." Her mouth opens with her lips forming a gaping hole. She doesn't say anything, but I can tell she's touched. I know what I just told her was cliché, but it's also what I really believe.

Trying to appear humble but still fishing for more compliments, she replies, "Yeah right. You're too nice to me. I wish more guys were like you." Note: if you're a woman, never tell this to a man. It's comparable to us telling you that you look good in whatever dress you try on, even if you try on seven or eight. On the surface, it sounds complimentary, but it's never what you want to hear.

"Well, you're the only person I have any desire to be nice to Ashby," I tell her as we place our napkins and trash on our trays so we can get back to the action.

"How did I get so lucky?" she says in a mildly satirical tone, but I know she really means it. We throw our trash away and begin to walk toward the Teacups, I put my hands in my pockets, and she sticks her left arm through my right arm. "Franklin?"

"Yeah."

"Boys suck. I hate dating. I'm really glad I have someone like you in my life no matter what happens."

I really want to tell her that I won't be available forever, so she should take a chance on me sooner rather than later. But naturally, I just say "Thanks Ashby. I'm lucky to have you too."

We walk silently for about fifty paces and she says, "Anton, can we make the deal that all best friends make? If we aren't married by the time we're thirty-five or whatever, we'll get married?"

My heart races. She just called me Anton. In all the years I've known her, she has *never* called me Anton. I have no idea what this means, if anything. My hands start shaking; I'm so nervous. I don't even know if I should be nervous, but it's such a curveball. Obviously, my initial reaction is to jump at any opportunity involving a long-term commitment with Ashby. What I want to say is something like, "Can we make it thirty-five *days* from now?" But true to form I panic and coolly reply, "Oh sure. But can we make it forty? I don't think I'll have everything out of my system by then." Why in the world is it so hard for me to be sincere in this very moment? Granted what she is proposing is purely hypothetical and highly unlikely, but why does my insecurity thrive at the most inopportune times?

She looks at me with those eyes that break down any defenses I have and doesn't say a single word. This is the kind of power she has over me. And all I can respond is "OK, thirty-five works." Then, she smiles up at me in a way that insinuates she is happy, but at the same time implies she's just proud she has control over me. Like I said, I am awful at reading women.

"Perfect. Now, let's go ride some Teacups."

As we're walking through Tomorrowland, or Neverland . . . it's one of the "Lands," we see a group of children gathered around some of the Disney characters wearing those large plush suits. As we get a little closer, I can tell that Mickey Mouse is present, as well as Snow White and Peter Pan. I know Ashby will want us to take a picture with one if not all of these characters. For one, she loves these costume employees, primarily the ones that aren't obviously human. More importantly, given her love of animals, I wouldn't be surprised if she has Donald Duck panties on at this very moment. And the thought of that excites me greatly, almost enough for me to ask if my suspicions are even vaguely credible.

"Oooh Franklin! Come on, let's get our picture taken with Mickey," she says as she takes her camera out of her small purse. I want to object, because there is only one side of the camera I like to be on. By now though, I think I've established a pattern of behavior that will clearly dictate how I'm going to respond to her request.

"OK Ashby, but only because *you* want to," I tell her with mild enthusiasm. She is probably the only person aside from my parents who can convince me to be the subject of a photograph.

"Great!" she says, and then quickly turns around and approaches a group of parents hoping to find one willing to spare a minute or so to snap our photo. Not surprisingly, given her panache, she finds a volunteer immediately. She thanks the woman, kind enough to help us, and we take our positions on opposing sides of Mickey.

Ashby immediately goes into a funny pose and flashes her biggest grin. "Franklin, put up your 'Mickey Ears.'"

I give her a dumbfounded look because I adamantly opposed buying those souvenir black hats with the plastic ears on them. "Huh? We didn't buy them remember."

"No, silly. Like this," she says as she puts her flat hands on the top of her head, palms facing out. I can only assume that her hands are supposed to resemble the ears of a mouse.

"You're joking right?"

"Come on Franklin. Just do it ya big baby."

I decide to just suck it up and get it over with. The sooner we take this picture, the sooner we get on the Teacups, which means the sooner we hit the Matterhorn. The main reason I like this ride is because Ashby and I sit in the same coaster car and I get to hold her super close. It's not like a traditional roller coaster where everyone has their own seat. It's more like a log ride. I put my hands on my head and nod at the woman who is ready to take our picture.

"OK, smile and say 'cheese' everybody," the woman tells us enthusiastically. She has likely done this enough times today that her zeal is completely fabricated and she is functioning in a repeat mode. After she says the word "cheese," Mickey rubs his tummy because mice are supposed to like cheese. I roll my eyes because the person in this suit probably does that every single time he takes a picture and hears the word "cheese." What's worse is I'll bet the person in that suit is amused by it every time too. I put up an actual genuine smile despite looking ridiculous, because I know this picture is actually a big deal to Ashby, and I'm hoping she'll give me doubles. The woman snaps the picture, and hands the camera back to Ashby.

"Thank you ma'am," she tells the lady, then turns back to Mickey, and gives him a big hug. "Yeah, Teacup time!"

"You got it. Which way are they?" I ask.

"Follow me, it's not very far," she says as she begins walking at a quick pace. Even when I kick it into high gear, she is still about three steps ahead of me. After about three minutes of walking, she spots the ride and exclaims, "Oh yes! The line is really short. See? I told you this was a good choice."

"OK, you're right. But are you sure you want to go on this ride immediately after eating?" She looks at me as if I'm just being a jackass, but my query is actually sincere. "Hey, I'm just saying, those things can get spinning around pretty fast Ashby. And I hope you don't think I'm gonna take it easy on ya."

"Bring it Franklin. I can take it," she tells me with the utmost confidence as we reach the back of the line, which is only about twelve people long. The ride that was in session while we were talking has begun to wind down. After everyone has exited the circle of massive rotating cups, the ride attendant opens the gate, and people begin jumping into their favorite color dish. Ashby bolts out of the gate shouting, "Oh yeah! The blue one, we got the blue one." I honestly think she would have killed a puppy in order to get the blue teacup. Rarely have I ever seen her this passionate about anything not related to animals.

"All right, good choice," I say as I get in the cup and close the small door behind us. "You know, these things spin faster in one direction than they do in the other. I forget which is faster, clockwise or counter-clockwise, but we're gonna find out," I tell her with a cocky sneer.

"Yeah right. I could spin this thing faster in my sleep than you could on your best day Franklin." I raise my eyebrows, accepting what I interpret as a challenge. Just then, the attendant's voice comes over the loudspeaker and reminds us to keep our hands inside at all times. As cheesy as this ride is, the music is actually pretty fun. The sounds of whistles and tooting teapots begin, and the cups gradually pick up pace. "Oh yeah, here we go!" Ashby passionately shouts.

"OK, you asked for it," I tell her as I grab the wheel in the center of our blue teacup and begin spinning it clockwise as furiously as I can. One of the biggest smiles I have ever seen on anyone appears on Ashby's face; she is obviously having a great time.

"Yeah Franklin! Is that all you got?" she yells, daring me to spin it even harder. I put even more muscle into the motion, and even though my effort probably appears to make us spin faster, I'm fairly sure we were already at the maximum speed those little cups are capable of handling.

While I'm putting every ounce of energy I have into spinning this wheel, all I can focus on is how happy Ashby looks. The perspective you get from these teacups is actually quite extraordinary. In effect, what ends up happening is the people in the cabin with you all appear to remain still, because in relation to you, their position never changes. However, the rest of the world around you is whipping by at the speed of light. Everything outside the realm of your teacup is a blur. And with Ashby looking as beautiful as she is, it's like I'm staring at a famous painting. If Michelangelo were to paint Ashby's portrait over the top of just about any work by Van Gogh, that would pale in comparison to what I'm looking at now. I really wish I had a camera with me right now. Although I doubt I'd be able to hold a steady enough hand to take a good shot. Luckily, this image is so striking it will be easy to etch it into my mind for the rest of my life. The ride begins to slow down, which makes me glad because my arms were getting really sore. Once the cups finally stop completely, we hear the voice over the loudspeaker to tell us where to exit, as well as remind us not to forget any of our stuff.

"Oh man, Franklin. That rocked! You weren't kidding about how fast you could spin that thing," she tells me. After only about two minutes of walking, I can tell she isn't feeling well. She puts one hand on her stomach and with the other thrusts her purse into my stomach. "Take this," she exclaims as she runs for a bush off the main walking path. I follow her quickly, but not nearly as fast as she is running. She makes it off the trail and hunches down over a bush. I tuck her purse under my armpit, and with both hands free I bunch her hair behind her back in an attempt to keep her from getting puke in it. It is only a matter of milliseconds between when I pull her hair back and the time vomit flies from her mouth. As tempting as it is to comment on the fries or her idea of Mickey-shaped hamburgers, I don't say a word until she is totally done.

"Aw, you poor thing. Are you OK Ashby? You need anything, some water or something?"

"Yeah, water would be great. And a napkin too. Thank you so much, you're the best."

"You got it," I tell her and begin to walk away toward a snack stand. But before I even take two steps, Ashby bends over and resumes throwing up. I rush back to her and grab her hair again. As I'm gently patting her on the back, I feel so badly for her. I hate seeing her like this. But as much as I want her to feel completely healthy, there is a part of me that is so thrilled to feel like she needs me right now. All I can think is that I would gladly hold her hair behind her head every day of her life rather than hook up with any other woman ever again. Although the circumstances are less than ideal, there is nowhere else I'd rather be.

14

"Come on Ed! This is pathetic. My mom can drink faster than you," I yell at my therapist as he is in the middle of downing his third Jaeger Bomb in about thirty minutes. I rarely go out drinking, particularly if there is no prospect for sexual activity at the end of the night. But when my psychologist suggested we go out to a bar, I thought that was pretty cool. I have not been this wasted in many years, and my behavior seems to be regressing to how I acted in college.

"There," Ed exclaims as he slams his shot glass on the bar top. "That's how you do it Anton. That was a free lesson in how to drink like a man. You can feel free to start any time now."

I've clearly never seen this side of Dr. Polk, and I really like it. When he said he was going to start talking to me as a friend, I had no idea that would involve shots of Patrón and pints of Anchor Steam.

"All right, not bad Ed. You do OK for an old man. I hope that in a few years when you're blowing your social security checks at the local pub, you'll still invite me along."

"Ah fuck off. What are we drinking next?" I shrug my shoulders, partly because I don't know what I want to drink, but mainly because I'm not fully convinced this is real. I have to contemplate for a moment to check and make sure that this is in fact my life. "I know," Ed perks up and looks for our bartender. "Hey Bobby," the guy behind the bar looks up at Ed, "let me have two shots of Maker's Mark and two pints of Guinness."

"Shit Ed, I can't do anymore shots. I think I might have to go soon anyway."

"Oh I see," even when we're not in his office, he finds a way to work that phrase into the conversation. "Well Anton, I understand," he says dryly, "Just don't forget your lunchbox, and don't talk to strangers on the way home, OK? Are your shoes tied?"

"Oh yeah, very funny Ed." In my drunken state, even the weakest insult carries a lot of clout against my ego. "All right Bobby," I say to the bartender, "Make mine a double."

"That's the spirit." Bobby sets the whiskey and beer in front of us, we pick up the shots, and Ed asks me, "What are we drinking to?"

My response to his question is delayed because the song *Two Tickets to Paradise* has just begun playing throughout the room. All the alcohol coursing through my veins forces me to ponder why he actually purchased two tickets. He is in fact going to Paradise, the epitome of wonderful vacation destinations, so why wouldn't he be satisfied by going alone? Surely even a lonely person can have fun in Paradise. After those questions roll around in my head for a few moments, my focus shifts back to my drinking companion. Slurring every other syllable and barely making sense I tell him, "To not . . . to well . . . um . . . Fuck Ed, we're drinking . . . we're drinking to me not gettin' any."

"Bullshit Anton! We both know that's not the problem. You can get laid, but that's not all you're after anymore right?" I bury my head, "Hey, look at me." I look up at him, "You've got your sights set on something better right?"

"Yeah, Ashby!" I shout like a kindergartner who just got two toys in his Happy Meal instead of one.

"Good, that's what I thought. So tonight, we're drinking to " . . .

I interrupt him and shout, "To Ashby!" as I raise my shot, spilling a few drops on my pants.

"Nooo, not yet. We're drinking to Machiavelli."

"Oh yeah, good call." After a long pause, I look at him and say, "Ed, you're really smart Ed. I think that's pretty cool man. I wish I was smart like you Ed."

"Well thanks Anton, that's nice of you to say. But you are smart, don't forget that. You went to UC Berkeley, that's no small feat. And you're very well spoken, definitely one of the more articulate patients I've had." I silently mouth the words "Thanks Ed" to him, and he continues, "OK, enough of this sentimental shit, bottoms up!" I nod; we click our glasses together, and throw back our whiskey.

"Oh man! I'm gonna feel that in the morning," I say as I cringe and shake my head violently. "Give me some beer."

"Here ya go," Ed says as he slides my pint closer toward me.

"Thanks." After a few sips, a light bulb inside my restrictively functioning brain goes off. "Hey! I'm gonna call Ashby!" I scream as I pull my cell phone out of my pocket and hit the buttons to call her via speed dial.

With quicker reflexes than a Zen Master, Ed snatches the phone from my hand. "Whoa! I don't think so buddy. Give me that phone."

"Hey, that's mine. Give it back," I say while reaching across Ed's torso as he pulls the phone further away.

"Anton, I'm doing you a favor. As much as I want to see you drunk dial the woman of your dreams, my conscience won't allow me to do that. You'll thank me tomorrow." He raises his hand to get Bobby's attention, and the bartender comes right away. Ed leans over the bar close enough to whisper something into Bobby's ear. When he's done, Bobby backs away and nods his head to confirm he properly heard the instructions. Then, Ed hands him the phone and some cash of an indiscernible denomination.

"Ed, what are you doing? That's my phone, get it back man." I'm definitely overreacting, in true drunken fashion.

"Calm down, you can have the phone back tomorrow. I gave him forty bucks to make sure you don't get your hands on it tonight."

Making a melodramatic facial snarl, I bitterly say, "Thanks a lot Ed, that's super nice of you."

Appreciating my sarcasm, he responds in a similar tone, "You're quite welcome. Now, enough of this nonsense. Drink your beer."

"Good idea, Ed," I tell him as if everything that transpired right before now did not even take place. I take a few sips, and sit silently for a minute, calming myself down.

"So Anton, I've got a question for you . . . if you don't mind that is?"

"Yeah, sure man. Go for it."

"Well, I remember in one of our earlier sessions, you said you had some kind of sentimental attachment to FDR."

I have no idea if I said this or not. First of all, I'm quite drunk. But more importantly, this is the guy who could never remember my name or occupation. Did I really tell him this, or is he fucking with me? "Yeah, that's right. Well, it's really more my grandfather, but I guess I do have a fondness for the man."

"Well, would you mind telling me the story?" he asks, as the tone of our evening has gotten just slightly more serious.

"Ed, honestly I'd really like to. The problem is though, you see . . . Um, well . . . I don't really know the story."

"What?"

"Well, basically what happened was one day my grandfather met FDR during his presidency, and apparently it had a really big impact on his life."

"Interesting!" He rolls his eyes around in his head expressing curiosity. "Well, if you ever remember the story, or if someone tells it to you, I'd love to hear it."

"Sure Ed, I'd like that." I tell him this as if Ed is the first real friend I've ever had in my life. That is definitely not the case, but in my frame of mind, it feels like it. "What I remember, and I could be wrong on this, is that my grandpa was working as a waiter in a diner in Georgia, and Franklin Delano Roosevelt came in to eat one day. That's really all I know though."

"OK, well that still sounds pretty neat. Maybe another day though."

"You see Dr. Polk," he said I could call him Ed, but I switch back and forth, "my grandfather has only ever told that story to a handful of people in its entirety."

His interest is mounting. "Really?"

"Yeah, he has only ever told it to his son. You know, my dad. And I think he also told a couple of his childhood friends. But apparently, he told my dad to tell me the story only when he thinks I would really need to hear it. I keep telling him I need to hear it, but I think he's reading that as boy who cried wolf."

"Well, that sure is something."

"But I'll definitely let you know the story when I hear it. Deal?"

"That's fair. Thank you."

"You're very, very . . . welcome. Ed?"

"Yes Anton?"

"Why did we drink to Machiavelli? That name sounds familiar, but who is he?"

Laughing at the absurdity of my inquisition, and also questioning my sincerity, he responds, "Ha-ha, that's funny. Remember, *The Prince*? That book I gave you? It was written by Niccolo Machiavelli."

After I think about it for a second, I rejoice, "Oh right! I knew I'd heard that name. That was a really good book by the way Ed. I've read it probably like 250 times."

He looks at me in disbelief. "Is that so?"

"OK, just kidding," I say as if my hyperbole was the funniest joke ever. "But honestly, I really have read it four times I think."

"Wow! That's very impressive. So I guess you like it then?"

"Oh yeah Ed, it's incredible."

"Well good, because now that you're familiar with it, we're going to start applying it more to your daily life and relationship goals."

"What? Come on Ed, now you're just shittin' me. I mean, the book is good and all, and I know I'm drunk, but isn't the book about war, power, deceit, and fear?"

"Exactly. Haven't you ever heard the phrase 'All's fair in love and war?' They can be synonymous."

"Well, then could you please explain to me how that is supposed to help with *any* woman, especially Ashby McHale?"

"Absolutely. It's actually quite simple." He takes a sip of his beer, followed by a deep breath, and goes on, "How about this? You pick a certain part of the book that you find compelling, and I'll tell you how it relates to women and relationships?"

What he is proposing is very intriguing. I have no doubt the fact that my BAC is approaching a whole number must be contributing to this. I take a moment to ponder what he has just said, and respond, "OK Ed, you're on. Give me a second to think though." In a very blatant drunken and sarcastic stupor, I say, "I know that you probably can't tell right now Ed, because I have such a high tolerance and all . . . but I'm kind of drunk."

Joking back with me, he responds, "Is that so? I never would have guessed. By all means Anton, take as much time as you need."

I close my eyes in an attempt to give the impression that I am very deep in thought and throw in some twisted facial expressions for emphasis. After sometime to recall what I have read recently, I turn to Ed and say, "OK Ed, I've got one. Well, I guess it's not so much of a specific example, but I know Machiavelli talked a ton about using inequality to be an effective ruler. You know, he should be vicious and ruthless."

"I think the word you're looking for is *iniquity*."

Acting genuinely impressed as if Dr. Polk is filled with more knowledge than a Jeopardy trivia board, I emphatically reply, "Oh yes! That's what I meant. Infinity."

Pretending that I didn't just slaughter the same word twice in as many attempts, he chooses to take two steps forward rather than four steps back. Posing the question in a way that he's hinting at the obvious answer, he asks me, "OK, well what about iniquity is it that you find unappealing?"

"Well, I mean come on Ed. That's like common sense."

"How so?"

"Well, I mean no one likes a liar. That's pretty basic stuff here Ed."

"Now, before I respond to that, I think it's more important that we clearly establish an objective. What is it you want?"

"Duh Ed, I want a relationship."

"Right. But does everyone in the dating world seek the same thing?" he asks me in what I like to refer to as his "therapist tone."

Thinking briefly, wondering if this is a trick question, I respond with what appears to be evident, "I guess not. I mean, some people just wanna screw, while others want to get married, start families, and stuff like that."

"Exactly. So given one's intentions, iniquity can work in a variety of ways."

"No Ed, nobody likes a liar." I'm pretty sure that there is an ingredient in all alcoholic beverages that induces redundancy. Seriously, there must be something in liquor that makes people repeat the things they've just said.

"Do you mean to tell me you've never told a lie to a woman to sleep with her?" he asks me in a tone that insinuates I'm guilty.

Ashamed of myself, I reply, "Well . . . yeah, I guess so."

"OK, and you probably did that because your objective was to have sex and likely not much more."

"That's true, but that is obviously not going to help me with relationships Ed."

"That's not entirely accurate Anton. Sometimes small lies can be effective." Did he really just say that to me? "Let me put it like this Anton," looking me in the eyes to make sure I'm actually paying attention and not about to pass out in a puddle of Guinness, he continues, "Let's say you're dating a woman that you are very compatible with."

"OK? So I should start lying to her once we've been together for a while? I'm sorry Dr. Polk, I'm really lost here."

"That's OK, this is good. This is why we discuss things. Just listen though. So you've been dating a woman for a few months, and you're clicking in many ways." I nod my head, trying to see where he is going with this. "Well, hypothetically speaking, let's say the two of you made plans to meet up for dinner one night."

"Sure, sounds good."

"OK, well let's say that you agree to meet at 7:00 p.m. at your favorite Chinese restaurant. But then, at 6:45 p.m., you get a call and you can tell your date is a little frustrated." I continue to nod. "You can hear the tension in her voice; she isn't calling to cancel, but she will be a little late."

"Well that's fine, it happens."

"Right, but let's say she is so caught up in whatever it is that's bothering her that she completely forgets you planned to have Chinese. And you were *really* craving your favorite dish from this restaurant." I make a frown because the thought of missing out on Lo Mein from *The Silk Dragon* is not all that enticing. "Well let's say she really wants some lasagna or another form of pasta dish."

"OK? What's your point?"

"Here's what I'm getting at: you clearly want Chinese food, but are you going to tell your girlfriend who has clearly had a rough day that she can't have fettuccine alfredo because there is no way you can go another minute without chicken chow fun?" I giggle for a minute because the fact that he just said "chicken chow fun" is quite amusing. But what's even better is that it is an actual name of a dish.

"Well of course not Ed. That would be stupid."

"Naturally. But by telling her that you 'don't mind' having pasta or that it's 'no big deal' might not be exactly true. Granted it's not a life-altering lie, but it is straying from the truth. And sometimes, that's OK. People make sacrifices and concessions. Please understand that I am not saying you should just give up and give in anytime you argue or butt heads with a partner, but sometimes to make the people you love happy, you sacrifice a little bit of comfort."

Trying my best to soak in what he just said, I reply, "You know what Ed? That kind of helps. Thanks man."

"And remember Anton, Machiavelli did not say iniquity was the *only* way to achieve a desired end. There is ingenuity or creativity as well. He also said that a smart prince will learn from his predecessors. Successful people will study what made those before them triumphant, and what lead to their demise."

"OK, but how does that help? The only people I've really learned *anything* from about talking to women were complete jackasses. Their only objective was getting laid."

"And you don't know *anyone* who meets the criteria necessary to instill better values in you?"

"I guess not."

"What about your parents?"

"Oh yeah my parents rock."

"So you would say their relationship is stable and functional then?"

"Oh absolutely Ed, my dad would do anything for my mom and vice versa."

With more passion and fervor than I've seen in all his prior statements combined, Ed shouts, "Bingo! Well there you go! Learn from them. Ask your dad for advice about women. He obviously knows a thing or two about treating women well and what it takes to make a relationship work."

"My dad? Ed that's weird man."

"I know it can definitely take you out of your comfort zone, but just think about it is all I'm saying."

Pausing for a while to think about all the times I've seen my parents smiling together, I reply, "OK Dr. Polk, I'll do that."

"Good. Now, what other parts of the book do you have questions about?"

I am trying diligently to recall what I read in the book, but nothing is coming to mind. "I'm sorry Ed, I really did read that book a bunch, but I'm not exactly thinking too clearly right now you know?"

"I understand. Well then would you mind if I just discuss some of my favorite parts? Please feel free to ask any questions you have at any point."

This is a great idea because my brain was working way harder than it likes to with this much booze flowing through my system. "OK Dr. Polk, that sounds like a good idea. What else ya got?"

"Well take the part in chapter nine when Machiavelli discusses one way in which a prince may come into power, that being through outside people. That would include either the wealthy elite or the common people."

"Sounds vaguely familiar." Truthfully, I'm not sure how much that rings a bell. He probably could have said the author was commenting on the changing of the seasons, and I wouldn't have known the difference.

"OK, well he states that a ruler is more likely to be successful if he is given power by the common people as opposed to the wealthy elite. Just think about that for a minute, Anton."

"Um, OK." I think about it for a while, and I spit out, "Well, he's probably saying that women who are only interested in your money are bitches, and you need to show 'em the door."

He grins and chuckles at my diction and continues, "Well, that's actually not bad. He goes on to state that commoners are very willing to listen, but at the same time, they do not want to be oppressed. That sounds to me like the beginnings of a viable relationship right? Shouldn't a couple be willing to listen to each other, but at the same time have enough autonomy to stand alone and not let the other walk all over them? Relationships require compromise right?"

It's as if everything that is coming out of Dr. Polk's mouth is the most intelligent stuff I've ever heard. My brain is racing; I can't get enough of what he's telling me. Jubilantly, I exclaim, "You're absolutely fucking right Ed! Damn you're good!"

"Well thank you, but there's more. He goes on to proclaim that a good prince will think at all times of ways in which his people will feel a need for the state and himself."

Getting a little lost, I inquire with mixed sincerity and humor, "OK, but a woman is only one person, not a whole big group of them. Are you saying this only applies if I'm hooking up with multiple women?"

"Well, it could I suppose, but that doesn't apply to you. Remember now, we're focusing on your efforts, which include just one woman." I nod in agreement, and Ed continues, "What I want you to take from this is that a good boyfriend, husband, or whatever will always be thinking of ways to impress his partner. Relationships will always have their ups and downs. Just because things are going perfectly between you and a woman, doesn't mean there isn't the potential for them to go sour."

Reminiscing to several of the times I've upset women, I throw in, "Tell me about it brother."

He smiles again, clearly amused by how vulnerable and calm the alcohol has made me. "Remember how I said love and war are often the same thing?" I vigorously nod, focusing intently on what he is about to say. "Good, well Machiavelli said that war should be the number one focus of any prince. Now clearly, I don't want you to literally fight and get violent; we're using this work as a metaphor. But he also says that to be effective, it is essential to focus on the prospects of war even *more* in times of peace than in times of war."

"What does that mean exactly? If things are going well with a woman, I should be getting ready for the next time we get into an argument?"

"Well, I suppose that could apply, but that's not exactly what I'm getting at. Think of it like this: when you are single, you probably spend a lot of time thinking of how you are going to impress a woman and how you can win her affections."

"Very true Ed. You know your shit man."

"Yes, well I'm glad we agree on that. Try this, I want you to think of the times you are pursuing a woman's affections as wartime, and when you are in a relationship with her as peacetime."

I squint and raise one eyebrow out of confusion, "But I thought if I'm arguing with a woman, that would be wartime Ed. And from what I've heard, marriage and relationships are usually anything but peaceful."

"Although it certainly can be, you're mixing up the metaphors. It's the pursuit in question here. And when people are not actively pursuing a mate because they are in a committed relationship, they have a tendency to grow complacent. Just because things are OK with your girlfriend, doesn't guarantee that it will be smooth sailing for the rest of time. And especially in the early stages of dating, there is a very good chance that someone else is interested in the same woman that you are. So just be on your toes at all times."

Suddenly, my mind goes back to the moment in his office when Dr. Polk initially gave me his copy of *The Prince*. "Right! Just like when we were in your office, and you told me the part about how war can never be avoided. But that instead I think it's just delayed or something like that, right?"

"Yes, I believe the phrase is 'deferred to your disadvantage,' but I think you get the point."

I do a silent fist pump to celebrate my retained knowledge. "So, I should basically just always be thinking of ways to impress and care for my girlfriend even when things are going great?"

"*Especially* when things are going great. Just remember to never become complacent. That is probably the best way to sum things up."

I pick up my glass and finish my pint of beer, set it down on the bar, and look Ed directly in the eyes, "Ed, you're a good man." Becoming much more candid, I go on, "I mean, I'm really glad I stuck with you as my therapist."

"Thank you, Anton."

"No, I mean, I really wanted to switch for a while. For the longest time, I thought you were a complete idiot."

He is clearly mildly insulted, but he brushes it off quickly because he knows it's primarily the alcohol speaking. Subtly averting an argument, he says, "Well, either way, I'm glad I have been able to help you."

"Yeah, me too Ed . . . me too."

Unbuttoning his sweater, Ed tells me, "I want to show you something. It's a tattoo I got a very long time ago. I got it shortly after that incident in the movie theatre I told you about, remember?"

"Of course I do, that was pretty rough."

"It sure was. But I also learned a great deal from that."

Showing me the mark on his torso near where his pectoral muscle meets his shoulder, I say, "That's pretty sweet Ed, but what is it?"

"It's an archer. You know, a man shooting a bow and arrow."

And right as he says the word "archer," despite my inebriated state, I am able to recall the section of *The Prince* where the author discusses pursuing objectives similarly to the way an archer aims for a target off in the distance. Getting very enthused, I perk up and say, "Yeah, yeah, yeah. Aim high right? When you see something you want, aim big. Set your goals way higher than what you're reaching for, so by the time you get there, you'll actually achieve it right?"

Clearly impressed that I not only recalled that very short section of the book, but that I was able to articulate a coherent statement in my drunken state, Ed says, "Very good young man, I'm quite impressed." With every gesture Ed makes indicating my growing knowledge of the topic, I become more and more pleased with myself. The grin on my face is getting so wide it's beginning to hurt. It's a clear sign that I've been over-served, but I'm too excited to care. And for the record, I don't really consider that I'm ever over-served, but more that I'm underfed.

Eventually, my giddy state subsides, and I push my slanted frame of mind aside and admire Ed. "Hey Ed," I say calmly in order to get his attention.

"Yes?"

"When did you study this stuff so much? I'm not talkin' about the whole relationship stuff. But more like, when did you study this whole Machiavelli and *The Prince* as it relates to dating? Clearly, I've never studied the stuff in-depth, but I just doubt that it's a common topic of study."

"Well, I'm probably not the first person to draw the parallels that I've laid out here tonight, but yes, it is not what one would find in a typical psychology curriculum. For me, I noticed some similarities the first time I ever read that book early in undergrad. But my passion for it and my deeply held concrete opinions were really developed because I wrote my Master's Thesis on the topic." My interest grows because I realize this is quite a laudable feat. He continues, "Yeah, way too many pages and hours spent arguing that men who followed the principles outlined by Machiavelli were much more fulfilled in their sex lives."

Confused, I counter, "But Ed, I thought that being promiscuous wasn't the main objective. Rather, I mean, at least it's not my goal . . . anymore."

"Ah, but you're twisting my words. I said they are more *fulfilled*. That doesn't necessarily mean that they have more sex. It just means that the sex they are having, they are truly enjoying. But yes, there are undoubtedly many men, particularly of the college age, who live life like this and are perfectly content sleeping around. You have to remember, Anton, that everyone has different goals. My job is not to tell people what is right and wrong, but rather to help them understand *why* they want the things they want."

There he goes again with his middle of the road nonpartisan bullshit. *This* is the Dr. Polk I know.

"Finally, let me just say one last thing."

"Go ahead, Ed." I chuckle to myself at the unintentional rhyme. Ed is amused a little as well, but not at the rhyme. He thinks it's hilarious that I am so easily entertained.

"Foundation." All I can think is that I hope he's not asking me to wear makeup. I expect him to elaborate, so I wait a while, and then begin tapping my fingers on the bar.

The silence goes on for too long and eventually becomes downright annoying, so I break in, "Well? What about it Ed?"

"Remember that word 'foundation?' Among other things, it will be very instrumental in your search for meaningful relationships."

"How is that Dr. Polk? Like I'm supposed to build a house and then women will want me?" I inquire sarcastically, but in my condition, I consider it somewhat of a legitimate question.

He smiles, "Well, not exactly, although I'm sure that would certainly help your cause. But it's similar. You see, of all the people I counsel, not just males, when it comes to relationships and matters of the heart, there is one major common thread."

"What's that?"

"Well, many people have a tendency to focus on *one* specific person. Males are especially guilty of this. You have no idea how often I hear something to the effect of 'I won't be happy with anyone but her.' Those people are running a race with their feet anchored to the starting blocks. They're at a disadvantage before they've even begun."

My interest continually growing, "How so?"

"Anton, placing conditions on your happiness is a terrible mistake. By saying you will only be happy if a certain criteria is met, you set yourself up for an atrocious letdown. Obviously, everyone has preferences, and I fully support activities geared at attaining those goals. But people need to keep their options open."

The word "foundation" does in fact sound like something I read in *The Prince*. I think I might have a slight idea of where he's going with this, but encouraging him to get to his point more succinctly, I say, "Ed, this is great and all, but where are you going with this?"

He rolls his eyes, and I can only conjecture that he is accustomed to this reaction, given his often verbose explanations, when he does in fact utter more than his usual "I see." "Several times throughout the literature in question, he states that it is very important for a ruler to be local to the area he governs over. Part of this is because he is familiar with the area. It is also because he has many friends in the territory. All of this leads to what is essential: a foundation. Just as it is advantageous for a leader to preside over people and a land with which he is familiar, it is in your best interest to know *lots* of women."

I know he's getting frustrated that I continually misinterpret him, but nonetheless I interject, "But Ed, I thought the point was to not know a lot of women. I'm trying to cut back on casual sex, remember?"

Although he wants to explode and lash out at me, Ed takes a deep breath and composes himself. "Anton, listen closely, OK?" I lean in. "I said it benefits you to *know* lots of women. I never said anything about sleeping with them. There is a difference between the two." I nod, acknowledging my ignorance while simultaneously asking to be pardoned for it. "It's really quite simple. If you set your sights on only one woman, you may or may not get her. But if you allow yourself to really get to know many women, really learn about their interests and quirks, you are more likely to find one that suits you. Assume you go out on a date with a woman, and the two of you have a good time. You feel like the two of you have some chemistry, but after a few dates, she decides that it would be better if the two of you were just friends. What do you think of that?"

"Aw, that sucks Ed! No one likes being just friends. The whole point of dating is to go on a few dates, and it either turns into a relationship, or maybe just some fooling around, or even nothing at all."

"I see." There it is again, that little phrase I've grown to despise. He takes a sip of his water that has been on the bar since we arrived, sets it down, and then slaps me across the face as hard as he can.

"*Ouch*! Ed! What the fuck was that for?"

"Anton, you're missing the point. If she doesn't want to date you, then you have nothing to lose by being her friend. Whether you see her on a 'just friends' basis, or never again at all, it seems likely that you two will not work out from a romantic standpoint."

Still fuming from being slapped, I shout, "I know Ed, so what's the fucking point?"

"The point is if she wants to be friends with you, she obviously sees something valuable in you. And since she is a woman, I would assume that she has female friends. The more women you know, the more women you have potential to meet, and therefore there are more women who are potential partners for you. Think of it like building a portfolio. Too many men get frustrated because things don't work out immediately with a woman they have an interest in. More often than not, that is a good thing. When couples rush in, it often leads to disaster. And as I was saying, the more women who find you charming, funny, intelligent, take your pick of adjectives, the more likely it is that they will want their girlfriends to meet you. I know that what I'm about to say is one of the worst things I can say. It's cliché, and everyone hates hearing it, but it's true."

All I can think is, "then don't say it Ed." I know where this is going though, so humoring him I ask, "What is that Ed?"

"If you really are serious about finding a long-term commitment, it is simply going to take time. You can't rush it."

There it was, he said it. The proverbial dagger through the heart. But deep down inside I know he's right, which ultimately means that I am wrong. And this isn't a time that I want to be wrong. Moaning, I concede, "I know Ed, it just really sucks man."

"No shit Anton. Welcome to life." He takes another sip of his water and then asks me, "So, you want another round or are you ready to go home?"

"Well, I think I've had plenty to drink tonight, so I won't be needing another round. But I'm not ready to go home just yet, either."

Intrigued, he replies, "OK, well what did you have in mind?"

"I don't know about you Ed, but when I get drunk, I get hungry. Alcohol seems to wake the sleeping dragon in my stomach, and only a burrito or slice of pizza can tame the beast."

"Tempting. I could go for a slice." I jump off my stool in excitement, we begin putting our jackets on, and he adds, "But there's also a great taco stand about two blocks away, if you'd prefer that."

I take a moment to think, really allowing all that we've discussed tonight to sink into my brain. After my mind absorbs as much as is reasonably possible, I tell Dr. Polk, "Well Ed, that depends." He peaks his eyebrows, "Which one is closer to the nearest tattoo parlor? The pizza place or the taco stand?"

15

"Hey Johnny, are you gonna clear off that table or not? I ain't payin' ya to sit on yer ass am I?" an angry man spits out with a thick southern drawl.

"Oh yes sir, I'm sorry. I'll get right on that," a scrawny young man wearily tells his boss who is drenched in a combination of sweat and cooking oil.

"That's what I thought. I shouldn't have to remind you, but I'll do it anyway, cuz I know you ain't the brightest kid I ever met." The kid swallows out of fear; the bulge in his neck gives the impression he just ingested an entire chicken. "It's the third Sunday of the month, and you know what that means?"

The young man nods emphatically because everyone in Warm Springs, Georgia, knows what happens on third Sundays. "Yes sir, I'll have these tables cleaned up in no time," he says as he puts a rip in his step and begins clearing tables as if he had entered a competition.

"That's what I like to hear, Johnny. You might not be as much of a shit head as I thought."

The young man finishes wiping down the last table, takes the dishes and utensils to the kitchen, and the front door opens immediately upon his return. "Hello gentlemen, welcome to New Deal Café." Despite the fact that he has seen this same party of men accompanied by two women several times over the past year and change, he still addresses them in a very professional tone, never forgetting he is at work.

"Good morning Johnny, is our table ready?" a muscular man in a pristine suit inquires.

"Of course it is sir, right this way."

Every single patron in the place turns and stares at the group of people as they walk a few steps behind Johnny. They move at a casual pace so as not to disrespect the one in their group constrained to a wheelchair.

"Johnny! Order *up*! You're killin' me damnit!"

Turning toward the group he has just led to the table, he pleads, "I'm sorry, I'll be right back. Is everything OK?" Johnny asks while he makes his move for the kitchen window.

"It's fine Johnny, take your time."

Once the young waiter reaches the plates of hot food waiting to be sent to the respective tables, his boss greets him with, "Don't screw around kid. I ain't got any tolerance for your slackin' and goofin' around today. Now get going, and don't make me look bad, OK?"

After he delivers the steaming plates of pancakes, eggs, and bacon, Johnny immediately scurries over to the table he seated moments before. "Hello everyone, I'm so sorry about that. It won't happen again," he tells them with a quaking voice, well aware that his boss is watching his every move like a hawk.

"Johnny," the man in the wheelchair says, "please just calm down. You don't have anything to be sorry for."

Hearing that certainly helped, but the visual of his boss berating him in front of the entire restaurant is etched in his mind. "Thank you, mister, um . . . sorry, sir. Excuse me. May I take your orders, or do you need more time?"

"Same as always Johnny." All of the members of the group nod in unison, indicating that they will have the same dishes they always get.

"Well, not today, Johnny. I mean, not for me that is," says the man with neatly slicked hair and glasses, backing his wheelchair away from the table and turning directly at Johnny. "Son, today instead of my normal hash browns, coffee, and sausage, I will have wheat toast. Hold the butter. No jam either. Thank you."

Johnny looks at the man while confusion overtakes his senses. He has no idea if this is a joke or possibly a test. Did his boss put him up to this?

"Sir? I mean no disrespect sir, but are you serious?"

"I sure am, young man. You heard me, wheat toast, dry, and a water, please."

Although the order is overtly simplistic, Johnny takes his notepad out and begins to write it down. With his boss overseeing the exchange, Johnny starts to scribble, but drops his pen on the floor. "Oh, I'm sorry," he says while bending down to pick it up. "Is that all then?" Again, they all nod up and down. "Great, well, I'll be right back with some waters and a pot of decaf for everyone then."

"Thanks Johnny," the group says in unison.

He arrives at the kitchen window, and the shouting commences. "Damnit Johnny, what the fuck are you doing? Dropping stuff like it's your first day on the job!" His boss scolds him loud enough that everyone in the place can hear. The admonishing isn't loud enough to be easily understood, but his tone is unmistakable.

"I'm sorry."

"Yeah, I've heard that before." He calms down slightly and asks, "Now, are they all having the same as usual?"

"Yep. I mean, yes sir."

"Then what were you writing down?"

"Oh right. Everyone is having the usual, except that he will have wheat toast, nothing on it."

"Don't fuck with me kid. Now is not the time."

"No sir, that's what he said, honest. I even asked him again to make sure I heard him correctly."

Giving him a harsh look, but not really knowing what else he can say, he replies, "OK, well, if that's what he wants, I'll get right on it."

"Thank you sir. I'm going to get them their water and coffee now."

"Yeah, you do that," the gruff man states in a very assumptive tone.

Johnny nervously delivers the beverages to the table, and avoiding small chat out of fear of embarrassing himself, he moves on to the other customers in the restaurant, knowing that just because there is an esteemed party in attendance, that is no excuse to ignore everyone else.

After about twelve minutes of frantically rushing around picking up plates, refilling water glasses, and taking orders, Johnny is startled by his boss, "Hey! Johnny! Order up kid. I ain't gettin' any younger!"

Just like a perfectly trained pet, Johnny instinctively darts for the kitchen to retrieve the food waiting on the shelf. He precariously stacks all of the plates on his arms, opting not to use a tray. Johnny's boss, still not fully trusting him on the wheat toast debate, follows a few paces behind him. "Here you are everyone," he says as he begins laying the plates out in front of their respective patrons. "And wheat toast for you sir. Will there be anything else?"

Looking down at the toast in front of him, the man in the wheelchair quizzically asks, "Excuse me young man, but what is this?" Upon hearing that, Johnny's boss moves closer to the table, his aggravation becoming much more obvious.

Sweating more profusely than ever before, Johnny responds, "Um, sir, it's wheat toast sir. Isn't that what you ordered?"

"Is everything OK here?" the boss butts in.

"Well, it's not exactly going to ruin my day, but I ordered my toast dry. And this has butter on it. Not on the side, but actually on the bread."

"Oh, I am so sorry, sir," Johnny jumps in.

Picking up the plate of toast, his boss calmly tells the man, "My apologies sir. Give me just one minute. I'll be right back with fresh *dry* toast. Johnny, would you come with me please?" As the two head back for the kitchen, everyone at the table keeps their eyes on their food, but their ears remain fixated on the interaction in the kitchen.

"Johnny! What is your damn problem kid! He told you he wanted his toast *dry*!!! How hard is that to get right? I'm not fuckin' around kid, one more screwup, and you're done!"

Merely two minutes later, the two men return to the table with a fresh plate of wheat toast stacked high.

"Mr. President, I am so sorry for the misunderstanding. It won't happen again. Johnny here is a little out of it today I suppose."

"Please, don't worry about it. Thank you for the fresh toast."

"You're quite welcome. And please don't hesitate to let me know if there is anything else you need." He takes a small little bow out of respect, and walks back for the kitchen.

"Mr. President, I am so sorry about that. I really thought I told him that you wanted the toast dry. I guess I'm still just messin' up." He makes a similar gesture as his boss and starts to walk away.

"Johnny, please come back here, son." Looking at him with a stern but thoughtful stare, the man in the wheelchair asks, "Why do you take that?"

"Excuse me, sir?"

"Why do you let your boss yell at you like that?"

"Well, sir, he is my boss, and I did screw up. It was my fault. He was right to discipline me."

"Johnny, that's nonsense. You're a very good waiter. You've served us countless meals and honored our requests without hesitation. In fact, if you were a few years older, I might have room for you on my staff. I have no doubt that you told him I wanted my toast dry. I can say with absolute conviction that this mistake was all his."

"Well, thank you sir."

"Johnny, come here," he tells him, even though he is only a few feet away. "I want to give you some advice. Please listen closely to what I'm about to tell you."

16

WHY IS IT that every time I've had a hangover, I've sworn off drinking? But for some reason, I've never followed through. Do I expect my body to somehow get *better* at processing alcohol the older I get? These are the thoughts racing through my head when I wake up on Ed's couch the next morning. Well, racing isn't really an appropriate description. I'd say the thoughts are more like rioting in my brain. They're flipping cars and stealing television sets left and right, and it's complete bedlam at the intersection of Occipital Lobe Drive and Cerebellum Parkway. Although it would have been more convenient to take a cab home last night, Ed and I just kept shooting the shit late into the a.m. hours, and he said I could sleep on his couch. Despite the pain shooting through my skull, the blanket he gave me last night is doing its fair share to comfort me. I look at the time on the DVD player, and see that it is only 7:00 a.m. As much as I want to go back to sleep, I find that it's not quite as easy as it should be. I'm about to get up and look for some water or Gatorade, when I hear a noise at the front door, most likely a key trying to open the lock.

When the door eventually opens, a woman who I immediately assume is Ed's wife steps inside. Judging by her attire, it's safe to say that she has just returned from a morning run. Although it is likely a minimal forty degrees or so outside, she is wearing only a sports bra and tight running pants. Well, she's wearing sunglasses too, but I highly doubt they provide much warmth. She closes the door, goes to the fridge to get a bottle of water, and begins stretching. Now, I am not at all proud of this, but I could not help but pull the blanket over my head, just to the point where I am fully covered, with the exception of my eyes. If I go by how old I think Ed is, his wife is probably in her sixties, but she has one of the most amazing bodies I have ever seen. It's no wonder she shows it off every chance she gets. She has obviously worked hard for that, and I don't blame her, as I think any rational person would do the same. Her abs are so incredibly toned that if I ignore her silver hair pulled back into a ponytail, I could easily be convinced that I was staring at Danielle, the stripper's flawless stomach. Her butt is incredible. It is tighter and shapelier than the vast majority of the models I have ever seen. The fact that she is sweating just enough to accentuate all of her visible muscles isn't providing any incentive for my erection to go away. Thankfully, I have a blanket to help conceal it, because I can't imagine how uncomfortable that situation would be. And yes, I know that women prefer to think of perspiration as a "glow," but I'm a male, so she's sweating, and it's a good look for her. She stands up from her stretch and focuses her gaze on the mass slumped on her couch. I adjust myself below the belt while I'm still concealed, knowing that I'm going to have to stand up and talk to her in just a moment.

"Hello? How are you feeling this morning? It's Anton, right?"

It appears Ed has filled her in on what happened last night, which quickly relaxes me, so I poke my entire head out of the blanket. Shifting into polite guest mode, I tell her, "Oh hi. Yeah, I'm Anton. You must be Ed's wife. Thank you so much for letting me sleep here last night, I hope I'm not too much of an inconvenience."

"Oh don't worry about it. Ed told me you two had a rather eventful evening. Well good for you." She now shifts into her wonderful hostess mode and says, "How are you feeling?" I groan to show my discomfort, and she responds, "Oh, you poor thing. Can I get you anything? Some water or some juice perhaps? We also have cereal. You'll have to excuse me, but we don't have too many guests, so our food supply is rather sparse. I don't know if you'll like what we have though, because I am really into eating healthy."

Yeah, milk does a booty good. I think the granola movement has their new spokeswoman. "Oh, that's fine. Some water would be awesome." Looking into the kitchen, I spot a bowl of fruit, "And would it be cool if I had a banana too?" I begin to get up and head toward the kitchen, but she prevents me from doing so.

"Oh, don't get up, silly. You just sit right there, and I'll get it for you. From what Ed tells me, you two did more than just drinking last night?"

When she says that last part, I assume she is referring to our trip to the tattoo parlor. Although I was drunk, I wasn't so wasted that I don't remember it this morning. "Oh, he told you about that huh?" She nods with a smile on her face as she brings me a big glass of water, a banana, and a wheat bagel, as I sit up to receive it.

"Sorry, I don't keep a lot of spreads and cream cheese around. I hope you don't mind it plain."

"Oh, please, this is just perfect. It looks delicious." Getting back to the topic at hand, I say, "Yeah, it's true, I got a tattoo last night. It's really small, nothing major."

"May I see it?"

I'm a little thrown by my preconceived notion that all people my parents' age or older abhor tattoos. Her interest is surprising, which I find refreshing. "Oh of course, check it out," I tell her as I lift up my shirt.

"Oh that's cool! Is that a keyhole? I like that. Any special meaning behind it?"

"Yeah, there is. It's a really long story, but to make it short, this keyhole is kind of an inside joke that I have with one of my best friends." I want to explain to her the rationale behind it, but don't quite feel ready to do so. "I apologize, but it's kind of personal, and I don't know if I'm comfortable talking about it just yet. I don't mean to be rude."

Surprised that I'm apologizing for keeping my personal feelings to myself, she responds, "Oh darling please. I understand completely. You can tell me or anyone else whenever you want. Or you don't ever have to tell anyone if that's what you prefer."

I am truly impressed by her understanding, and I tell her, "Wow! Thank you. I really appreciate that. I guess you can relate a little bit, I mean, when did Ed tell you what his meant?" I ask her, referring to his archer that he revealed to me the night before.

She lets out a little laugh, and says, "Oh, you mean that man shooting the bow and arrow? I like it, but I remember when he got that, he was biting his tongue so hard I thought he was going to cry." Her laughing gets slightly louder as she reminisces.

"You were there when he got it?"

"I sure was. It was quite a sight."

"But I thought Ed got that before he met you?"

She chuckles again, "Is that what he told you? That's too funny. Look, whatever my Eddie told you about that tattoo, it was probably a lie."

Very intrigued, I inquire, "Really? How so?"

"Well, when I first met Ed, I was in the Marines, and I had this," she says as she pulls her socks down revealing two small words written in script, one on each ankle. "It says 'Semper Fidelis.' It's the credo of the Marines."

My infatuation with this woman is growing by the second. I am so thankful that my boner is hidden beneath a blanket. "Wow! That is so cool. So Ed saw that and got one to impress you then?"

"Well, basically. He'll argue otherwise, but I really think that was what happened."

Hearing this story is one of the most amusing things I have heard in a while, so I begin to laugh and grin with her. "That is too funny. But you didn't encourage him to get it?"

Taken aback as if I'm accusing her of stealing my wallet, she responds, "Oh of course not. Don't get me wrong, I don't think he needed it, but who would I be to discourage him given the fact that I had mine?"

"Well, that's very noble of you. But do you like the meaning behind it? You know the whole Machiavelli and dating analogy?"

Immediately after I ask her that, an enormous grin comes across her face. "You know, when I first met Ed, I thought he was completely crazy. He was one of the most annoying men I had ever met. Not at all in a mean way, but he was incredibly persistent. I guess he thought the fact that I was in the Marines meant I would be enamored with talk of military conquests and the like. At first, I just wanted him to leave me alone. Let me ask you this. What do you do for a living?"

"I'm a photographer. Mainly fashion, but I do some personal work on the side that I sell on my web site."

Her eyes widen with intrigue, "Oh wow! Very nice. Well imagine if every time you went somewhere, there was a woman who continually approached you, and all she wanted to talk about was photography. Would you be very interested?"

Seeing her point, I reply, "No, I guess not."

"The last thing I wanted to talk about in my free time was war and his thoughts on it. I might have been more willing to listen in the beginning if he was in the force as well. But he was in school studying psychology, and it simply did not interest me."

With every word she speaks, my fascination with her and my therapist reaches new heights. "So what happened? How did he win you over?"

Again, her smile widens. "Like I said Anton, he was very persistent. I still remember very clearly what he said to me that forever changed my mind."

Very eager to hear this, I ask "Oh yeah? What did he say?"

"Well, trying to politely brush him off, I once asked him what it was he saw in me. I thought it was a reasonable question, because we didn't really have many common interests or hobbies."

"I see," and as the words leave my mouth I cringe just a little, afraid that Ed is listening in the next room, thinking I'm imitating him.

"And I'll never forget how he responded to that question. He looked me right in the eyes, and I almost burst out laughing. But he never cracked, and he said in his most calm and confident demeanor that he, and I love telling people this part," she takes a pause to replay the moment again in her head. "He said to me, 'I like you because I scoff at the mundane and despise the ordinary.' I was floored. So much so that I didn't even bother to mention that he was being redundant. He was so sure of himself that he pulled it off flawlessly. I can't say at that moment I knew we would get married one day, but it most assuredly changed my opinion of him, that's for sure."

"Wow! Way to go Ed. I hope I'm not being rude, but I have to say, Ed did pretty good for himself." She blushes so intensely that I could have smeared Heinz 57 on her cheeks, and it wouldn't even show. As cute as this is, I feel compelled to stop talking about Ed without him around. "So the Marines huh? That must have been intense."

"Oh, it certainly was. It changed my life to put it mildly. I have seen and heard things that until that point I never thought possible." Her facial expression shifts toward confusion and sadness as she recalls her time in the corps.

"Well, for what it's worth, I thank you for your years of service to our country."

Clearly touched as well as astonished by my sentiment, she replies, "Oh, well it was what I felt I had to do. I must admit though, I never thought someone like you would feel that way," she tells me as she points at my shirt that simply says "Berkeley" in big letters across the chest.

Immediately understanding what she means, I say, "Oh, well, not everyone at the UC is a pacifist. That's not to say that I'm not one. I'm not really sure what I am. I kind of fall all over the spectrum when it comes to common views affiliated with that school. I fully conform to some stereotypes, while completely defying others."

"Well, that's good that you keep an open mind. But I can understand, not a day goes by that I don't deeply contemplate my years in the service. Please understand Anton, I sleep well at night knowing what I did was right, but that doesn't necessarily make it easy to deal with everything I saw."

Not fully comprehending what she is referring to, but not wanting to pry into an obviously personal matter, I say, "I have no idea what that must have been like. A high school buddy of mine was killed during his second tour of Iraq not too long ago." I take a brief moment to ponder why they call it a tour. Rock bands go on tour; tours are supposed to be full of debauchery and fun, and I am skeptical that anything going on in Iraq falls into those categories. Rejoining our conversation, I add, "I've heard some of the stories. I'm not going to say that I fully support everything that our commander in chief does, but I also recognize that many people in this country do not fully understand everything that happens in military affairs."

Impressed by my statements, she simply responds, "Exactly." I wonder if she got her mastery of dialogue from Ed, or if it's the other way around.

"I've actually been to Iraq, during the war I mean."

Raising her eyebrows, she says, "Is that so? Please forgive me, but you don't exactly strike me as a fighter." I'm not sure if this is her hinting that I am in fact a "lover," which would mean that she's flirting with me. I ignore the pending innuendo because I'm aware the greater likelihood is that she is calling me a wimp. "You weren't in the service and then discharged, were you?"

"Oh no, but like I said, I'm a photographer." She nods upon seeing the connection. "I work for a fashion magazine currently, but a few years ago, I was doing freelance work and was able to make it out there to document what was going on." Shaking my head and letting out a huge gasp, I tell her, "Saying that it was intense would be an understatement." And as I am about to continue my story, the front door opens, and Ed walks in.

"Oh hey there! Good morning you two. Hi honey," he says as he walks toward his wife and gives her a kiss on the lips. "How are you feeling Anton?"

"You know Ed, I'm actually doing surprisingly well. Your lovely wife," I pause and turn toward her, "I'm sorry, I just realized that I don't know your name."

She smiles, and says, "Oh that's OK. My name is Caroline."

"Thank you Caroline," I tell her, and turn back toward Ed. "Yeah Ed, I'm doing pretty well. Caroline has been a very lovely hostess; she got me a glass of water and some food, so I should be back to normal in no time." Suddenly, realizing that Ed not only appears fully functional, but that he was in fact out and about incredibly early in the morning, I inquire, "So, I guess you're recovering remarkably well, considering last night? How much do I owe you for the tab, by the way?"

With a look of genuine confusion, he asks, "Yeah, I am feeling great. I'm sorry, should I be feeling ill? As for the tab, it was practically nothing. I took care of it, so don't worry about it."

Becoming increasingly perplexed, I ask, "Well, I mean, you had just as much to drink last night as I did, if not more." I look at Caroline to gauge her reaction at the mention of her husband getting drunk with one of his patients, but her facial expression remains fettered. Returning my attention toward Ed, I ask, "How many shots did you have last night anyway?"

Without hesitating, Ed lets out a rather large laugh and says, "Oh Anton, I'm sorry. You still don't know?" he asks as he looks at his wife. Their visual exchange is so sinister that I begin to suspect I might secretly be on a reality television show.

Deeply fearing how he is potentially going to respond to my question, I dig deeper for the answers I don't really want to hear. With my vocal chords wavering, but not quite cracking at a prepubescent level, I go on, "Um, know what Ed? What do you mean? You got drunk last night with me. Please, I know I was out of it and all, but I sure as fuck wasn't alone." I look at Caroline and silently mouth "sorry" for my use of a profanity in her home.

"Oh Anton, I apologize. I assumed my beautiful wife had filled you in."

Suspecting the worst, but not wanting to delay the inevitable, I pry deeper with an agitated timbre, "Fill me in on what Ed?"

"At the bar last night, you were drinking shots of whiskey, tequila, vodka, and so on. Whenever we were served beer, I had a beer with you. But when you were taking shots of the alcohol in question, I was taking shots of water, Sprite, Coke, and random juice mixtures. You know, whatever Bobby was serving us last night, mine was the virgin rendition. So by the night's end, I had probably consumed, oh, I'd say four pints at the most."

In complete shock, the only response I can generate is, "What?"

He breaks an uncomfortable silence with his patented laugh that is sure to promise I will not like what he is about to say. "You see Anton, this was another part of my method." My eyebrows peak while my eyes widen. "I had to get you drunk last night to get you to fully loosen up. But it wouldn't have been very professional of me to get you drunk in my office. I needed you to talk to me while free from reservations and inhibitions. But at the same time, I had to have a clear enough mind to understand what you were saying." Realizing that Ed has once again played me like a rook, my blood begins to boil. And I especially like how getting me drunk in his office is unprofessional, but for some reason outside of his office falls into the realm of the ethically sublime. Before I can break out into a tirade, he continues, "You see, Bobby was helping me out. He used to be a patient of mine. I helped him with his triclosan addiction." His wife rolls her eyes and then mouths the word "soap," while mimicking washing her hands. For some odd reason, I was actually aware that triclosan was the active ingredient in soap, but her little gesture was much appreciated. Ed continues, "He knows that whenever I come in with someone, I am not allowed to drink liquor. That is of course, unless I specifically tell him I am not there on business."

As Ed is relaying this information to me, and I reflect on the situation, I am torn with a surplus of emotions. Part of me wants to whack him square in the balls with a 2 x 4 while wearing a mirror-mask over my face. This way, every time he gazes into a reflective surface, he will associate his own likeness with pain in his groin. Although I'm sure this would aggravate him initially, he would most likely appreciate the fact that I demonstrated knowledge of Pavlovian responses. (Surely, a psychologist would get a kick out of that, right?) But at the same time, I want to high-five the fucker for being so underhanded. Was this part of his Machiavellian teaching? Was he trying to instruct me with an example of deceit to get what he wanted? I'm really not sure how to interpret what has recently transpired. The one thing I do know for sure is that my respect for Ed is growing on a regular (but not daily) basis. He might not always act in a conventionally logical fashion, but at the very least, contrary to how I viewed him for the longest time, he is not boring.

I am so confused; the only thing I can think to do is leave. "Ed, you're a weird guy. Keep it up. Well, I should be going. I've got some stuff to do before I head out for work later tonight." As I stand to gather my wallet, keys, and shoes, I remember that my cell phone is at the bar. "Oh, and I have to go back and get my cell phone. You know Ed, I'm still mad that you gave my phone to the bartender, but I will gladly concede that you were right."

"Right about what?"

"That I shouldn't have called her. That would have been a huge mistake. So although I'm not exactly thrilled with you, I'll let it slide buddy." Did I just call my therapist "buddy?"

"Oh, well, don't worry about it. I've been in your shoes . . . just glad to help." As I make my way toward his front door, he interrupts me, "But hopefully this will redeem me at least a little bit." After he finished his sentence, he pulls my cell phone out of his pocket. "I got it back from Bobby last night before we left. When you went to the bathroom right before we got some food, he handed it back to me. I hope you understand." And right then, he tosses me the phone.

Ed is one of the most nefarious jackasses I have ever met. I really must constantly remind myself to never end up on his shit list. "Hey, thanks Ed. You're OK." I put the phone in my pocket and head for the door. On my way out, I give Caroline a farewell hug. Had it been any other sweaty half-naked sixty-year old woman, I might have been grossed out. But she is pure muscle, and I'm a little embarrassed to say that I enjoyed that hug much more than I should have. After we break our embrace, I shake Ed's hand, and I motion toward the door.

"Thanks a lot for everything you two. I really appreciate it."

Simultaneously, they both say, "You're welcome, Anton."

I wave good-bye and leave through the front door, closing it quietly behind me. Judging by the neighborhood, I think that I am almost four miles from my place, but I have plenty of time before my flight, and it is a gorgeous day outside. I make the executive decision that I will walk about two miles of the distance and then look for a cab. In the unlikely event that after two miles I'm still feeling active, I'll just walk the entire distance. With the sun shining down on me early in the morning through the crisp air, I am resolved to make this a fantastic day. When I approach the first intersection on my journey home, I remember to check my cell phone. Once I turn it back on, I see the little phone logo indicating a new voicemail. Although last night is slightly blurry, I still vividly recall dialing Ashby's number on my phone before Ed ripped it from my grasp, which means that in all likelihood this voicemail is from her. I have no idea if Ed ended the call before she heard any of the commotion or what, so if the message is from her, the subject of her voicemail is anybody's guess. I decide to wait until I get home to check it though, because I want to enjoy my walk on this beautiful morning. Therefore, I attempt to simply enjoy the moment and revel in the fact that I recently became close buddies with my psychologist.

As diligently as I try, I cannot remove the thoughts of Caroline's pristine abdominal muscles. Her back was nothing to be ashamed of either. I have always had a thing for women with toned back muscles and stomachs, and here is why: most men enjoy large breasts and sculpted buttocks. Now, I enjoy them as much as the next guy, but I also pride myself in having a rather strong work ethic. Simply put, that is what abs and a spectacular trapezius represent. Any person with a few thousand dollars can buy a nice set of boobs or get surgery to enhance their body parts. But you can't fake muscles, those you have to work for. And I'm coming to realize and appreciate the fact that Caroline has spent a lifetime working on her physique, which I find very alluring.

However, as much as the thought of seeing the rest of her bare flesh entices me, that is all it will ever be: *thoughts*. First and foremost, she is married to my . . . well, I guess Ed is my friend. I would never even attempt to betray that. But more importantly, Caroline would most likely throttle me in the sack. Given her evident physical prowess, I would most assuredly be the one at risk of hurting themselves or pulling a muscle.

The fact remains though, that Ed's wife is undeniably stunning. Now, I think Ed is great and all, but never in a thousand years would I have envisioned him with a wife of such paramount anatomical construction. All I can do is wonder how in the universe that sweater-vest wearing clown-puncher ended up with a babe such as Caroline. With that in mind, I am coerced to give his Machiavellian philosophy on dating some serious consideration. I have read the work several times, and I truly enjoyed it. However, despite him giving me the book with dating principles in mind, it is my nature to read it as a treatise on government and philosophy. Luckily, I do have some recollections of last night's conversation surrounding the disquisition, so that should provide a solid starting point. I am resolved to read *The Prince* a few more times cover to cover, all the while taking notes regarding anything that might be remotely related to sentimental relationships. The more I consider what I am about to undertake, the more my anticipation builds. As my mood escalates, the pace of my feet gradually gains steam, and I become inexorable. About forty minutes into my endeavor, I decide to take a cab the remaining distance. Fatigue is actually not a factor because in my current disposition, I feel as if I could walk five hundred miles. But as the visual of me actually taking on that challenge pops into my head, I begin to hear the opus made famous by *The Pretenders*, and I realize that it is in my best interest to get as much rest as possible before my trip to New Orleans.

Immediately after stepping through my front door and getting naked, I take one of the most refreshing showers I have ever experienced. I could have easily spent a rampant amount of time in there, but I kept it to a slightly opulent twenty minutes. After exiting my steam-filled bathroom and dancing like a fool while making my way to the closet, I eventually put on some respectable clothing. Once dressed, I jump onto my bed to rest, but quickly remember that I have a voicemail waiting for me to listen to. I cross over to my dresser where I placed my phone upon arriving home, and hop back onto the cozy mattress. I nonchalantly hit the button to dial up my mailbox, and wait for the pending message. Following the automated voice indicating I have one unheard voicemail, I hear Ashby's elegant tone say:

"Hi Franklin, it's me. Sorry I missed your call, but it only rang once, and then I don't know if you hung up, or you probably just got cut off with bad reception. But I just wanted to call you back since I haven't talked to you in a while. I have some great news: I think you already know, but I made the Olympic speed-skating team, and I am so thrilled about it! Aaaand you'll be happy to know that I am *finally* a real veterinarian. I know, I know, it took long enough, but I'm moving to Portland shortly after the games to work at a clinic up there. I can't wait! You're probably out right now livin' it up, so enjoy your night. Oh, I'm so sorry, now I'm just rambling. But I'll be free pretty much all weekend, so please call me back. I need to know what you've been up to. OK, talk to you soon, bye."

I don't know what it is about her voice, but I seriously think there is something in the resonance of her vocal chords that reacts with the chemicals in my brain, which causes me to lose all sense of time, place, and anything resembling logic. The fact of the matter is that I did know about her trip to the Olympics, and I am very proud of her because she has worked incredibly hard to get there. Making the Olympic team is obviously difficult enough, but Ashby put in all the hours to train while working on becoming an animal doctor. But it is a really good thing that she mentioned that little tidbit concerning the Olympics via a recording. Because if I had heard it from her live, I undoubtedly would have revealed that I am going to be there for the magazine as well. Normally, I jump at any opportunity to see Ashby and spend as much time with her, but the Olympics are a special exception. From what I've been told, Olympic athletes screw like they're dependent upon it for survival. The engage in so much sex that one could make a legitimate claim that they do in fact not have a respiratory system like the rest of us. Instead, they breathe through their sexual organs, and fucking like crazy is the only way they don't asphyxiate like fish out of water. Apparently, they hand out condoms in Costco-sized proportions in locations frequented by athletes.

When I first heard I was going to the Olympics and that Ashby would possibly be there, I knew I couldn't tell her because the last thing I wanted to do was have the woman of my dreams know that I'm sleeping with snowboarder chicks and slalom ski bunnies. However, thanks to Dr. Polk, I am past that desire. Up until a few weeks ago, I had planned on making my trip to Vancouver entirely focused on banging as many gold-medal winning European women that I could meet. But I've come to realize that Ashby is my gold medal. Even if I were to sleep with hundreds of medal-clad women during my trip to Canada, at best, they would combine to make me feel as though I've won silver. I am completely resolute that this is a race I plan on winning.

17

"Do you seriously not have drive-throughs in this town dad?"

"That's right son, San Luis Obispo placed a ban on them, oh I'm not sure, around twenty-five years ago I think."

"That's awesome," I tell him with equal amazement and admiration. "I wish every city in America would do the same. Those things annoy the shit out of me."

"Well, it really makes no difference to your mother and me, since we cook most of our own meals. And when we do eat out, we usually go for something a little fancier than Bert's Chicken Shack."

I have to admit, San Luis Obispo has more than grown on me over the years. Near the end of my freshman year at Berkeley, my parents decided to move up north from Mission Viejo to get a taste of the SLO life. For the first couple of years, I really had no idea why anyone would want to live here, but with every return trip I make, this town takes hold of a larger piece of my heart.

"Yeah I know what you mean. I think I've sort of outgrown that phase of my life where greasy fast food dining had a pull on me. Not that I mind it from time to time though," I say with a smirk.

"Well, your mother should be home from the farmers' market any minute now. She is so excited to have you home, Anton." I look at him, hoping to guilt him into saying, "And so am I son, of course. She is even making your favorite lasagna for dinner tonight."

My belly begins to growl with anticipation of the evening's feast, "You have no idea how much I love hearing that. Nothing beats mom's lasagna, especially when the majority of your meals come straight out of a box."

"Well, she was planning on making it tomorrow, but since you have to hit the road, it was rather easy to convince her to make it tonight. I'm sorry, I completely forgot to ask you, how was New Orleans?"

"Oh it was incredible dad, you have no idea. Aside from all the flavor of the city, the shoot was so much fun." I recently returned home from a photo shoot in New Orleans. *Velvet Rope* is getting ready to run a piece on Mardi Gras and all of the elaborate masks and costumes. It was quite a trip to say the least. The Olympics start in just a few days, and they are going to consume my life for the few weeks to follow. Luckily, I was able to persuade my boss to allow me to use some vacation days to take off the time between my trips to the Big Easy and Vancouver. I decided to use the time to take a little road trip up the Pacific Coast. Rather than simply flying into Canada as I normally would, I opted to rent a car and see some cities and people I haven't seen in a while. This was a huge step for me because I loathe driving with unrivaled passion. I don't even own a car in Los Angeles, perhaps the least pedestrian friendly city in the world. But I had begun toying with this idea shortly after I heard I was being sent there, and thought I might be able to swing by Corvallis and see Ashby. Unfortunately, she will be in Vancouver by the time I reach Oregon, but I am consoled by the fact that I will be seeing her in just a few days regardless.

"That's great to hear. I still remember when your mother and I went there shortly after we were married. We had so much fun partaking in all of the amazing things that city has to offer." The tone in his voice implies that he isn't referring simply to the jambalaya and po-boys. "So where are you headed on the rest of your trip before the games begin?"

"Well, tomorrow I'm going up to the Bay Area. I'll probably stay in San Francisco with an old roommate from college, but I'll definitely swing by campus for a visit." Just as I finish my sentence, I hear the door open.

"Who's visiting what?" my mom yells as she trudges into the kitchen with three large paper bags full of food. Oddly enough, one of those bags is all dog food. Although my parents had a little bit of "empty nest" syndrome when I left, they quickly resolved that by buying a puppy.

I stand up to help her with the bags and give her a hug and a kiss. "Hi mom, great to see you. I can't wait for your lasagna. The smell has been making me so hungry. Always good to be home. Oh, as I was saying, I'm heading up to San Francisco tomorrow morning, but I was telling dad that I'll take BART over into Berkeley so I can hit up Telegraph Avenue and visit campus."

"Oh I love BART. It's so much easier than driving and having to park."

"Tell me about it."

"Well, I'm going to get the salads and bread ready while the pasta bakes. Why don't you two grab some beers and watch some football or something."

My dad politely responds, "Honey, that's a great idea." Turning toward me with a look encouraging me to play along, he says, "Come on Anton, let's go watch the game. Grab a couple of the Full Sails on the bottom shelf would ya?"

When I meet him in the living room, I notice he's watching Jeopardy! "Here you go dad, what channel is the game on?" I ask as I pick up the remote control.

"Oh don't worry about it. You know your mother. She is well aware that there are no football games on the schedule for today." I give him a bewildered glimpse, and he tells me, "She just wants us to do some male bonding, that's all."

"Oh. Got it." I love my parents so much; they are hands down the nicest and smartest people I have ever known. But I have never felt comfortable talking to them about relationships and women. I'm sure the fact that I've never really had a long-term functional bond with a woman, at least in the romantic sense, has a lot to do with that.

After taking a swig of his beer, my dad staring at the television asks, "So, how is Ashby?"

I already know where this is going. It is not an exaggeration to say that my parents adore Ashby more than I do. I have no doubt in my mind that if they could pick any woman in the world for me to marry, it would be Ashby McHale. They wouldn't even care if I changed my last name and became Anton McHale, so long as I ended up with her. Whenever my parents mention her name in conversation, my body fills with trepidation. Every muscle and nerve contained in my frame tenses up. I have gotten remarkably effective at changing the subject whenever they do this, and I'm about to add one more to the tally, until I remember my drunken night at the bar with Dr. Polk. "Oh she's great dad. She is a veterinarian now, and she'll be working in Portland after the Olympics. You do know she's in the Olympics right?"

Because they are her biggest fans, my mom shouts from the kitchen, "Yep! We'll be watching every speed-skating match from start to finish, cheering her on all the way."

"Does that answer your question?" my dad asks.

I laugh a little and very quietly continue, "Yeah, and then I think I'm going to marry her." I say this with highly sarcastic overtones, but I know my dad is thrilled to hear me say anything that even insinuates it.

"Wow! That's great to hear. She's a good girl. And I've always wanted to have a daughter-in-law who has an Olympic medal."

I give myself an imaginary pat on the back for saying something I never envisioned happening. But I can only make small strides, and I decide to change the subject, but not as drastically as I'm known for. "Hey dad, can I ask you something?"

Noticing I'm not likely to bring up something trivial, he responds, "Of course Anton, anything you want. What's on your mind?"

Speaking softly so that mom doesn't hear, I ask him, "When did you know that mom was the one for you?" Hearing those words come out of my mouth feels so bizarre. I have no idea why, but thinking of your parents as romantic and emotional beings just seems so unusual.

"That's easy. The moment I met her."

"Oh come on dad. None of this love at first sight business. When did you *really* know?"

"Anton, I know that my answer sounds about as cliché they come, but I'm serious. I first saw your mother at an audition for a play back in college. Now don't get confused. I said the moment I first met her, not when I first saw her."

"OK? Well when did you meet her?"

"Well, she got cast in that production, and I did not. This is going to sound very cheesy, but she was Juliet in *Romeo and Juliet*. I met her following the opening night performance to tell her how much I enjoyed the show." Right now, all I can think is that my dad said this to her to try and hook up with her, and that visual makes my stomach swirl just a little bit. "She really was amazing in that show. Now as an actor, I was fully aware that she was portraying a character. But I had to meet her because something about her just stood out to me. It had to be a number of things, but she was the only one in the room I could think about. Finally, I had the guts to talk to her, and when she first shook my hand and told me her name, I was in another world."

I'm still not entirely sure that I buy into all that my dad is telling me. I definitely had feelings for Ashby the moment I met her, but to say she was the one for me was probably a stretch. However, one thing is for sure. My dad loves my mother about as much as any man can possibly love a woman. Ed was right; I need to take notes from this man, because whatever he did back then obviously worked. Remembering that night in the bar, I think back to the FDR story. "Hey dad, I have another question."

"Go for it."

"Well, I'm named after Franklin Delano Roosevelt right? That is where my legal first name came from right?"

The expression on his face tells me he knows where this is going, and he replies, "That's right. And your middle name, as I'm sure we've told you thousands of times, is after Anton Chekhov, the playwright."

"Well, if it isn't too much trouble, could you tell me the story of why that is? I mean, what happened between him and grandpa that was so significant that you named me after the president?"

With a brazen fervor, he tells me, "Wow! I've been wondering how many years you were going to wait to ask me that. I know you've hinted at it in the past, but it never seemed as if you were genuinely interested. I'd love to tell you the story son." And for the next fifteen minutes or so, he describes in great detail the day my Grandpa John was working in a diner and received some very valuable advice from none other than Franklin Delano Roosevelt. He mentions something about wheat toast and follows that with, "You're never going to believe what happened next. I don't think Grandpa wanted me to tell you this, but " . . ."

And just as he is about to follow that final word, my mom interrupts by coming into the room and says, "The lasagna needs a few more minutes in the oven, but the salads are ready. Come and eat."

18

Do YOU EVER reflect on moments of your life, or even your life as an entity, and wonder why you didn't do something differently? Thoughts of that nature have consumed my existence for the past two days, ever since I left San Francisco. Nothing out of the ordinary happened there. I was not involved in anything groundbreaking or revolutionary. But being back there simply reminded me how much I love that part of the country. Simply put, I am so relaxed when I'm there, I feel as though most of my problems disappear. I partook in the things I normally do: a walk along Telegraph Avenue, lunch at some mom and pop restaurant downtown, and a stroll through campus and the surrounding neighborhoods. Visiting destinations you hold dear to your heart is hard to describe. Upon returning after an absence of a couple years, things always appear considerably different; yet, somehow they're exactly as you remember. That is the best way to describe how I felt while in the Bay Area. Sure the shops might be different, the students are obviously much younger relative to my age, but I still feel as though I never left.

However, there was one thing from my time in college that did not change. Catching me entirely by surprise was the tweaker who always walked around various districts enveloping the UC. Now, I realize that does not even come close to narrowing it down in Berkeley, where people fit that description almost as often as they contradict it. More specifically, this guy would often walk around wearing an umbrella hat and a poncho, carrying an acoustic guitar, and shouting rather loudly that he could play "any song ever recorded." When I saw him just a few days ago, I was astonished that not only was he still alive, but that he didn't look much different than the first time I remember encountering him well over a decade ago. It would be foolish to think that there is anyone on earth who could actually live up to the lofty expectations this man proclaimed. But, to his credit, whenever you asked him to play a song that he did know, he was quite talented. One of my favorite memories during college was from junior year, while walking back to my house after a night at the bars. My friends and I were headed back to pass out, when we heard his rather presumptuous announcement. We'd all heard it before; yet, none of us had ever actually put his merit to the test. I decided that this was the time to see what he was made of. For some reason, whenever drunken people see a person with a guitar, one of them will inevitably request *Free Bird* or *Stairway to Heaven*. My friends did not disappoint on this night, but I quickly shut them up and asked the man if he could play *Train in Vain* by The Clash. My friends thought I was crazy for this request, and admittedly, I knew it was a pipe dream.

But he fucking knew the song. Not only did he know it, he nailed it. Once I recovered from being stupefied that he was actually playing, and playing it well, we all began dancing on the sidewalk like the drunken jackasses we are. It was a moment that lasted a mere three minutes, but I remember it vividly to this day. So you can imagine my surprise when I ran into him midday on Telegraph Avenue, and put his skills to the test once again. I thought about requesting something else, but I really wanted to hear *Train in Vain*. I guess I get that nostalgia thing from my parents. Despite the fact that it was many years ago, I felt like I was listening to a recording of that night when my friends were with me. I know there is no way he remembers that night from many years ago, and I wouldn't expect him to. But hearing that again almost brought a tear to my eye. Even though he will likely never know how happy his song made me, I had to show him my gratitude. I gave him $10, as well as bought him a burrito and a soda. It was the least I could do.

Berkeley is really special to me. It is a bizarre feeling to walk around a place where so many of the most crucial moments of your life occurred. You are primarily struck with a sense of thankfulness, but you also realize that what made it so special were the people you spent those times with. Even if you were to move back there that very second, in some ways it would be exactly the same. But in many ways, you wouldn't recognize anything in your surroundings.

Unfortunately, I was only able to spend approximately a day in the area, but it's more than most people, so I really can't complain. I left San Francisco early in the morning a couple of days ago and headed for Portland. I had never been, and I was very excited. But like I said, I hate driving. The computer map told me it was roughly ten hours from San Francisco to Portland. I probably drive forty cumulative hours in a given year, and I was not about to expend an entire quarter of that amount on one continuous stretch. I spent that night in Ashland, a town just north of the Oregon/California border. I really did not do much except rest and watch some television in my hotel room. Splitting up the drive to Portland was definitely the way to go though, since I was very refreshed when I arrived. It made my sightseeing much more enjoyable, and I got some fantastic pictures of Mount Hood covered in powder. I was planning on stopping in Portland even before I found out that Ashby is moving there in a few weeks. But once that information came about, my fascination with the city grew exponentially. I am fully aware that I might be building it up in my head, but in an ideal world, I will be spending a substantial portion of my life in Portland in the coming months and hopefully years. I had to get a feel for the city, learn where the nicest restaurants and coffee shops are. From what I've seen, I love it here. I could certainly see myself settling down and starting a family here. Did I really just use that word? As long as I've known her, Ashby has never been able to shut up about having children. More than likely, she only wants two or three, but when you listen to her go on about the topic, you get the impression that she would be thrilled having one in the oven every nine months for the rest of her life. I never thought in a million years that I would ever want children. My opinion of little kids is tantamount to my view of animals. Rather, it was. The more I think about her, and the more I reflect on my life in general, the more I think that my own family is what I want. But I can only think about this kind of stuff for a few minutes and then I get migraines. No joke, it literally hurts my head to think about growing up. So I turn up the volume on the radio, and *Everybody's Working for the Weekend* is playing. All I can think is that as great a song as this is, it is really only enjoyable on Fridays and Saturdays. If someone ever played this song on a Sunday, the ensuing blue balls that I would receive would be more than enough to make me throttle them. And I don't even have a standard work schedule. I can only imagine how much that song must infuriate a typical nine-to-fiver on a Tuesday morning.

I am now entering Seattle, and my enthusiasm is immeasurable. I am not even going to my hotel first to drop off my stuff. Instead, I am headed for my favorite place in all of Seattle, and if I'm going to speak hyperbolically, my favorite place on the entire West Coast. I'm not referring to the Space Needle or Pike Place Market. Nope, I am talking about Green Lake. Undoubtedly, the best walks I have ever taken in my life have been through the neighborhoods surrounding the UC campus in Berkeley. But I also have four years of those in my memory banks. Green Lake is a walk I've only made a few times, but I love every minute of it when I get the chance.

I finally arrive in the neighborhood and find a parking spot in the small lot on the North side of the lake. I adore this walk so much that I am going to take pictures to document it. But because I want really nice photos that I can also sell on my web site, I'm going to use my very expensive work camera, not just my digital that I bought for personal use. Much to my surprise, there is a Starbuck's about two hundred feet away. It must be my lucky day since I was able to find one so easily, in Seattle of all places. As I'm about halfway through the crosswalk, I notice a cyclist coming at me full speed. From my perspective, it is fifty to sixty miles per hour, but in reality, it's probably more in the twenty-five miles per hour range. Still, I totally freak out and leap back just in time to avoid getting hit, because this dude sure wasn't going to stop for me. Once I collect myself and check the camera for any damages that I know do not exist, I continue my voyage across the street and enter the building, preparing to pledge my allegiance to the two-tailed siren.

"Hello sir, what can I get started for you today?" the barista asks me.

As I've undoubtedly mentioned countless times, I've always had a propensity to go against the grain. Since Seattle is the coffee capital of the Milky Way, I tell her, "I'll have a *venti* peppermint hot chocolate, please."

She begins writing on the cup with a Sharpie and inquires, "Would you like whipped cream on that sir?"

"Light, please. Thank you." After I pay for my drink, I make my way to the perimeter wall in order to make room for the several other patrons waiting for their drinks. Behind me is a hallway. Located on the near side are the restrooms, and on the opposite side is a door with a small window that leads into what is either the stock room or break area. Either way, it is obviously off-limits to customers. Just as I hear another barista call out my name to indicate my PHC is ready, the door swings open. In that split-second when I was able to get a clear view of the room, I caught a glimpse of something that is nothing less than unmistakable.

Jenny Desmond. The infamous "slutty barista" picture that jumpstarted both of our careers is staring at me. I haven't seen that shot in a couple of years, and seeing it again is just odd. I don't know why, I have no resentment toward her, and I am fairly certain she has none for me. Nor do I still have affection for her. She is gorgeous, no doubt about that, but my heart belongs to Ashby. For some reason, just seeing that picture manifests in me this uncomfortable feeling that I can't fully comprehend.

"Excuse me sir, can I get around you, please?" another green-apron clad teenager holding a large bag full of garbage asks me.

Returning to reality from the daze that momentarily engulfed me, I step out of his way and let him pass. I go up to the counter and pick up my peppermint hot chocolate, and as I approach the door to exit, the same young man is returning from his trash expedition. The social instincts in me kick in, and I stop him to ask, "Excuse me, but where did you get that picture?"

"Um, what picture sir?"

"Oh sorry. That picture of the girl in the apron. I saw it on a wall behind that door. Was that Jenny Desmond?"

His eyes light up. "Oh yeah, that's her man. Smokin' ain't she? Yeah, all of us guys here are huge fans. I'm not sure where that came from. It's been on that wall ever since I started working here almost two years ago."

I shouldn't be surprised at all that he doesn't know where it came from. In all likelihood, this kid was playing with Legos and watching the Power Rangers when that photograph was first published. Even though I am now certain it is my photo, I still talk to the young guy in an oblivious manner. "Oh OK. Yeah, I thought that picture looked familiar. I actually know the guy who took it." His eyes widen as his interest builds. "I actually know Jenny Desmond. I mean, it was a while ago, but I've hung out with her." I give him the information in this way, because I know there is no way he will believe that I actually dated and slept with one of the most famous current actresses in Hollywood.

"No shit? I mean, really? Dude, that is so cool." His voice becomes even quieter, "Did you ever hit that?"

I heard him very clearly, but I still ask, "Excuse me?"

"You know, I mean, she's so hot. Did you ever bang her? I would do anything to get a piece of her. She's like, totally hotter than a double *venti caramel macchiato*." I think he threw about seven other words often found in a coffee drinker's vocabulary into that description, but I zoned out after the first few. Making a really annoying perverted facial expression, he says, "I hope she left room for cream. Know what I mean?"

I am literally biting my tongue to prevent myself from yelling at this kid in front of about twenty-five people. But part of me knows that ridiculing him would be hypocritical to put it mildly. I'm not proud of it, but I used to talk and think of women in the same manner. For some reason, I guess you just take it much more personally when the subject of the conversation is someone you care about or at least know. Gaining my composure, with my teeth clenched together and my jaw frozen, I force the words out through my mouth. "Yeah, well, she certainly is a very attractive woman. But I really don't think you should talk about her like that." And as I hear myself say those words, I have to leave the store. Not only did saying that feel peculiar, but I think I actually meant what I said. I turn around to leave, and the kid just stands there frozen in place.

As I exit the store, I'm not exactly in the most cordial mood, but the anticipation of my walk around Green Lake calms my nerves at least partially. I am only a few feet from the crosswalk, when the cyclist who almost hit me, now on foot, approaches me with another person at his side. They are holding clipboards and a variety of colored pieces of paper. People like this are all over Berkeley, and I'm sure they dominate the Seattle area as well. Odds are that they want a signature on a petition, or maybe a donation for a cause. Although nine times out of ten I have no desire to support whatever group is lobbying for my succor, I always at least stop and find out what their cause is. Personally, I don't think I could ever stand outside and ask strangers for a minute of their time. So if someone believes in something strongly enough to donate their time to a cause, even if I disagree with it, I like to at least hear them out. I do realize that some of these people are paid for their time, and I guess I talk to them more out of sympathy. I would go crazy having people ignore me and scowl at me all day long. However, this guy is not exactly in my good graces considering he nearly sent my camera and me to the pavement. I take a deep breath, then a sip of my delicious peppermint hot chocolate, and prepare for the ensuing conversation.

"Excuse me sir, do you have a minute to talk?" the cyclist with one pant leg still rolled up asks me.

"Yeah, I think so. What's up?" I say, trying to be civil.

"Oh awesome. Well, we are here representing the ACLU. Are you familiar with the group?"

This is absolutely no surprise whatsoever. I should have known that this jackass with no regard for the rules of the road would be endorsing what is quite possibly the most ridiculous civil rights group ever formed. I always joke with people that ACLU stands for another condom left unused, because I consider the group to be like an expired condom. Basically, they aren't much good to me. If I was in a situation where I needed protection, and absolutely no other options were available, they are certainly better than nothing, but I would never trust them with my life. And as it happens, this organization was highly active and commonly supported back in Berkeley. So yeah, I am quite familiar with this group. Hopefully, I can avoid getting into an argument with this guy like I did so many times back in college, but that is asking a lot. Trying not to indicate that my mind is already made up about the ACLU, I politely tell him, "Well yeah, it's the American Civil Liberties Union, isn't it?"

Genuinely impressed, he responds, "Very good. Most people don't know that. Well do you know what kind of work we do, and what we stand for?"

I have a pretty good idea, but again, trying not to sound biased and giving him an opportunity to enlighten my mind, I say, "Um, not really. What kind of viewpoints does your group endorse?"

"Well, do you know what the Patriot Act is, sir?"

I do, and I am pretty sure I know what he is about to tell me, but I continue with my act. "You know, I've heard the phrase so many times, and I probably know what it is, but it's not coming to me at the moment."

"OK, well that's fine. Well, are you aware that because of this legislation the government is now able to wiretap your phones? Doesn't it worry you that they can listen to your conversations?"

Actually, it doesn't bother me at all. If I were a criminal, if I bought or sold drugs, if I planned an attack on congress, this law might worry me. "Well, to be honest, I think it is a little odd, but truth be told, I don't think it's that big of a deal."

He is clearly shocked by my answer, "I'm sorry. What do you mean? It's a violation of civil rights. How is that 'no big deal'?" The fury in his voice has risen slightly.

"Well, fact of the matter is I'm certainly not perfect. But I don't do anything so nefarious or illegal that the government is going to care. In all honesty, I think the law is kind of a good thing." As I tell him this, I can feel the temperature jump about five degrees as his blood begins to boil. Now, I do stand by this opinion to an extent, but I'm also exaggerating it because I really get a kick out of fucking with these people. "I mean, sure it is annoying to know they might be listening to my private conversations, but if you're not doing anything wrong, then you have nothing to worry about. And if it helps out our national security and prevents a terrorist attack, then how can that be wrong?"

I love that I can tell how livid he is on the inside, but he also knows it does his cause no good to yell at me. I don't think he will be able to keep the act going for long though. With a coerced tranquility, he says, "But it violates all kinds of civil rights, most notably, the first and fourth amendment. That honestly does not concern you?"

"I don't mean to upset you sir," well, that isn't entirely true, "But you see this camera? I'm a photographer." He rolls his eyes. It's an expression I get very frequently whenever I tell someone I'm a photographer. He takes this as "Oh, you're a photographer, just like riding a bike makes me a cyclist in the *Tour de France*." So I continue, "I'm a photographer for a fashion magazine. It isn't just a hobby. I'm well aware of the first amendment. I deal with its implications on a regular basis."

"And it doesn't bother you to think that the government can restrict what you do for a living?"

"Truthfully, it does worry me slightly, but when I look at my body of work, as well as the things other people put in the public eye for profit, I think that maybe restrictions aren't such a bad thing." This is a sentiment I never thought I'd find myself saying in a million years. Despite my disdain for this group, during my college days and several years after graduating, I was adamant that freedom of speech should be entirely unrestricted. Needless to say, things change over time. "I mean, some of the endeavors that I've made a lot of money from, probably should not have been allowed. And don't even get me started on pornography."

I can tell this is a dagger through his heart. I'm not insinuating that he enjoys, hates, or even watches porn, but I know that he will defend the right of a woman to defecate on a leprechaun while fellating a horse until the day he dies. I am clearly getting to him, but to his credit, his composure is still intact . . . for now. "Well, OK, you are definitely entitled to your opinion. After all, it wouldn't be very fair of me to try and force you to agree with me. But are you familiar with the 2005 case in Pennsylvania that dealt with the teaching of evolution versus intelligent design in middle school science classes?"

Surprisingly, I am. My parents are very avid Catholics, and when this decision came out, I heard all about it. I'm no saint, but I have to agree with my parents that this ruling was absolute bullshit. What's even worse is that this guy honestly believes this conclusion to be congruent with the rest of the ACLU's perspectives. Deciding to let him get his view out untainted, I tell him, "No, I don't think that sounds very familiar. I mean, Pennsylvania is so far away and all."

"All right, well basically what happened was that a public school district in Pennsylvania was requiring science classes to present intelligent design as a viewpoint for the creation of the universe."

"OK, so what's your point?"

"Well, that violates separation of church and state. If you want to learn about creationism, parents are free to send their children to private schools. However, we at the ACLU very strongly endorse a nonsecular approach, that being evolution. We helped to win the case, and the judge ruled that teaching intelligent design was unconstitutional."

At this point, I've heard enough. I have to very calmly point out the inconsistencies in the beliefs that his group stands for. Subtly mocking him, I say, "Oh OK, well *that* makes sense." He nods his head in agreement, not realizing what I'm actually getting at. "So to get this right, your group endorses Darwinian Evolution?"

"That is correct."

"OK. Now, it's been a while since I've discussed Darwin and/or evolution. Please refresh my memory: if you were to sum up the main principles laid out by Charles Darwin, what would you say?"

He is grinning, now thinking that we are on the same page, that maybe he has made at least a small impression on me. "Oh, that's easy, survival of the fittest."

Yes. He said it. I cannot wait to make him eat those words, but only after he says grace to give thanks for the meal he is about to eat. "Right, so when you say "survival of the fittest," you mean that the strongest will make it and thrive, while those who are weak and lacking a general prowess will falter and eventually die out."

A cocky smile coming across his face, he says, "Yeah, that pretty much sums it up. Would you like to know more about our group? I will admit that not every member of the ACLU agrees with every single policy we have, but I think you can see that as a whole, it is a valuable organization."

"Well, actually I do have a question." Finally, the moment I've been waiting for has arrived. I take a moment to collect my thoughts, and find the hammer and nail that I'm going to drive into the coffin of this conversation. "Correct me if I'm wrong, but isn't this the same group that defended, how can I put this? Pedophiles."

"Excuse me?"

"At some point in the past, didn't the ACLU defend a NAMBLA member accused of raping a young boy? Or they argued that age of consent should be younger or something like that?"

"Well, yes. But it's not that simple, sir."

"No, actually it is. Because you say that you believe in survival of the fittest, but you apparently have no problem defending some of the weakest members of society. Now, you can preach this 'we're free to make our own choices' stance to me as long as you want, but the fact remains that what those men did was wrong. They are weak, maybe not in a physical sense, but certainly their morals have degenerated to a level so low it is almost unthinkable. If you really believed in survival of the fittest, you would let the majority opinion that NAMBLA is fucked up, prevail, and the system would take care of this."

"Sir, I don't think you're being rational about this."

"No, I'm pretty sure that I am. Now, I'll be the first to admit that I'm no saint, and when I die I sure ain't gonna be considered a martyr. But you're group is so demented. You can find an excuse to defend anyone and anything, just so long as it gives you a reason to argue."

At this point, he can tell that I'm clearly not going to give his group any money or even so much as a signature. "Well, sir, I think that you should go to the library and do some research. You clearly don't have all the information. Have a good day."

Much happier that I've gotten that out there, I start to head for the lake to take my six-plus mile walk. But as I turn around, I see a bicycle secured to a street sign, and am reminded that this asshole almost took me out. "Oh, but one more thing. You are full of shit. I'm not talking about your group now, although I don't care for them either. But you almost took me out with your bike in that crosswalk over there not too long ago because you ran a stop sign."

"Well I'm sorry, it wasn't intentional," he tells me with overwhelming insincerity.

"Can you please tell me why it is that cyclists are so fixated on 'sharing the road,' but they have absolutely no desire to obey the rules that govern it? You run stop signs, you don't wear helmets, and you'll jump up from the street to the sidewalk and ride through a crosswalk if it makes your trip just a bit faster. Which is it? Are you a pedestrian or a vehicle?" He absolutely despises me right now, and I'm fine with that. He is snarling at me, not saying a word, because he has no idea what he can actually say that will defend his stance in a logical manner.

"Well, at least our riding is environmentally conscious. When was the last time you took public transportation? At least our bikes are pollutant free. Can you say that about whatever vehicle you drive?" I can tell he is struggling for a legitimate argument.

"You know, you'd have a point, if I did in fact actually own a car. I personally hate driving, and over the course of a year, I'll probably drive around five hundred miles." I'm very tempted to start singing *I Would Walk 500 Miles*, only substituting "walk" with "drive," but I suppress the urge.

"OK, well whatever, I think we're done here. Thanks for your time. Have a wonderful day," he adds on in an egregiously sarcastic tone.

And now, he is basically telling me to leave, which is odd, considering it's coming from someone who is apparently so concerned with the semantics of free speech. For the record, I never raised my voice. I learned long ago that the fastest and easiest way to lose an argument is to yell. Quite simply, if your argument is solid, then the facts and words will speak for themselves. It's only when you know you're on the verge of defeat that you resort to yelling and slandering. It's a sign of weakness, and in this case, survival of the fittest is absolutely relevant. I begin walking away, and tell him, "OK, well you have a nice day too. But I hope there are no hard feelings. I'm actually on my way up to Canada for the Olympics, and I'm a little stressed out about some personal issues."

Not buying my explanation, he just says, "OK fine, well good luck with that."

"Thanks, you too. I mean, it's such a nice day," I tell him, even though it's January in Seattle, which means overcast, gray, and shitty. "I can't wait to take a couple laps around the lake. And then, when I'm done, I think I'm going to parade around the front of a Planned Parenthood dressed as Santa Clause with a petition trying to reverse the nineteenth amendment. Oh, and one more thing: why is women's right to vote called suffrage, when really it's the rest of society that pays the price for it?"

19

WITH THE OPENING ceremonies only two days away, one would think I'd be much more thrilled to be in Canada than I actually am. I mean, British Columbia is nothing like I expected. I was fairly certain that when I crossed the border, I would see a plethora of drug dealers with bad teeth, but I have yet to see even a single person picking coffee beans while playing cricket. What can I say? I stereotype just a bit. One time, I was on a date, and the girl actually called me a racist because I said Mexican people like burritos. She was looking at me like I was Eli fuckin' Whitney and I'd just invented the cotton gin, propagating a demand in slavery. And right now, the temperature outside my rental car is even colder than the look she shot me over our bruschetta that night. And I don't handle cold very well. What I deal with substantially worse is driving in snow. The fact that they drive on the left isn't helping matters much either. Granted, the snowfall I'm currently rolling down the road in would be described as flurries at worst. It isn't even piling up on the ground, but it is horribly overwhelming to a person who spends more time annually at The Academy Awards than he does behind the steering wheel of a car. I don't do this, and by "this" I mean drive in snow. I hate driving, and I'm not exactly about to start a fan page for snow either. Add to that a map with directions I can't really make out and the jackass behind me driving way too close, and yeah I'm getting a bit flustered. I know I'm probably going about half the legal speed limit, although I'm not very good at converting mph into kilometers, so my actual speed is anybody's guess.

"Why is this fucker following me so closely? Just pass me already!" I shout out loud to myself even though I'm completely alone in my rental car. Every three seconds, my focus shifts from the road ahead up to my rearview mirror, hoping that somehow he will see the look of contempt reflected back at him and realize he needs to back off. "Oh, and of course, this asshole is on his cell phone . . . just wonderful!" My nerves are certainly getting the best of me as this enormous white van is close enough that the driver could reach through his windshield and touch up my hi-lights. Just when I notice the van put on its turn signal to change lanes, a dog dashes into the street from out of nowhere, and I have to hit the brakes rather forcefully to avoid hitting it. I hear my tires squeal along the wet pavement, and the sound is quickly followed by a loud noise and simultaneous rocking of my vehicle. The only reason I stopped for that dog is because the love of my life is a veterinarian, and I don't think it would serve me well to intentionally increase her business.

"*Shit*! Damnit, what the fuck?" Have I mentioned that I don't like driving? Fortunately, it was just a mild tap from behind, and I'm completely fine. It rattled my nerves, but I regain my composure and slowly open the door, making sure not to step out into oncoming traffic.

Once I step out, two men get out of the van, and the driver begins yapping a mile a minute in a language that I'm pretty sure is German. Fortunately, the passenger speaks English. "Hey man, I am so sorry. Are you OK?" I don't say a word, my frustration still getting the best of me. He asks, "Sprechen Zie Deutch? I guess you don't speak German then? Um, do you speak English? French?"

I snap out of my daze and respond, "Oh, um, yeah, I'm American. I mean, I speak English."

"Oh OK, great. Well, we're really sorry, but we're all in town for the Olympics. We just arrived at the airport, and we're looking for our hotel. And not that it's any excuse, but we're used to driving on the Autobahn. And no offense, but you were driving so slow I think I saw a turtle pass you by."

"Actually, you mean a tortoise, they're land dwellers." But because they're also in unfamiliar territory, I settle down slightly and I'm able to empathize with their situation. "And I'm sorry about my speed. I'm here for the games as well, and I'm actually looking for my hotel too. Definitely not used to driving in this kind of weather though. So what do you do? Are you guys reporters or just here as spectators?"

"Oh no man, you're looking at the German ski team. Well, part of it anyway. Gustav here is a biathlete, and I do moguls. What about you?"

"Hey that's awesome. I wish I was competing, but my bobsled skills aren't what they used to be. I'm a photographer, actually." Realizing we haven't actually formally introduced ourselves, I extend my hand for him to shake, and say, "I'm Anton, by the way."

Shaking my hand with a grip that could turn an apple into cider, he says, "Ben. Nice to meet you."

A little confused by his flawless English and lack of accent, I inquire, "Nice to meet you too Ben. Do you mind if I ask where you learned English? I mean, you're perfectly fluent, and I don't even detect a German accent."

Chuckling, Ben says, "Oh yeah, it's kind of a long story, but I grew up in Colorado actually. My parents are German, and after pulling way too many strings, I was able to gain residency in Deutschland in order to compete for Germany. I know that kind of thing is frowned upon, but I felt I had a better shot at making the German team. So here I am."

"Interesting. Well hey, whatever flag you'll be saluting on top of that medal stand, I think it's pretty cool that you're even in the Olympics."

Appreciating that I'm insinuating his success, he says, "Well thanks man, we'll see though. The competition is always tough, and I'm sure you know, this is as big as it gets, so it won't be very easy. But man, am I excited." Just then, Gustav starts speaking to Ben in German, and Ben provides a very terse response. "Well, hey we have to get going, so can we exchange information and all that? I'm really sorry again man."

Just wanting to get out of the snow and find my hotel, I tell him, "Hey man, it doesn't even look like there's any damage, and nobody was hurt, so I don't even really care. But let's exchange phone numbers, just in case my bumper falls off later tonight or something."

"Really? Are you sure?"

"Yeah Ben, no worries. I made sure to get the $7 a day rental insurance." We pull out our phones and exchange numbers, along with hotel information, just to be safe. As we are about to part ways, I ask, "Hey Ben, where are you guys staying? I mean, I'm guessing my hotel is probably near the Olympic Village, so we should celebrate your victory after you're done competing."

Jokingly he replies, "Sure thing man. After I win gold, I'm drinking all night on your tab."

I smile and nod, then get back into my car. The van pulls into the street from behind me, and after checking my directions again, I do likewise. My novice level of driving experience becomes even more evident as I near my hotel, but after circling the area where I thought it would be, I still can't find it. How did it become so difficult for me to follow directions? I'm a smart guy, and I cannot comprehend how this rather simple task is providing substantial impediments to my sanity. Fortunately, my redeeming quality in this situation is that I'm not a typical proud male; I have no qualms whatsoever stopping to ask for directions.

If I weren't so tired, I would probably be more amused that the hotel I am looking for is simply several blocks up the street on the right. Apparently, when I wrote down the address, I either erased or forgot the "1" in 2192, and simply wrote down 292. After I get over my temporary embarrassment, locating my residence for the next couple of weeks is quite simple. Had I not stopped for directions, I probably would not have found this tiny hotel wedged in between the mammoth Marriot and Sheraton. The building itself is a moderate size, but the sign is almost impossible to read. The sign hanging above the door to my lodgings says *Le Petit Batteur*. I was told not to look for the sign though, because it is rather small and covered up by plants. The woman at the gas station told me to keep an eye out for a small bronze statue of a boy playing a drum. When I heard this, I put 2 and 2 together and figured that "*batteur*" meant drummer, since "*petit*" obviously means small or little. I park in the Marriot garage since I have no idea what parking, if any, my hotel has.

"Bonjour, Monsieur," a man greets me as I am about to open the door to the hotel. Had it not been for his nametag, I would have figured him to be a tourist since he is fully decked out in Olympic paraphernalia.

"Hello," I tell him, quickly trying to establish that I would like to conduct this conversation in English. "Thank you for holding the door for me," I tell him very slowly, carefully enunciating each syllable in case he has no idea what I'm actually saying.

"Bien sur. You are quite welcome, sir," he says with a thick accent and even thicker derision. "May I take your bags, Monsieur?"

Assuming he is the bellman, I allow him to take my things and set them on a cart. As he wheels my things near the elevator door, a woman welcomes me in English from behind the front desk. Although the bellman's attire is amusing, I am pleased to see that she is dressed a little more professionally. Had the entire staff been wearing bright T-shirts and hats, I might have thought a rogue group of tourists bound and gagged the usual staff just for fun.

"Welcome sir. Checking in?"

"Yes. Last name Bradley, first name is Anton."

After a long series of keystrokes at her computer, she hands me some papers and calls out to the bellman, "Quatre-cents quatre-vingts-deux." The bellman nods acknowledging that he understood the room number correctly. "Enjoy your stay sir," she concludes.

"Thank you," I tell her as I nod and head toward the elevator.

I step inside, my bags and the nice man already waiting for me, the number 4 already illuminated. "482," he tells me. "You're room number is four-hundred eighty-two."

"Oh, thanks." My French is a little rusty, but I had actually figured that out in my head. I don't tell him that because I know he is only being helpful and not trying to insult me. The doors close, and we ascend the three flights up to the fourth floor. I am so exhausted and cannot wait to get to my room and pass out. The doors begin to open. I step toward the back of the elevator to let him lead the way, since he obviously knows this hotel much better than I do. When the doors open completely, I take my focus from the digital number "4" above and look straight ahead. My eyes nearly pop out of my head when they lock onto the woman who is standing in front of me.

"Franklin! Holy cow, I can't believe it!"

Ashby McHale is standing a mere two feet from me. Far more thoughts than the human brain is capable of processing at once run through my head. "Hello," would be a good start, but I have no idea what to say. I don't know how it's possible, but somehow she gets more beautiful every time I see her.

20

THE ELEVATOR DOORS open, and I quickly step outside and make my way to the large conference room where the party is being held. I can hear the bass of whatever band was desperate enough to play this gig blaring down the hall. A sign over the double doors reads "Congratulations Class of '95." The enormous room is decorated from floor to ceiling with balloons, streamers, and a plethora of other flashy things. Every girl is wearing a dress or skirt manufactured from an average of two square feet of fabric, enough to cover only the no-no parts, as they've been waiting four years to dress like this at a school function.

"Anton! What's up bro?" my friend Scottie shouts from the middle of a group of approximately seven people. "Get over here dude." At his request, and since he is the first friend I know at the party thus far, I accommodate him. Yes, I recognize almost everyone in the room, but I would only consider a nice portion acquaintances, and even fewer would I classify as friends.

"Hey, what's up Scottie? Congratulations man. Feels good, huh?" I say as I reach out my hand to shake his.

"Oh tell me about it man. I'm so over high school. In a few months bro, college is gonna be sick! Where are you going again?"

"Berkeley. Cal. How about you?"

"Oh man, congratulations! That's fantastic. I love it up there. I'm actually going all the way out East to Boston College."

"Hey, way to go man. That's a great school. I've never been to Boston, but I've always wanted to go."

"Dude, tell me about it. I mean, I went a few months ago to check out the school, and it was fucking freezing, but I'm really stoked for a change of pace." And as he is finishing his sentence, I see Ashby walk into the room with the biggest fuck-head in our school, and arguably all of California. Jack Walter, my arch nemesis. I know they went to prom together, but I hope with every fiber of my existence they aren't dating or something like that. The sight of them together makes me so furious I might just punch a clown.

"Hey, hold that thought. I've gotta go say hi to somebody."

He looks in the direction that my head is facing, notices Ashby, and says, "Oh, right on bro. Good luck man."

"Thanks. I'll see you soon, OK." And I head over toward Ashby and Jack trying not to make it obvious that I even noticed they showed up. As I make my way through the crowd of people, Ashby is dragged away by a few of her girlfriends, and she doesn't even see me. I don't know if that is a good thing or a bad thing, given the fact that my stomach is quaking because I'm so nervous. Since she is obviously preoccupied, I turn around so I can either chat with Scottie some more, or just enjoy the band that is playing a pretty decent cover of The Clash's *Train in Vain*. I make my 180, and before I've even taken three steps back toward where I came from, I feel a firm hand squeeze my right shoulder.

"Well, well, well. How's it going Fag-ton?"

I knew who it is before I even turned around, because no one else is as lacking in originality as Jack Walter. "Oh, hey Jack. Pretty good I guess. You know, just excited to be done with high school. How are you?"

"Oh man, I'm great. You know what? I'm better than great."

"Wow. That's awesome dude," I tell him, completely apathetic to his overall level of contentment. I like most people. By and large, there are not many people I would intentionally do wrong toward. But Jack is an exception. I would give him a Muddy Gorbachav. That is, I would love to wipe my dirty ass with my bare hand and smear it on his forehead, leaving a nasty brown streak for all to see. And I would feel no remorse.

"Hey Anton, I need to have a word with you. About prom."

I already know where this is going. It was only a few weeks ago that the tension between us escalated to an all-time high. But feigning obliviousness, I ask, "Oh really? What about it?"

"Dude, you know exactly what I mean. I'm not a fucking moron." Well, he is certainly entitled to his opinion, even if it is undeniably false. He is in fact king of all morons. "Everyone in school knows you've got a major hard-on for Ashby McHale. Well guess what dude? She doesn't like you. She feels bad for you. She told me herself. Even she knows you like her, but she said she keeps you around because you do whatever she asks." Right now, my lividity is approaching a personal record. Admittedly, I am a rather sensitive person, but there is no way I'm letting this lecherous reprobate talk to me like this. As of two this afternoon, the ties between Jack and me were severed forever. We are high school graduates, and after tonight, I honestly plan on never seeing him again. He continues, "The way you cock-blocked me at prom, that was pretty impressive. I have to give it up to you. You went to some pretty extreme lengths to stop her from going to that hotel with me. But I've got some bad news for you dude. Not tonight. Tonight, it's on. I'm gonna be all up in her, and there is nothing you can do about it. But don't worry man, I'll take good care of her . . . *real* good care," he says as he makes a thrusting motion with his hips.

Just as I'm about to open my mouth to offer some empty threat, Ashby comes running up to me, "Franklin! We did it! We're so done with this place!"

"Hey Ashby, great to see you too." She must have gone to the stylist between the graduation ceremony and now, because not only does her hair look elegantly styled, I think it's a few shades darker, although it is kind of difficult to tell given the dark lighting in the party room. And the dress she's wearing. Holy shit. There is no way her mother saw her wearing that dress. To my knowledge, Ashby doesn't have any friends who are sex workers, but I'm fairly certain this red dress is on loan from a hooker. "Congratulations," I tell her. "Did you get your hair done? It looks great."

Jack rolls his eyes, but Ashby blushes, "How could you tell? You are so observant," she shouts at me with tremendous enthusiasm. She sounds and looks like she's had a few.

I don't like where this is going. The woman of my dreams, the woman I would kill and die for, is going to have sex with the biggest asshole in the entire universe tonight. Not wanting to witness anymore of this, I figure it's in my best interest to admit defeat and just go home now and get the crying underway. Ashby has now moved closer to Jack, and his arm is around her waist. "Well, it was great seeing you two, but I think I'm gonna head out."

Jack's hand has now moved below her waist onto her ass. The rage that he has been forcing to build inside of me is about to manifest. I can feel the Bruce Banner massive green man doing warm-up stretches inside my abdomen. Ashby pleads, "Wait, you're not leaving are you? We just got here; the party just started."

"It's cool, babe. He's only gonna make this party lame anyways," Jack says with a smirk on his face.

"Yeah, see. I should get going," I respond with a fair amount of contempt in my voice.

"Well, at least I got to see you. Call me tomorrow; we'll go do something," Ashby says as she gives me a final hug.

Jack so eloquently leans into my ear and adds on, "Yeah, but don't call her too early tomorrow. I don't think she's gonna be getting much sleep tonight."

I am fuming so intensely right now. I have no idea how to handle myself, because I have never experienced this much disdain for any single person.

As I turn around to leave, I hear Ashby say to Jack, "Hey I'm thirsty; can you get me a drink?"

"Well, the table is over there. You know how to pour soda into a cup, don't you?" he says with a snarky tone.

I turn around and say to her, "Hey, don't worry about it. I'll get you some punch."

Jack laughs and says, "Wow babe! You were right. He really will do anything you say." Immediately, Ashby's eyes connect with mine, and a tremendous look of panic shoots across her face.

I have had enough. I am light-years beyond my breaking point. I say to Jack, "I wasn't talking to her. I meant you."

With a look of confusion, Jack inquires, "What the fuck do you mean?"

And without looking at Ashby first, I ball my hand into the densest fist I can make, step up closer to Jack, and smash him across the face as hard as my body will allow. I'm definitely not the biggest guy, and I've never hit anybody before right now, but my anger combined with the fact that he was definitely unprepared, dropped Jack straight to the floor.

"*Ouch! What the fuck asshole*!!!!!" He is in such shock he doesn't even attempt to retaliate. I'm not sure if he even believes what has just transpired. He puts his fingers in his mouth. "I think you knocked out one of my teeth!"

"You *think*? Well you better check and make sure, because if I didn't knock it out completely, you're gonna have to stand up so I can deck you again and finish the job," I tell him while the adrenaline is still pumping, and confidently walk out the door.

21

"CAN YOU BELIEVE how amazing the opening ceremonies were last night? I mean, the dancing, the costumes, and the special effects. It was incredible!" Ashby says to me shortly after we are seated at the *Northern Lights Diner* near the Olympic Village.

"Yeah, tell me about it. It was quite possibly the most fantastic show I have ever seen. And you guys looked very nice in those jumpsuits they gave you."

"I know, aren't they nice? I saw something like it in a store for almost $400. And we all got them for free."

"Well, I guess being an Olympic athlete has its perks," I say a bit irrefutably. "But as good as Team USA looked, I'd have to say the women of Norway were definitely looking the best," I tell her, hoping to make her just a little bit jealous.

"Oh right, and how could you even tell?" Her tone definitely indicates that she is at least mildly annoyed by my assessment. It's not much, but I'll take it.

Pompously I unzip my jacket and reply, "Oh, you didn't know?" I take out a laminated badge hanging around my neck, and show her my press pass. "You see that? 'All Access.' How you like me now? I can go anywhere and photograph anyone. Not bad huh?"

Reaching over to grab it and verify its authenticity, she spits out in awe, "Wow! That is so cool." After all these years, I still think it is so adorable when she gets so worked up over these passes. I've been doing rather large gigs for a few years now, but every time I tell her about a job she drills me, questioning whether or not I'm telling the truth. "Where are you going to go next?"

As I am about to tell her my agenda for the next few days, our waitress arrives, and we give her our orders. After she leaves, I continue my train of thought. "Well, let's see . . . I've got some figure skating tonight, a couple of hockey games tomorrow, and " . . ."

"Ooh hockey! Which game?"

"Well, I'm pretty sure that it's the first round match between the United States and Russia. It's definitely not 1980's Miracle on Ice, but it should still be pretty cool."

Her jaw drops. "You're kidding? My brother and I are going to that game too. He got tickets through a friend that he played hockey with in college. I think the guy plays for the Islanders now. That's why he came out to Vancouver so early. My event isn't for another week, but we're both really excited to see an Olympic hockey match. And I still can't believe that you and my brother ended up in the same hotel. Small world huh?"

"Tell me about it. And not just the same hotel, but the same floor. I was so shocked to see you standing in front of me when the elevator doors opened." And never one to pass up an opportunity to compliment her, I add, "But it was definitely the nicest welcoming gift I've ever received." She blushes on cue.

The waitress soon returns with two glasses of water and our milkshakes. Even though it feels like single digits outside, and in terms of Celsius it certainly is, we have a tradition of always getting milkshakes when we go out together.

We each slurp the thick ice cream through our straws, and I can tell hers is better than she anticipated. "Oh wow! Anton, you have to try this shake. I know it's a stretch, but it rivals the ones we used to get back at Roxy's."

Taking the cup from her hand, and fully suspecting that her embellishment skills need some work, I say, "Yeah right. Give me that. Nothing beats Roxy's Oreo, Peanut-Butter, Caramel Swirl Apex." I dip my spoon into the glass and shovel the ice cream into my mouth. "OK, wow! Wow! That's really good. I mean, that's *really* good. I don't know if I can ever go back to Roxy's with a straight face now. I think she's been trumped . . . by Canadians no less." I am addicted to the confection in front of her, so I slyly try to sneak a few more bites by saying, "Hey, since you're still preparing for your event, aren't you on some kind of strict diet? I mean, I'm pretty sure your coach wouldn't approve of you consuming this many calories just a few days before your race."

She looks at me like she is a mother bear protecting her cub. There is no way she is parting with her shake. I can plainly see this, and she knows that I know. Since we are clearly on the same page, she continues our conversation, "So, tell me about your trip up the coast. How are your parents? And what did you think of Portland? Isn't it amazing? I can't wait to live there."

"Oh it was fantastic, well, minus the whole driving a car thing." She chuckles because she knows how much I loathe being behind the wheel of an automobile. "My parents are great, and they ask about you all the time." Of course, they ask about her all the time. My mother wants Ashby as a daughter-in-law more than a hipster wants a pair of pants that fit. I honestly believe that my mom likes Ashby so much, that given the opportunity, she would trade me for her. "And San Luis Obispo grows on me more every time I go up there."

"Well, that's good to hear. I know you didn't really react well when they first moved out there."

"Yeah, very true. But I kind of like it now. And well Portland was gorgeous. You're really lucky to be moving there soon. I didn't do too much stuff while I was there, but I did meet up with an old college friend that I haven't talked to in years. His name is Rick. I don't think you've ever met him."

"No, that doesn't ring a bell, but that's cool. How was that?"

"It was nice. He seems to be doing well and enjoying himself. But his friend was hilarious. And by 'hilarious,' I mean he was about as pleasant as a scrote-waxing."

She cringes a little. Even after all these years, she still hasn't fully adjusted to my crass descriptions. "Eww, gross Franklin. What was so wrong with him?"

"Well, my friend works in hospitality and nightlife type stuff, so he invited me to the club of one of his clients. Naturally, clubs are synonymous with loud music."

"Obviously."

"Well, Rick and I are chatting, or rather yelling into one another's ears, and his buddy sees him and comes to talk to us. So this guy starts talking to Rick, and after about thirty seconds, Rick cuts him off and introduces him to me. Keep in mind that the music is playing at a rather intense volume." She nods her head. "So Rick says to me, 'Hey Anton, this is Ryan.' The guy reaches over to shake my hand, but I didn't fully hear what Rick said, so I ask this guy directly what his name is. Now this is the best part. He leans into me shakes my hand and practically screams, 'My name is Ryan. I've nailed women hotter than any you've ever even talked to.'"

Ashby makes a very peculiar face, wondering how I replied to such a ludicrous introduction. "Wait, he actually said that to you?"

"Yeah, but it gets better. He walks up and starts talking to me like I'm some nobody. I mean, who does this guy think he is? He's struttin' his stuff like he's fuckin' Snoop Dogg or something, and I almost bust out laughing. He immediately begins to brag about his conquests, and seriously who talks like that? So instead of getting defensive or inquiring for more detail, I gave him a blank stare for about ten seconds. In situations like that I only know how to respond one way, so I eventually say to him in a very bland tone, 'I once ate 53 Pop-Tarts in an hour.' You should have seen the look he gave me, it was priceless. And then I walked away."

She flashes a cute smile at me, the kind that burns its image into your brain for the rest of time. The kind that consumes so much of your memory it causes you to forget useful facts like state capitals and cardinal directions. She's definitely amused, but also impressed that I have the bravado to talk to strangers like that. "Shut up. You are too funny."

I smile more than is necessary at the compliment. "Yeah, I was pretty happy with it. But other than that, not much else happened while I was in Portland. I thought it would be a little bit more eventful."

Her grin fades, not into an all-out frown, but the enthusiasm is clearly gone from her demeanor. Making a bit of a pouty face, she asks, "Does that mean you're not going to come visit me when I live there?"

I hate it when she does this. She must know what kind of control she has on me, and I have no clue how to interpret statements like these. Is she saying she will be disappointed if I don't come visit because that means she won't see me much, or is she bummed because maybe I've gotten over my obsession that has lasted roughly half of my existence? I have no clue, and when she makes faces like this one, the rational parts of my brain become even less useful than normal. Trying not to sound resentful, rude, or overly eager, I coolly reply, "We'll see what happens." This conversation is bordering on serious, which is making me apprehensive, so I try to change gears and tell her more about my story. "Oh, and guess what happened the other day when I first got into town. This actually happened shortly before I ran into you at my hotel."

"What's that?"

"OK, so I was driving slow, and I mean slow even for me. But the roads were wet, it was snowing big-time," she rolls her eyes because she knows how badly I'm exaggerating, "And I was trying to keep an eye out for my hotel. Anyway, a dog runs out into the middle of the street, and I had to slam on my breaks to avoid hitting it."

"Aww, Franklin, that's wonderful. I knew you had a spot in your heart for animals. I could always tell that you were all talk."

"Nope, it's not talk, I can't stand them. If I had it to do all over again, I would have kept cruisin'. Reunite the thing with Old Yeller," I tell her with great facetiousness.

"Well, you can say what you want, but I don't believe you," she retorts with her patented smile, annihilating any ability I have to keep up the act.

"OK fine, but the downside to me stopping so abruptly was that I got rear-ended." Her eyes bulge with concern, "I'm fine though, luckily we weren't going very fast before it happened. I was still plenty upset, don't get me wrong. I was just about ready to punch the dude driving until his friend started talking."

"Franklin, please. You know you'd never hurt a soul."

Getting a little defensive, I counter, "Hey, that's not true. I hit that guy that one time."

Recalling the evening of our graduation, she looks at me and appears to be harboring doubt as to if that night even actually happened. "I still can't believe you hit Jack like that."

"Yeah, me neither. It was the first and only time I've ever punched anyone. But I had my reasons." This subject has come up numerous times in the many years since that monumental night, and I've never told Ashby the *real* reason why I did it. I always go with something like "he was talking trash about my mom," or I always "suspected him of stealing money out of my backpack." Generic excuses really . . . anything I can tell her to avoid the truth. I'm terrified of how she'd react.

"Yeah about that. Are you still not going to tell me why you *really* did that? It was so uncalled for. I mean, he didn't do anything to you."

Is she actually defending that asshole? "OK, you're right. To answer your question by dancing around it, I'll only say that I had my reasons for doing what I did. And I stand by my conviction to this day. But it was so long ago, could we just drop it?"

Frustrated she responds, "OK, fine. We can drop it . . . for now. But don't think I'm letting you off the hook forever."

"I don't even know why you liked him. Or why you went to prom with the guy, he was so bland."

"You're going to lecture me on the guys I've liked?" She switches to her best manly voice impression, "Mister, 'I've banged Jenny Desmond and countless other models who've spent more money on their boobs than most families spend on their mortgages.'"

Point taken. I know she's right. But why is it that men don't exactly have conniptions when it comes to refusing to abolish this nefarious double standard? "All right fine. You win, but I'm just saying, there were so many better guys you could have spent senior year hanging out with."

"Well, what do you want me to say? I was young and foolish, and definitely easily impressed by the popular boy that all the girls wanted. I wasn't thinking with my brain. I just got caught up in how hot he was." As much as I want to yell at her for that, unfortunately I can't refute that logic. But I'm getting better about that. She takes a look around and then sips her shake. After a brief pause, she raises her eyebrows and looks at me so intensely I feel every muscle tense up. She continues, "Besides, no one else even asked me to go to prom with them." And right now, everything I know is wrong. Left is right and up is down. What is she saying to me? Am I reading too much into this, or is she implying that I should have asked her? Fuck. Why am I never able to think straight when I'm around her?

Trying to be complimentary, but not wanting to look like a total jackass, I reply, "Well, at least you learned from it. And as for prom, I honestly have no idea why thirty or forty guys didn't ask you. They must have been too intimidated and just assumed they didn't have a shot with you." Although I definitely believe that last sentence to be true, I'm also using this as a covert way of expressing my thoughts that have been suppressed for far too long.

Playing with my mind some more, she says, "Well, that's the problem with most guys. They're too afraid to take risks when it comes to women. They always just assume that they don't have a chance. We're not that much different from you guys, you know?" I nod to concede her point. "I think guys would be surprised at what might happen if they just approached women with sincerity, and not lame-o pick up lines."

"I know you're right and all, and I hate overstating the obvious, but it's easier said than done, Ashby."

"No shit Franklin. But I'll bet you could probably count on one hand the worthwhile things in life that don't require taking chances." She takes a deep breath, "I saw this saying on a placemat at a coffee shop once. It was way back in high school, but I remember it to this day. It said, 'Progress in life is like a turtle . . . you'll never get anywhere unless you stick your neck out.' I love that proverb, or whatever you would call it I suppose."

And at this moment, the room feels like it's spinning. She just said something about a turtle. There is no way that the tortoise she gave me for my birthday all those years ago was just coincidence, is it? But what if it is just a fluke? But it can't be.

"So, what happened to Leviathan by the way?" she asks.

I see our waitress approaching our table, and instinctively in a panic I'm about to ask for the check, when from behind me someone puts their hand on my shoulder.

"Hello Mister Anton Bradley. Long time, no see, yes?"

I turn around and look up. It's Svetlana Stalin, and she looks pissed.

22

THE REF STOPS play 5:17 into the second period, with the score tied 1–1. "Number 25, Kravchenko. Two minutes for high-sticking," I can faintly hear the ref tell the scorekeeper or whoever keeps track of that stuff. I know the basics of most sports, but I'm a little bit lost when it comes to stats and things of that nature. But I do know that the United States is about to go on a power play in their first match of these Olympics. As the ref gets ready to drop the puck, I prepare to document whatever they're about to do with their man-advantage. To clarify, none of these shots are for the magazine. However, when I get a press pass that allows me to go pretty much anywhere I want, I never hesitate to take full advantage of the opportunity. But in case you're wondering what the Olympics have to do with fashion, well it's quite simple. People idolize athletes. People buy what athletes endorse, and they wear whatever they wear. If Shaun White hits the half-pipe wearing a tinfoil sombrero and lavender gauchos, well you can rest assured that kids all over the world will be sporting the same attire on their next snowboarding excursion. In all honesty though, it's highly likely that a fashion magazine like *Velvet Rope* won't use any of my shots with the exceptions of figure skating leotards and/or the opening and closing ceremonial costumes. It's a bit frustrating when I think about how much time I spend doing this, and realize that in total roughly four or five seconds of my work is what actually appears in public view. On the other hand, I get two free weeks in Canada, so things could be worse.

The puck drops, and immediately Russia clears the zone. As the American goaltender stops the puck and his teammate retrieves it, the Russian team is uncharacteristically pressing hard. Dominic Brendan passes the puck across the centerline to his left, and just as the American wing starts to control it, Dmitri Mikhaylov intercepts the pass and shoots past the two American defenders between him and the goal. He quickly skates into the United States' zone on a clear breakaway. Eric Stahl, the goalie, comes out of his crease a few feet to try and cut down the angle, but he's in trouble, as Mikhaylov is one of the fastest skaters in the NHL. He approaches the net, and fakes as if he's going to take the puck to his right, but Stahl doesn't flinch. I'm frantically snapping away, trying to get some awesome action shots for my web site and personal collection. With only a few feet of real estate left, Mikhaylov is forced to choose where he wants to put the puck, and in the blink of an eye, he tries to flick it between Stahl's legs, but the goalie reacts more quickly than I've ever seen, and the puck bounces just a few feet in front of him. He quickly falls on it, and the whistle blows to stop the play.

Normally, I wouldn't be paying so much attention to a Russian hockey player, but as Svetlana so graciously informed me (on multiple occasions by the way), Dmitri Mikhaylov is her newest plaything. It's not that I'm jealous, because I did in fact walk away from *her*, which was no minor accomplishment. But something about the situation is still very unsettling. And as her new boy toy is denied access to the goal via Eric Stahl's five hole, I begin to wonder how bizarre this must be for him. Now that he's dating Svetlana Stalin, it's highly probable that he has grown accustomed to being able to put anything he wants between a pair of legs. I want to walk up to him, very gingerly mind you, because ice is slippery, and tell him that I was there first. I have no idea why this is frustrating me so much, in fact I should be thanking her for interrupting the conversation Ashby and I were having about Leviathan. Any time she mentions the pet, which happens every few years, I panic. My first instinct is to always turn it into a joke and say I sold him for an ice cream sandwich or gave it to some little leaguers for batting practice. She knows I'm joking, but I really don't like telling her the real story about the pet tortoise she gave me on my eighteenth birthday. I just don't know how she'll react.

But as I stand here, feeling slightly outraged by something that really doesn't pertain to me, I spot Ashby and her brother Tim up in the arena.

She looks super cute in her Team USA hockey jersey. I wave up to them, but I don't think they notice me. The ref drops the puck to resume play, and the Americans get three or four decent shots on the power play, but the Russians are able to kill it off, and Maksim Kravchenko is out of the penalty box. Just as he is storming out, American center Mark Winslow is skating up ice, not on a breakaway, but in good position. Kravchenko comes sprinting toward him from behind, and as Winslow winds up to shoot, the Russian slides in front of him and deflects his shot into the stands in the vicinity of Ashby and Tim.

A number of people in the stands duck out of the way, as the deflection only mildly slowed the puck down. It disappears into a group of people, but then all the fans in the area begin gathering around. My first instinct is that it hit Ashby and she's badly hurt, but I know that I tend to overreact. However, whatever just happened is definitely serious, as the crowd surrounding the commotion is growing larger, and throughout the arena everyone can hear someone yelling, "We need a paramedic over here, *now*!"

I can't really tell what's going on as so many people are bunched into a small area. Medical help arrives quickly, and they part the crowd with Moses-like precision, splitting the swarm like the Red Sea. After a few minutes of silence, the EMTs assist someone out of the arena, and everyone applauds due to our elation that this person is up and walking under their own power, but I think it's safe to assume they got hit rather hard by the puck, and might have some bleeding or broken bones. I say a quick prayer for them, and a few seconds later, play resumes. The next few minutes of the match go by, and not much happens. The Russians are called for icing, and there is a stoppage of play. I figure that this is a great chance to try and get Ashby's attention and look for her in the stands again. But when I look up to where she was sitting, there are now two vacant seats.

My heart skips so many beats I begin questioning whether or not I actually still have one. Was she the one that got hit with the puck? Maybe she's just in the bathroom or buying snacks. But where is her brother? Did the puck crash into Tim's face? Oh fuck, I can't take this. But then I realize that maybe the person I thought was Ashby wasn't even her at all. There, that's right; she and her brother are probably sitting safely up in some press box that they got hooked up with via his connections with the New York Islanders. I feel a lot better, knowing that she's all right. Yet I can't stop a surge of guilt from plaguing me, because in taking comfort in her well-being, am I then essentially saying I'm glad it happened to someone else? I don't know what to think. My nerves are becoming so precarious that I have to pack up and leave. After I get outside the arena, I know the only way I'm going to calm down is to give Ashby a call and hear her voice. I dial, and it rings . . . and rings . . . and rings . . . and then goes to voicemail. Maybe she can't hear it ringing inside that noisy venue though; that's perfectly understandable. But still, a rush of trepidation overpowers me, and I decide to call Ashby's brother. I dial again, and it rings . . .

After two rings, I hear Tim's voice on the other end. He is speaking unusually quickly. "Anton, now's not exactly the best time. Can I call you back in about fifteen minutes?"

23

"YOU KNOW, I gotta say, this Ashby chick is one lucky lady Anton. I mean, if you weren't so obsessed with her, I might try to make a move on you," my friend Janine tells me.

"Aw, well thanks Janine. But don't get all sappy on me. My methods haven't really been all that effective now, have they?"

"Yeah, whatever. But take it from a girl, if a guy did for me what you're doing for her . . . well, let's just say you'd be spending a lot of time horizontal," she tells me as she is applying some sort of makeup to my face. "Now sit still and let me finish this up, OK? How much longer until she gets here?"

I look at my phone, "Well, supposedly she will be her any minute, but she's had a rough twenty-four hours. So I'll be thrilled if she even shows up at all."

A few moments of silence pass, and Janine says, "All done. Ouch, you look pretty messed up . . . damn I'm good. Go take a look in the mirror and let me know what you think."

I step into the bathroom of my hotel room to check out Janine's artistry in a large mirror. I am absolutely horrified by what I see reflected back at me. "Wow! I mean shit Janine. If I didn't know any better, I would really think I had just been in a fistfight or even worse. How long have you been doing this again?"

"I've been doing hair and makeup since I was a little girl, it kind of runs in the family. But I only got into theatrical and special effects makeup about five years ago. Remember that Halloween shoot we first worked on together?"

"Yeah, that was fun. That massive scar you put on that Frankenstein's face was insane. It looked so real."

"Hey thanks, I appreciate that. Well, that was my first paying gig in special effects makeup."

Surprisingly, I reply, "Bullshit. Really?" She nods. "Well, it's no surprise then that you're one of the most sought after makeup artists in Hollywood. I'm just really lucky that you're in town for the Olympics too. Those opening ceremonies were ridiculous."

"Tell me about it," she says. "When I got offered a gig up in Canada doing makeup for the opening festivities of the Olympics, I was ecstatic."

"I know isn't this unreal? Have you done anything exciting yet?"

"Yeah, yesterday I went to " . . ." her response is interrupted by a knock at the door. We both look at it and I freeze in shock that she actually showed up. "Well, are you gonna answer the door or not?"

I nervously make my way to the door. I saw Ashby at the hospital briefly yesterday, since I had to shoot the figure skating event of the evening. She was in rather high spirits, but I was still stunned when she agreed to hang out with me today. Her face was bruised rather severely. Fortunately, her elbow slowed the puck down substantially as it went up to shield her face. But it still smacked her pretty hard on her right cheek. Her cheek and face were a little swollen and discolored, but the x-rays were negative, which was a huge relief.

I put my hand on the doorknob, take a huge breath, and open the door. "Ashby?" I ask to the person standing in front of me. She is wearing huge sunglasses, a big baggy sweatshirt, a scarf covering the lower half of her face, and a baseball hat. Honestly, if I wasn't expecting her, I don't think I would have recognized her. Having an expected female guest whom you know quite well show up to your hotel room dressed in a disguise is a very unusual feeling. This must be what it feels like to be a member of congress.

Quietly, and with her head down, she says, "Hi. Yeah it's me. Can I come in?"

"Absolutely. Please, come in and sit down. Grab a water or soda out of the fridge if you want." I open the door all the way and step to the side making room for her to pass. It isn't until she is about ten feet into the room that she looks back at me and notices my face.

"Franklin! What happened to your face? Are you OK?"

I chuckle a little. "Oh this. Yeah, I'm fine. It's makeup, but it looks real doesn't it?"

A little uncomfortable, she asks, "Makeup? Franklin, what's going on?"

"Ashby, I'd like you to meet a friend of mine. This is Janine."

Janine steps forward to shake Ashby's hand, and says, "Nice to meet you. Anton has told me a lot about you." Janine turns to me and says, "You're right Anton, she is a knockout."

I bite my lip and shake my head as I stand frozen in a cube of awkwardness. Now, Ashby knows that I was talking about her to other women and complimenting her no less. Is that good or bad? I think if I knew the answer to that, I'd have had more serious girlfriends than the zero that currently occupy my resume.

Trying to take the pressure off myself, I say, "Ashby, Janine is a friend of mine from Los Angeles. She just so happens to be doing some freelance work at the Olympics as well. Janine here did this to my face." Not wanting to insinuate that Janine is a catalyst of domestic violence, I add, "She's one of the top makeup artists in Los Angeles."

Starting to uncover my plan, but not wanting to be overly eager, she tries to blow it off. "So Franklin, what did you want to do today? I'd really love to see a movie." Her suggestion of a dark locale doesn't surprise me at all.

"Well Ashby, I kind of had some other things in mind. But I've got to go run a few errands, so why don't you and Janine hang out for a little bit, and I'll be back in about an hour." Without giving her a chance to respond or protest, I quickly make my way out the door. However, I catch what appears to be a smile forming on Ashby's face out of my periphery as I'm turning around. I don't have anything planned for the next hour, because my "errands" are clearly an excuse to give Ashby some privacy while Janine gives her a mini-makeover. The funny thing is that I was quite surprised Janine said that she would need an hour to do her makeup, since she did mine in practically no time at all. But I assumed that she just wanted to have some girl talk with the object of my affections. And when I think about this, it makes me rather nervous. Am I digging my own grave by leaving them alone? Realizing that it's too late now, I go to a nearby café and kill sometime drinking a soy *chai latte* while perusing my visitor's guide to Vancouver.

When I get back to my room, I knock on the door even though I have a key, just in case the two of them weren't done verbally assaulting me. But

Janine promptly opens the door and whispers to me, "Good work Anton. She is thrilled! You are sooo getting laid tonight."

Taking her comment in stride, I jokingly say "Wonderful." As I get further into the room, I see Ashby come out of the restroom, and she is striking to say the least. The first thing that actually catches my eye is her hair. Janine must have cut and/or styled it because it is amazing. And obviously, I notice the remarkable makeup job. Even as I walk right up in front of her, I would have no idea that Ashby had been injured if I had not seen the bruises myself. "Wow! Ashby you look great. Not that you didn't look great before, but . . . well, do you like it?"

At first, she tries to remain calm as if what I did was no big deal, but that only lasts a few seconds before she screams "Are you kidding? *I love it*! Thank you so much . . . both of you!" She throws her arms around me giving me one of the biggest hugs I've ever received. Her enthusiasm is so strong it literally almost knocks me backward onto the bed.

"Well, I'm glad to hear it." In reality I'm more than glad. Words cannot convey how happy it makes me to see her smile given the situation, and it makes me even happier knowing that I'm part of the reason she is smiling. "So, unless you two have more work to do, I was thinking we could do a little sightseeing or check out more of downtown?"

"Oh great idea." It is incredible how drastically her demeanor has changed from the few seconds I saw her this morning. "What did you have in mind?"

"I was thinking of going to the Capilano Suspension Bridge. It's not too far from here. And then maybe heading into Gastown for some food or something?" I know how much Ashby loves nature and things like that, and when I heard about this mammoth bridge from the bellhop, I knew this was where I wanted to go with her.

"Oh no way! That's awesome!" She is so animated I honestly feel that I could have suggested we go to the library or look for a Dairy Queen and she would have reacted just as passionately.

"Great. Well I'll go get the car and meet you out front in a few minutes, OK?"

"Sounds good. Oh, Janine, would you like to come too?"

Instinctively she replies, "Oh thanks babe, but I'm busy today. But maybe we could all meet up for drinks or something later?"

Now Ashby and Janine are conversing like they're best friends reunited on *Oprah*, and Ashby says, "Oh great idea. You've got my number right?"

I'm definitely going to need a strong martini tonight. And I'd love to buy you a few too."

"Sounds great darlin'. I'll call you later on."

"And Janine, thanks again so much. I really can't tell you how much I appreciate this."

"You're quite welcome dear. But it wasn't all me. It was Anton's idea after all."

Getting a little uncomfortable but also a little full of myself, I say to Ashby, "All right, well I'll see you downstairs in a few. Janine thanks again. We'll see you tonight."

I've been fortunate to have seen a lot of beautiful sights in my lifetime, and the park where the Capilano Suspension Bridge resides is definitely up there. Although the sky was a little gray, Ashby was so happy you never would have known anything was even remotely unpleasant. I got so many great shots of the park, the bridge, and the river. It was truly a fabulous experience, and it was made even better by the fact that I shared it with someone I care for so deeply. After the park, we drove back into downtown Vancouver to an area known as Gastown to grab some lunch. I assume this town was named for the clock and that it's not merely coincidence, but Gastown is home to either Vancouver's or Canada's first steam clock. I forget what our waiter at lunch told us, but I do know that it is a local landmark. It's also apparently the most photographed subject in the entire city. Normally, I make it a rule to never photograph methods of time telling not directly linked to the position of the sun or made in Switzerland, but what kind of photographer would I be if I didn't capitalize on such an opportunity?

After I took a few shots of the clock, Ashby insisted that the two of us take a picture with it as well. I reluctantly gave in after a brief debate, and asked a nice woman walking by to take our picture. She happily obliged, but I could tell the "bruise" on my face frightened her a little bit.

She took three or four shots and handed the camera back to me. And what happened next was one of those moments that makes you just sit and wonder.

"Thank you very much ma'am. Have a great day," I told her.

"Oh, you're very welcome. I hope the both of you enjoy your stay here in Vancouver," she responded. It was really cute though, because Canadians really do have that accent they are credited with. When she said 'both,' it most definitely sounded like 'booth.' I smiled a little and thanked her again. "You're a very lucky man to have such a beautiful girlfriend you know. Take care of her OK?"

I'm fairly certain that what she meant was that I was lucky any woman would be seen with me in public in my current condition. But that wasn't what struck me as odd. In all the years Ashby and I have been hanging out, strangers have probably referred to us as a couple at least thirty or forty times. And every single time, she promptly tells them we're not together. But that didn't happen this time. Instead, Ashby just looked at me and smiled. When her eyes met mine, I have to admit that my stomach got a little queasy. But it was definitely the good kind of sickness you get in your stomach when you like someone. The kind of swirling you feel inside when you forget how to talk, and even when you do eventually say something, your ability to enunciate has vanished... and it feels sensational. Even when your mangled words are incoherent, they're the only way to accurately express everything you're feeling.

After I came back down to earth from that moment, Ashby told me that she was supposed to meet her trainer, but didn't really feel like it.

"What do you mean you don't feel like it? This is the Olympics we're talking about."

"Yeah, but I'm not really in the mood after yesterday. Let's go see some more of the city."

Although I would much rather spend time with her, I knew I had to knock some sense into her. "Ashby, what are you talking about? This is the *Olympics*. Your event is only a couple days away. I know that the last twenty-four hours have been rough for you. The bruises are going to heal. But you've been training for this for a really long time," she nods in agreement. "If you quit now... I just don't want you to look back on this in a few months or years and wonder what could have been. So please, just go meet your trainer. And we'll get dinner and drinks afterward. I need to clean my face up anyway. I'm not used to having makeup on, and every time I touch my face, I smear it more and more."

She laughs a little, "Yeah, you're starting to look like a really depressed member of KISS, Franklin."

"Oh great, just what I was going for."

"But in all seriousness, you're right. I have worked really hard to get here."

"So?" I ask in a leading tone.

"So yeah, you're right. I'll go work out with Marty, and then we'll get dinner and drinks with Janine."

"Awesome! That's what I like to hear." We start to walk back toward where we parked, and I look at her and ask, "Hey, when you say I look like a depressed KISS member, you mean that in a Gene Simmons kind of way, not a Paul Stanley way, right?"

24

"So WHAT ARE we toasting to tonight?" Janine asks as she raises her pomegranate mojito.

"Oh that's easy doll. We're toasting to you," Ashby adamantly replies while hoisting her martini toward the sky. "Not only did you make my year when you did my makeup this morning, but you were such an angel to do it *again* before dinner."

"Yeah, well, I know as well as anyone that a gross and sweaty workout is not usually cosmetics' best friend. But you don't have to thank me anymore; it was totally my pleasure."

"Well, as grateful as I am for Janine and what she did, I would like to make another toast," I add just after the ladies put their glasses down. "I can't believe that in just three days, I'll be able to brag to everyone I know that my best friend is an Olympic gold medalist." I raise my drink and say, "To Ashby McHale, future Olympic champion." She blushes a little, but we all click our glasses together to celebrate the moment.

Trying to sound humble but really coming off as rehearsed, Ashby responds, "Well thank you Franklin, but I'm really just happy to be here. I mean, making the U.S. Olympic speed-skating team is an honor by itself." Both Janine and I give her a look imploring her to tell the truth, and she concedes, "But yeah, a gold medal would look pretty good framed on the wall next to my DVM in my office right?" Janine gives a quizzical stare. "Oh, Doctor of Veterinary Medicine," Ashby says to clear up any confusion.

We all cheer in agreement, and as I look toward the entrance of the bar, I see a group of seven or eight men walk in. Most of them look like an average Olympic athlete: tall, muscular, and foreign. But I definitely recognize two of the men. "Ben! Hey Ben!" I yell to Ben and Gustav at the front of the room.

"Do you know those guys?" Janine asks me as she begins to salivate over the prospect of a hot German piece of ass.

"Yeah. Well, I met a couple of them the other day. We got into a minor fender bender. Nothing serious, we're all fine," I tell them to allay any concerns.

Ben doesn't seem to notice me, so I get up to go say hi and invite his team over. "Excuse me ladies, I'll be right back."

I head toward the side of the room where Ben and his team have set up camp. And before I am able to surprise him, he recognizes me. "Hey, Anton right? What's up man?"

"Oh nothing much Ben. How about you? Win any gold medals yet?"

"Nope, not yet. My events start tomorrow. I'm pretty excited."

Not wanting to tell the man how to live his life or prepare for his forte, my curiosity gets the best of me regardless. "Well, sounds great, good luck to you all. I hope you don't mind my asking, but I read or heard somewhere that Olympic athletes go dry until after their events are over. Isn't drinking tonight going to affect your skiing?"

Right then, Ben looks at me with utter disbelief. He starts to laugh hysterically, but quickly moderates it to a modest chuckle. "Oh man, that was a good one. No, I think I've heard the same thing too, and that's probably true. But you have to remember this: we're representing Germany. Although I don't live there, I've still spent my fair share of time there. Have you ever been?"

"Well, actually I have, but it was on business, and I didn't get to see much."

"Oh cool. Well, I'll just tell you that I'm putting it mildly when I say these guys here drink beer for breakfast. The German food pyramid literally has hops and barley on the bottom layer." I know he's kidding, but he sure doesn't act like it. "You have to understand that alcohol is probably part of most German athletes' workout regimens. They train year-round under the influence of a few Meister Braus. So if they showed up to competition sober, well who knows how that would affect their performance."

I can tell by now that he's definitely exaggerating, but I understand his point. "All right, I guess that's fair. Well, when you're done with that beer, let me buy you another one." And the instant I finish my sentence, Ben puts his mug to his lips and chugs the remaining 80 percent of his beer.

"Wow! look at that. What a coincidence. Come on, how 'bout some Jaeger while we're at it?"

Amused by his gusto, I follow him as he clears a path toward the bar. The bartender stares at us for our order without actually uttering a word. A slight head tilt upward is universal bartender talk for "what the fuck do you want?" The bar is significantly more packed than it was when Ashby, Janine, and I arrived; so I raise my voice and shout, "Let me get two Kitsilano's and two shots of Jaeger please."

"No problem," he tells me as he quickly puts a glass to the tap.

"What did you just order us?" Ben asks.

"Oh, it's called Kitsilano Maple Cream Ale. I had one the other day at lunch. It's made by a local brewery around here, really good stuff. I try my best to always sample the fruits of the local brewery's labor whenever I travel."

"Agreed. There are so many good beers in the world, and the only way to try them all . . . is to try them *all*."

"This one is especially nice because they put real Canadian maple syrup in it, which gives it that little something extra."

"OK, there you go guys," our bartender says as he sets the beers and shots on the bar. He then looks at me and asks, "Are you paying in U.S. or Loonies?"

"I should have a tab going actually. Last name Bradley." I started a tab when I bought my first drink. Even though I offered to buy a round for the ladies, Ashby insisted on buying one for Janine after all that she did. As he turns around to mark the toll on my tab, I grab his attention. "Oh hey, see those two women over there?" I ask while pointing toward the beautiful entourage I showed up with. "They're on my tab too."

"You got it," he says and then immediately moves onto the next person craving liquor.

"Hey thanks man. What are we toasting to?" Ben asks as we pick up our shots.

My initial thought is to toast to gold medals or something affiliated with the Olympics, but while I'm holding my shot, my mind flies back to the night I spent at the bar with Dr. Polk. This in turn reminds me of what he apparently told his wife that blew her away. The phrase "Scoff at the mundane" has been coursing through my brain ever since Ed's wife divulged that information to me. "To being awesome," I say. "After all, it is recession proof."

After a very long pause accompanied by a heinously baffled stare, Ben finally tells me, "Anton, you're a weird fucking dude . . . I like it! Cheers man."

"Right on. It's like, when people act lame, they're just a bunch of paper tigers trying not to get caught up in a vicious hornets' nest of redundancy." I highly doubt that what I'm saying makes sense. For some reason, I have the tendency to attempt and hide my drunkenness by using as many big words as possible in every sentence. "Yeah, I tend to think that the things that make life incredible are not typically derived from the status quo. I mean, what makes someone awesome isn't simply being famous. Anyone can be famous, and anyone can have money, but being awesome is more than " . . ." and in mid-sentence, Ben gives me a look that can only mean "Dude, shut the fuck up and drink." The weirdest part is that I have no idea what I'm saying, even though I'm still aware that I'm saying it all. I think I know what I'm trying to say, but even after just a couple drinks any thoughts I have never leave my mouth the way they're intended. And what I find even more perplexing is that I'm bashing the rich and famous, when in reality they are responsible for the majority of my income. I hate that I get so philosophical when I should just be saying things like "Let's drink to getting laid," or "I would like to toast to big titties." Why can't I make a normal brainless toast like that? I only linger on that thought momentarily before Ben and I both put our shots down our throats and move onto the microbrews.

"Mmm, good stuff. You know Jaeger goes really well with pancakes," he tells me. I have no doubt that he is absolutely serious this time.

I contemplate asking him what hard liquor goes best with pop-tarts, but I'm interrupted when Janine taps me on the shoulder. "Anton, I can't believe you're doing shots without me." She's not upset she didn't get any Jaeger. She wants to meet Ben. I don't blame her; he's an attractive gentleman, and I think he's even wearing deodorant. Based on stories she has told me, that would be a huge step up for her. "And who is your friend here?"

"Oh, my apologies. Janine, this is Ben. Ben, Janine." They shake hands and spit out the requisite "nice to meet you." I hate to sound bitter, but I really hate when people say this. I know it's customary, but more often than not, it's not really all that "nice" to meet someone. I'm not implying that it's atrocious, but I'm pretty sure that the vast majority of scenarios in which people meet for the first time, they rarely ever see one another again.

Personally, I'm a fan of saying "hi," and that's it. I will deviate from that however if it's someone I anticipate seeing again, such as a new neighbor or coworker. Oh, and I always make sure to get on a first name basis with any pizza server I come across. "Well Janine, I just opened a tab, so if you're craving a shot, go ahead and get whatever you want."

"Oh, you don't have to do that," she tells me with a wide grin.

"OK. I offered, have fun paying for your own booze tonight."

And right then she hits me with her purse. "Jerk." And though I don't blame her for hitting me with her handbag, I'm somewhat appalled that she willingly subjected her genuine Coach to such torture. I work in fashion. I know how much that thing is worth. I can also spot a knock-off from the other side of a zip code, and hers is the real thing.

"Hey, come on, I was kidding. Although maybe I should cut you off. You're already getting belligerent, and I don't think I want to witness how hostile you get once you put a bottle of Ouzo in your system." To anyone else listening to this conversation, it sounds like an arbitrary choice of booze. But Janine knows exactly what I'm referring to, and not wanting to test me, she grabs Ben's hand and quickly moves to the bar so they can do shots together. I look back toward our table, but it's completely vacant now. I spin a full 360 looking for Ashby, but don't see her. The bar is pretty packed by now, so I'm not exactly shocked that I'm having difficulty spotting her, but I figure it wouldn't hurt to stroll around and see if I can find her.

After I complete three back and forth trips across the room, I finally spot her chatting with some tall dude. She doesn't really seem too interested, but I can tell he's attempting to be as suave as possible. I don't recognize him, and I highly doubt I know him. But I do know this: Right now, I have more contempt for him than the suppositional teenage child parented by Ann Coulter and Noam Chomsky. Fortunately, before I'm coerced into punching my second person in as many decades, Ashby spots me and rubs her eye, which is the signal to come rescue her. We've had a bulletproof system for years. If one of us is talking to someone and we need to be bailed out, we vehemently begin rubbing our eyes. Once there is a clear understanding that there is no chemistry, the person looks to the ground in order to search for their "dropped contact lens." Once Ashby is certain that I've acknowledged her plot, she puts both hands out and looks straight down, and I make my move.

"Hey honey, there you are. You need another drink?"

"Oh, not now baby. I just dropped a contact. Can you help me look for it?"

I quickly bend down like a loyal boyfriend and say, "Absolutely. Shit, I can't believe this happened again. I think that's got to be like the third time this month."

"Actually, I think it's four. Remember two weeks ago when you were having a poker night with the guys and I went with Carol to look for bridesmaid's dresses? Well, I dropped one into a cake at the bakery."

Trying not to burst out laughing, I surprisingly stay in character, "No way! That is too funny." And as I'm about to comment on how amusing a contact lens embedded in a three-tier wedding cake is, I look up and see Ashby's suitor has long left the area. "Wow! We're getting pretty good at this. I think that might have to be some kind of record."

"Seriously, we get better at that every time we try it. Just like a fine box of wine, we only get better with age. You know what's even better?" she asks.

"No, what's that?"

"That guy's name was Slate, his *first* name. Seriously, that cannot be his real name. Doesn't Slate sound like an actor from *Dawson's Creek* or something?" Ashby asks me with a wide grin. I can tell she's a little tipsy now, and I have no idea how many drinks she's had since I last saw her. All that I know is she's not holding a martini glass, so she's clearly not on her first drink. After smiling at me for what feels like ten minutes, she breaks the silence by saying, "Come on Franklin, let's do a shot."

"Are you sure you want to? I mean, you've got to see Marty tomorrow don't you? And your event is coming up really soon."

In a very somber and seemingly sober manner, she says, "In all seriousness, I probably shouldn't be drinking tonight. OK, I know I shouldn't, because Marty will kill me if he finds out. But honestly, I've had a rough couple of days. Don't get me wrong; today was great. But going to the hospital . . . well let's just say it wasn't my first choice of sites I wanted to see in Vancouver."

I immediately empathize with her situation. This, combined with the fact that I have about as much success saying "no" to her as a deadhead does to brownies in Amsterdam, I tell her, "OK, what are we drinking?"

"That's more like it. I'm thinking Cuervo. Tequila makes me . . . feisty," she tells me with the most seductive look I've ever received, as she grabs me by the belt and pulls me toward the bar. My first instinct is to remind her that the only liquor I refuse to drink under any circumstances whatsoever is tequila. But right now, she could tell me to guzzle kerosene laced with ammonia, and I'd be all for it.

"Sounds great, make mine a double." My extraneous gusto in this scenario is a classic example of how the things she says to me annihilate any logic I might have.

We get up to the bar where about five other people have been waiting, but Ashby does whatever it is that women do, and she has the bartender's attention immediately. I know the other people are pissed off right now, but I'm not sure what annoys them more: getting passed over for alcohol by the bartender, or the fact that they think I'm hooking up with this bombshell.

"Two shots of Cuervo, please. Doubles!" she half-shouts while holding up two fingers. Within seconds, two enormous glasses of liquid punishment are sitting in front of us on the bar. "They're on his tab; it's Bradley," she says after picking up our shots. She hands me my glass. I can smell it from two feet away, and I know this is going to be a terrible idea. Before I can even protest, she interjects, "Cheers Franklin."

"Oh of course. A toast . . . to the Olympics," is all I say.

Slurring her words slightly, she rebuts, "Nah, screw that. We're drinking to . . . to . . . to sticking your neck out." I'm not exactly sure what that means, but at this point I imagine that any dispute from me will be ineffective at best. I nod, we tap our shots together, and send them on a voyage to our livers. The tequila isn't even halfway down my throat before I feel it start to come back up. Luckily, it's just a minor gag reflex, and I keep everything down. She on the other hand looks about as happy as I've ever seen her. She smiles at me with the widest lips one can imagine, and then says to me, "Come on, let's get out of here."

"Yeah, that's probably a good idea. You do have to focus on your skating after all. Come on, I'll walk you outside and get you a cab."

"Oooorrrr, we could share a cab, and you could come hang out at my room?" she utters flirtatiously.

My mind instantly flounders. Is she suggesting what I think she is? Does she want to hook up with me? I'm not saying she's trying to sleep with me, but maybe she is. Maybe she just wants to make out all night. But maybe she just wants to talk about how stressed she is. Confusion is running at an all-time high, but in moments like this, rationality takes a distant back seat to the slim chance of requited love. Trying not to sound overly eager, I aloofly tell her, "Yeah, sure whatever. I guess I can chill for a little bit before I head home."

At this point, she smiles and grabs my hand, leading me for the exit. I've never had many reservations about being crass. But right now, even I don't feel proper giving a vivid description of what's taking place below my belt. I keep telling myself to play it cool; just don't blow it and everything will be fine. Once we're outside, the freezing winter air quickly brings us out of our euphoric state. Her hand goes up in the air to signal for a cab, while I huddle behind her, rubbing her arms up and down in an attempt to keep her warm. Luckily, we wait no more than thirty seconds for a taxi to arrive. He comes to a stop, and we hop in the cab.

"Hey there, you two," he greets us with an extremely friendly smile. "Where to?"

Ashby replies, "The Olympic Village please. Back to the dorms."

"Oh, an athlete huh? Wow! Good for you," he tells her. Even though I'm sure he has met several over the past few days, his fervor seems genuine. "What's your event?" he asks as he slowly pulls away from the curb.

Just as Ashby is about to reply, I interrupt, "Oh hey, stop the cab please."

"What's wrong?" she asks with a look of concern.

"Oh, nothing major, but I left my credit card at the bar." I am notorious for doing this. Being drunk doesn't exactly help the situation.

"Oh OK. I thought something was really wrong. Well, do you want to just come back tomorrow?"

"No, it's cool. I'll go back inside and get it now. I should just get it over with."

"OK, no big deal. Can you just wait and leave the meter running, sir?" she asks the driver.

"Don't worry about it, sir. It was getting busy in there. It might be ten minutes or more before they even acknowledge me. Just go on without me, and I'll be there before you know it."

"Are you sure?"

"Yeah, it's cool." Opening my wallet, I give her some money, "Here, this will definitely cover it. It's American dollars, but he should be cool with it."

Overhearing the conversation, he says, "That's fine young man."

Looking a little disappointed, Ashby makes a funny gesture with her lips. "OK, well don't be too long. You know where it is right?" I nod yes. "Great, well call me when you get near."

"You got it," I tell her with an overly cocky wink. "See you in a few," I tell her as I begin to shut the door.

"Oh hey, babe." I look around, then realize she's talking to me. "I'll miss you."

"You too," is all I say before shutting the door and heading back into the club. During the brief chilling walk back to the bar, I ponder what exactly she meant when she called me "babe." And the way she said "I'll miss you," it was like she was trying to take my pants off with her words. But I am a little drunk; I'm probably just imagining this. Yeah, I'm sure that's it. I'll get back there, and we'll have a nice all-night talk about everything from work and money to the best milkshakes we've ever had.

I reenter the room and head toward the bar, preparing to retrieve my credit card. For the first five minutes, I don't think anyone on the other side of the rail noticed me, and if they did, I'm sure the massive smile consuming my face freaked them out. They probably thought I was on a cocktail of every narcotic ever created. I wait another couple of minutes with similar results, when from behind me I hear a woman shout my name.

"Anton! There you are!" I turn around and recognize Janine, a few sheets to the wind. She looks very amused, but not nearly as happy as Ben does with his arm around her waist. "Get over here!" she shouts while frantically waving me toward her with her free hand.

"Hey Janine. Hey Ben, what's happening?"

Cutting to the chase, Janine blurts out, "Where's Ashby? I saw you two walk outside together. I had my fingers crossed."

"Oh, well we were about to head back to her room, but I forgot my credit card at the bar. I just came back to get it really quick, and I'm going to meet her once I'm done."

She begins to jump up and down, "Ahhh, yes! I'm so happy for you," she exclaims as she gives me a huge hug. "I knew you two were going to get together. How thrilled are you?"

"You know, I always dreamt of this moment. Well, I'm not even sure if she wants anything to happen. I mean, she might just want company," I tell her modestly.

"Anton, seriously? That girl wants you . . . *Bad*. Trust me, it's on tonight. Take it from me. I'm a girl, and I can see the signs."

I start to beam, but restrict it, not wanting to gloat. But something isn't sitting right with me. "Janine, don't get me wrong, I have thought about tonight for many, many years. But I guess . . . I don't know, I just thought it might happen under different circumstances."

"What do you mean?"

"Well, let's be honest. I don't mean to deprecate myself, but think about it. Ashby was really drunk. And you were at dinner. She didn't eat very much. I know she's vulnerable right now, and I'm not saying she has no feelings for me at all. But, well, don't you think that maybe she's just into me right now because she's in a fragile state of mind?"

A few moments pass with Janine just staring at me, her approval growing with every passing second. "Anton, you are so sweet. I wish more guys were like you. I think that's really nice of you. If you really don't think getting with her tonight is a good idea, she will totally understand. In fact, I'm sure she'll want you even more because of it. But I'll be straight up with you; I do think she really likes you. Sure, the booze might be talking a little, but from what I've seen, I think she wants you no matter what."

In my elation, not wanting to embarrass myself, all I say is "Thanks Janine, I really appreciate that."

"So, do what you think is best. Honestly, I think whatever you decide will be fine with her." Ben whispers something into her ear, and Janine gives me a hug. "Well, let me know what happens, but we're going to head out," she says as she gives me that look that only materializes when someone knows they're about to get laid by an Olympian. I don't exactly know what that face looks like, but I imagine her expression is about as close as you get.

"Have fun you two," I say as Ben and Janine walk toward the exit. After standing there reflecting, I decide that it's best for me to just get my credit card and call Ashby telling her I'll see her tomorrow. As much as I want tonight to happen, I really do want the circumstances to be different. It's funny because I have often gone over this moment in my head, under multiple conditions. No matter the circumstances, the end result is always she and I ending up naked together. But now that this scenario is actually playing out, something just doesn't feel right. I walk over to the bar to get in line once again. All I want to do is get my card, go home, and rub one out and forget about passing up the most amazing sex of my life.

This time, only about three minutes pass before a woman behind the bar asks me what I'm drinking, but I tell her "Oh, I'd just like to get my tab please. The last name is Bradley." She quickly heads back to the stack of credit cards and starts pushing a bunch of buttons. While she is doing that, another bartender puts a shot of something in front of me; it looks like whiskey.

"Oh, I didn't order that," I tell him.

"It's from her," he says, as he points to the other end of the bar. I see a beautiful blonde staring back at me; she raises her shot, puts it back, and begins walking toward me.

"Hey there. Do you know Ben?" she asks upon arriving in front of me.

"Excuse me?"

"Ben Crandall. He's a skier for the German team. I thought I saw you talking to him earlier."

"Oh yeah, Ben. Sorry, I got mixed up for a minute. Yeah, I met Ben a few days ago. Is he a friend of yours?"

"Yeah, me and Ben go way back. We grew up near each other in Colorado. I've known him since I was like seven."

"Oh cool, are you a skier too?" And finally remembering my manners, I say, "Oh, and thanks for the shot by the way, but I think I should pass. I've already had a few tonight."

She gives me a look of extreme disapproval. "Not quite, I'm a snowboarder."

"For Germany as well?"

"No, my parents raised me with a sense of loyalty. And my grandpa always taught me that treason was a bad thing. He would lecture me for hours to 'never turn out like Benedict Arnold.' I compete for the Red, White, and Blue all the way."

"Well, that's very noble of you. I salute your patriotism."

"Really? You don't seem all that impressed."

"Excuse me?"

"Well, I just bought you a shot, and you aren't even going to drink it?"

"Oh, well it's just that I've already had a ton of drinks tonight."

"Oh come on, just celebrate with me by having one little shot. That's all I'm asking."

At this point, I realize we haven't even had an introduction. "Well, first, I'll say congratulations, even though I don't know what you're celebrating. Second, my name is Anton. I feel kind of weird for not asking your name earlier."

Shaking my hand, "Hi Anton, nice to meet you. My name is Alexis. Alexis Donovan."

"That name sounds really familiar. Are you an athlete?" I like how in my drunken state I still require her to repeat the information she gave me less than a minute earlier.

Smiling, she replies, "I am."

"What event?"

"Snowboarding, half-pipe."

And right then it clicks. I don't follow winter sports all that closely, but I've definitely seen her on ESPN and in some other magazines. "Oh shit. No way! Now I think I know who you are! Your event was today wasn't it?"

"It sure was," she responds, not trying to gloat.

"And how did it go?"

"All that glitters is gold. It's the only way I roll."

I almost pass out knowing that an Olympic gold medalist is not only talking to me, but also possibly hitting on me. I mean, she did send a drink my way, that's usually a sign of interest, right?

"That's so awesome. Seriously, you have no idea how cool I think that is."

"Well, thank you Anton. So now you have to drink that shot, otherwise you're going to put a serious damper on my celebration party." Even though that is a pretty strong argument by itself, she then gives me the look that I've never been able to say no to.

"OK, I think that's fair," I say as I pick up the whiskey and use all my strength to keep it down.

"Yay! Good work. Now we have to do a shot together." And before I can object, she is already back at the bar ordering more booze. My check is sitting on the bar waiting to be signed. I scribble my name and finally accomplish the one thing I came in here to do. Before I know it, a huge glass of what I believe is Knob Creek is staring back at me, mocking me. If this were any other woman (besides Ashby McHale) I would have a mild chance of saying no to this. But I'm drinking with an Olympic gold medalist. It's not necessarily my biggest fantasy, but it's up there. When most guys back in junior high were jerking off to Playboy, I kept the Mary-Lou Retton commemorative Wheaties box in my room for such occasions. Women who dominate what they do are very alluring.

"OK, ready?" she asks as she hands me my glass.

"Probably not, but let's do this," is all I can spit out before I choke down a few ounces of a pending disaster. "Wow! That was rough. Thanks a lot, but I really do think I need to get going. I have to work early tomorrow." That's not entirely true. Although I do have to work tomorrow, 3:00 p.m. hardly qualifies as early.

"Come on, I just got here Anton. You can stick around for one more, can't you?" she asks me in her most flirtatious tone. Her dimples are staring back at me with a more ominous presence than any knife or weapon I've ever witnessed. Why do women have this control over me? Why can't I just say "no" when I know it's in my best interest to do so? Why can't I just call Ashby, tell her I'll see her tomorrow, and go back to my room? . . . Alone.

"Well, I guess I can stay for one more. I do have to make a quick phone call though."

Why the fuck did I leave my credit card at the bar?

25

"UGH. I CAN'T believe I let you talk me into that last shot of whiskey," is my morning greeting. Alexis is up and moving just past 10:00 a.m., although it feels like I just fell asleep.

Moaning, I contest, "What are you talking about? You were the one who kept passing me drinks all night long. This is gonna be an awful morning." Mainly, I'm referring to my headache. But right now, last night is so vague that the notion of piecing it together worries me severely.

"First of all, there are no such things as bad mornings. There are only good nights. Second of all, thanks for everything. It was, well . . . interesting. I had a great time. But I'm gonna head out."

Not really sure what to say due to the nature of last night's events, I begin to get dressed so I can walk her downstairs. "Oh, OK. Well, just let me find a clean shirt, and I'll walk you down."

"Don't worry about it Anton. You did enough last night. I can make it from here."

Just then, I stand up to stretch and give her a good-bye hug, but my back is so sore from the contorted position I fell asleep in last night. I don't think passing out on the floor at the foot of the bed was in my best interest either. "Whatever you say, Alexis," I say as I walk over to her to exchange a very uncomfortable good-bye.

We give each other a hug, I open the door to my room to let her out, and she says, "Well, thanks again. Maybe I'll see you around."

"Yeah, I hope so," I tell her, fully aware of how awful it will be for each of us if we run into one another in public.

"OK, well, I'm gonna go get some breakfast."

"Sounds good, have a great day." She starts to walk down the hallway, and I remind her out of courtesy, "Hey Alexis, you've got your gold medal with you right? As much as I want to tell people it's mine, I'd feel really bad if you lost it."

She pats the pocket of her coat and says, "Yep, right here, but thanks for checking." She makes a turn toward the exit but quickly stops. "Oh and Anton. Good luck with Ashby. She sounds like a really great girl."

And just like that, she's gone. As nice as it was for her to wish me luck with Ashby, I really don't think last night helped my chances. I mean, Ashby was throwing herself at me, wasn't she? And now, all I can wonder is if I just made the biggest mistake of my life. I'm about to close the door to my room and finally get some decent rest, when I hear a familiar voice calling me from down the hall.

"Good morning Anton. Looks like you had quite the night," Ashby's brother says to me in a highly bitter tone. "My sister sure knows how to pick 'em I guess."

Oh fuck. "Tim, I can explain. It's seriously not what you think," is all I can come up with. I storm down the hall in my boxers hoping to catch him and explain my side of the story before he tells Ashby.

"Really? Because last night I happened to be in the lobby downstairs when you and that chick that just left came stumbling through the door. She was all over you man."

"Yeah, I know, but Tim, it's really not " . . ." and he cuts me off immediately.

"Bullshit asshole. And whatever you want to tell me, it's too late. I just had breakfast with her. She knows what you were up to last night. It was bad enough to do this, but you didn't have to call her and leave her that message last night you know. See ya 'round," he growls in his most demeaning tone, and takes off for his room.

My heart is pumping so fast at this moment. I honestly think this is what it must feel like to have a near brush with death. A freefall from an airplane minus the parachute probably wouldn't horrify me as much as this does right now. The only thing I can think to do is run back to my room and call Ashby.

Over the next three hours, I make thirty-seven calls and leave fifteen messages, until her mailbox becomes full and refuses to let me leave anymore. Obviously, I should be able to take a hint, but coming to grip with reality has never been my strong suit.

The amount of stress this is putting on me is doing nothing to help my hangover, so I decide to give up calling her for the time being and find something to eat. Not too far from my hotel is a nice little park, and just on the other side of it is a strip of restaurants. Although there are several appealing options, there is only one food I can rely on in a time like this. Pizza is my comfort food, my Ben & Jerry's if you will. The first pizza place I find is called *Canucklehead Pizzeria*, and I'm sold on the name alone.

I love the decor inside. It's a bit of a dive, but still very cozy. One of those places where people sign money and tape it to the wall. Every time I see this, I'm tempted to pay for my food or drinks with it, mainly just to see what kind of reaction I would get. I step up to the counter and smile minimally for the first time all day. "Hey how's it going?" I ask the kid behind the counter. "Can I get two slices for here, please?"

"Sure thing. You just want plain cheese?"

My smile gets a little bigger; personally amused by the ridiculous question I'm about to ask. "Oh, well, can I get one of them just plain cheese, but on the other," I pause to look at the menu. "Let me ask you a question. What do you guys call Canadian bacon up here in Canada? Is it just bacon, or is it still Canadian bacon?" Only in Canada can I get away with a question this ludicrous. Anything this asinine would never fly in the Bronx or The Windy City.

"Ham," is all the kid says.

"Oh OK, cool. Well, let me get one slice plain cheese, and . . . you know what, I think both cheese will be fine." The kid rolls his eyes and rings it up.

"You want a drink?"

"Yeah, I'll take a medium soda too, thanks." I pay the kid and grab my slices once they're out of the oven. It's probably because I haven't eaten in almost eighteen hours, but it looks and smells amazing. After it cools down enough so I won't burn the roof of my mouth, I dig in. Instantly, I can tell that it is among the best pizza I've ever had. Not the best, but easily top seven. And sadly, I'll never be able to fully enjoy it. All I can do is dwell on how I had everything I wanted, or at least had it within my grasp, and then pissed it all away. Instead of tasting like undeniable victory, these slices of cheese taste like supreme rejection. It's comparable to having every denial by every girl you've ever liked broadcast in Times Square right before the ball drops.

As I'm halfway through my second slice, I hear a kid at the table next to me brag to a man I assume is his dad that he's eaten four slices. Normally, I'd give the dude a high five, or at least keep my mouth shut. But in my given state, being difficult seems the more logical route. I look over at the kid and say, "You know, it doesn't really count as a whole slice if you don't eat the crust. And with as much crust that you've got sitting on that plate, I'd say you've eaten two and a half slices at most." The dad's expression immediately goes sour. He's staring me down as if I just kicked a nun in the shins in a dark alley and stole her shoes. It makes me very apprehensive, so I quickly finish my slice and get up to leave.

"Thanks again man," I tell the staff of the pizza place as I throw my trash away and step out the door. The pizza helped, but not nearly enough. Fortunately, the weather is pleasant enough that a walk in the park is definitely doable. Walks always help me clear my mind, although I rarely have issues this big tearing me apart. Because I seem to flourish on self-loathing, I call Ashby one more time. Why do we always think that for some reason the 115th time will be the charm, as if all failed attempts prior to right now were just flukes? Again, it goes straight to voicemail, but I can't leave a message because her mailbox is full. In my frustration, I'm tempted to smash my phone on the ground, but fortunately, I have just enough composure to refrain. However, I do shut it off so that I don't have to look at it every ten seconds to see if by some divine miracle she has called me back.

The park is busy this afternoon, occupied primarily by joggers and people sitting down and reading. But the shittiest day of my life wouldn't be complete if there weren't several people out walking their dogs. More than likely, these Canadian canines are turning this park into a doggie doo-doo landmine field. For the vast majority of my walk, my head stays down, keeping an eye out for dog poop. Like I said, with the day I'm having, stepping in it seems like my oedipal tragic prophecy. Despite the fact that I don't really get to enjoy much of the scenery given the position of my head, I am able to calm down a little bit during this walk. And then, a thought occurs to me. What do I have to be sorry for? Obviously, I am crazy about her, but it's not like Ashby and I were dating. She never even really insinuated that anything was going to happen last night. Do I really have anything to feel bad about? I dwell on these thoughts for a while, but the solace they bring me is fleeting. No matter how I look at it, I still feel like shit. My nerves get the best of me, or maybe it's the three liters of whiskey in my liver, and I have to sit down and rest.

After about fifteen minutes or so of sitting under a tree, I'm on the verge of passing out, when I'm brought back to full attention by my least favorite sound of all-time.

Barking. Horrendous, mind-numbing barking.

Naturally, leave it up to a dog to add to the pile of my disastrous day. My first inclination is to attempt to ignore it and hope it shuts up, but then I see what is going on. Whatever kind of dog this is, I'm not really sure. All that I know is it's a big dog, and it looks mad. The owner is pulling on its leash trying to calm it down, but the dog is lunging with all its strength. The leash is stretched so tight that the dog is testing its tensile strength with all its might. To make the situation worse, it's flipping out in the vicinity of a group of kids. My only instinct is to stand up. I wish I were inclined to do something, but I get scared of Chihuahuas with bedazzled collars.

But this fucking dog will not stop, despite countless pleas from its owner. I slowly start to walk forward, my pace increasing with each step. My heart is throbbing as I sense the impending calamity. I'm not sure why it took so long, but finally all the kids in the area simultaneously scatter. As I see them begin to run away in panic, I shelve my inhibitions and begin running toward this dog. I'm only about ten strides into my sprint when the dog liberates itself by yanking the leash out of its owner's hands. The moment I see this, I double-time it. As I get closer, I can tell this dog is either a German shepherd, a Doberman pinscher, or a pit-bull. Like I said, dogs aren't my thing. All I know is that I'm praying the dog's bark is worse than its bite, because I can't even fathom the opposite holding true. Just as I get within a twenty-foot radius, (or roughly seven meters) of this seemingly possessed dog, it stops in its tracks, looks around, and begins sprinting for a little kid not far from me. This little boy is shaking unlike anything I've ever seen. His screams are deafening, even with his face buried in his mother's chest. I can tell the dog has set its sights on these two, and begins to run their way.

It's a footrace between this slobbering rabies machine and myself. I have to beat it to the kid. Even though I'm very seriously concerned Ashby will never talk to me again, I know that part of the reason I'm even entertaining thoughts of what I'm about to do is because of her. And right then, it all comes back to me: last night, when she toasted to "sticking your neck out." She was telling me something. That was her telling me to make my move.

That was why she gave me Leviathan all the way back in high school. No wonder she's so pissed off about last night. She's wanted me to make my move for years. And as I imagine the whole tortoise versus hare parable, I realize that I'm the turtle, and I'm fated to win, right? But at this moment, this dog has got a solid step on me, and the gap is closing. I have no choice but to lunge out in front of the boy and his mother as she runs away gripping him tightly.

As I leap to shield them, I actually fly over the dog. But luckily, my knee grazes the dog's back, or top, or whatever it's called. I don't knock it over or anything, but I definitely distract it. Whatever I did was enough to draw Cudo's attention over to me, giving the kid and mom enough time to flee for cover.

And right now, I'm so glad I only had two slices of pizza, because I'm fairly certain that anything inside my body won't remain there for long. As this dog begins barking away and trying to bite me, I cover my face with my arms. I really have no idea how to protect myself from a dog attack, as I've kept a large distance from them pretty much my entire life. And suddenly, I feel a sharp stabbing pain in my forearm. I don't look because I'm so scared, but I feel liquid drip onto my forehead. I begin to roll around, which would probably be a great idea if I were either on fire or being attacked by bees. Unfortunately, the son of Cerberus is unrelenting, and I feel another bite. This time I look and see my right arm covered in blood. I scream for help, look around to see if anyone is coming, and close my eyes again. I wish I could recount what happened next, but all I see is . . .

Blackout.

26

THE LAST TIME I opened my eyes in a hospital to find myself surrounded by medical personnel, I was squeezing my way out of a vagina. My mother's vagina to be exact. And after that dog got the better of me, I find myself in one again. A hospital that is, not a vagina. Fortunately, round two has a lot less screaming, crying, and gooiness. When my parents found out what happened, they flew to Vancouver as soon as they could. Although I would prefer seeing them under different circumstances, it was such a relief to have my mom be the first person I saw when I opened my eyes. Interesting how it seems we always come full circle.

Her eyes light up as she sees mine open, and she begins rubbing my forehead. "How are you feeling honey? I'm so glad you're OK. Is there anything I can get you?"

"Hey mom. Wow! I can't believe you guys made it. No, I'm fine right now. Where's dad?"

"Oh, he just went to the bathroom. He should be back any minute."

I sit in silence for a while, looking at my cuts and bruises, then say, "Thanks for coming mom. It really means a lot to me."

Almost laughing, she tells me, "Oh honey, don't be silly. Of course we were going to come see you. You're my baby after all," she adds as she rubs my forehead some more. And just then, dad walks in the door.

"Hey dad, great to see you."

He leans over to give me a hug but then reconsiders, assuming it might do more harm than good. Instead, he just pats me on the shoulder. "Hey buddy, how ya feeling?"

"Well, I'm not gonna lie, I've been better. But I can honestly say that I feel better than I look."

They both look at one another, then at me, and smile. My dad continues, "I was just speaking with your doctor out in the hallway, and she thinks you'll be able to leave in a couple of days. She said that you're very fortunate not to have any internal damage, mainly just a lot of lacerations and surface scars. No infections either."

"Yeah, I spoke with a nurse earlier this morning. You have no idea how relieved I was to hear that."

A tear starts to seep out of my mother's eye, "I'm just . . . so glad that you're OK."

I know that it's my responsibility to console my mother, so I tell her, "Thanks mom, but it really wasn't as bad as it looks." In reality, I have no idea if that is true or not, since I passed out at the onset of this ordeal. I did luck out big time though since there was mailman taking his lunch break in the park. From what I hear, he jetted over to us as soon as he could and knocked the dog out with some pepper spray. I know that I've been making minimal efforts to become more appreciative of animals, but this incident is quite a setback. I'm not saying I think the dog should be put down, but I'd be lying if I said I was opposed to it either. "How long are you guys in town for?" I ask.

"Oh, well it's open-ended. But since you seem to be recovering just fine, we'll probably take off tomorrow," my dad explains. "Hey, has Ashby been by yet?"

Not really wanting to get into this at the moment, I simply say, "Um, no. But she's really busy training for her big event. I think the prelims are sometime today, and the semis and medal round are tomorrow."

Smiling as if she were her own daughter, my mom adds, "Oh, I'm just so proud of that girl." And right then, I can see something in my mom's eyes that I've honestly never seen before. I would love to describe it, but like I said, it's foreign to me. Clearly, her emotions are a factor, but she flat-out asks me, "So Anton, when are you and Ashby going to get together?" And there it was. Just like that. The question I know that both she and my dad have been wondering for years. I guess moments like these that really make you focus on the fragility of life force you to be more upfront.

"Well mom, you know she and I are just really good friends, and I" . . . and I'm interrupted by my dad.

"Son, that's all well and good, but what do you really *want* to come out of that friendship?"

"Excuse me?"

"Look, I know how hard it is to take a chance when emotions are so intense, but you'd also be a fool to let someone so wonderful pass you by." Even though I fully agree with what they're saying, it is still taking time to soak in. This is seemingly coming out of left field.

"Well, yeah, that's true. But, I don't know, I mean . . . I don't really know what to do. It's just a really complicated situation. We're really good friends, and I know that neither of us want to jeopardize that."

And this time, my dad is the one whose eyes grow wide, and he and my mother share a knowing glance. "Son, I think now is the perfect time for me to finish telling you the story about the time President Franklin Delano Roosevelt gave your grandfather some life-changing advice."

Eager to *finally* hear this, but also surly from the medication, I reply, "Sounds good. Let's hear it, I'm not going anywhere."

"OK, well, I can tell you need sometime alone, so I'll try to keep this brief."

"Sorry dad, I didn't mean it like that. Please, tell me all the details. I would love to hear the story."

"OK, well as your grandfather told me, FDR and his entourage would come into the diner where he worked from time to time. There was a rehabilitation center in Warm Springs, Georgia, where the president went on occasion to treat his condition."

"Really?"

"Oh, yes. And I'll try to pick up where we left off, but I think last I told you, FDR had ordered plain wheat toast, a departure from his normal order. Grandpa thought this was odd, but when the president orders wheat toast . . . well, that's what he gets."

"Good point."

"And when the toast arrived, it had butter on it. President Roosevelt said that's not what he ordered. The manager of the place got really upset with your grandpa, really laid into him later."

"Seriously?"

"Well, as Grandpa told me, it was his boss's fault, and the president made sure he knew that. Your grandfather was still feeling down, and FDR could really see that. And that's when he told Grandpa to listen close to what he had to tell him."

At this point, the anticipation is eating away at me. Despite feeling very tired and weak, I sit up in my bed to give my full attention. "Yeah?" I ask like an eager kindergartner. "What was it?"

My dad continues, "Well, he leaned in, and the president took his hand and squeezed it. And I know he was a young boy at the time, but Grandpa told me the president squeezed his hand so hard he nearly squealed."

"But wasn't FDR in a wheelchair?"

"Exactly. I'm sure that's what caught your grandpa by surprise. Anyway, he leaned in, trying not to grimace, and the president told him something that Grandpa bragged about as long as he lived." He takes a long, dramatic pause.

"Well?"

"President Roosevelt said to your grandfather, 'Johnny, don't let anyone talk to you the way your boss does. Don't ever let anyone tell you that you can't do something, or you don't deserve it. Look at me. I'm in a damn wheelchair, and I'm the president of the greatest country in the world. You can do anything you want, never forget that. Simply ignore anyone who tells you otherwise, because they're just a coward. That's all."

Impressed, all I can ask is "Really? That's so cool. So what happened next, did Grandpa go all Jerry McGuire and quit his job?"

Laughing, my dad says, "Not quite. But he definitely didn't take as much crap from his boss. Grandpa certainly took that advice to heart."

"How's that?"

"Well, there was this really pretty girl that came into the diner all the time with her family. Whenever he told me this story, he gave very in-depth descriptions of her, so it's safe to say he liked her very much."

Interrupting, I say, "Oh OK, I get it. The woman was Grandma; they fell in love and got married, right? That's so emo."

Laughing again, he tells me, "Nope, not even close. But he had wanted to ask this girl out for a long time. And the day after the president was there, he asked her out . . . and she shot him down."

"Ouch."

"Sure, but he didn't let it stop him. He was persistent; he asked her out every week until she said yes."

"And then she finally agreed, and it was Grandma?" I say with a cocky tone.

Grinning, he says, "Nope, according to him, she shot him down twelve times."

"Well, that sucks. So what exactly is the lesson here?"

"Well, before that, your grandpa was too shy to ask any girl out, and didn't handle rejection well. But after meeting FDR, he slowly changed."

"So this story doesn't have any really happy fairytale ending then, does it?"

"I didn't say that. Your grandpa was preparing for rejection number thirteen when he went to wait on her table. But this time, another girl was with them. It was a neighborhood girl who had just moved to town. And Grandpa took one look at this girl, and never even acknowledged the first one. He walked straight over to their table, introduced himself, learned that she was new in town, and offered to show her around."

"Well " . . ."

"OK, now you can say it."

"And *that* girl was Grandma?"

"Yep. He took her out for sodas the next day, and they were inseparable from that moment on."

"Wow! Good work Grandpa. Great story Dad." I reflect on it briefly and grow more curious. "So are you saying that I should go for Ashby's friends?"

"Son, look. Do whatever you want. My point is mom and I know that you are in love with her. And we think the only thing stopping you from going for it is that you think you don't deserve her." I bow my head in shame as I recall recent events. And almost as if they know what happened, he adds, "We all make mistakes, and no one is perfect. But don't let flaws in your past prevent you from happiness the rest of your life. You deserve the best."

My mom adds, "And so does she. And we know you can give that to her."

After I deliberate all of this for quite sometime, I change subjects by saying, "Well, thanks a lot guys. We'll just have to see what happens. But can we watch some TV now? The Olympics are on."

"Of course," my dad replies as he picks up the remote and finds the Winter Games. And there she is, gliding along in a glorious spandex one-piece. "Hey, that's her!"

"Wow! That's Ashby! Come on darlin', you can do it!" For the next forty-five seconds, we watch the remainder of her first-round race. She sails across the finish line easily, beating her Danish competitor by a full two seconds. As she finishes, we all cheer at the top of our lungs.

After the commotion settles down, my parents gather their things to leave. "OK, well have a great night Son. We'll try to stop by before we leave tomorrow," my mom tells me.

"Wait, you're not leaving without me, are you?" A look of confusion fills their faces, unsure of whether I'm joking or delusional.

"Son, you need your rest. Sleep tight. Love you," my dad says.

"Bullshit. I don't need rest. There's something more important I have to take care of. Now get me out of here."

Rushing toward me to prevent me from getting out of bed, Mom says, "Nonsense. You're so weak you can barely even walk. You'll fall over."

"Then get me a cane or some crutches, because I'm not staying here another minute."

"Son, are you crazy?" my dad wonders.

"Probably. But look at it this way: it'll make a great story at my inauguration."

27

IF SOMEONE TOLD me back in high school chemistry class sophomore year, that I'd be at the Olympics cheering a girl I'd just met toward a gold medal, I would have laughed in their face. And although the setting isn't exactly ideal, being here to cheer for Ashby is breathtaking nonetheless. The down side: I still haven't spoken with her since the debacle of a few nights ago. The plus side: Thanks to my press pass and dilapidated state, I have an excellent view. However, getting in was a little bit more difficult than I anticipated. I was denied access by the first two security guards I talked to, which I'm pretty sure is a result of my boss still being pissed off at me for what I did the other day. Luckily, I happened to run into Big Ron. He does security for big events, but he also does a lot of traveling tours for rock stars and stuff. I met him a few years back at a U2 show. What can I say? I like to network.

Not that I'm exactly elated about it, but the fact that I'm walking with a cane allowed Ron to give me my own little area so I have some personal space. If anyone who knew me saw me right now, they'd get quite a kick out of it. I look like the forgotten love child of Elvis and Willy Wonka. I'm wearing the most ridiculous outfit I could find, simply because I don't want Ashby to recognize me as she skates by. I realize that she'll be moving around fifty miles per hour (which I think equals roughly 375 km/hr), but still, I wouldn't want to distract her during her big moment. Come to think of it, my crazy velour jacket and pompadour might have had something to do with being denied access earlier.

Although this is not my first Olympic event, it is my first gold medal match in any sport. I don't know if I'm just getting caught up in the moment, but something about it seems so unreal. From the moment one enters the arena, they can immediately tell that the stakes are higher than they've ever been. People are waving flags from all over the world, and the clothing in the crowds represents every color of the spectrum. The first gold medal race is the 1,000 m final, and it was preceded by a very close bronze contest. The 1,000 m is a very quick race, only two and a half laps I believe, as I've been told the oval is 400 m around. As the competitors remove their warm-up suits and casually glide to the starting line, the crowd goes crazy. The Canadian locals are particularly vocal, as a hometown favorite is representing the maple leaf in this race. She is a very tall woman with obscenely muscular legs. Her challenger is from Poland, so red and white are pretty much the only colors one can notice at the moment.

The gun goes up, a quick snap is heard, and the women sprint off the line, with the Canadian skating in the outside lane. I've never seen people move so quickly without the help of mechanical devices. I feel like I'm watching a pair of eagles on speed going at it as if it were business as usual. After I take a few shots, I sit down to rest my leg, and notice the next group of racers warming up. I see Ashby talking to her trainer. He's waving his arms all over the place, contorting his body in every direction. Although she is at a distance, I don't stare too long for fear of being noticed. Suddenly, everyone in the arena stands up, and the volume is raised to glass-shattering decibels. The hometown girl has a healthy lead as they make the final turn, and she wins easily. I never knew that they did the medal presentations so quickly after the race, but just a few minutes after it's over, the Canadian flag is hanging in the air, with that of Poland and Finland on either side.

I'm not exactly what one would classify as an imperialist, but I do genuinely enjoy living in America. However, there is something so impressive about watching thousands of people sing *Oh Canada* in unison to celebrate a national victory. It is so moving that it actually gives me goose bumps.

Once they have cleared the area, a voice comes over the loudspeaker announcing the next race: the bronze medal race in the 3,000 m distance. It features a woman from Russia, as well as another Canadian. Despite the crowd screaming as loud as they could, the woman from Russia takes the race by a few strides. I'm not certain, but I believe that Ashby defeated her in their semifinal race.

And suddenly, here we are. This is it. I pick up my camera to document every moment of this race, but the potpourri of emotions coursing through my soul prevents me from keeping a steady hand. I take a big gulp of water, a deep breath, and finally compose myself. She looks so adorable in her spandex suit with that hood that makes her head look so smooth. The announcement is made, so Ashby and her German competitor take their places. Ashby is starting in the inside lane. I tell myself that is a huge advantage, but in reality, I have no idea if it makes any difference. All it means to me is that on each odd-number lap, she'll be a little bit further away from my lens, but that's what a zoom is for.

The gun goes up, followed by a popping sound, and the race is underway. They don't start off as rapidly as the 1,000 m contestants, but their velocity still blows my mind. For the first four laps, the racers exchange the lead on a regular basis. It isn't until the fifth lap that the German takes a noticeable lead. As they enter lap number six, they switch lanes, and Ashby trails by roughly ten meters. Not insurmountable, but her window of opportunity is closing. The skaters round the turn and are now approaching my station. I put my camera up to my face and begin taking shots as fast as my trigger finger can possibly move. Ashby has drawn a little closer, but still trails by a few strides. The two women fly by me within a fraction of a second of the other, and the instant they pass, I break character.

"Come on Ashby, you can do it, dude! Don't give up!" I yell at the top of my lungs. The people in my immediate vicinity turn and stare, but the arena is so noisy that I highly doubt anyone else heard me. Maybe it was coincidence, but just after I finish my cheer, Ashby makes her move. The German girl is definitely winded, and is trying desperately to hold on to even the most miniscule lead. Within seconds, the women cross the line where they started, and have entered the seventh lap. One and a half more times around and this race will be cemented in history forever. It is so intense that I can barely stand to watch. My stomach hasn't had an internal quarrel like this in years. As they round the turn and begin their approach toward me again, the ladies are dead even. If the race ended right now, only technology could determine the victor.

I put my camera up on cue and begin snapping away. And from the looks of it, Ashby has taken a *slight* lead. They pass me more quickly than the blink of an eye, and once again I yell, "Let's go Ashby! Don't give up now. You're so close!"

They finish the seventh lap dead even, and after all that has transpired; it will all be decided in the final 200 m. I'm seriously about to throw up, I can't handle this. I know people will say it's "just a race," and I suppose that when push comes to shove, that is true. But from a metaphorical standpoint, which is how I've lived too much of my life, it's so much more.

I've had the good fortune (or curse, depending on how you look at it) of being close to the finish line for this race. As the racers tear across the final meters of ice, I prepare to take one final photo of this monumental event. The ladies approach the line seemingly joined at the hip. They both lunge forward trying to gain any advantage possible. The instant they cross the line, they slow down and stand up, panting heavily. The arena is cloaked in silence. It is so quiet that anyone inside could hear two mosquitoes knockin' boots (I think the whole "pin drop" analogy had a good run, but a new comparison is called for).

Everyone looks up to the sky where the scoreboard will display the results. Normally, these come up instantly, but given the extremely close nature of the finish, someone is undoubtedly reviewing the video. I held my breath for the entire thirty seconds it took for the results to be posted, but it felt like a year. And just like that, the results flash across the sky. Everyone in the crowd lets out a collective gasp, followed by an amalgam of cheers and groans. Ingrid Krause has won the race. Ashby missed out on a gold medal by 0.02 seconds.

28

"YOU'VE GOT TO be shitting me. She lost the race by *how* much?" Ed asks me. Although he offered to meet me at a bar, I told him I would much rather prefer a more serene environment. Instead of going to his office though, he was quite insistent that I meet him at his house.

"Two. One-hundredths of a second. That's zero point zero two seconds, Ed. It was insane. I'd never seen anything like it."

"Wow! That is unbelievable. I'll have to see the replay on the Internet. Hey, did I ever tell you about my brother and YouTube?" Without hesitation, my eyes bulge to the size of softballs. I was not amused, and he can tell. He makes the blatantly evident observation, and wisely shifts gears. "So Anton, aside from that, how was your trip?"

I called Ed when I got back into town a couple days ago, telling him I needed a session. I gave him a very brief synopsis in my voicemail, but nothing too intense. Even though I had originally planned on staying for the full run of the games, I left the day after Ashby's event. "Well Dr. Polk, the simple version is that I'm a wreck." He peaks his eyebrows. "I have to admit, when we started these sessions a while back, I was very skeptical. But over time, I really felt like you were getting through to me. I mean, I think

I was definitely making progress in some major areas." I take a long pause and look down at my feet.

"And?"

"Well, I . . . I had a . . . relapse I guess? All I know is that I fucked up, I fucked up big time, Ed."

Maintaining a calm exterior, he gently asks, "And why do you say that?"

I stand up because right now it is impossible for me to remain motionless for any duration of time. I begin pacing around his living room, and I'm fairly certain it's making Dr. Polk nervous. "She wanted me Ed! She wanted me to come back to her hotel room. She wanted me! I don't care what you call it: fucking, sex, making love, gettin' it on, banging, screwing . . . whatever you call it, she wanted me! And I. Fucked. Up."

He takes a deep breath, and I can see all of his possible responses cycling through his head like lottery balls. Dr. Polk carefully chooses his words, and tells me, "Anton, I need your help understanding something. I know I haven't always had the most orthodox approach with you, so please forgive me if I go astray here. Now, correct me if I'm wrong, but wasn't one of your major goals to cut back, if not give up, one-night stands?"

Trembling, I reply, "Well yeah Ed, in general that's true. But Ashby was the exception to that!"

"The exception? But haven't you been telling me that you have a very intense level of attraction toward this woman?"

"Yeah?"

"So how did you mess things up by *not* having sex with her? I'm going to go out on a limb and assume alcohol was involved?"

Furious and very defensive, I shout, "What Ed? Are you saying the only way a woman would want me was if she was wasted? Thanks a lot."

"What I mean is often times when two people have known each other for so long, any feelings they want to express become even more difficult than normal. Most people have enough difficulty expressing emotion to new partners. I see it all the time though; people who have been friends for years, secretly holding an attraction for the other. And so often the way they deal with it is by having intercourse while inebriated. That way, they get what they want in one way, their curiosities are satiated. If things go awry, they can hide behind the excuse of being drunk. So I apologize if I offended you, but please understand that it's very common."

"I'm sorry for shouting. And yes, you're right; we were both drunk. But that's what is so weird Ed. I don't even know how many times I've pulled the pin on my man-grenade while thinking of sex with Ashby. And when I had the chance, I passed on it."

"Anton, that's not a bad thing. It sounds like you were a totally respectable gentleman."

"Well . . . I was for a while."

"A while?"

"Unfortunately, I made the mistake of continuing to drink that night after I sent her home in a cab. Long story short, the next morning her brother caught a woman coming out of my hotel room. Or, according to him, he saw us the night before, but you get the point. News travels fast."

A sullen look comes over his face. "I see." If I had a nickel for every time he used that phrase . . .

"Ed, it just sucks so bad man. I mean, I had the whole thing planned out. She was going to win a gold medal, and then during the ceremony, I was going to pull some kind of insanely romantic stunt. I didn't have a speech written, but I know whatever I said would have been amazing. That was my chance. I was going to make everyone in that arena cry. Every woman was going to turn to her boyfriend and ask 'How come you never say stuff like that to me?' It was supposed to be my time to make Lloyd Dobler look like a fugitive. Anything that Cameron Crowe or John Hughes ever wrote was going to crumble into ruins all because of me. I mean, even though she didn't win the gold, had I not fucked up so badly, I could have still pulled off the speech."

He's writing on his trademark notepad, and asks me "Who's Lloyd Dobler?"

I almost throttle him, but quickly realize that it's actually a legitimate question, so I calm myself. "He's a character in *Say Anything*. He's played by John Cusack."

"Oh, is that the one where he holds the radio above his head?" he asks with genuine intrigue.

"Yes."

Smiling, "Oh, I love that movie."

"*As I was saying*," I mutter through a clenched mouth, "that was supposed to be the moment I made it all work out."

"So, why can't you do something about it now? I don't mean to be rude or cliché, but just because you missed an opportunity doesn't mean you can't do something about it now."

"Yeah, but I haven't even heard from her since that night. It's like when she lost that race, the universe was trying to tell me something. It was like a metaphor for our relationship. We were always so close wherever we went, but no matter how hard I tried, I always come up just a bit short," I say in an increasingly dejected tone.

Ed continues to write things down on his notepad. "Anton, would you mind getting me a bottle of water from the fridge while I finish writing some notes? Feel free to help yourself to anything you'd like as well."

"Sure, Ed." I change my course and walk over to the fridge. I take out two bottles of water off the middle shelf, set one down so I can open mine, and take a swig. As I pick up the second bottle to give to Ed, someone grabs me from behind. The bottles immediately drop to the ground, and my head slams onto the kitchen table. My arms are twisted around my back in such a precarious manner that I'm on the verge of tears.

From behind me, I can feel a hot breath burning down my collar. A female voice asks in a low tone, "What the fuck do you mean, 'no matter how hard you tried?' From what I've heard, it sounds like you haven't done a damn thing."

Even though I can't see her face, I know this is Ed's wife. There have been numerous occasions when I wondered just how strong she was, and if she was actually ever in the Marines. At this point, I'd have to say that I'm pretty sure she was telling the truth. "What? Ouch. Please let go, this hurts so fucking bad."

"Oh sure, you'd like that. Things get tough, so you just expect everything to acquiesce to your needs. Sorry Anton, it doesn't work like that. You see, I've been listening to you, and I think you're full of shit."

"What? What are you talking about?" I ask in a high-pitched voice.

"Well, all I hear you talk about is how hard you try, but as far as I can tell, you've never even told her you love her, or have these feelings at all. Just because she might suspect they're there isn't enough. And let me ask another thing."

I like how she seems to be making a request. This is actually rather humorous, given the fact that she has all the control in this situation. "Yeah go for it," I say as I bite my lip, trying to keep from screaming.

"Well, if you want her so bad, why aren't you wherever she is? I mean, just because she isn't picking up your phone calls doesn't mean you can't talk to her."

"Huh?" At this point, my vocabulary has been condensed to one syllable sounds.

"If you want her as badly as you claim *Lloyd*, do something about it. John Cusack wouldn't sit here complaining."

Actually, he might.

"He'd go out there, do whatever it took to find the woman in question, and make an ass of himself in the process. No matter what it took, he would find a way. You're just sitting here talking, when what you should be doing is devoting every minute of your existence to finding her, and doing all you can to win her over."

"OK." At this point, I'll say anything to get her to let up.

"Now, let's be honest; it might not work. But that's life. I didn't spend fifteen years of my life sleeping in muddy ditches and risking my life so that you could be a little bitch. Here's a lesson I learned in the military: war is not avoided, it is merely deferred to your disadvantage."

"Actually, that's from *The Prince* by Machiavelli."

Her grip becomes more intense, "Oh, a fuckin' wise guy. I like this kid Ed. Even under pressure, he's still got some mettle. All right Anton, since you seem to be such an expert on literature, what do you know about *Fight Club*?"

Oh shit. There is no way this can lead to anything good. Squirming, I tell her, "I've never read the book, but I've seen the movie."

"OK, well that's a start. Let me give you the quick version. There's a part in the story where either Tyler Durden or the main character, I think they're switched in the book and movie, but never mind about that. As I was saying, they're in Project Mayhem, and they go into a convenience store. One of the guys forces the clerk to go outside behind the store. Do you know what he does next?"

I have no idea, but I'm sure it wasn't throwing him a surprise party with a stripper hiding in a cake. "No," I tell her, "I have no clue."

"He puts a gun to the back of this guy's head and starts asking him a ton of questions. He asks the clerk if he dreamt of working in a convenience store to which the guy obviously replies no. Then, he asks what he really wants to be, to which the answer is a veterinarian. So next, he takes the guy's wallet and finds his driver's license. He tells the clerk that he now knows his name and where he lives. If within the next six weeks, he is not taking strides toward becoming an animal doctor, he will find him and kill him. After he lets the man go running free, he explains that the clerk will wake up tomorrow and have the best breakfast he has ever had. You know why?"

I'm really hoping the answer is all-he-can-eat pancake buffet, but I doubt it. "No," is all I can spit out.

"Because he was that close to death. And now Anton, so are you. This is my gift to you. I know it doesn't seem like it, but you'll thank me later. I'm not going to kill you, but I most definitely could have."

I look at Ed, and he shakes his head up and down. The terror in his eyes makes me wonder if he got this same death-grip before he proposed. "Thank you."

"But that doesn't mean you can just go about your normal routine. Anton, you have been given so many opportunities, don't waste them. So many people miss out on love because they're too scared. If you really believe that you've done all you can do, then fine, forget everything I've said." She finally lets go of me, I desperately try to catch my breath, and I turn and face her. "But somehow, I think you have one last blaze of glory left in ya."

After about two full minutes of heavy breathing and water consumption, I speak. "I don't know what it is about you and your husband, but you have, without question, the *worst* methods of counseling people that I've ever seen . . . Thank you," I say, and I give her a hug. "This was exactly what I needed. *Once*. I think I've got the message. Now, if you'll excuse me, I must be going." I walk over to Ed, shake his hand, and head for the front door.

As I open it, they say together, "Good luck Anton."

I stop in the doorway, face them, and say, "You know what the best part of your *Fight Club* parable is?"

"What's that?"

"Ashby is a veterinarian."

"Hmm. Isn't that something?" she adds.

"Now, I'm off to win the woman of my dreams. But first, I need to go see a doctor." Ed gives me a nasty look, and I elaborate. "Sorry, I mean a 'turn-your-head-and-cough' kind of doctor. Not a 'turn-your-head-and-*scoff* kind of doctor."

29

I F I HAD a calendar, or a date-book, or even just a pad of post-its, I would make a note of this moment. Right now, sitting here in this waiting room, I am more nervous than I have ever been. I am fully aware how much I exaggerate much of what I tell people and how I describe things. However, I am being absolutely serious. My stomach feels like it's hosting a fight-to-the-death with everything I've eaten over the past decade. Although my scars are healing, the muscles are still very tender. And to top it all off, my appointment was for fifteen minutes ago. I know just as well as anyone that things happen, and schedules get thrown off. But this minor delay is doing nothing productive to help calm my nerves. Trying to take my mind off of everything that has transpired over the last couple of weeks, I pick up the first magazine I see. The only one that is near me features an article entitled *Are You Afraid of the Bark?* It's a fucking magazine featuring dogs wearing Halloween costumes. Great, just when I thought I couldn't feel any worse, I pick that up. I quickly set it down and consider walking the ten paces required to get another periodical, but the receptionist speaks to me.

"Um, Anthony, the doctor will see you now. Please go into room number three."

"Thank you," I say as I stand up and open the door that separates the exam rooms from the waiting room. The reason she called me Anthony is because that's what I told her it was. For some reason, when I write Anton, people often have a tendency to get confused. I just add the extra couple of letters to make everything easier for everyone else. I slowly make the walk down to room three, and step inside, closing the door most of the way, but not entirely shut. I gently set my things down, and slowly lower myself into the chair that looks the most comfortable. My options aren't exactly great, but one has padding and one doesn't. My choice was made for me. I'm glad to finally be inside the actual exam room, and not the waiting room. However, all that really means is that the intensity of my nerves has multiplied tenfold. I slide a small trashcan toward me, just in case. The next four minutes are the longest of my life. I fidget uncontrollably, looking at the posters on the wall, when I hear a knock at the door.

"Come in," I say.

"Hello, Anthony, thanks for coming in today," Ashby says to me, as she is looking down at some paperwork. "What can I help you with today?" And then, she looks up, and sees who I really am.

"Hi Ashby, it's great to see you," is all I say. It took every bit of strength and courage just to come up with that. She closes the door and stares at me in silence for an excruciatingly long time.

"Franklin. Wow! I . . . I can't believe you're here. What are you doing here?"

Trying to take the edge off a very tense situation, I tell her, "Well, I have rabies. I mean, I *think* I have rabies," and then I start to force saliva out of my mouth. Despite her best efforts to stay upset with me, she momentarily cracks a smile. "OK, but seriously, I need to see a doctor."

"Well, I can tell. I heard that you got pretty banged up. But I'm sorry I can't be of more help to you. I'm an animal doctor, remember?"

"Oh, I didn't mean for me. I need to see a veterinarian for him." She gives me a puzzled look, not seeing anyone or anything else in the room. And right then, I pick up my duffel bag and take out a small case. "You remember Leviathan, don't you?" I would gladly retire from photography forever if it meant I could have one solitary picture of how her face looked when she saw that tortoise. I legitimately think she almost fainted.

An entire egg seems to slide down her throat. Then she softly asks, "Is that . . . the present I gave you back in high school?"

"Of course it is. I've kept everything you've ever given me."

She pulls up the nonpadded chair and sits herself down. "But I thought you killed it, or lost it, or it died, or " . . ."

I cut her off, "Yeah, I know I told you all that stuff, but I was kidding. The truth is I've had this little guy ever since my eighteenth birthday. I always tell people that I'm such a bad 'Dad' to the tortoise that I keep buying new ones, because I didn't want them to know how much he meant to me. Some people probably think I've owned about nine or ten tortoises over the years. I had a reputation to uphold after all."

"Reputation?"

"Yeah, well it's no secret that I'm not exactly the biggest fan of animals. But this little guy was different. I've loved having this guy every minute since you gave him to me. He's actually quite simple to take care of; all he does is sit and eat cereal. He's a big fan of Frosted Flakes, but he will never say no to Kix." She chuckles again.

Trying to remain professional, she asks, "Wow! That's amazing. So is something wrong with him?"

"Well, yeah, I think there is. Obviously, I'm no expert, but I'm afraid that something is wrong with his stomach."

"OK, may I have a look?"

"Of course," I tell her as I hand her the little green animal.

After looking at it for a little while, she says, "Well, he looks fine to me."

"Are you sure? I mean, look at that mark on his belly."

"Franklin, I know it's been a while, but hasn't that mark always been there?"

Acting aloof, "Oh, you know what? You're right. What was I thinking? The keyhole is how his name kind of got started."

"Yeah, I remember that."

"Well, since he looks fine, can I ask your opinion on something else?"

"Sure."

Lifting up my shirt, I ask, "What do you think of this?"

"Is that a tattoo?"

"Yep, pretty cool huh?"

She stands up to get a closer look. "What is it? Wait, is that a keyhole?"

"Sure is." And right then she gives me a very puzzled look. "Ashby, I need to talk to you. I mean, I need to tell you something. And I understand if you're mad at me, and I'll definitely understand if you want me to leave right now. But I'm begging, please give me a few minutes?"

She takes a deep breath. "OK, that's fair. But please make it quick. I do have other patients I need to see."

"Oh, absolutely. That's fine." I close my eyes, breathe in heavily, and look her right in the eye. "My whole life . . . well, for most of my life, I've always told people how hard I work and how they should go for what they want. And lately, well I've come to realize that it's time I take my own advice." I take a pause to collect my thoughts, but am unsuccessful. Instead, I just decide to start talking, and hope that whatever comes out doesn't dig my own grave even deeper. "You know how people always say they try to live life with no regrets. Well, for the most part, I think I've honestly done a pretty good job of that. But there are definitely things I've regretted, no question about it. And, well, I know I'm probably going to regret what I'm about to say. But I lose more respect for myself every day that I don't do something about these feelings I'm having." I stand up out of my chair and continue. "Ashby, the day we met back in high school was quite possibly the best thing that ever happened to me. I honestly remember every detail of that moment. Where we were sitting, what we were wearing, even the stupid diagram on the blackboard. Having you as a friend and in my life has been something so incredible that I have no idea what I did to deserve someone so amazing. Ashby, what I want to say is . . . I am so in love with you that it's making me crazy. I've had a thing for you ever since I met you. I don't know what I'm trying to accomplish by finally telling you this after all these years, but if I hold it in any longer, I might literally explode. And I know that I fucked up really bad back in Vancouver, so I'll understand if you want to forget all about me, but I know the only way I'll even sleep somewhat decently is if I get this off my chest. I definitely don't want to lose you as a friend, and I'm so sorry I jeopardized that. And if you're at all interested in still being 'just friends,' I'm totally fine with that." I pause and think about what I just said, "Wait, scratch that. I'm not totally fine with that. I love you, and I don't want to be just friends anymore. But if that's all we'll ever be, then I'll do my best to accept that, but it won't be easy. Because, well, you're the most beautiful, gracious, and stunning woman I have ever met. And . . . well, I guess . . . I don't know, I think that's pretty much what I came to say."

Following my soliloquy, there is a pause so long I honestly start to think she hasn't heard a single word I just said. Finally, I can take no more. "Ashby? Please, just say *something*. Anything."

And right then, just when I expect the most vengeful response I've ever received, she reacts by doing the last thing I ever thought she would. She grabs me behind the head and gives me the most passionate kiss I've ever tasted. It is so good; my knees begin to shake. All of the nerves in my stomach immediately disappear. I am not distorting the details when I say that this kiss was honestly better than about half of the orgasms I've had in my life. Even though I've waited almost half of my life for this moment, I would gladly wait another fifty years just for the chance to do it again.

After she pulls her tongue out of my mouth, I have to ask, "Um, I'm *not* complaining, but . . . could you please explain what that was all about?"

"Franklin! Do you know how long I've been waiting for you to say this? It's about fucking time!" she says with a small jump in the air.

"But I thought you were mad at me for Vancouver."

"Well, I certainly was. I was livid when my brother told me he saw you with some other woman. Especially since you'd called me saying you didn't want to come over because you weren't feeling well."

"I know, I just said that because I knew you were drunk, and I thought I'd be taking advantage of you."

"And that's one of the many reasons I adore you. I know how difficult it must have been to pass that up. But thank you, I really appreciated it."

"So when did you decide that you weren't so mad about me and that other woman?"

"Well, let's just say I found out what *really* happened?"

I have no idea what she's talking about. What does she mean by "what really happened?" "Excuse me? What in the world are you talking about?"

"Never mind. It's my little secret."

My first instinct is to debate with her, but then I realize that she's forgiven me for being a total asshole, and I know better than to question that. Now that my bravado has been restored, I decide to up the stakes. "Ashby, can I ask you another question?"

"Of course, Franklin. What is it?"

And at that moment, I get down near the floor, on one knee. When I look up at her eyes, I can tell she is thoroughly freaking out. I don't care; I've been waiting so many years to ask her this question. "Ashby?"

"Yeah?" she replies with blatant trepidation.

"Will you *please* stop calling me Franklin? I've always preferred Anton."

She breathes a refreshing sigh of relief. Now laughing, "Of course. Now stand up and kiss me, *Anton*."

Our mouths connect again for about another forty-five seconds, when she hesitantly breaks away and says, "I'm so sorry, but I have other patients I have to see. But can we have dinner later tonight?"

"Of course we can. I'd really like that."

"Awesome. There's a great diner a few blocks from here with amazing cheesecake."

"Well, if you want cheesecake, we can definitely do that. But I was really hoping to take you to some place with a sommelier and a dress code. I mean, if that's OK with you?"

She forces back a grin and simply replies, "Sounds perfect. I'll call you when I'm done with work." She begins to walk out of the room and onto her next appointment, but I have one more thing to say.

"Oh hey, Ashby?"

"Yeah?"

"Um, seriously though. You really should get checked for rabies. I did get attacked by a dog not too long ago."

30

"THERE YOU GO, one rum and Coke. Anything else?"

"No, I'm good for now. But could you please turn up the volume on that TV right there? I'm a hockey fanatic, and I think the United States is gonna win gold this year."

"Well, not if Michael LaFleur and the Canadians have anything to say about it," the bartender says with a wink and a smile. "But sure, I'll see what I can do." He grabs a remote control and ups the volume.

"Thanks a lot. What's your name?"

"I'm Guillaume."

"Oh, cool name. I'm Alexis, nice to meet you," the woman in the Team USA jacket says.

"Nice to meet you too Alexis. Just yell if you need anything else."

She nods and quietly sips her drink, making funny poses anytime something vaguely exciting happens on the television. It is midway through the second period, and the United States leads Sweden 2-1. As the game goes to a commercial, Alexis excuses herself to the restroom. Right then, a woman with large sunglasses enters the restaurant and takes a seat at the bar.

"Hey there, how's it going?" Guillaume asks as he throws a cocktail napkin down.

"Well, I've been better, that's for sure."

"I'm sorry to hear that. Can I pour you a drink? It won't make things totally better, but it should help."

"Yeah, that sounds great. I'll have a Midori-sour, please."

"Sure thing." Guillaume makes the drink and places it in front of the woman, then begins to walk away.

"Oh um, how much do I owe you?"

"It's on me," he says with his moneymaking wink and smile combo.

"Wow! Thank you." The woman begins to sip her beverage and watch the hockey match, when Alexis returns to her seat. Although she notices the stranger wearing tinted spectacles indoors, she doesn't say a word. Five minutes go by, and each reaches the bottom of their glasses. Guillaume, the gallant bartender that he is, has another drink ready for each just as they begin to make slurping sounds. Each lady thanks him, and before anyone can say anything else, Alexis erupts with excitement.

"*Yes*!!! Nice shot Samuels. Keep doing that and the gold is all yours."

Breaking the ice, the woman next to her asks, "Are you a fan?"

"Oh, yeah, most definitely. All of my brothers played hockey, and growing up in Colorado, it kind of gets ingrained in you."

"Tell me about it. I grew up in Minnesota, my brothers played too. I was actually at the Unites States versus Russia game a few days ago."

"No way! Ugh, I'm so jealous. You know, it's funny you mention that. Just the other night I was hanging out with a guy who was at that game. He was doing photography or something like that I think."

Her interest suddenly peaks. "Really? Hmm, I went with my brother."

"Well, that's cool. I really want to make it to a game in the next couple of days, now that my event is over."

"Yeah, I saw your jacket. That's great, what event did you do?"

"I'm a snowboarder. And I don't mean to brag, but I won gold."

"No way! That's so cool. Congratulations."

"Yeah, I wish the guys I'm into were as impressed by it as you are."

"Excuse me?"

"Well, the night after I won gold, I went out to celebrate. Pretty standard, right?"

"I think you deserved it."

"Right. Well, I start chatting with this really cute guy. Actually, he is the photographer I was telling you about. And we hit it off. Well, long story short. We both get really drunk, and I practically invite myself back to his hotel room."

"You mean, he didn't invite you back?"

"Not exactly. I asked him if we could split a cab, and when the driver asked him where he was going, I acted surprised and said I was staying at the same hotel. Well, when we got there, I explained that I had told a little fib. I asked if I could come into his room to use the bathroom."

"Nice. I've used that one before," she says insincerely.

"I know. Well, I come out of his bathroom wearing nothing but my underwear and a gold medal."

"Oh wow! I'll bet he liked that, huh?"

"No, I couldn't believe it. I literally jumped on him, and he kindly set me down."

"What? You're kidding me. Did he say why?"

"Yeah, and although I was furious at the time, it turned out he was such a sweetheart."

Her curiosity growing by the second, she asks, "How so?"

"Well, he told me that he was definitely attracted to me, and if it were any other night, he wouldn't have even thought twice about hooking up."

"But?"

"Story of my life, there was another girl. Naturally, I was pretty annoyed. But you should have heard the way he talked about her. Her name was, Ashley I think. Like I said, I was pretty drunk. But he was talking about this girl like she was the only woman he'd ever met. I just remember wishing that some guy would talk about me like that one day."

"Wow! No kidding?"

"Yeah, and this part is so cute. He tells me how much animals make him nervous, but that this chick gave him a turtle back in high school. And even though he pretends like he doesn't have it anymore, he still has it to this day. He said it was the best gift anyone has ever given him."

"You're right, that is really cute," she says while she blushes.

"I know. And then, he's telling me about how this Ashley was at the USA-Russia hockey match the other night, and got hit with a puck. Apparently, it bruised her face pretty bad."

"Ouch, that's awful."

"Seriously. But then he's telling me how he had a friend of his help her cover it up with makeup. Like, how sweet is that?"

"Wow! I wish I could meet this guy," she says with an ever-growing smile.

"Oh, and you know how I said he was a photographer?"

"Yep."

"Well, he's here at the Olympics for work. And from what he told me, his boss wanted him to go to Los Angeles for an assignment for a few days, then come back for the closing ceremonies."

"Well, that doesn't sound so bad. I'm sure the weather down there is a lot better than it is up here."

"Right, except this chick he's in love with is a skater or something, and her event takes place during the days his boss wanted him in Los Angeles"

"Bummer, that sucks. So I guess he went to Los Angeles for a few days?"

"Nope. He told me he quit his job, just so he could watch her race."

"Shut the fuck up," she says, not fully aware of how loud she's speaking.

"I know, I couldn't believe it. I mean, whoever this girl is, she is so lucky. Honestly, it's like straight out of a fairy tale. What girl wouldn't want a guy like that?"

Smiling, the woman removes her jacket, revealing a T-shirt that says "USA Speed Skating." "I know if I ever found a guy like that, I'd think it was too good to be true. My, I can't believe I'm still wearing these things, it's not *that* bright in here," she says as she removes her sunglasses, revealing a small bruise on her cheek.

Alexis watches her as she does this and notices the shirt and bruise. She stares at this woman in awe, reaches out her hand, and says, "I'm sorry, I didn't even introduce myself. I'm Alexis."

"Hi Alexis, it's nice to meet you."

"Well, do you have a name?"

"Oh, I'm sorry. I'm still in shock from hearing that story. My name is Ashby McHale. But I try not to get too attached to it, because I like the sound of Ashby Bradley much better."

ACKNOWLEDGMENTS

Endless thanks to my parents, my friends, Hope, and anyone who read this and offered me suggestions. Megan Roe, for sparking my interest in reading for enjoyment. Any of my professors who ever told me my writing style was "too casual." All of the random strangers who unknowingly provided me with great material. Most importantly, Lauren Conrad. Thank you for making me realize that if you can publish a novel, so can I.

Get Published, Inc!
Thorofare, NJ 08086
03 November 2009
BA2009246